Hazel Hucker was a teacher, magistrate and much-travelled army wife and is now writing full time. She is the author of several novels for Little, Brown including, most recently, *The Real Claudia Charles*. She lives in Richmond, London.

Also by Hazel Hucker

The Aftermath of Oliver
A Dangerous Happiness
Trials of Friendship
Cousin Susannah
The Real Claudia Charles

Changing Status

Hazel Hucker

WARNER BOOKS

A *Warner* Book

First published in Great Britain in 2000 by
Little, Brown and Company
This edition published by Warner Books in 2001

A CIP catalogue record for this book
is available from the British Library.

ISBN 0 7515 2573 1

Typeset in Melior by M Rules
Printed and bound in Great Britain by
Bookmarque Ltd, Croydon, Surrey

Warner Books
A Division of
Little, Brown and Company (UK)
Brettenham House
Lancaster Place
London WC2E 7EN

www.littlebrown.co.uk

To Michael,
with love and gratitude.

1

Donna looked as she always had, only that she was a woman now. The schoolgirl skirt and blouse beneath her navy coat and the impetuous dishevelled look deceived him as she jumped from the car, so that he flung open his arms for her kiss, but this was not his darling daughter, this was a raging adult who evaded his embrace to let fly at him.

'You miserable sod, how could you do this to me? You've spoiled everything. You realise you've mucked up my whole life, don't you?'

Alex Lindridge actually retreated, embarrassed by her ringing contralto, her tossing luxuriant hair and breasts, her aura of sheer animal femaleness. He prayed no neighbour was about.

'For Heaven's sake, Donna, if you mean having to change schools I'm sorry about it, but it's not the end of the world, surely? After all your moans about being at a snobbish day school with only silly girls around, I thought you'd be happy to leave. There'll be boys at your new school next term, won't you enjoy that?'

'No,' she retorted. 'They'll be spotty.'

His wife, Fenella, brittle and thin as a dried-up bean pod, emerged from the car to drawl: 'Donna's mad at having to leave some damned art teacher. I've told her, there'll be perfectly competent teachers at the comprehensive, there's no need for all this drama.'

'It won't be the same,' Donna said. 'Come on, how often do

you get really brilliant teachers? Most of them are useless.
And the syllabus is bound to be different. Different in every
subject, too. Get real, Dad, I have to stay where I am.'

Beneath his greying hair, Alex's thin face had a pallor
almost of illness, with dark smudges under the eyes. He
clenched his jaw, the pain of what he saw as his inadequacies attacking him like knives. He should have told her
himself, not allowed Fenella to get there first. For most of her
sixteen years Donna had not been an easy child to live with
but he loved her as he'd never loved anyone else. 'And you
give in to her too easily,' Fenella would say: 'That's something you'll pay for.' Donna was so different from him; even
as a toddler she'd been sure of herself, a lively dark-eyed
child who argued in screams of passion for the right to do as
she wanted. She'd been bright, too, early with every step of
her progress, and he'd acknowledged compliments on her
behalf with his heart swelling. Now circumstances were forcing him into letting her down and he cursed himself for
lacking just that brilliance he saw in her.

'I'm sorry, darling, but it can't be done.'

Fenella interrupted. 'Your father's forced early retirement
from the Lord Chancellor's department means everything
has to go, Donna, not just your school.' She was looking over
her daughter's shoulder along the drive, as if Donna didn't
really exist. Her voice was as bitingly cold as the December
day. 'Your father thought himself so well established on the
ladder that he'd never need to worry over the snakes, poor
fool. But they managed to slide him out just the same and
now we're all suffering. Think of others as well as yourself
for once.'

She pivoted on a heel to stalk off into the house, but the
too-fashionable shoe betrayed her and she staggered, letting
out a curse like a parrot's squawk. Father and daughter's eyes
met in momentary glee but then Donna stared after her,
frowning. 'What does she mean, everything has to go? Suffer
what? Dad!'

'My income was halved. We thought we could manage till
you both left school, but we can't. We shall have to live quite

differently. We shan't be able to stay here, for a start. We're moving near to Winchester. It's not too far from London, but the price of property is lower in Hampshire.'

'You can't be serious.' A pause. 'You *are* serious.'

He nodded. They walked into the house, each clutching bags of the schoolbooks she thought she'd brought home merely for the holidays, dumping them in the hall. There was an insistent smell of the scent *Poison* hanging on the air. Alex thought in a disjointed way that his wife's aroma preceded her like a warning, lingered like a shade. To escape it he prowled into their oversized drawing-room and looked out of the French windows at the big frosted garden. There was a strange bluish sheen on the Roman-style swimming pool, it must be something to do with the cold. Oh, he was so tired. It seemed impossible that he could ever have swum in that pool, ever changed, laughing with friends, in the pool-house with its row of Doric columns that he'd always suspected were way over the top. To shut Fenella up he'd taken out a second mortgage to pay for that lot, and now the repayments were beyond him. The boundaries of his life had changed and shrunk. At fifty he was no longer a senior civil servant, he was, oh God the filthy word, *unemployed*, a state that was once to him merely part of certain unfortunate statistics, but which he now saw, as he was sure Everyman in the street would, as exemplifying yet another waster, another failure. He was losing his sense of identity, while his mind was corroding with repressed rage that all his talents and efforts had come to nothing. How could this have happened to him, a man who had always worked with dogged energy and loyalty?

Donna stood beside him smelling of something light and pretty, but her presence didn't change anything. She was in an electrically charged mood that reminded him horribly of Fenella, her questions drilling holes in his pride. What had he done to have to retire early? Why couldn't he find another job? Why Hampshire? 'I have to do my GCSEs where I am. Mother says you're letting Duncan stay at Lancing. You're being sexist. It's grossly unfair.'

'No. Duncan has his A levels in six months time, and there's no way we'd dare mess him about – though God knows where the money's to come from. For you it's different. The comprehensive school uses the same examination board as your school did. I've checked it out with them and they think you'll be fine in most subjects. Where you're not I'm sure we'll be able to find you coaching. There must be someone. I promise, darling, it will be all right. And I'll make it up to you somehow.' The weariness was making him incapable of clear explanations. He wanted to be brisk, resolute and responsive but he could hear himself instead being bumbling and indecisive and wretchedly emotional. Part of him wanted sympathy from his daughter, but another part loathed the thought of her pity.

He made a last effort. 'Next autumn you'll go to the Sixth-form College. It's an old foundation and their results are good. What's more there's a far wider choice of A level subjects there than at your old school and you'll be treated more as a student than a child.'

She gave him a hard look, her eyes glittering with the diamond brightness that he connected with intelligence. 'You worked all this out weeks ago,' she said, 'without asking for my views on *anything* and you've probably already found some awful little house . . .'

'We didn't want to worry you . . .'

'What's wrong with talking? So, have you?'

'A flat,' he said. 'Reasonably large, in a handsome old house . . .'

'Huh!' she said. 'I'd better check it out. You and Mother never did have any taste in architecture. Look at this awful suburban palace for a start.'

Where in hell had she acquired such adult disdain? 'Donna—'

'*Listen!*' she said with fury. 'I'll go to the Sixth-form College next autumn, if it really is reasonable, but there's no way I'm going to a bloody comprehensive school where everybody's been friends for years and where I'll barely know my way around before it's time to leave. I'll work at home.'

'You can't,' Alex began.

'Yes, I can. We've virtually finished the syllabus in most subjects and I'll revise like mad. If you aren't working you can help me with English and history and things – you've got a decent degree after all – and I don't mind being coached for the rest. So that's it, Dad, final, finished.'

'You're only just in time to avoid a burnt offering,' the Judge's wife commented in resigned tones, juggling with pans on the hob as she turned her head to kiss her husband, Hugh Thorne. 'What was it this time? Some meeting you forgot to put in the diary? Lousy traffic?'

'Traffic. What else? A lorry spilled its load at Hanger Lane – tailback three miles long. A dreadful journey. And the rain made it worse.' He returned her kiss and stepped back to assess her mood. He quailed at the thought of the ignorance he must shortly enlighten. Celia couldn't guess as she prepared her mouthwatering chicken dish that he was about to jerk the flow of her agreeable life right out of its course, but that's what his news would do. Guilt gnawed at him, yet along with the guilt was annoyance that events had forced him to this crisis in order to make his own life bearable. For once, watching her deft hands fly about was not giving him the familiar feelings of pleasure, easing away his tension after a difficult day in court; today she was going to erupt with fury and something in him resented this.

She poked potatoes with a fork, turned and smiled at him. 'Two more minutes. Pour us both a drink, will you, while I make the sauce?'

'Yes, certainly.' At fifty-six she was still the most attractive woman he'd ever met, his Celia, prematurely white-haired or not. A small woman, small beside his six foot three that is, she still retained the intelligent grey eyes, the lively smile and the perfect proportions – high breasted and long-legged – that had made him ache to tug off her jeans within minutes of first meeting her. He looked at her, still sexy, still dressed in trousers with floppy pullovers or loose shirts, living in her own unbothered way, never wanting for occupation – she was a botanical artist – but, thank God, never dashing about in the frenzied way that so many of his friends' wives did.

Oh hell, thought the Judge, drawing a deep breath. Better pave the way a bit, enlist some sympathy for himself before the blow hit her. 'You know I'm not a carping man by nature or given to complaining, Celia, my treasure, but it does seem a trifle inequitable that you should pass the days painting the flowers of the earth amid the charms of Richmond, while I'm dealing with the criminal elements of east London in the insalubrious environs of Snaresbrook Crown Court, miles of stinking roads away.'

'Very unfair,' she agreed, adding in turn tarragon, white wine and cream to her pan and stirring. 'But you find the work fascinating, don't you, Hugh? You've always said so.'

'I do. But I'm not genetically designed to crawl for up to four hours a day round the North Circular in the company of diesel-belching lorries. That's for the brain-dead.'

'But you're waiting for a transfer to Kingston Crown Court. Then you'll drive through Richmond Park with the deer for company instead. Pure pleasure.'

'That'll never happen.' He removed the foil from the bottle he'd been clutching, took off the wire, then tilted it at forty-five degrees and grasped the cork firmly with his left hand.

She swung round from dishing up sugar-snap peas to stare at him. 'Why not?'

'There are a dozen or more judges in front of me who'd relish sitting in a large new court centre where they're taking Old Bailey work. Not a hope in hell.' He rotated the base of the bottle slowly, allowing the cork to rise and leave the bottle with only the faintest of pops.

He was avoiding her eyes, the bottle he was opening was champagne, the set of his shoulders was tense. Celia and Hugh had been married for more than three decades; it needed no Pythian powers to sense that her husband was up to something. 'Hugh, what's going on? Why the champagne?'

He poured it out slowly, delicately. 'The circuit administrator spoke to me this afternoon. I do have a transfer; it's to Winchester.'

'Winchester? You're joking! Seriously, where?'

'Seriously Winchester.' He held her glass in his fingers, watching her, estimating her reaction should he pass it to her. Would she drink to a move so favourable to him – or chuck the champagne in his face? Celia might be endearingly vague much of the time, but she could also be sharply direct. 'George Torrington who was there died recently. Heart attack. They want someone who can move swiftly to fill the gap, moreover someone, like him, licenced to deal with rape and child abuse cases.'

She exploded. 'But you can't move quickly. And get this clear, Hugh, we're not leaving this house, not ever!'

A blast of wind threw rain against the windows. Now what? his brain demanded as he put the bottle down. Face anger with anger, call her a selfish bitch, have a shouting match? That might be an outlet for the tension but would take them nowhere. He was heading for sixty and the very essence of his nature precluded the screams and flying crockery of younger couples. They had to talk this through. But his mouth was thick with bitterness.

'Let's eat,' he said. He hoped his face looked as stern and tired and wretched as he felt. 'I'm starved and this looks good. Here, take this champagne. We both need a drink. I'm sorry about the shock.'

She pushed the glass away. 'Shock? I can't believe this. Have you accepted?'

'Mmm. In principle. Though I said I'd have to talk to you. We don't have to sell this house in a hurry, I can stay with my Manningford cousins at Abbotsbridge during the week, be home at weekends. No, wait, please. Let's discuss it quietly over our meal.'

He carried the glasses to the cherrywood table at the other end of the roomy kitchen with Celia dashing to and fro past him, crashing plates and dishes down with ferocity. But Hugh felt, abruptly, just as thunderous. Did he want to leave their house halfway down the slopes of Richmond Hill? Yes, he did! They'd lived in this tall, gaunt mid-Victorian house of no great architectural merit for twenty-three years and it was more than enough. The trouble was that Celia had been born here and apart from art school and the first ten years of their marriage, she had lived nowhere else, nor wanted to. She loved its lofty ceilings, its ornate cornices, its melancholic corners, and she'd transformed it as only an artist could, softening its austerity with full curtains and decorative tapestry hangings, and warming its cold spaces with wallpapers by Charles Voysey or William Morris in shades of old rose, honey and willow green.

An only child, she had inherited it after her parents' deaths in a sailing accident. From the young Thornes' viewpoint of a cramped Pimlico terrace, its spaciousness had seemed munificent; almost overnight little John and Anna had a playroom, Celia a studio, Hugh a study and – oh bonus of all unbelievable bonuses – they were mortgage free. But now, with John married and a law lecturer at University College and Anna working in an advertising agency and living with her partner in Chelsea, the house seemed ludicrously too big, the pair of them hallooing to each other about the place like climbers from valley to peak. It was absurd, and expensive too: top rate of council tax, endless repair bills, an eczema of flaking plaster in the second-floor bedrooms and the roof distinctly dubious. 'But I love it,' Celia had said simply on the one or two occasions when he'd hinted at the possibilities of a move. 'My roots here go too deep to shift, and I never shall.' The Judge sat down, helped himself to the delicious chicken and took a few mouthfuls, but his hunger had vanished. He put down his knife and fork. In the car he'd been lulled by dreams of a Crown Court overlooking a venerable city, of a cathedral in its quiet close, perhaps the two of them living in a period house nearby with rooms of sensible proportions and a garden where one might unearth ancient artifacts. Most vivid of all had been his vision of escaping the treadmill of the North Circular.

Staring accusingly at his wife as she ate with every appearance of enjoyment, he took the plunge. 'Celia, I can't go on like this, you know. Not unless you want me to end up having a heart attack like old Torrington.'

If he'd hoped for sympathy, he was out of luck. Celia's brain had been busy. She swallowed her food, licked her lips with the thoroughness of a cat, braced herself.

'The Winchester offer didn't come out of the blue,' she spat at him. 'You're a south-eastern circuiteer and Winchester's western circuit. You planned this and asked for it – *and without having the decency to address one word to me about it.*'

'I said nothing because I was told it would never happen. As likely as winning the national lottery they said. It's because they're desperate that they recollected me.'

'There are other courts where you could sit.'

'Not really. In any case, I *want* to go to Winchester. Listen. You were brought up in this house and you love it here. I was at school in Winchester and I love it there. We've lived in Richmond for a long time and it's been great, but now the house is too big for us, quite ridiculous. And expensive to run. Celia, out of the blue I've been given a chance to live in *my* place. Fair shares – how about that?'

'Not interested. You've been a bastard, Hugh, hatching this plot behind my back, a thoughtless, self-centred, inconsiderate brute. Maybe if you'd given me time to come to terms with this idea, maybe if I believed you'd bothered about my needs, my wishes, my life here, I might, just might, have felt sympathetic to your problems and agreed to moving. But since you clearly haven't given fair shares to my self-respect or my feelings for a house whose every corner has memories and meaning for me, then the answer's no!' She tucked more food into her mouth and chewed it savagely.

After a moment's silence he raised his eyebrows. 'I thought we could discuss this like mature people but you're screeching like a three-year-old throwing a tantrum. What about my needs, my wishes, my life? You've had your way in everything for years and you don't give a damn about anyone but yourself, you miserable hypocrite.'

Celia half-choked. 'Don't you call me foul names. This is my house, I'd like to remind you, which you're making God-like assumptions you can sell to go somewhere I don't want. And I earn every penny of the expenses you're complaining about—'

'We have a shared account! How the hell do you know whose money you spend?' he interrupted.

'Never mind that. You know what I mean, Hugh, and you bloody well know why I'm angry, too. Why not unzip and flash the truth – the truth of all the male resentments you must have been bottling up for years to make you do something this mean?'

'That must be the most unjust thing you've ever said to me. Well, in view of your own nastiness, there's no hesitation left in my mind. I take the Winchester appointment and stay with James and Arabella for the first month or so and if you still refuse to consider a move to Winchester, then I'll stay in a hotel every Monday to Friday and we'll have to manage like that.' He shoved his food away from himself and stood up. 'You can throw that in the bin. Somehow I seem to have lost my appetite . . . among other things.'

He strode out. The sounds of the rain gurgling in the drains reminded him of a need to pee. Washing his hands afterwards he was assailed by morbid thoughts. Made a complete mess of that, didn't you? he observed silently to his image in the glass over the basin. For a once competent advocate, you couldn't have handled your case worse. In fact you pretty much destroyed it. Lost your temper, caused Celia to lose hers. What's the matter with you, old man? Old man? He surveyed himself. White hair, curly over his ears, faded hazel eyes, unexpectedly dark eyebrows. An arresting face, people said. It was pale tonight, looked mean, too, like that of the thin-lipped defendant he'd given a five-year custodial sentence a few hours earlier. God, he was tired, but then he always was on a Friday.

Fifty-nine, not sixty yet, more than ten years on the Bench

to go. You wouldn't want to be alone in bed all the working weeks of all those years, he told himself, you're too fond of Celia's warm curves beside you, you'd miss the sensuous way she presses herself against your rump when she wakes in the mornings, the kisses planted on your neck, the reactions that make you turn and pounce on her . . . Oh hell. He wouldn't get much of that for a while, not after tonight's disclosure.

He struggled to distinguish the various layers of thoughts that swirled around in his mind: Celia's anguish, the dead albatross of the house round his neck, his work, his children and grandchildren, (dear little Elaine and tiny Joshua), Christmas in no time at all . . . Make it up with Celia, calm her down, sort it out. (He was an uxorious man and his wife was his best friend.) But you aren't going to kill yourself spending sixteen to twenty hours on that vile road each week, he told himself, not even for her. That wasn't the life you studied so hard for at Balliol, all those years ago. Then he'd thought he'd be young for ever, now he tired more easily, found the cases that he dealt with ever more worrying and depressing. Once he'd been able to turn the disturbing thoughts aside, sometimes with an effort, but he could do it, yet recently there had been a downward shift in his view of society and his mental security felt imperilled. He knew he needed a change, to make an investment in his own well-being, and he longed to go back to the scenes of his youth that he'd loved, to have time to fish for trout on the Test. He must try again to make Celia understand. No, leave it to the morning, the future's unclear and thick with dangers, the mood's wrong. He remembered hearing on the car radio that there was a Mozart concert tonight. He'd listen in the bedroom, try to unwind. Maybe the morning would bring inspiration, though he couldn't imagine what. He trudged upstairs. An early night wouldn't be a bad idea. God, he'd had enough.

Something woke him at twenty to four in the morning. He opened his eyes and the light of the street lamp through the curtains was eerie and there was a dramatic silence in the

room as if some person had just stopped speaking. His heart
was thumping and he was cold. At first he thought the coldness was because he was alone in the bed, but then Celia's
warm hand hit his left thigh with some vigour and her voice
announced: 'I've solved it.'

'What?' he mumbled, bemused.

'The house, idiot, you going to Winchester. If I hadn't been so
shocked I'd have seen it before. I can't think why you didn't.'

'Tell me then,' he said carefully. For the harridan who'd
picked that quarrel with him only hours earlier she sounded
quite reasonable.

'We don't move to Winchester lock, stock and barrel,
Hugh, we buy a cottage – like a weekend cottage, only it'll be
our weekday cottage, making this house our weekend place
instead. We can afford it, can't we? My only stipulation is
that I must have a studio there with the right light. And if
I want to be in London midweek for a lunch party or an
exhibition then I'll drive up. I suppose it's not *that* far.'

The rain was falling softly against the window now, a
friendly sound. He moved towards her warm humped shape
across the dividing inches of cold sheet. 'Sounds too good to
be true. But I can't think of anything wrong with it.'

'Of course you can't. I told you I'd solved it. Now say I'm
brilliant and you love me passionately.'

He buried his face in her shoulder, and said: 'I'm brilliant
and you love me passionately!'

'Big-headed bastard,' she retaliated cheerfully.

'Takes one to know one. I love you just the same.'

'That's sorted, then. Now go back to sleep.'

'I don't think I can,' he said. 'I'm far too wide awake.
You'll have to put me to sleep.'

'Now how do I do that?' she enquired in an innocent
voice.

'Oh, I think you know,' the Judge said. 'Better than anybody.'

And that was how they came to buy their flat at Brambourne
Manor.

2

It had snowed from seven o'clock in the morning, insubstantial gusts of snow that swirled along the grey bulk of Winchester cathedral like smoke, and sent icy dust-devils dancing up and down the narrow High Street. Despite its flimsy nature, by late morning perhaps two inches had settled on old roofs and windowsills, and those who ventured out grumbled of fuzzy vision and noses and ears that stung.

'It is pretty, though,' Betty Upcott observed to her husband as they trudged up to the estate agents to collect the keys to their new flat, the snow crunching beneath their feet.

Major Martin Upcott was in no mood to notice its beauty. To him it was like fog, muffling sounds and making familiar places seem unreal, ghostly even. Blinking the stuff from his eyelashes he said in a resigned voice: 'Impossible weather for the move. You know half the furniture was wet before we left Farnborough, don't you?'

She glanced at him from under her own wet lashes and said: 'Well, it was a bit damp. But those nice lads swathed everything in paper blankets after I mentioned bumper slices of chocolate fudge cake when we have lunch. It'll be fine.'

Martin frowned. Her determination to look on the bright side of things stung him with his own inadequacies and failures. Besides, he'd never liked snow. It put him in mind of death, partings, the cruel indifference of nature. He sighed with a shiver that encompassed all his untold fears for the years ahead, plus a bittersweet nostalgia for his Army past, a past where the bounds of his life were set and where his income had been comfortably adequate. Today, faced with moving into a flat barely half the size of the house on the Church Crookham side of Farnborough that he'd bought six years ago on early retirement, and with his income chopped to something less than a third, he felt about as useless as that chap in Scott's expedition to the Antarctic, Captain Oates, the man who'd walked out into the snow to die. At times Martin found himself craving a similar oblivion.

Betty steered him into the estate agents. 'Here we are, just got to sign for those keys, then we'll be on our way.'

The estate agent, a plump, hearty thirty-year old in a blazer, was apologetic that he couldn't hand over the keys quite at this moment, the money wasn't through yet from their purchasers, nothing wrong he was certain, but these things could take time. He leaned shiny knuckles on his untidy desk: how about a coffee and wasn't the weather terrible?

A woman working at another desk rose and silently lifted a cafetière to pour coffee which Martin muttered to Betty was about as bitter and cold as the weather. They sat waiting. After a minute Betty took the particulars of their new home out of her bag to gaze at the glossy photograph on the front. Their place might be small, but it was in a lovely old manor house with splendid country views. She smiled to herself. Martin thought she was being brave about it, but she wasn't: no need to feel ashamed of living there. She read the words she'd read dozens of times before.

Brambourne Manor is attributed in Nikolaus Pevsner's 'Buildings of England' series as having a late Georgian façade with two prominent bows of brick under a hipped and gabled clay-tile roof. The property is situated in the west wing and is self-contained over two storeys. The manor house, more than two centuries old, stands within ancient walled gardens in the centre of the delightful Hampshire village of Brambourne, beside its charming mediaeval church. The gardens, which are

communal, encircle the property to the south and west.
The extensive amenities found within Winchester's city
centre are within nine miles and the property is well
placed to afford easy access to riverside walks along
the course of the River Test, with its world-famous trout
fishing. There are five units in all . . .

England, it was real old England. Martin and Betty had
lived in Army quarters in so many places – Malaysia,
Cyprus, Germany, Ireland – and she'd liked them well
enough, but she'd dreamed of somewhere like this. She had
to admit she'd miss her half-acre garden in Church
Crookham, though, where she'd spent so many happy hours
at work. She'd loved the autumn digging with her robin for
company and the smell of the rich brown earth in her nostrils, and then the winter, a quiet time of waiting. Her young
twisty willow would be looking amazing now with its
corkscrew twigs outlined against the snow, but who would
feed her friend the robin the crumbs of cheese he loved?
And it would be horrid not to see everything shooting up
when spring came again, great sweeps of yellow and white
narcissus around the lawn and the apple trees vibrating to
the humming of bees among the blossoms – then later, as
summer came, the blousy beauty of the roses and the delicious scents of lavender and philadelphus . . . No, she
mustn't think of it. You could fall in love with a garden like
you could with a person; plants were living things, after all,
and she could have sworn that the depressed little lilac she
had transplanted to a sunnier spot had been saying thank
you when it flowered spectacularly the following year.
Saying goodbye had been painful, but it was no good looking
back. She wondered whether she'd be allowed to contribute
anything to the communal gardens at the manor, now a sadly
muddied patch after the developer's men had stored building
materials all over it. She could always try.
   The front door opened and a tall white-haired man with
startling black eyebrows came in. The agent leapt to his feet,
caught up a bunch of keys lying on his desk and pressed

them into his hand. 'Ah, Judge, you didn't have too bad a
drive down from London in this treacherous weather, I hope?
Good, good. Here are the keys then, and may you have many
happy years in your new home.'

A pair of hazel eyes surveyed the keys, and a baritone
voice stated: 'Three keys here, I am expecting four. Looking
at them I imagine it's the garage key that is missing. Could I
have it, please?'

The young man looked quite put out. 'Ah yes, of course, of
course. I put them all out ready for you first thing, it must
have been moved by some careless idiot.' He grappled with
the mess of papers at his desk, peering under them, clumsy
fingered with haste.

The Judge raised his black eyebrows at Martin and Betty. 'I
hope you're not mad enough to be moving today too?'

'Afraid so,' Martin acknowledged. 'We're awaiting the
release of our own keys. The long-range forecast never mentioned snow.'

'Ah, but then the British Isles are at the convergence point
of five weather systems, which accounts for the lunatic irra-
tionality of our weather changes.'

'Really?' Martin laughed. 'So we're not to blame for being
caught unawares?'

The Judge gave them a grin. 'Never!'

The woman at the next desk gave her struggling colleague
an expressionless look. 'You used a key to scratch your back
earlier, Alun. It's probably in your pocket.'

The key discovered, the Judge took it and nodded at the
Upcotts. 'Well, the very best of luck in your move.'

'And you too,' Martin said.

'What a nice man,' Betty murmured as the door closed
behind him.

The estate agent turned to them. 'Just popping out for a
minute or two, but when I come back I'm sure it'll be all systems go.' He opened the door, a spurt of snow blew in and he
blew out.

A girl stuck her head round a door beyond them; she had
a round face, immaculately made up, and the latest sleek

short haircut to her blonde head: 'Here, Liza, the photocopier isn't working.' The expressionless woman rose from her desk, pushing an impatient hand through her own hair. Betty noticed a wedding ring. Through the door she could hear mutterings and then, clearly: 'Did I ever tell you that men are a bunch of wasters? Well, I'm telling you again. This machine's run out of toner, but *he* doesn't put any more in, does he? Like all males, Alun waits for a woman to do the chores.'

'They're useless,' the younger girl agreed. 'And they're martyrs, too. Last night mine said to me: "I've done the washing-up for you!" in a tone like he'd walked through boiling oil. I said: "For me? For you, you mean. Most of it's your own yucky stuff."'

'Typical,' said Liza. 'Sometimes I call to Steve when I'm stuck peeling boring old potatoes and carrots, why doesn't he come and chat to me? But he moans the kitchen stools are too hard for his bum – truth is, he's terrified he might actually have to do something.'

'Mine's always got urgent business with his car. I yelled out the window at him on Sunday: "What's the car got that I haven't?" and then all his mates who were hanging about started sniggering, sod them. Sometimes I ask myself what I'm doing with him, anyhow.'

'Look, watch me,' said the woman Liza, 'then you can do the refill next time. Someone has to and I can tell you this, it won't be Alun. You're right, the average man's a waste of space. D'you know, ninety per cent of crimes are committed by men. Shows you, doesn't it?'

'Worthless. Girls ring up when you're ill, want to know how you are. Your partner doesn't bother. I can feel a cold coming on, it'll probably turn to flu with this weather, but all he'll think about is his stomach and his dick.'

A giggle rose up in Betty, but she suppressed it. The two women were funny but they were sad too. Oddly, they made her feel better about Martin's shortcomings. He might have made a mess of the wine business he'd set up with that man Gavin Farmer he'd thought so clever, but at least he did communicate with her, and, now she thought of it, he was terrific with machines. He'd always repair her household appliances and when they'd had two cars she'd never had to think about washing hers, or checking the tyres or getting it serviced. Organisation was his thing. But then he'd been in the Royal Corps of Transport, of course. She sighed. The Logistic Corps they called it now, joining several regiments together, shedding officers and men.

She shifted in her chair. Why did it have to change? Why did anything have to change? As a child she'd thought her world secure, its structures as solid as the mountains, but now she saw it as more resembling the sea. Those abiding horizons were an illusion, everything was in a state of upheaval, and unsuspected currents were wearing down the cliffs and grinding away the rocks she had thought indestructible. Rocks like the Army. As an officer, Martin should have had a career for life, such as her own father, Wing-Commander Pierce, had enjoyed in the RAF, but the Cold War had ended, the Iron Curtain had been torn down, and people like Martin were surplus to requirements. Redundant. Binned. It was happening in other places, too – the civil service, the City. 'Never dwell on sad thoughts, think positively,' was what her father used to say. She watched the snow swirling against the window, and shivered. It was hard to be positive, especially since Martin's stream of rejection letters made it clear he was never likely to find another job, not at fifty-two. Her heart ached for him.

The door to the street opened and the telephone rang simultaneously. The man called Alun nipped back in and seized the receiver. 'Good, good, good.' He turned to them, his shiny face beaming. 'There we are, all sorted out as I said. Now, Liza, where're those keys?'

Alex observed his angular wife as she stared from the window of their new flat: stupid black wool dress more suited to a drinks party than the unpacking of books and china, chunky shiny jewellery that made his eyes ache. Why couldn't Fenella have dressed in old jeans? Silly question, she wanted to impress her new neighbours. In the pale midday light that reflected off the snow she reminded him of the late Duchess of Windsor; something about that over-sleek dark hair, the long nose and chin, and, yes, the identical squared-up shoulders. He'd never cared for the Duchess of Windsor. What was Fenella griping about now?

'Just look at this,' she said, pointing with a bony finger. 'Two great removal vans parked end to end and entirely obstructing the drive. Suppose I need to go out?'

'But you don't,' said Alex. 'I did a vast food shop yesterday so we could sort the flat out today without interruption.'

'That's hardly the point. The people moving in must be very thoughtless. If you won't deal with it, then I shall. We have to start as we mean to go on.'

'Leave it . . .' Alex began, but she was already stalking from the room, her head pushed forward like a bird of prey about to pounce.

He peered from the window. Two large sinewy men, surrounded by half-a-dozen equally muscular lads, were stamping their feet and haranguing each other in the snow.

'Look,' came the aggrieved voice of the foreman of the rearmost vehicle. ' 'Ow are we supposed to unload the big stuff in 'ere when you've blocked off 'alf the entrance? You gotter move forward, mate, haven't you?'

'You got as much room as we 'ave,' said the driver of the first van, his breath smoking from his mouth. 'Only you ain't got organised right. See, what you gotter do is back out an' turn and come back in t'other way round. Then you ain't got no problem.'

Then Alex heard Fenella's high voice: 'Hold on, men, I don't see that either of you can leave those great things here, you're blocking the drive entrance and the exit. Suppose I want to get my car out? Suppose we have deliveries arrive?'

'We deal with that when it 'appens,' said the first driver, hitching his trousers and looking contemptuous. 'Unless you wants to come out this minute. Do yer?'

Fenella's voice became edgy: 'I could well do just that. Now look here . . .'

A mellow baritone intervened in calm but firm tones: 'I'm sure these men will move their vehicles any time you want. And my wife and I will do our best not to be a nuisance. Now tell me, are you by any chance a resident here?'

A searing feeling ripped across Alex's gut, a terrifying suspicion that he knew the owner of that voice. He leaned forward, caught a glimpse of a white head. He did. Dear God! He hurtled from the room and rushed for the front door.

'Judge Thorne!' he gasped. 'Well, how extraordinary! And pleasant. How do you happen to be here? Friends in the neighbourhood, perhaps?' Gabbling like an idiot, thrown completely off balance. Pull yourself together, man. 'Have you met my wife? Fenella, this is Judge Thorne.' Emphasis on the judge bit, stop Fenella from making fools of them both in this tiresome bossy manner. What would Hugh Thorne make of his overdressed wife? Most men, he suspected, secretly disliked her while finding her sexually challenging, a situation which too often led to exchanges of the sort of leering banter Alex detested, but at which his wife excelled.

Hugh Thorne's eyes examined the pale sphere of her face, the thinly arched eyebrows, the flashing fuchsia-lipsticked smile. His hand touched Fenella's, he murmured: 'How do you do?', then turned back: 'Alex Lindridge. Well, hello, good to see you. Surprising, though. Have you been moved to the Western Circuit?'

Alex shook his head, the remembrance of his disaster sweeping through him. 'No, I've . . . well, I've retired. Early. It was when the new Court Service came into being and my grade was scrapped.'

'I'm horrified. What are you doing?'

'Apart from moving here two days ago, nothing. I thought I'd find a new job but people of my age aren't wanted.'

'What a waste of a good man.'

Fenella, huffy at being ignored, was strutting into the flag-stoned hall giving no evidence of hearing these words, but Alex was certain she had. Salve on the wound. His mind continued to stagger around the oddity of the Judge's presence here. 'But – what are you doing here yourself?'

'A transfer to Winchester. Unexpected but very welcome as a refuge from travelling across London to Snaresbrook. My wife refused to consider selling our Richmond house for sentimental reasons, so we've bought the first-floor flat here as a pied-à-terre. Are we to be neighbours?'

Neighbours. Alex's heart thumped with shock. 'It seems so. We have the ground-floor flat,' he said lamely. 'It's very nice. At least, the drawing-room is.' Nothing in comparison with Judge Thorne's house in Richmond, of that he had no doubt. Alex had wanted to escape from the people he knew in Wimbledon, from his erstwhile colleagues in the Court Service and their condescending sympathy in his enforced retirement. Some had even said they envied him: 'Wish I could escape from the daily grind, pop off for a holiday any time I wanted.' Stupid, insensitive clods. Hadn't it occurred to them that he'd missed out on those last most productive years for paying off the mortgage, so that decent holidays would be out of the question? Or that he'd be bored out of his mind hanging around the house? Every day his existence seemed more shoddy and useless, the weight of his shame more suffocating. But he was not to be allowed isolation. He should have known he couldn't escape. And yet, there was a certain comfort in its being Judge Thorne who'd turned up here. He was known as a tough man, with a sharp and driving intelligence, but he was all right. He treated you with the same friendliness he'd extend to someone on his own level.

A car shot into the drive and braked behind the rearmost vehicle. A middle-aged man and woman emerged with haste.

Hugh Thorne stared. 'I don't believe this,' he muttered.

'Keys released at last, sorry about the wait,' the man called to the removals team, who were jumping gloomily back out from the van into the snow. 'All systems go now, but you'll need to back up a bit.'

'Back up?' the driver said. 'Owjer mean? We can't lug stuff no further'n this, not with all this ice and muck around, you'll 'ave things damaged.'

'It's all right,' the man reassured him in a brisk no-nonsense way, 'we're moving into the west wing, this door back here.'

From the first pantechnicon a male snigger came; the second driver muttered something presumably not compli-mentary, swung himself into his cab and backed up in a noisy display of irritation. When he switched off his engine the silence was deep and frosty. The Judge broke it, moving forward to speak to the new arrivals.

'Hello, we met at the estate agents, didn't we? That stupid fellow must have known we were moving to the same place, yet it never occurred to him to introduce us. How ridiculous. Let me make amends – I'm Hugh Thorne and my friend here is Alex Lindridge.'

'Hello. I'm Martin Upcott, and this is my wife, Betty.'

They shook hands. Martin, an upright stocky man with short sandy hair and a strained look, wore beneath an open mack an elderly regimental blazer and battered flannels, while Betty, shorter and on the plumpish side, was clad in the sort of clothes Alex wished his own wife would wear: a dark green car coat and thick pullover over those Black Watch tartan trousers Fenella had sneered at in the shops a couple of years ago, 'I'd look like somebody's aunt,' she'd said, 'you surely wouldn't want that, Alex?' But he would. He'd liked his aunts; sensible, comfortable women in sen-sible, comfortable clothes. Betty's face was the tanned outdoor sort that theirs had been, crumpled rather than lined, and her straight light brown hair was twisted into an untidy knot at the back. She was smiling, but like her hus-band, she had a strained look. Maybe this move was upsetting for them, too. Fleetingly he thought how com-forting thoughts of other people's troubles were when you were suffering yourself.

He said: 'Well, it does seem presumptuous from someone who only moved in himself two days ago, but welcome to Brambourne Manor.'

'Thank you,' Betty said, then, 'oh, my goodness, Martin, we'd better get the front door open and start organising

things or we'll be in trouble – look, the men are taking packing cases out already and by the look of that darkening sky
there's more snow coming.'

'I'm afraid you're right,' said the Judge, rubbing cold
hands together and swivelling on his heel, 'and my wife will
be cursing because I'm not inside directing operations. She's
already busy checking that everything's connected that
should be.'

'Wait,' Alex told them, his brain whirling. *My friend*,
Judge Thorne had called him. He felt charitable towards the
whole world. 'Look, you must all come to us and have . . .'
What? A meal sometime? Drinks? He could hardly invite
them to dinner, not for days, not with all of them in turmoil
and Fenella in a foul mood. Besides, there was the expense.
What then? They must start as they meant to go on, as
Fenella had said, but if he could manage it, it would be on
very different terms from what she envisaged. 'Come to us
for coffee tonight after dinner and a drink or two. To relax
and take a breather. A meeting of neighbours. And your wife,
naturally, Judge.'

'Hugh, please,' he said, poised to go. 'If you're sure that's
all right?'

'Half past eight, then. And strictly informal. No need to
change.'

Hugh strode off. The Upcotts' tired eyes swivelled towards
one another in a brief wordless question. Then Martin
answered for them both that this was very kind of . . . Alex,
wasn't it? They would look forward to it.

3

Hugh and Celia worked hard for the next few hours. While he darted from doorway to doorway with the removals men, assigning pieces of furniture brought from Richmond to their exact locations according to Celia's plans, she was busy in her roomy kitchen establishing places for her shining new cookery equipment and copper-bottomed pans. She'd refused point-blank to cart anything culinary around: 'If I'm to be living in two places at once I want something of everything in both. Imagine what a pain it would be if I forgot your favourite Winemaster corkscrew!' Now, glimpsing her choice of white-painted Edwardian table and cane-seated chairs already in place at the far end of the room, delightful against the leafy green wallpaper and greeny-grey dado, Hugh pondered the alluring nature of new possessions. What was it about them that was so stimulating? Was it their celebratory mint condition of colour and form? Did they induce a fresh-start feeling akin to the advent of spring? For there was no doubt that Celia, despite all her grumbling, had a bounce in her step.

Taking advantage of a lull in the removals men's activities, he paused in the doorway. 'It's going to look good,' he told her.

She withdrew her head from a cupboard to survey her territory. 'Better than good, great!' she stated.

Her satisfaction was reminiscent of the artist Celia choosing flowers to paint. 'Isn't that enchanting?' she'd say, gloating over a candelabra primula or a Cardinal de Richelieu rose. He liked her enthusiasms. And he thanked God that she also had the hoarding instincts of a squirrel, instincts that had enabled her to retrieve a good-looking assortment of old walnut and mahogany furniture from their Richmond attics to furnish these rooms, together with a dilapidated Venetian mirror she'd spent her evenings restoring, and, rolled-up beneath the eaves, a blue needlework rug with a stylised design of yellow and white flowers which Celia swore she'd never seen before in her life. 'But it settles my drawing-room colour scheme.'

He returned to the drawing-room, with its great curving bay of sash windows, and was fascinated to see how the room was gradually taking on a character of its own as piece by piece the furniture was put in position, lamps set on their tables, the Venetian mirror hung above the chimney piece. Tomorrow the ample old mahogany desk he'd discovered in a Winchester antique shop would be delivered and he thought he'd have it in front of the middle window. He could prepare his summings-up there on summer evenings, lifting his head to gladden his eyes with the Hampshire countryside beyond. Then he let out an impatient mutter: it wasn't summer now; he should have ordered logs for the fire.

Two men staggered in with a bookcase. 'In the alcove flanking the fireplace, and then its pair on the other side,' Hugh directed them, lending a steadying hand and then heading for the kitchen and Celia's list of *Things to be Done*. As he scrawled down *Order logs*, he recollected that they were to have coffee and drinks at the Lindridges after they had eaten.

'You mean I have to have a bath and look respectable tonight of all nights?' Celia protested. 'Who are they? What are they like, anyway?'

'Alex was a member of the Lord Chancellor's Department, took early retirement. Good man, you'll like him. And he specifically said not to change.'

As Betty walked into the Lindridges' drawing-room she was

Hazel Hucker

grateful that she had changed her elderly trousers for something smarter. Her hostess, sleek in a black wool dress with a black and gold silk scarf floating from her long thin neck, looked as though she had this minute emerged from Harrod's designer clothes department, while the Judge's wife, Celia, though more simply clad in knitted top and trousers, looked distinctly stylish. Unlike the room, Betty thought, accepting a cup of coffee from Fenella. Its furniture was of mixed origin: a modern drinks cabinet, squishy off-white leather sofas and smoked-glass coffee tables conflicting with a pair of cherrywood cupboards and two tub-shaped chairs that she suspected were Biedermeier – the unadorned Germanic good taste of a hundred years ago. Over the fireplace were pictures of sand and putty-coloured rectangles superimposed with apparently floating blue and green shapes. Not unattractive, but curious in their eighteenth-century setting.

As she drank her coffee, Betty looked at the teenage boy and girl lolling on the far sofa with an air of bored detachment. Both were wearing faded blue jeans, he with a fraying oversized blue pullover, she with a skimpy purple mohair affair. When Alex pronounced their names: 'My son, Duncan, my daughter, Donna,' the boy nodded, the girl simply stared, or, more accurately, glared. What could they be thinking, feeling? They had just moved house, they were among strangers, yet they showed no wish to be friendly with their new neighbours, as she would have done at their ages. As indeed she had been anxious to do each time Martin had been posted somewhere new. In Army quarters abroad you lived marooned on a cabbage patch of British solidarity where your colleagues were also perforce your neighbours and friends. Creating positive relationships wove lifelines for times when troubles struck, held loneliness at bay and made friends for the youngsters. You were all much of an age, you all had families – after all, what else was there for the wives to do but produce babies?

Young people today baffled her. Her own son, Adam, a tall, dark, driven young man, now twenty-five years old and working in New Jersey, was remote from her, and not only by the width of the Atlantic. That this had been virtually inevitable in view of their nomadic Army life and the years of boarding school separation, failed to comfort her. She wanted to be near her child in his thoughts and beliefs, but he could have come from another continent, an alien culture. He was a scientist, an engineer; he read nothing but abstruse engineering journals or computer magazines. She loved poetry, good fiction, gardening, the countryside. He was dismissive of such incidentals to reality; his work was his life. He was fond of her in an offhand way, responding to her regular telephone calls pleasantly, even, in moments that she treasured, calling her 'Mother dear', but she knew in her guts that the moment he put the telephone down he switched her from his thoughts. Two years after Adam's birth Betty had miscarried at five months; the dead child had been a girl. Often she yearned for that child; a daughter stayed close to her parents, would have been a friend. This girl Donna appeared scornful and darkly smouldering; Betty would never have indented for an adolescent with such a scowl, and yet there was something appealing about the way the thick lashes of the downcast eyes lay on the chubby downy cheeks, something unresolved and vulnerable about the slumped young body with its unexpectedly womanly curves.

Alex Lindridge removed her coffee cup and handed her a glass of claret. She sipped and blinked with pleasure. Martin would relish this. Wine was still his greatest interest. While they lived in Germany their holidays had invariably taken them to wine-producing areas, the Rhône, Burgundy, the area round Bordeaux, driving from vineyard to vineyard, château to château, tasting, comparing, cogitating, Martin's eyes aglow with pleasure as he stowed case after case in the car. Sometimes his colleagues had asked him to select wine for them, but even when he'd bought at special discounts he had refused to take a profit. 'Not from my friends,' he would reproach her. Occasionally she resented the cost of his obsession, but then she'd acknowledge that she did enjoy the sun-drenched vineyards, and remind herself that there were plenty of officers with sillier or more expensive hobbies –

better good wine than showy cars, or horses with vets' bills as long as your arm. She sighed and finished her glass. Immediately Alex crossed the room to refill it.

She smiled, thanked him. 'It's excellent.'

'It is indeed,' the Judge said. (She couldn't think of him in any other way, though he'd said to call him Hugh.) 'First class. You have a sound palate, Betty.'

She looked across at her sturdy upright husband. 'It was Martin who educated it. He's the expert,' she said.

'How did you acquire your expertise, Martin?'

'It was always a hobby with me, and then after I left the Army I was in the wine business for, oh, five or six years.'

'In the Army, were you? What regiment?'

Martin told him. 'For more than twenty-five years,' he added.

'I did my national service in the Green Jackets,' the Judge said. 'And enjoyed it. In fact I wouldn't have minded the Army life myself if I hadn't had my career already mapped out. So you retired as what? A major? Yes. And took the redundancy money when it was offered.'

'Yes, it looked like good money then, so I accepted it and went into the business with a friend.'

'Brave of you. How did it go?'

Martin stared into his glass, swirling the wine around. Betty watched him. She knew he would set out his words with care, an exercise in damage limitation to his pride. He'd flamed with anger at Gavin Farmer when dissolving the partnership had first been mooted, pacing the bedroom floor at four in the morning, muttering at being cheated and betrayed – for the second time. 'First the Army rejects me, then my friend. What's happened to the world that you can trust no one?' That he felt mistreated and disillusioned she knew only too well, but it was not something he wanted to reveal to outsiders. His jawline tightened and the faint new tic in his cheek started up.

He said evenly: 'It was not a success. I went into it with the best of intentions. The Army offered me a course in business management and I took it, but no course can replace experience and that I lacked. The friend I was working with was optimistic, over-optimistic, I see now, and neither of us had reckoned on matters like the recession or rising interest rates.'

'Or the growing competition?' Alex asked.

Martin shook his head. 'We were buying unusual wines — from Turkey, Bulgaria, Latin-American countries – as well as the more usual stuff, trying to establish our own niche in the market. It went all right for a while, we met a lot of people in the area, made a lot of friends. They'd come to the wine-tastings all right, promise to buy, but the real business failed to materialise. Then Gavin, my business partner, pulled out. I cursed him at the time, but I suppose he was right. We were undercut by the big boys; they could afford the flamboyant special offers, the big discounts for companies' entertainment requirements and so on, we couldn't. Then Oddbins set up almost next door. Previously the competition had at least been at a distance, but that finished it. I pulled out too.'

'And moved here, where it's charming but less expensive,' Betty said protectively.

'It was hard luck,' the Judge said.

'So you, like me, Martin,' Alex said moodily, 'are living in restricted circumstances, on a lesser pension than you'd expected.'

'You too? In the same boat?'

'Yes. From the civil service. Age discrimination. Infuriating, isn't it? But there are many of us about.' He sat down on the far end of a sofa from his wife, picking up his glass and hiding his thoughts behind it, hating the admission he'd just made, trying still to grapple with a shock of change he'd never anticipated. He'd been brought up with the belief that a post in the civil service was a job for life. But then so many aspects of life had changed equally dramatically.

'It's the current atmosphere,' the Judge said, stretching out his long legs. 'Nothing's to be taken for granted any more. The government's been squeezing the civil service and the armed services to save money; a deliberate reduction in numbers. The trouble in both is that men trying to save their empires become ruthless, shedding others to save themselves.'

Alex looked up. 'You describe it exactly. I remember discussing with my immediate superior the need to make cuts, defending my people. Too late I realised that I should have been guarding my own position. I was over fifty – I was expendable.'

His wife shifted irritably at the other end of the sofa, wriggling her shoulders and tugging the black wool of her dress down towards her bony knees. She breathed deeply through her nostrils. 'I told him he was a fool to be so trusting.'

The Judge glanced at her and away. 'They were fools to let you go,' he said to Alex. 'In my opinion you were making a valuable contribution and always would.'

Alex's eyelids blinked at this forthright support. He shrugged and muttered: 'Oh, I wouldn't know . . . I mean, I was never going to set the Thames on fire.'

'I've never seen any point in setting the Thames on fire,' Hugh returned with caustic humour. 'Yes, we need the occasional genius, but there's a bigger need for the solidly reliable who do the hard graft, the consolidating, the sorting out of the daily problems. Those who understand how the structure has been built over past years, and why, who can grasp ideas and translate them into action – and more important still, who bring along with them the people working alongside them. Chaps like you, fifty or not.'

'Thanks, Judge, you're very generous,' Alex said, his voice rough, his cheeks reddening. He sucked in air, glanced at his white-faced wife, at his slumped son and daughter listening with enigmatic faces, and burst out: 'You know what really sticks in my gullet? It's that all the awful people had the exact same retirement package as me. You know the sort – the idle, the ones who go off sick every time the pressure's on, the ones who feel up the typists in the lifts – people one despises. It's sick. The computer spits out your seniority – but your real input counts for nothing. The computer can't quantify it, so who cares?'

'What can I say?' Hugh replied. 'I know, I sympathise, it's wrong. But don't think you weren't appreciated, because you were, and by others as well as me.'

'I'll hang on to that.' Alex picked up the wine bottle from the smoked-glass table beside him. 'Here, let me refill your glass.'

'With pleasure,' Hugh said. 'It's just what I need after the hardest day's physical work I've done in years.'

'If the wine's so good,' Donna interrupted from her sofa, sticking out her glass to her father, 'then pour me more too. Come on, Dad, fill it up.'

Alex hesitated visibly before half-filling her glass.

'What's this?' she demanded, holding it up to the light. 'Wise up, will you? I'm growing up, so you keep telling me, time *I* started to develop a palate. That's one of the smart things of life, isn't it, Mummy darling? Like playing good tennis and riding well and knowing which designers are the *in* names for this season and who's having it off with whom.'

Her brother turned his lolling head towards her to say with a grin: 'But there's nothing smart in not knowing when you've had enough, Donna. I saw you sneaking the stuff before they came.'

'Oh, shut up,' she snarled. 'I'm all right.' She pulled herself upright and sipped her wine with exaggerated delicacy. 'But I could do with cheering up. Maybe some good news for once. But that's not available and this is.'

There was an almost tangible hostility about the girl. Betty noted the abrasive voice and wondered why the bitterness. She hesitated to probe, and besides, in life it is not easy to make real contact with strangers' minds. How can you ask the right questions when you're starting from nothing and you've no idea what you're searching for? Words are exchanged on a superficial level of good intentions that in the end creates its own fog of misunderstanding – with adolescents, almost inevitably so. But this girl wasn't to be a stranger, she was their near neighbour.

She leaned forward to ask Donna whether she disliked the move but recollecting the words of a counsellor friend

she paused; questions must be neutral, never framed in a
way that suggests an answer, worse, a negative answer.
Conscientious Betty reframed her question. 'How do you feel
about living here, Donna?'

A shrug. 'Could be worse,' the girl conceded.

'Where have you come from?'

'Wimbledon.' Her voice was grudging, irritable. Slumped
again, she lowered her chin on to her chest and a swirl of
dark hair flopped over her eyes.

Betty pondered her, determined for some unfathomable
reason not to relinquish her concern. School, was that it?
Where would she go now? She asked: 'What about school
here? Or have you left?' A deft touch there, implying she'd
reached that desirable stage.

Donna shook her head, flicking the hair back. 'Wish I had,'
she said sourly. 'But I've got years to go yet and exams to
pass. I was all right till this happened but Dad losing his job
and then the move's mucked it all up. I have to change
schools and it's wrecking my life.'

'The move has been a trauma for us all,' Fenella told her
guests with an impatient gesture. 'We've had to leave our
very nice six-bedroomed house in Wimbledon with its swimming pool to live almost entirely on Alex's pension in this
little place. He's lost his post in the profession he'd believed
would be his for all his working life. I've lost my friends and
my interests. Well, one copes, I suppose, but it's hardly what
I, for one, expected, to be brought to this level at our age. Yes,
Donna's had to change schools, but we're told the Sixth-form
College is excellent. She'll find friends there; the change
won't be as disastrous as she thinks. She'll even have a wider
list of subjects to choose from.'

Betty intercepted the fury of Donna's glare at her mother.
'It's desperately hard for anyone . . .' she began, but Donna
overrode her.

'I'll never get a better art teacher than I had at St Hilda's,'
she exploded. 'Mrs Peel really understood where I was at.
She was special. She ran our art club and we looked at developments in art history and things. Her pictures were

brilliant, too. She was always selling them. Get over it? Hah! You don't understand, Mum; you'll never understand.'

Fenella sighed. 'Donna wants to go to art college simply to paint,' she shrugged, 'though I can't imagine the appeal. You find such strange types in that sort of place, grubby, rings in their noses, involved in drugs, drink, God knows what. She's an intelligent girl; she's always done well in art and I know she's good, but she can aim for something better, something steadier. Combine painting with lecturing, perhaps. Women need a secure career these days when men lose their jobs in an instant. As much as anything's secure. Painting's all right for a hobby, an interest – I'm interested in modern paintings myself – but it's no good for a steady income, is it? I'd rather she had a professional qualification behind her.'

'Graphic artists are in demand, surely?' Betty questioned, tensing at Fenella's words. 'And then there are book illustrators, people like that.' She knew she was speaking from ignorance, but she was suddenly so sorry for Donna that she had to contradict Fenella. Her irritable pronouncements, her lack of concern for her daughter's feelings, her scorn of art students – they filled her with such distress that she nearly choked on her wine. Perhaps she herself could help Donna sort out her problems and her awkward mother. Adam was gone but Betty had not discarded her interest in young people; yes, she could talk to her. A spasm of warm, preoccupied, older-woman concern tugged at her chest. Happiness was far more important in the long term than professional success; it did not occur to her that for some the two were synonymous.

Softly, coolly, Celia was saying: 'I am an artist. I went to art school in London and in Paris.'

Silence in the room. Donna blinked. 'Seriously?'

'Seriously. And I've sold my work without problem.'

'Celia's a botanical artist,' Hugh told them.

'That's different,' Fenella conceded. 'I mean, it's highly refined, highly specialised.'

Donna jerked her head forward, appraising Celia. 'Why a botanical artist?'

Celia laughed and explained how at school she had thought herself all set to spend her life painting wonderful perceptive portraits. She had found faces fascinating, and bodies too. That was why she had gone to Paris, for the life class at a famous art school. It was a summer course run by a professor everyone had assured her was brilliant. And he *was* brilliant – at stripping any students he thought unworthy of every scrap of hope or pride. The class was to have a final exhibition, he was to judge which of their works were deserving, talking them through each one in class, dissecting its strengths and its weaknesses. It came to Celia's turn and she had stood up – to be destroyed. She had no sense of anatomy or form, worse, she had attempted to follow the latest modern style without the least comprehension of its underlying concepts, she had proved herself a mere copyist . . . 'I won't go on,' she ended. 'Suffice to say that at the end of his denunciation I burst into tears and sat down with a bump – smack on to my sticky palette, laid down on my stool. Disaster! I leapt up with the thing stuck to my trousers, the class fell about with glee – and relief that it wasn't them, no doubt. I ran, never to return.' She gave a huge sigh and pulled a face.

Her audience laughed sympathetically. 'Poor you!' said Alex.

'Terrible,' Donna shuddered. 'Christ, I'd just die if that happened to me.'

Celia shook her white head. 'Don't be depressed by my cautionary tale, Donna, it was, in fact, very much for the best. At home a kindly aunt who wanted to console me commissioned me to paint her favourite roses. I took out my watercolours, I did my best, she showed the results to her friends, and suddenly I was in demand. And they paid me! So I studied the botanical construction of plants and how best to depict them, and I've never looked back.'

'Ah, I like that story,' Betty said.

'How do you work?' Donna wanted to know.

'I try to work every day, every morning at least. I suppose you could say that I work as I'm inspired – but then that's limited by what's available at the time.'

'You couldn't work at this time of year then,' Fenella remarked dismissively.

'Oh, no, there's plenty of material available in January,' Betty contradicted her. This was something she knew about; while planning her own garden she'd studied books and read articles so that she could have plants in flower through every month of the year. 'Apart from the berried plants there's, oh, witch hazel, winter jasmine, several of the viburnums and chimonanthus flowering, and of course the lovely helle-bores – Christmas roses to you, I suppose,' she added almost rudely.

'I scent a gardener,' Celia commented. 'Passionately so? Then I'm glad we're to be neighbours.'

Donna brushed aside the chitchat. 'Do you work in water-colours or oils or what?'

'Watercolours totally for botanical work – though when I'm on holiday I use gouache for landscapes. No oils, I find them too messy. I paint all morning inside the house, it's no good outside, there's too much light and of course it moves.'

'It does, doesn't it?' Donna giggled unexpectedly. 'It mucks up the shadows.'

'Sometimes I'll draw outside,' Celia added, 'perhaps a sun-flower, balancing myself on a step-ladder. Neighbours think I'm mad. But I'm inside again to paint it. And I'll tell you this, one has to be quick because flowers will go over if they can. But before I start I look at their construction. I use a lens and I really do work at it.'

'There's nothing impressionist about Celia's work,' Hugh said. 'It's absolutely meticulous and that's why it's so beau-tiful and convincing.' He put down his wineglass and stood up. 'There are two or three in our hall waiting to be hung. I'll show you if you like.'

'Yeah, please. So go on,' Donna urged Celia. 'How do they get sold? That's what my mother's bound to want to know.'

Celia sighed. She disliked the atmosphere in the room and she was tired. She longed to go back to the flat, ignoring its chaotic state, and tumble into bed, to sleep and sleep. She had been up since six o'clock. But the bed still had to be made, and this odd, tense girl Donna, gazing at her, must be answered. 'Well, there are commissions, and exhibitions. Then there are the prints which I have made in Italy on very fine paper and most years I sell them at the Chelsea Flower Show. That's great fun. Lots of people around with money to spend – and my prints are easier to take home than the plants other exhibitors can sell only on the last day. It's the best show there is, Chelsea. I take twenty to thirty copies of each print and I usually sell the lot.'

'Pour us some more wine, Alex, will you?' Fenella instructed her husband before turning to Celia to enquire off-handedly: 'What sort of prices do you charge for an original painting?'

'A price in four figures,' Celia answered with cool disdain. 'No, no more wine, thank you.'

Donna's full childish mouth was open. 'Wow!'

'The name Celia Thorne is familiar to the *cognoscenti* in these matters,' the Judge observed as he returned through the half-open door.

Betty felt a distinct frisson of pleasure as Fenella first stiffened and then visibly underwent a transformation, her body inclining towards Celia in consideration of such affluence and celebrity status, her cheeks blotching with patches of red. 'Fascinating, goodness, how fascinating. Celia, I thought you were speaking of a hobby, but this is different. I had no idea . . .' Her voice trailed away and she covered up with a cough. 'I do admire you.'

Donna told her derisively: 'And you said money can't be made in art!'

Hugh Thorne propped his wife's work on two chairs, flung out his hand in demonstration. 'Hellebores, painted in the New Year by my wife, and winter heathers.'

Betty fished in her bag for her spectacles and perched them on her nose. They're exquisite, she thought as she focussed on Celia's work, goodness, how enchanting. She opened her lips to say so, but Donna was there before her.

'Hey,' she exhaled, squatting down before them, 'that's something different. That's clever. Those shadows – Duncan,

Dad, look – white flowers on white paper and yet they're so real you feel you could pick them off it. And the detail's stupendous! They're out of this world!'

Young Duncan, actually upright and leaning over to see, informed his sister that the ribs and veins of the leaves were so fine they must have been put in under a magnifying glass by the steadiest hand in the world. 'And you couldn't do that after what you've drunk, Donna.'

Celia was looking embarrassed, her eyes meeting her husband's with an unreadable look that could have been vexation. Perhaps, thought Betty, she felt her husband's affectionate display of her success to be out of place when others were mourning their descent into the black pit of unemployment, their displacement from the worthwhile. But no, she reasoned, the Judge wasn't like that, he had said all sorts of kindly things to Alex Lindridge. She had a certainty that his display of the botanical paintings had been to interest and reassure Donna (and snub that snobbish mother of her's), never to make Martin or Alex feel bad. He was a nice man; she'd felt that when they met at the estate agents' that morning – was it truly only a few hours ago? And the pictures *were* wonderful.

'I love them,' she said. She might persuade Martin to give her one or two of the prints for her next birthday – if they could afford it.

In a moment's silence she heard the soughing of the wind round the house. She hoped the snow had stopped falling, pretty or not, because when you were moving house the dirty slush got walked everywhere, horrid stuff. And to think of the cost of the carpets made her nervous, even though they had bought them direct from a factory in Wiltshire. 'Just stop fretting,' Martin told her, 'we ought to be able to afford them, after all.' He made Betty cross sometimes over money; she didn't think he understood it properly. What had *ought to* got to do with keeping the bank account in credit? You either had the money or you hadn't, in which case you made do. Martin refused to admit this nasty truth. He still drank wine every day at dinner; when she reminded him that water was free he looked shocked. 'One must have some standards in one's life,' he said. But he didn't mind Betty drinking water.

Celia and Hugh were rising and saying their goodbyes: 'A delightful evening . . . so pleased we've all met . . . so kind.'

Perhaps the look Betty had seen was their marital code for *Come on, let's go, darling.* Tiredness overwhelmed her. She must catch Martin's eye, signal her own message. Oh, she was thankful she'd thought to make up the bed before they came. She ached to climb between those worn sheets, to lay her head on the kind cotton of her pillows and seek oblivion. 'Goodbye everyone . . . an unexpectedly pleasant evening . . . So glad . . . Good night.'

4

Celia liked solitude, it affected her much as others are moved by being in church. She felt peaceful, light at heart, at the edge of revelation. When Hugh drove off for his first day in Winchester Crown Court the next Monday morning, she poured herself a second cup of coffee, leaned back in her chair and reflected on the charm and desirability of her new kitchen, so neat, so clean, and, up on the first floor as it was, full of pale light, so different from the semi-basement gloom at Richmond. She felt changed here, and to confirm that feeling she ate, unusually, a second slice of toast, hot and buttery, topped with her own special three-fruit marmalade. As she licked her fingers it occurred to her that the strange pale light must be a reflection of the snow. She rose and from the rear window saw fields and low downland glistening white under the winter sun – remote and beautiful, yet bleak in their emptiness. She cleared the dishes, and from the window over the sink found a less chilly, more congenial outlook along the lane that joined Brambourne with Abbotsbridge. Here were cottages, thatched or slated beneath the snow, an ancient inn, the church tower with its gilded clock, a black cat licking its paw on a flint wall. She stood transfixed, a cloth in her hand, as the clock chimed. She must paint that view, that slanting apricot sunshine. She visualised it at winter's end and wondered whether there would be celandines and primroses in the churchyard. The idea of a series of wild-flower paintings leapt to her mind.

She thought of the blue viper's bugloss, an older generation's remedy against snakebite, and valerian, white, pink and red, used as a sedative as late as the First World War air raids, and honeysuckle for headaches and lung diseases. She remembered with affection childhood walks down country lanes with her grandmother, who had taught her all the names of the flowers and their uses.

In the dining-room she unpacked china. When later she ventured outside to find the dustbins, it was an unsmiling Donna who told her where they were.

'There,' she gestured, jumping with care, up, down and round on the snow that covered the manor-house courtyard. 'Look, the green door.' Pant, bounce, a sigh of impatience. 'It must have been a tackroom. Yeah, that's it. Gotta keep bins out of sight.' Another jump, eyes on the ground, woollen scarf flying. 'You've got smart new ones. I saw.'

Celia deposited her binbags full of packaging material, shut the door and turned. Donna had vanished. A pity her footprints had smirched the purity of the courtyard. But then as she ran back upstairs she saw from the window that the girl had not spoiled the snow, rather she had made patterns; comically, clumsily, but recognisably, she had created two flowerheads, the prints of her trainers the petals, a twisted sole the central disc. Daisies? A strange fancy.

Alex finished organising the clothes in his wardrobe, bundled two more pullovers and a dozen assorted socks into his chest of drawers, and thought, that's it, the bedroom's done. He'd even hung Fenella's latest picture, *Woman with a Lemon*, above the bed, where the pale intersecting planes of the mouth, cheeks, nose and eyes of the sub-Picasso female it depicted with her acid-yellow fruit would haunt his every dream. He perched on the windowsill and glowered at the snow, shuddering at the white emptiness that seemed to stretch for ever. Today the world appeared particularly brutal, and the winds of his circumstances so merciless and disheartening that he would have liked to curl up in bed with the purple duvet over his head and retreat into a semicomatose existence like a prenatal child. But there was no hope of that, not with Fenella's constant carping about the hundred-and-one tasks she had awaiting him. Still, he could have a coffee, and he might just manage ten minutes in an armchair with the newspaper. He clapped his hand to his forehead. Oh hell, no papers ordered yet.

Take a grip, Alex, he admonished himself. OK, go to the shop in Abbotsbridge, a mile away, and order the papers. Tell Fenella it's too slippery to drive, walk instead, take a break from sorting out the flat to her machine-gun rattle of instructions. His wife was in the kitchen, he could hear her on the telephone. 'Darling, what fun!' she purred. 'On Wednesday . . .?' Something in the pitch of her voice made him stand still, scarcely breathing. 'No, of course I've still got my own car.' A high-pitched laugh. 'It is *my* car, don't forget. My emotionally dysfunctional husband may be financially stagnant, but *I*'m still pretty well off, thank God.' Really? He doubted it. Fenella used her money for her own amusements: all those designer clothes, her horrible pictures, her smart cars, her expensive lunches with friends, the Mediterranean holidays – they must have made inroads into her capital, mustn't they? On the other hand, she'd paid less towards their joint expenses. 'Suppose anything happened to you, Alex? How could anyone manage on half your pathetic pension? I have to protect myself. Besides, look how much I save you.' As a free housekeeper, she meant. True enough. What was she saying now? 'Oh awful, terrible, you can't imagine the slog and the boredom of this move . . . You will? That's sweet of you. Till Wednesday, then, darling.' Click.

Darling? Man or woman? His fingernails bit into the flesh of his palms. Please God, a man, please, God, someone to take her cold eyes away from his shortcomings. He felt at this moment, a prickling of hope. She'd had the occasional lover in the past, he was pretty certain. He'd ignored it, hadn't wanted to know. He wouldn't have been able to cope with the children and the house if she'd walked out on them in those earlier years, not given the long hours he worked for the Lord Chancellor's Department. At least a lover put her in a good mood, for once oblivious to the faults that otherwise were reiterated daily. Besides, at those times she wanted little to do with him sexually, and that had been his greatest relief. In bed Alex found her scrawny, chilly flesh about as exciting as a flatfish. He loathed loveless sex. Hard labour, followed by a forced feverish release. Maybe he could contemplate a love affair himself, now. Or could he? Come to think of it, when had he last had an erection? Was it weeks or months ago? The bastards had emasculated him. You wimp, he told his unresponsive penis. His momentary feeling of hope slid away. Maybe she was right, maybe he was useless.

He pushed at the kitchen door. 'I'm going to the post-office stores in Abbotsbridge, Fenella. Do you need anything?'

A shocked jump away from the telephone, a burnt-out stare. Her bony hands tore a piece of paper from a notepad to thrust it at him. 'It's all written down there,' she said. 'Don't leave anything out.'

Betty straightened herself from stowing cleaning materials beneath her sink and stared out at the snow. She longed to muffle herself up and stride out into those fields, following the prints of birds and foxes and maybe even deer along the hedgerows, making her own prints beside theirs. It was tantalising to see the sun burnishing the countryside from that intensely blue sky, yet to know that steadily, surreptitiously, it was destroying the very view it was enhancing. Already she had heard the creak and slither of snow on the steep roof of the west wing and seen the first flop of snow from the branches of the cedar in the garden. If this warmth persisted, by tomorrow the snow would be shrinking, its surface stained and blotched with earth. Oh, never mind that, she had to push on. There was a pile of furniture about the place, all to be allocated to some space, somewhere, and a dozen packing cases of china and books still to be unloaded.

Martin had marched into the living-room this morning, stood a moment staring, then announced with bitterness: 'You know we've brought too much furniture here, don't you? You understand we'll never fit it all in? Not unless we live in a virtual junk shop.'

'I know, I know,' Betty had said wearily, thinking of their reduction to just one living-room and two bedrooms. Yet she was loath to sell any more belongings than they had already forced themselves to do. Theirs were pleasant family pieces and you never knew when good times might not come again. Perhaps Martin would find a job after all. Or perhaps Adam would return from America and want to marry and settle down. Surely he wouldn't say no to his great-grandmother's pretty burr-walnut display cabinet or his great-uncle's mahogany davenport? If you sold such pieces you might gain badly needed money, but their elderly charm and the memories would be gone for ever. The thought made her shrink inside. She didn't want to lose more than she had already.

She grasped a couple of empty packing cases, lugged them outside and dumped them in the snow. Martin seemed to have disappeared. An age ago he'd gone to put the garden tools at the back of their garage that had once been a coach-house. She peered in that direction. 'Martin?' An echoing silence.

From behind her a voice said: 'Your husband's gone off with my dad to order the newspapers at Abbotsbridge post-office stores.'

Betty whirled round. 'Oh! Donna!' Her heart thumped.

Brown eyes examined her: 'I don't suppose he told you.'

'No, he didn't.'

'Mother says men are useless. They never . . . you know, make connections.'

'Martin's not bad,' Betty said with grumpy loyalty. 'It's just that I can't deal with some things on my own.'

'Like I said, he's not here,' Donna reiterated impassively. 'So, want me to help?'

Betty's first reaction was to refuse and hang on to her grievance. But the girl was offering, and Abbotsbridge and its store were a mile away. Besides, she wanted to get to know her. 'Thanks. Would you?'

'What then?'

Betty took a deep breath. 'Help me shove the furniture in the living-room into place so that it looks good? Some of it's heavy and it definitely won't be easy.'

Donna went past her into the west wing, a farmhouse-looking part with uneven old walls. 'Christ,' she uttered, standing in the sitting-room doorway, taking in the crammed state of the room. 'Yeah, well, you've got problems.'

'I hardly know where to start,' Betty admitted.

Donna stripped off a heavy sweater to reveal a woollen red-checked cowboy shirt and rolled up her sleeves. Grabbing two dining chairs and swinging them into the hall, she said: 'You start by lugging half this stuff out. Here, grab hold of these!' she added, and two pictures followed. 'Now this desk thing. Got to make room to get it sorted, haven't you?'

'Yes,' Betty said meekly, fielding the objects flung at her and stowing them to one side of the hall. 'You're right. Of course you are.'

When the room was half-empty Donna stopped to survey it, panting. A long rectangular room with a low ceiling and pleasant old casement windows, it overlooked the village street and the church as well as a side-garden. There was a wide brick fireplace and hearth.

'Not bad,' she approved. 'Now, big things first. What about this sofa and the chairs?'

'The sofa facing the fire and the armchairs on either side,' Betty suggested, shoving at the stout sofa, heaving at a chair.

Donna stopped her, creasing her brows in concentration. 'No, too sprawly. Look, there'd be no space behind the arm-chairs for other pieces and you can't afford that.' She pushed with huge young energy. 'Look, sofa *opposite* the two arm-chairs – at right angles to the fireplace. Put a rug between and the coffee table on that.'

Betty joined her, tugging the sofa round. 'You're right. A conversation piece.'

Donna grinned with a faint malice. 'Like in smart *Country Life* houses. We take that magazine because Dad thinks it's upper class to have around. He doesn't read it, though. I do.'

Betty glanced at her. There were things she ought to say, but couldn't . She substituted: 'Do you like the country?'

A shrug. 'Don't know yet. I like old houses, though. Interesting ones. Like this.' She helped Betty unroll a rich red and blue oriental rug, straightened herself and gestured around the room. 'Three hundred and fifty years. Think of all its inhabitants. My Grandma Lindridge told me once her old cottage is full of ghosts – sort of lingering feelings that have never dispersed. It's like . . . you come down her crookedy winding stairs hanging on to rope banisters and there's something about that makes you glow inside, but then there's an east bedroom that never feels right, not even when the morning sun's streaming in. She says there's a . . . a potency – you know, from all those births and deaths and hatreds.'

'And love scenes?' Betty smiled at Donna's fancies. 'But this house isn't so old. Two hundred years, maybe.'

Donna shook her head so that the luxuriant hair flew about her face. 'Uh-uh. It was started about the time King Charles lost his head, that's what our architect next-door neighbour in Wimbledon thought. I showed her the estate agents' photograph of the manor house and she was fascinated. She said the great bow windows with the grand front door between were a façade, um . . . superimposed on a much older building, a late Georgian squire's chintzy way of being one up on the neighbours.' She picked up one end of the mahogany coffee table. 'Now this,' she ordered.

Betty obeyed, setting it down on the rug, but her mind was on dates and historical settings. Her education as a child had not been of the academic sort, but history had been a favourite subject, particularly the larger-than-life Tudors and Stuarts. Could this part of the house truly be that old? How lovely if it were. She looked up. The big brick fireplace did have a tremendously wide chimney . . . supported by that big beam . . . and then there were those low diamond-paned windows. Elation rose in her. 'I'm going outside to look at the house.'

Donna followed her and they stood in the snow together

staring upwards. 'See,' Donna pointed to where the side wall of the bay swept back to join the west wing. 'Look at the hipped and gabled roofs. They don't fit those bows at all.'

'They don't, do they?' Betty took a deep breath. 'And most of the other windows are casement windows, older than the sash ones. Brambourne's original manor house was a rambling farmhouse till your pretentious squire decided to slap his handsome front on it.'

'Or his new wife talked him into it!'

She laughed. 'Yes, probably she demanded a touch of polish to the rural life.'

'My architect friend said the main roof beams here could be real oak timbers from old ships, since we're near ports like Southampton and Portsmouth. The old folk built to last and they looked for stuff that was seasoned and tough. Apparently if you look carefully you can see notches and things in them where lines or spars were attached.'

'That's an enticing thought. Shall we sneak up to see? I always dreamed of living in an interesting old house after years of blank-faced Army quarters, and this is turning out even better than I expected. Hey, thank you, Donna, you've made my day.'

'Good, isn't it? No, I tell you what, I bet your Martin and my dad are in the pub. They could have come and gone to the stores three times by now. We'll work fast and get your room perfect and amaze Martin when he gets back. And then we can nip up to the attics and really explore it all.'

Alex and Martin were seated side by side on a high-backed settle in The Bull in Abbotsbridge, each with a second pint of real ale before him.

'Good, isn't it?' Alex said, gesturing with his tankard.

'First rate,' said Martin, lifting his in return. 'Good place, good atmosphere. I'm glad you brought me.' His thawing feet were relishing the heat of the fiercest log fire he'd seen in years. 'My sort of place.' There were old prints and pictures of Hampshire above the oak wainscoting on the walls, comfortable elderly furniture and a Jack Russell terrier asleep in a corner chair.

'The White Hart in Brambourne's a decent bolt-hole as well.'

Martin grinned and gulped at his ale. 'Like that with you, too, is it?'

'Fenella,' Alex said carefully, 'is remarkably articulate in voicing her indignation over my dismantled career, and her performance as a martyr is worthy of an Oscar. I think she feels the indignity more than I do. It's her friends. They see her as married to a failure.'

'Betty, I have to admit, has been saintly. She wears this brave and suffering face, and she's terribly, terribly kind to me. About everything – like having no money, and having me underfoot all day, and all the rejection letters, and having to move from her adored house and garden, and, and . . . sometimes I damned well wish she'd scream at me, but she's never been that sort.'

'Makes you feel bad, does she?'

'Guilty,' Martin brooded, crunching peanuts from a bowl before him. 'I am guilty, of course. Not about the Army, I don't mean, but about the wine business. I should have seen that disaster coming.' Betty had: she'd told him of her hunch that Gavin was planning to pull out but he'd refused to believe her. Not his oldest friend. 'Well, I suppose I knew things were wrong, but I couldn't admit it, I ducked it. So I lost more money than I needed.' He sighed and the tic in his cheek started up. It was his own uselessness that was so alarming. He'd thrown good money after bad and there was no way he could recoup a penny. 'Betty coped with Army life, she's coping with this. She's got women's chores to occupy her. What terrifies me is how there's no context to my life. I've thirty years to go perhaps, but already I'm at screaming point from boredom. What *do* retired people do with all that excess of time?'

'My brother-in-law is retired,' Alex remarked with a sideways look, 'but he and his wife take off round the world. India, Florida, Mexico – they've the money and they say it's wonderful, but the intrepid travellers' tales I hear are more of painful jabs and Montezuma's revenge than the glories of their far-flung destinations.'

Martin stuck out his lower lip. 'Then *that* grass isn't any greener.' He took a pull at his tankard and wiped his mouth. 'I've seen plenty of the world with the Army,' he told Alex, 'and it's made me recognise a truth, that of all the places on God's earth, England is the best. Americans say that of their country, why don't we? Not perfect, God knows, but the best. I'm content to be here in Hampshire. But I can't stand being looked on as walking dead. Ageism stinks. I may be over fifty, but I feel no more than thirty. Well . . .' a grin, 'maybe thirty-nine. Why should I be shoved in a corner to rust like some obsolescent machine?'

'That's how I feel. Outdated, surplus to requirements. Then everyone says: get involved in community work, Alex, computer-literate chaps like you are really needed and would be greatly valued. But when you don't receive a penny, how can you know you're valued? I could accept a low salary and feel philanthropic, but with nothing on offer I'd simply be a sucker filling a void. Besides, if I did find anything I'd chuck it for a paid job, have to!' He gave an embarrassed laugh. 'If it isn't a rude question, how many job applications have you made?'

'Running total's fifty-seven.'

'God. What we put ourselves through. I even booked myself into specialist agencies. They tried, then shrugged. Any interviews?'

'One, just one. I was so desperate I brushed that hair-colour restorer stuff through my locks to make myself look younger—,' a half-laugh, a mocking camp gesture, 'but my *deah*, my interviewers still weren't charmed.' He shrugged. 'That was my lowest point. Being ex-Army damns you. The stupid bastards picture a barking sergeant-major type and that's that.'

'They're not so different if it's the civil service. They don't look at my skills or my abilities. They're blinded by visions of fifty years ago, certain I'd be rigid and hidebound.

Old black-and-white films on TV have a lot to answer for, don't they? My total's twenty-three applications and three time-wasting interviews – conducted by jargon-spouting condescending young halfwits I'd never dream of employing myself.'

'I know.' Martin rose to kick a log into place on the fire, looked at him with sympathy. 'What exactly did you do? I mean, I understand how the Ministry of Defence works, but I haven't a clue as to your sort of thing at the Lord Chancellor's Department.'

'I was a courts administrator, concerned with a number of courts within an area, civil and criminal, looking after the fabric and the structure of the courts and the staff who work in them – including giving back-up to the judges.'

'Ah, that's how you know Judge Thorne. He was shocked about you, wasn't he?'

Alex said as if impelled: 'He thought I'd be made circuit administrator, not made redundant. That's what I bloody well thought, too.'

'That's why you're so angry.' It was a statement, not a question. Alex was scowling down at his snow-stained shoes. 'How senior is that? In armed forces terms, I mean?'

'Roughly, Brigadier, I suppose.'

Martin sucked in his breath. He admitted: 'My chances of becoming more than a half-Colonel in the RCT were exceedingly slim, and I didn't even make *that*, though I'd been given to understand it could happen. You were at a very different level. God, I'd be angry, too. Oh, to hell with it, let's have a whisky chaser before we go. Or two. My turn.'

Plodding over the snow on the lane back to Brambourne, Alex stumbled on an icy patch, recovered, and said: 'I think I've drunk too much.'

'Me too,' Martin admitted. 'Not that much too much, though.'

'No, but it makes you think,' Alex grumbled. 'Not sure that's a good thing.'

'Tell me,' Martin commanded him, kicking at a clod of snow. 'You can tell me. After all, we're in the same boat. I'm

glad about that, you know. Oh hell, not that, but you know
what I mean!'

'Yeah,' Alex said with a jerked laugh of acknowledgement.
'I do.' He picked up a lump of snow and flung it at a big beech
tree, where it exploded in a shower of white icicles. 'Well . . .
I was thinking how stupidly complacent I was. I enjoyed my
work and I knew I was good at it. So I let it become the major
part of my life. It was security, it was interest, it provided my
friends and – though I didn't for a moment see it then – it provided my support system together with the handsome house
and the swimming pool. When the blow came, well, it was
like a divorce and a death together. A black hole. You know
what you said about the excess time we've had thrust upon
us? Well, that emptiness scares me witless too.'

'Got to do something about it,' Martin told him thickly.
'Hang in there together. Find things to do.'

'But what?'

'I don't know yet, do I?' he retorted with injured dignity.
'But we will. Not Meals-on-Wheels, I draw the line at that.
But something. And we'll share the employment pages in the
papers. You'll be a *Times* man – I'm *Telegraph* myself. We'll
look out for each other.'

'Look out for each other when we get back.' Alex grinned,
glancing at his watch. 'Hell! It's nearly four. Fenella's going
to murder me.'

'What time is it? Oh Lord, Betty won't be too happy, either.
We were supposed to sort out the sitting-room this afternoon. And she'd made curried parsnip soup for lunch.'

'Before we rush on to our doom,' Alex said, 'I have to let
some of that beer out of my system.'

'Me too. Behind this hedge.'

The field was an unbroken blanket of white. They swore.
'Snow's ruddy thick.'

'Better get on with it right here, then.' They were awkward with their gloves on, two fumbling men, their shoes
sinking ever deeper as they stood.

'We'll stick together,' Alex said, surprising himself with
his expansiveness. 'Know what I mean?'

'Yup,' said Martin. '*A problem shared is a problem what-sitted . . .* You know.'

'Exactly.'

Companionably side by side, they pissed deepening yellow holes into the snow.

At Brambourne Manor there was again a removals van in the drive. The skin of Alex's scalp tightened. More people to discover his shame. Martin waved and turned off to his little west wing. Alex proceeded with caution; the snow on the driveway had turned to slush and his feet were painful with cold. These arrivals must be people destined to inhabit the second floor. He dreaded meeting them; any second now Fenella could glimpse him and come flying out with scoldings, unconcerned about any remnants of his dignity.

In front of the removals van he saw an elderly Peugeot, so covered in slush that it was hard to distinguish its colour. Blue, he finally decided. He glanced at the interior. It was piled with a mixture of objects that in his own car would have exasperated him, but in that car caused only a tremor of amusement. Pullovers, books, framed pictures, magazines, plants, on the floor, on the parcel shelf, on the back seat. And crowning everything, two Victorian dolls in elaborate outfits of velvet and lace, carefully wedged in with velvet cushions and a box of Kleenex. The dolls had pale porcelain faces, delicately pink and white, and they were infinitely more delectable than any he had ever given Donna. In the fading light he stopped and stared at them with enchantment.

His concentration was broken by the simultaneous arrival of Fenella and an unknown woman, presumably the owner of the car and the dolls.

'Where the hell have you been?' Fenella demanded of him.

'I hope my car isn't in your way,' the woman said apologetically, her voice soft with the faintest of West Country intonations. Devon, perhaps? 'If it is I must move it at once.'

If Alex had been wearing a hat he would have doffed it and pressed it to his heart. Was the attraction in the voice, the sea-green eyes, the tilted head with hair like burnished pewter, or the smile that transformed a plain face in a flash, impossibly, startlingly, into something beautiful? Her clothes, somehow endearingly comic, he saw as utterly right for house-moving on an icy January day: a huge silvery grey pullover over grey trousers just a shade darker than her hair, together with a woollen scarf around her neck whose ends hung pendant over full breasts. Her legs were long and on her feet were short black boots, which she was slamming sideways against her car to knock away the lumps of snow that clung to them. Was she perhaps in the early forties? It didn't matter. She made the chilly blood of his body prickle and thump with sudden warmth inside him.

'Not in my way at all,' he told her.

'Oh good. I'm Margaret Jessop, by the way, and this—' she looked round and indicated a tall youth sagging against the right-hand pillar of the front door, 'is my son, Sam. We're moving into the east flat.'

'Hello, and hello Sam. I'm Alex Lindridge, and this is my wife . . . Fenella, do please come and welcome our new neighbours.'

Fenella stalked a few feet nearer and produced a smile. 'Welcome to Brambourne Manor. I'm afraid we've only recently moved in ourselves, so we're horribly busy putting things straight, but I hope you'll find everything's all right in your flat.'

'If we don't,' Margaret told her in that soft voice, 'I'm sure we'll manage between ourselves, Sam and I. Sam's always helpful.'

With delight Alex recognised the delicate breath of a snub, and wondered whether his wife would.

Fenella shuddered, said briskly, 'Heavens, it's too cold to stand out here, do excuse me!' and went indoors. The stiffness of her back boded no good to Alex, but he couldn't have cared less.

'Lindridge,' Margaret said. 'That's a Devon name. I come from Devon – originally, that is, before I married. Could you be a Devonian too?'

'Yes, I was born there. South Molton. And your husband? Is he with you?'

'Neither Devonian, nor with me,' she told him composedly. 'He left me for his current squeeze six months ago. So Sam and I have moved here to restart our lives.'

Alex took what seemed to him the biggest breath of his life, icy fresh air down to the base of his lungs, and said with feeling: 'I'm so sorry. That's the hardest challenge to undertake at any time. When you feel rejected and lost.' Another breath. 'I know because I'm trying to restart mine after a forced early retirement.'

'Then that's two of us Devonians struggling to climb out of the pit. I'm sorry, too.'

At the sound of that voice, sympathetic, but not pitying, and sharing the accent of his almost forgotten youth, Alex felt a succession of feelings run through him – amazement, delight, and a sense of recognition that was swiftly joined by a sensation of strength. He wanted to hug her, to feel her warmth and imbue her with his own. And with the thought of holding her came another feeling, a stirring in his groin that made him want to laugh out loud: not such a wimp down there after all. But this was no time for such thoughts – and she was sneezing.

'It's cold and it'll soon be dark,' he told her. 'You must let me clear your car for you. You should be inside, in the warm.' The lumps of ice that were his feet no longer bothered him; the dusk had been irradiated with light. He could think of nothing he would rather do than help this courageous woman. He opened a rear car door, leaned into the back and pondered with a smile which of her possessions he should gather up first.

5

Martin leaned from his doorway: 'Alex, hey, Alex, come and view the transformation your artistic daughter has achieved in our sitting-room.'

Donna ducked beneath his arm to contradict him. 'Not just me, Betty and me together.' She added with a mixture of pride and reproach: 'You two men had vanished, so we pushed on with it. Probably did better without you.' Her eyes swerved beyond her father to peer through the dusk at Margaret Jessop. 'Hi. You moving in too? You know this house is older than it looks, don't you?'

'Is it?' Margaret sounded intrigued. 'How can you tell that?'

'From the sorts of windows and fireplaces and rooflines there are. And there are old ship's timbers holding up the roof – I mean, but *genuine*. We've been up there and seen them, Betty and me. And do you know what we worked out? The acorns for those trees they came from would have rooted themselves round the time of the Peasants' Revolt and the ships they were in could have fought the Spanish Armada along the Channel.' Donna was bouncing on the balls of her feet and hugging herself against the cold, her breathless voice suggesting that she was hugging herself mentally too. 'They're even sort of scarred. Come and see!'

Suddenly, amid the draining light of the winter afternoon and the litter of boxes and packing cases, a feeling of festivity seemed to develop among the gathering of new neighbours, the thought of being connected in their very different lives today with the turbulent days of their ancestors appealing to something primitive and romantic in them. They laughed and relaxed: 'Yes, let's have a look.'

'Shall we? We shouldn't stop, but it sounds too good to miss,' Margaret said. She turned to call, 'Sam, come and meet some people and see the ships' timbers in the roof.'

Her son levered himself off the door pillar and prowled towards them, a watchful young male neither boy nor yet quite man, his tight pullover and jeans outlining rippling muscles reminiscent of an elegant young cat. Greeny eyes glanced at them from beneath errant locks of dark hair that flopped from either side of a central parting as he nodded.

'The men will be pissed off if there's no one around to tell them where to put things, Ma,' he said. 'What is this, anyway?'

'Old places, old things,' Donna said, scrutinising him. Evidently he passed some test, for she turned away casually, saying: 'I'm Donna. Come on, you'll enjoy this. It's the real past, I mean, like, the past of real people's lives, things vital to them.'

'Sitting-room first and then upstairs,' someone was saying.

'Suppose I don't like history?' Sam asked, following Donna into Betty's sitting-room.

'Then you'd be a loser,' she stated with scorn. 'Don't you?'

'Oh yes,' he said, rubbing his nose and giving her a mock capitulating nod. 'That's why I'm reading it at the University of Exeter next year.'

Donna scowled.

From beside them Alex saw a long, low-ceilinged room snug with an abundance of small Victorian and Edwardian pieces, a crowded domestic scene that somehow escaped fussiness and made him ponder, not for the first time, how the perception we give people of ourselves is composed of the accumulation of many details. Here on shelves flanking the big hearth were rows of books, many in worn but handsome leather bindings, interspersed with intriguing carvings and pottery from the countries that were part of Betty and

Martin's former lives. There were tiny paintings of the Mediterranean, too, grouped glinting like jewels beyond the dining-table, and in the sitting area, faded sepia portrait photographs of late-Victorian matriarchs with their broods about them, gentle and kindly. Clearly the Upcotts did not reject the past, but rather made it a part of the continuous present. Fenella would reject almost everything in this room. She allowed no accretions to their joint image; it was strictly pinned to the most immediate, not to say ephemeral, of fashions, and permitted few glimpses of any of their interests or sensitivities. 'Alex, you wouldn't want us to look all earnest, would you!'

It was the same with her clothes. Clothes, he thought, spoke volumes about their owners. The gaudy, word-emblazoned T-shirts of the restless teenagers that shouted: 'Get me! Get me!', the tracksuits of determinedly healthy young motherhood, the lawyers' expensive pinstripes proclaiming their status, his own limp flannels and worn blazer betraying his lack of it. Fenella would wear nothing that lacked a designer label, such coarseness might bring her up in a rash. Her clothes shouted the importance of style, the immediate present and the body beautiful, while the heels of her Gucci shoes tapped her impatience with the lesser matters – biography, history, government and politics – that her foolish husband involved himself with. 'Boring, darling, boring.'

The Upcotts' room appealed to Alex with its indications of wide-ranging interests. He was particularly taken by the dried-flower picture above the crackling log fire: summer flowers fanned out with an almost seventeenth-century air across a background of palest green hessian. Beside him Margaret Jessop commented in her husky Devon voice: 'An unusual picture, that, delphiniums and lavender and Rosa Mundi. I could covet it for my own place.'

Betty sounded apologetic. 'It's just something I did a couple of summers ago for our bedroom. It was Donna who insisted it must go there. In fact it was her clever ideas that brought the room together. She saw what would fit where.'

'Her eye is good,' Margaret commented. 'That picture's

perfect against the old bricks of the chimney. It could date from yesterday or three hundred years ago. Donna couldn't be more right.'

Alex, dizzily gratified by this praise of his daughter's perception and elated to discover the closeness of their thoughts, longed to settle in the fire-warmed room with her for many hours, uncovering their life's stories together . . . as if she were some familiar spirit he had known in another time, another place, and they had light years to catch up on. Curiosity, replacing the shock of their meeting, began to plague him. Had she arrived here from Devon, or London, or where? Did she have other children? Was she a working mother or would she be free to go for long walks with him during the day? But this was the wrong time for such questions. She was caught up in the pressures of her move and, all too probably, wrenched by her husband's desertion. There was no rush, she would be here for the days and weeks and months ahead. He could wait for the slow burgeoning of their friendship, just as plantswomen like Celia and Betty waited through the dark days of winter for the light that brought the slow unfurling of the glorious flowers of spring. The blossoming of their affection would be altogether different from the onset of his relationship with Fenella; this would be no flashy, rushed affair, but something of sturdy, rational growth. He breathed deeply. Please God.

'Come on,' he said, touching her elbow, 'up through the house to see the roof, and then we must delay you no longer, as your son rightly says.' He watched the easy way her long trousered legs moved as she climbed the stairs in front of him and he anticipated helping her sort out the jumble from her car as something festive. Perhaps he could put up shelves for her over the weekend. Chores commanded by Fenella were invariably coated with grey gritty boredom, but he had an instinct that any toil done in conjunction with Margaret would be fun.

Hugh Thorne returned from the Crown Court at half past five. 'The snow's going,' he observed, appearing suddenly in the bedroom doorway. Celia leapt round from organising his shirts and pullovers into his wardrobe.

'Hugh, you made me jump! Heavens, are you always going to arrive home this early?'

'Nearly two hours sooner than from Snaresbrook. Hooray!' As she turned back to her task he flung his arms round her from behind in a bear hug. 'This is going to be a better life. Four hours more to live and do something positive in, each and every day. And have treats.'

'Treats? What treats?'

He laughed. 'A policewoman told my clerk, who told me, that when she first went to interview today's burglar defendant his sensible-seeming wife turned her away saying he wasn't available Wednesday evenings. Why not? Well, that was the time he had a treat – a tart in his bed – while she did the ironing. She couldn't interrupt him, could she? Come back tomorrow.'

'Well, you're not having any such treat,' Celia said with prompt indignation, pushing his seeking hands aside to deal with a pile of black socks. '*You* are going to put up four sets of curtain poles for me. Right away.'

Hugh clutched his white head with drama. 'I can't credit the brutality of such demands on a tired man. Come back the North Circular, all is forgiven!'

'You idle wretch.'

He kissed the back of her neck, sliding his hands round to weigh her breasts. 'Treat first, you gorgeous tarty piece. Then I *could* even lay the dinner table too.'

Margaret Jessop was a doctor, a general practitioner, Alex discovered during a day spent putting up curtain poles and lugging her furniture about. The boy Sam had helped with the heavy stuff, but retreated when his mother demanded advice on where to put their pictures, remarking loftily that debating such details wasn't his scene. Instead he flung himself on to his bed to read a huge tome that he proclaimed to be the most exhaustive account of the Russian Revolution ever written. Thus Alex was left blissfully alone with

Margaret, the more blissful since Fenella had announced at breakfast her intention to spend the day in London, shopping – 'And lunching with a friend.'

As he wiped the dusty glass of Margaret's picture frames with a damp cloth, Alex replayed the day's discoveries in his mind. She'd been a partner in a group practice in Basingstoke, now she'd be one of two doctors, both women, covering the local villages from a surgery here in Brambourne. Her ex-husband, Boyd, was the regional sales manager for a big engineering firm. 'He was away from home half the time so he'd plenty of opportunities to play and stray. He flung it all at me in the final stupendous row.' The bastard. The thought of her pain was unbearable. She had moved from Basingstoke to be away from Boyd and everything associated with him. She had dreamed of a country practice. 'So for the first time in years I did something that was for *me* – without being made to feel selfish. It was amazing.' She thought that living in this fine old manor house would be something to celebrate too; after all, it was special – his bright daughter had shown them that – and she looked across at him and smiled with such warmth that his heart turned over and he felt his habitual defensive tension disperse, relaxing him like a drug. The information that she was a doctor left him torn: caring for people was wonderful work, no doubt, but it was inevitably associated with long hours and he yearned for those hours to be his. But then he thought once more: take it slowly, slowly. So he asked about her son, Sam.

Sam, it transpired, was in his gap year. He had intended to work abroad, in Israel or Africa or India, a place that needed his contribution, where he could feel what he was doing was worthwhile. 'But then the break with his father came and he said he couldn't leave me to cope alone with the divorce and selling the house, all those beastly bits.' Now he had a temporary job as a scaffolding erector, making good money that he was saving in great chunks to make his years of student poverty bearable. 'I think it's an awful job, but he assures me it feels tremendous. From sixty foot up, he says, he can look down with scorn on the ant-sized pillocks scuttling below him. Macho stuff! I don't believe the divorce has done him half the damage I feared.'

Alex nodded. 'That's good,' he said, and meant it. He'd vowed when Donna was small that he would never allow her and Duncan to be caught up in the nastiness of a fought divorce, never inflict on her the battleground that had been his own parents' expiring marriage. He would wait for Donna to reach sixteen at least. Well, she was there now, but suffering traumas of her own. He must guard her from the scourge of the break until she was successfully through with those damned GCSEs.

He wiped a last picture and propped it against the wall, thinking of Fenella, of the flat they shared, of the furniture and the dismal pictures that looked so out of place here (he blamed her for that), and her thin ropey neck and her gold jewellery and the bills and the low but continuous rumbles of discord – facets of his failures.

He hammered in a picture hook for Margaret Jessop with measured, careful strokes. 'X marks all the spots,' she had said, blown him a kiss and disappeared to sort out saucepans and press curtains. He hung the picture, a watercolour of Exmoor, wild, remote and beautiful beneath a windy sky of torn clouds racing to beat their shadows across the purple heather. Devon. Fenella could never have come from Devon; she was a child of the affluent suburbs. Her father had made his pile in the City, in currency deals, pampering his daughter and his sharp-faced wife with everything money could buy. Dad had bought Fenella a flat in Kensington to share with a friend while they scrutinised their circle for the right husbands. She had found him instead. He was twenty-two, deeply tanned that year from a cheap student holiday in southern Greece and swaggering with delight at his shiny new first-class degree; she was twenty-six, bored, predatory and desperate.

He moved along Margaret's sitting-room wall, reached for another hook. He had never had a chance, not with Fenella towing him from party to party, theatre to theatre, to art galleries, smart eating-places and Bond Street shops, spending her income lavishly. 'Let me buy you this gold silk tie and *don't* worry about money, Alex sweetie. You may be only just starting out, but that needn't mean us missing out on the fun.' Fun! He'd had his fun all right and it had cost him. And what was that fun? All-night celebrity parties when Fenella dressed to vie with the celebrities in eye-catching clothes – embroidered, beaded, or peacock-hued, plunging to the navel or slashed to the thigh – he struggling to keep a drunken dignity in a hired dinner jacket; she noisy, tossing back the drink, quick with the slick repartee, her voice shrill above the guitars and the saxophone. Exhausted, he would stagger home at dawn for a couple of hours' sleep before he headed for the Lord Chancellor's Department and a hard day's slog – brain-dead as a boiled cabbage. And the celebrities? He picked up the hammer and knocked the hook in with short angry strokes. He recollected an actress who'd hit the headlines with her nocturnal gambols, a swaggering foulmouthed footballer, a TV weatherman whose sly camp wit had cracked them all up. He'd been mesmerised by the excitement of a life so different from his penniless undergraduate days, by the wealth everyone spilt around, by friends who said: 'Christ, you lucky bugger!', by the illusion those nights produced that these were people who somehow counted. Illusion? Delusion. But he'd married Fenella before disillusion had set in. Why had he married her?

It was at the dawn end of one of those parties that he'd found himself engaged. 'Spring's coming, let's have a big party,' some drunk had yelled, 'all day instead of all night, for a change. What'll we celebrate?'

'Alex and Fenella's engagement,' her brother had shouted. 'Yeah, come on Alex, what about it?' Someone had already topped up his glass of champagne. Had it been a cunning set-up? He never could decide. All he knew was that he'd found himself buying the ring as soon as the shops opened and had spent the rest of the day shaking with shock. He wasn't in love with her, never had been, but he'd been stunned by the generous presents, reeling from the fun life, enjoying the sex – not that she had been all that marvellous, but sex on tap was something he'd dreamed of rather than experienced in his previous all-male world of public school and Cambridge college. His friends considered him wildly lucky to have a rich girl chasing after him. Caught in that electric moment, how could he snarl: 'You must be joking!' and slink off when she had turned to him, laughing and waving her own champagne glass over her head, her eyes pleading? The one time the power had been wholly his – and he'd let it drop.

Alex hammered home another hook and hung two prints of Exeter Cathedral. He stood back to contemplate them. Above, the west front, below, the decorated Gothic interior of the cathedral. Memories crept from the recesses of his mind, of evensong in winter holidays with his father, the nave a place of mingled light and shadow and great soaring pillars; the choir singing the glorious anthems of Bach or Handel. Margaret's prints and the organ music coming from her kitchen radio were reviving his yesterdays: the warmth and security of his father's big body beside his; the sense of grasping the meanings of deep mysteries; the tranquillity of the ancient building. He had been happy then, sure in his own small family world. What had happened to those certitudes? Destroyed by the tornado of hatred that had been his parents' divorce, a roaring blast of rancour that had burst from his father on his discovery of his randy wife's persistent infidelities, flaying them all until his death from a heart attack two years later. The betrayals were the reason for their move from Exeter back to South Molton. Overnight, it seemed, everyone in the city was sniggering over the affair with the doctor, the rumours of the vicar among the tombstones, the scenes with a spurned lover on the doorstep. From then on the father he had admired, the man who had seemed as stable as the cathedral pillars to the adolescent boy, had turned first abusive, then paranoid and finally brutal. At his school's sports day his mother had arrived alone to tell him of their parting, her black eye inadequately hidden by a pink plastic eyepatch.

Alex started on a fourth and final picture hook. His main

grief on that occasion, he recollected with a grimace, had been her lack of applause when he'd won the hundred-yard sprint for his House, her failure to notice that he had broken the school record for the long jump. Neither of his parents had shared the ups and downs of their lives with him; prep school from seven years old had limited any closeness there might have been, but his father at least had swelled with pride at his successes and communicated his love of music to his son. Alex blamed his mother. When, on visits, she fluttered forward to kiss him, he twitched his head away. What was it she had said of that last lover? 'One piece of flesh stuck up another – what's the big deal?' Hell, how could she have been so stupid? He banged down the hammer so hard he broke the sturdy pin and swore.

Fenella's infidelities were repeating the pattern, but she, at least, was discreet. And he, unlike his father, didn't give a damn. A psychiatrist might suggest he'd married her *because* he didn't love her, the coolness of the relationship shielding him from the possibility of similar hurts to his father's. Had he? It didn't matter now. When he was ready he would divorce her.

Last picture, propped face to the wall; Alex turned it about and squatted to survey it. A pastel portrait of Sam, green-blue eyes like his mother's peering at him from under the floppy hair; a good likeness. He must get to know the boy, invite him to do things along with Duncan and Donna. He rose with the picture to ponder what, exactly. He'd time enough in his empty life, God knew. Country walks ending with a pub lunch by a mighty log fire? Visits to historic houses? A day at the Newbury races? He picked up a hook and a pin to secure it. If Margaret weren't working she could join them. Might she be interested in the Winchester cathedral concerts? Fenella wouldn't. He realised the music wafting from Margaret's kitchen was one of Handel's organ concertos. He hammered the pin home, smiling. Yes, they would go to those concerts.

He hung the portrait, turned to survey the effect of the pictures on the room and once more experienced the frisson of pleasure that had struck him on viewing the interior of her car. Junk, but good junk, attractive junk: a worn bamboo sofa piled with bright cushions, an octagonal bamboo table; old uphol- stered chairs draped in richly coloured shawls; a carved Chinese chest of a strange yellowish colour and, beneath the window, an ottoman on which reposed the two Victorian dolls in their elaborate lacy outfits. And every surface covered with bric-à-brac – a mingling of colourful curios that struck him with delight in the sense it gave him of a casual, almost flip- pant female who relished anything old and attractive. Margaret the magpie. And Margaret the laid-back, unbothered about smartness or what people thought. Breathing deeply against the bubbles of laughter in his chest, he became aware of an elusive scent of camphor mingling with lavender and a faint but growing smell of coffee. He swung round and there she was behind him, a mug in each hand.

'I take it you'd like coffee?'

'I would.'

'Milk? Sugar?'

'Neither, thanks.'

'I guessed right, you're like me.' Margaret handed him a blue and purple striped mug filled with rich black coffee, then tipped her head back to scrutinise the walls. 'They look good, my pictures. This room suits them.'

'Yes.' He sipped the coffee, staring at her over the rim. Beyond her lustrous pewter-coloured head the window was already dark, bleak with the country night's total absence of luminosity that he'd forgotten about in all the years of sub- urban living. He wanted to cosset her in the firelight. 'I'll hang your curtains next, if you like,' he offered.

'You're very attentive.' Her voice was uncertain.

'Why not? I like to be useful.'

'But you've been here on and off all day.'

He said, aware of a rush of resentment: 'Being unem- ployed leaves me with too many unoccupied hours. I loathe being idle, always have.'

She looked at him with thoughtful eyes. 'You're bitter about that forced retirement of yours, aren't you?'

'No, I'm trying to come to terms with it.' That sounded lame and contradictory.

'But you aren't succeeding.' It was a statement, not a question.

He lowered his face to his coffee mug, sucking up the dark brew and swallowing noisily through a throat that had tightened to near blockage point. What could he say? She was right, he wasn't. He mumbled: 'I never imagined being discarded like time-worn machinery surplus to requirement.'

She nodded. 'I'm bitter, too. Twenty years of married life that all seems a sham today. Wasted. I, too, was redundant.' She looked directly at him with a wry smile and he saw the faint lines on her face leap into prominence. 'But we're here now, we have to let go of the past or it festers. We have to make changes.'

'You're right,' he said, despising himself.

He was being shallow and weak in using his anguish to thrust himself into her life.

He thought: Fenella's so irritable and indifferent to my feelings that she makes me desperate, running my case through and through in my head to reassure myself it wasn't my fault, to exonerate myself from guilt and stupidity. But I should have been thinking of Margaret's troubles, her needs. Do I genuinely want to help her or am I manipulating the situation to gain her attention, her sympathy? No, I want to help. I must. She's on a cliff edge, in a crisis that's threatening the very grounds of her being. And I know how that feels. We can talk, explore our problems together, sympathise, empathise. He hungered for closeness.

He finished his coffee. He realised that the bothersome sounds he could dimly hear from downstairs came from Fenella, back from Wimbledon and her lunch with her charity shop friend, Jodie, and now calling his name with rising impatience. He grinned in another frisson of pleasure, this time from the nefarious glee of annoying her. He went to the front door of the flat, opened it, strolled on to the landing and called down the stairs.

'Fenella? I'm helping our new neighbours with some tricky curtain hanging. I'll be down when it's done.' He sniffed the air like a dog scenting an enemy, released a gust of breath and returned to Margaret, slamming the front door against the current of *Poison* that had almost felled him from two floors below. 'Now,' he said, firmly, 'hand me those curtains you've been pressing and let's make you comfortable in here.'

6

Walking briskly round the gardens of Brambourne Manor mid-morning on a cold February day, Celia acknowledged inwardly her enjoyment in spending the weekdays in Hampshire. Earlier, up at her kitchen window, she had seen a mist across the valley through which the hills had risen like islands in a milky sea. Now the sun had broken through, burning away the mist, reflecting light back from the frost crystals in a white and glittering beauty that made her feel she had been reborn into a new world.

At the top of the garden she stepped on to the flagged terrace, turned and stood for a moment, hugging herself. Nowhere in London could such tranquillity be found, not even in Richmond's great park; always there were people and vehicles and planes. Here was where Hugh had longed to be during those noisy crowded journeys round the North Circular. Remembering how she had rejected his need made her wince. Now she understood how these very different surroundings restored his sanity after strung-up days of trying cases of rape or child abuse. No longer did he zap the television from programme to programme in search of distraction each evening, or shout at politicians on the news programmes instead he'd perch on a kitchen stool as she cooked, to tell her of the pheasants he had seen foraging in the morning fields, or the deer half-hidden in the woods. Then after their meal he would read or listen to music, and she would do the same, savouring a quietness which somehow seemed connected with the peace they had known in earlier years after the children were put to bed. He even telephoned John and Anna for the latest happenings in their lives, something he'd left to her before, too tired himself to talk.

At times her own acceptance of the change startled her. She had always thought those friends who ran a second house fools to take on the work, but the flat was easy to cope with, while her old cleaner kept the Richmond house dusted and it survived their absences well enough. She had taken to walking at lunchtime when the rain held off. She had never lived in the country before, only passed the occasional week with friends in Cornwall or Wales or the Lake District, places of wildness and granite rocks; Hampshire was different, gentler. She liked the measured pace of her new life and its soft sounds: the caws of the rooks in the tall trees, the River Test lapping under old bridges where trout and grayling lurked, the bleats of the bulky fleeced sheep on the hills. Sometimes Donna would join her and they would pause for a while, beguiled by a heron flapping up from the reeds at the river's edge to find himself a fresh fishing post, or observing an owl on a gatepost. More material to paint, Celia had remarked; a winter series related to her changed existence.

There was also material for her thoughts among her neighbours at the manor house. Unlike her neighbours in Richmond, people almost without exception as successful as she and Hugh were, and as comfortably off, these were the dispossessed, folk who stared at the world with baffled resentful eyes as they struggled with lives abruptly changed for the worse. Celia had little respect for losers, the sickly, the lazy, the fat girls whom no one ever loved; perhaps because she despised them for not fighting harder against their disabilities, perhaps because she saw how easy it would be to be one of them. But she felt an unfamiliar sympathy for her neighbours. Some people, she thought, staring across the garden, messed up their own lives, while others had them messed up for them. She thought of Margaret Jessop and Donna, and sighed. As Celia grew older she was often struck by the unfairness of life. She wondered why she and Hugh had been so lucky and whether unknown odds were stacking up against them. She crossed her fingers superstitiously, grimacing.

Somewhere beyond her a door opened and she heard footsteps. She turned her head to see Betty Upcott six feet from her, a dish in her hand, smiling in her hesitant way.

'I feed the birds,' she explained.

'I should have thought of that, too,' Celia said. 'They'll be hungry in this frost. What have you got there?'

'Oh, breadcrumbs, nuts, some bacon fat, you know.' Betty leaned her head back to make chirping noises before scattering the food with wide sweeps of her arm.

The birds came, first one, then another, and then in a rush of wings there were a dozen or more, beady-eyed and greedy, jostling for position on the brittle frosted grass; great tits and blue tits, a robin, a chaffinch, three wood pigeons.

'You've fed them before.'

'Mmm,' Betty agreed, 'I've always fed the birds, wherever I've been.'

Yes, Celia thought, liking her, you would have. She was reluctant to move on; this unassuming gentle woman had not burst the bubble of stillness she had settled in with her own thoughts. Another bird came, bluish-grey with reddish flanks. 'Is that a nuthatch?'

'Yes. You often see them with the tits, especially in the winter. They all like nuts, that's the thing.'

'We should have a bird table,' Celia said.

'Yes, in stone, perhaps and old, put where we could see it from our windows. Oh, but then we'd have to have everyone's agreement, wouldn't we? Like over the gardens and what to do about them.' Betty threw more food and her eyes explored the developer's efforts at creating what had been described as . . *minimum maintenance gardens set along old-fashioned lines in keeping with the ambiance of the handsome manor house* and which here in the old walled garden behind the house consisted of three uncompromisingly straight beds flanking the walls, all recently planted with stalwart no-nonsense shrubs – berberis, mahonia, forsythia and spotted laurel – and in the centre of the lawn a mean little circular bed containing three gaunt shivering saplings. She gestured. 'That's not exactly inspired, is it?'

'It could be improved upon,' Celia agreed.

'I could do a lot with this garden,' Betty said wistfully. 'If it were mine I'd swirl those side beds forward in the centre, back in the corners, giving movement and shape – creating places for groups to sit a little separately, with a handsome bench or two. And then the central bed should be enlarged, with just one tree in the centre to give height and focus, a weeping silver pear say, with white or silvery plants around it – white roses and lavender and irises.'

'And clumps of narcissus for the spring,' Celia added. 'It sounds delightful.'

'Doing that wouldn't cost much, would it?'

'It'll come up at our committee meeting tomorrow, you can put forward your ideas then, though I don't know who would carry them out.' She shivered. 'Brr. This is too cold for me. I should be inside and painting.'

'We should grow plants specially for you,' Betty said.

At eight o'clock the following evening most of the adult inhabitants of Brambourne Manor were sitting on the off-white leather sofas in the Lindridges' drawing-room, drinking coffee and studiously avoiding one another's eyes, not from distaste, but, Hugh suspected, because they were afraid of becoming involved in unwanted commitments when the meeting came to demand action. It had all been described in the particulars and the leasehold documents: the occupiers of the property must each pay their proportion of expenses and outgoings, and form a residents' management company to deal with such matters as external upkeep, repairs to the house, cleaning of the common parts, and to maintain the gardens and drives.

Hugh looked upon the occasion as a spectacle to be observed with interest. He and Celia, both having demanding, full lives, were probably safe from being clobbered, unlike the Lindridges and the Upcotts and the new chap in the small flat opposite Margaret Jessop, who would be prime targets. Not that Fenella Lindridge appeared the sort ever to bore herself with such matters. He turned to Alex.

'Is Fenella busy elsewhere this evening?'

There was an odd, almost smug, look on Alex's face. 'In London; she has a dinner and theatre date with a friend,' he told him before calling the meeting to order and introducing Todd Steele, 'who has moved here from Southampton, where until recently he was the deputy headmaster of a comprehensive school.'

The elderly Todd was a tall, scrawny man – too scrawny, a bag of bones – whose bald pate was surrounded by a dry grey frizz of unkempt hair, and whose haggard face was creased with gloomy downward lines. He nodded at his neighbours unsmilingly and Hugh remembered someone telling him that he was a recent widower who had nursed his wife through some awful lingering disease. He looked as if he weren't far from succumbing himself. Poor man.

The meeting started with agreement over the election of a chairman – Alex Lindridge – and two directors – Martin Upcott and Margaret Jessop. 'As long as you don't expect me to deal with emergencies with ballcocks or any horrors like that,' Margaret said. Cleaning came next. At the end of the first week of ice and slush they had all balked at cleaning the hall and the communal stairs and a sturdy village woman had been employed. 'Lena cleans for me, too,' Celia reported, 'and she's not bad. Basic but thorough, and highly informative on village affairs – she's the sister of Nancy Chubb at Abbotsbridge post-office stores.'

'Another gossip?' This from Margaret, one eyebrow up in amusement.

Hugh let out a grunt of laughter: 'A steady flow, from what I've overheard. But not, I think, malicious.'

'We'll keep her,' they decided.

Alex moved the meeting on with the air of one accustomed to achieving rapid progress. Insurances, external window cleaning, gutters and drains clearance, repairs and redecorations were discussed and their decisions noted. 'Though there shouldn't be a need for repairs or redecorations for years yet,' Betty observed on a breath of thankfulness.

The gardens were the last item 'The choice here,' Alex directed them, 'lies between employing a regular gardener, or hiring one of those garden maintenance companies. The companies are more expensive, but then we wouldn't have the problems of dealing with an employee's tax or insurance, or watching weeds grow if he fell sick.'

There was a pause for thought. Alex added: 'I'm personally in favour of a maintenance company. Those people can deal with every aspect, including lopping heavy branches, for example, which one man on his own couldn't tackle. I've used them before with great success.'

Hugh recollected Alex's description of his previous garden: 'Big, with masses of purple rhododendrons and pink azaleas flowering in spring, and then in summer it was our roses that were a picture, each bed of a different colour and shape, rising to standard roses in the centre. And the lads did the summer bedding round the pool and the patio – varying the colour scheme every year. Tremendous. My only task was to turn on the sprinklers.'

Shuddering, Hugh leaned forward. 'I can't say I'm in favour of using a company for a country garden such as this. We could find ourselves with a different person every time – probably some half-trained lad who'd have no real understanding of the plants and dig up anything rare as a weed. And despite the developer's worst efforts, there's still stuff worth recovering here. My vote would be for a proper gardener.'

Todd Steele nodded his cadaverous head. 'We really should give employment to someone in the village.'

'After all,' Margaret added, only half joking, 'this is the manor house.'

Alex smiled at her. 'I see I am in a minority.'

Betty opened her mouth, shut it, then startled the meeting

by asking in a sort of muted shriek: 'Could I apply for the job? I know I've got the skills and I'd . . . I'd like to do it.'

Martin muttered at her in vexation: 'What are you talking about? That's not the sort of work you should do.'

'Yes it is,' she retorted with anxious firmness, 'it's exactly my sort, and you know it.'

Her husband tightened his mouth and shook his head at her in a wordless snub.

Celia flashed Hugh a look, then spoke with delicacy to avoid inflaming Martin's prejudices. 'You know, I'm rather in favour of Betty . . .' a search for the discreet words, 'taking on the care of the garden. It needs someone with her knowledge and taste to develop its potential. At lunchtime today Betty showed me several photographs of your last garden, Martin, and to me they revealed such a talent for colour and texture and shape that I think it would be an honour to have her undertake the development of our gardens here.'

'I have ideas, you see,' Betty said quietly to them all, 'ideas that I think you might like. And . . . and gardens in good heart do raise the value of properties, don't they?'

'Tell us your ideas,' Hugh invited her.

'Well, I've visualised the walled garden as a place of old-fashioned seclusion with roses and clematis twined on the walls and drifts of silvery stuff and soft colours in the borders. Traditional, but with an eye to low maintenance. Then by the west wing where the house is oldest, perhaps a paved herb garden with a central feature of a sundial would work well – I've a sundial from our old garden and there's a pile of old flagstones left behind the garages by the developer that we could use.' She glanced round at her audience, gauging their reactions. 'Then . . . then in the remains of the old orchard, a miniature wild-flower meadow, colonised by cowslips and buttercups in spring, followed by clover, scabious, yarrow, ox-eye daisies, poppies and so on. I visualise a sinuous mown path around those few remaining trees, and seats for contemplation. The upkeep would be minimal, just the occasional cut.'

Celia leaned forward. 'I think it sounds wonderful, all of it.'

'Far too ambitious for a place like this,' Martin snapped, the tic in his cheek jerking.

There was a pause, a silence of the sort wherein unseen currents move and visions alter. The residents looked everywhere but at one another. They were going to have to decide a matter beyond their remit, and worse, to intervene between husband and wife. Betty was hovering, apprehensive of confrontation with her husband, yet silently begging their support.

Todd Steele began, 'I'd favour it . . .' then stopped.

'Let's face it, Betty, gardening's basically a labouring job,' Martin was bringing out in a choked voice, rebuking her, 'and this would mean hours of hard digging and lawn mowing – nothing like your last dear little garden.'

Betty's face stiffened. 'Martin, you know something? You're out of date and you're suffering from hardening of the attitudes. What's more, you're being condescending. I need the occupation and we could do with the money. I know it wouldn't pay more than a few thousand but every little helps.'

He flushed with anger and shame. 'Betty, listen will you?'

'No,' she snapped. 'You listen. I've spent my adult life travelling the world as your shadow – and in your shadow. Now for the first time I want something for myself, something I can create and take a pride in, and you're trying to deny me.'

'Yes, don't be sexist, Martin,' Margaret said flippantly, 'Betty'll look lovely sitting on one of those motorised lawnmowers. I've always fancied that myself.'

There was a flash of fury from Martin. 'Maybe we come from very different backgrounds but I wouldn't expect Betty to be grubbing about in all weathers . . .'

Celia raced to defuse the situation and present a suggestion that had leapt into her mind. 'The National Gardens Scheme,' she exclaimed, 'that would be our aim, wouldn't it, Betty? All of you? Not just an everyday story of digging and mowing, but creating something of beauty here at Brambourne Manor. Our gardens could be opened to the public for charity once or twice each summer.' Support me, you stolid lot, support me, her eyes appealed, darting from face to face. 'There are already gardens in Abbotsbridge that open for good causes. Hugh's cousins at Abbotsbridge House took us to see two last summer and they were delightful. It would take time before we could offer ourselves to public view, but then Betty's work would make her known, Martin. Now that would be tremendously worthwhile.'

There was a further pause while her words were assimilated.

'It's an idea we should seriously consider,' Hugh commented.

'It would be a dream,' Betty brought out, showing her pleasure with a dazed smile.

'Jane Field, my new partner at the surgery, said something about she and her husband having one of those Abbotsbridge gardens,' Margaret contributed. 'Yes, that's it, he's an old-fashioned gardening rector and they raise money for the upkeep of the old church and Macmillan Cancer Relief and similar good causes. We could ask them about the scheme.'

Todd Steele, still solemn, said he'd never envisaged anything so ambitious as this when he moved in – deep breath – but after forty years of drab classrooms and bleak playgrounds he was all for a vision of something glorious. 'What's more, I'd not mind doing the mowing myself. Sometimes in summer at my school, well, I'd look out at the sports field from my classroom windows and envy the groundsman on his clattering mower with the grass whirring up behind him, out there with the sun and the air and the sweet smells.' His lips creaked to something resembling a grin. 'Like I say, I'd volunteer if Betty needed help.'

Hugh Thorne turned to Martin and remarked with a judicial air: 'There've been more great women gardeners than men, you know. Take Vita Sackville-West, Gertrude Jekyll,

Rosemary Verey, Beth Chatto, just by way of example. People like us may not think of it as a woman's world, but it is.'

Martin had the outraged expression of someone being put in the wrong when he was in the right. He muttered: 'And the cost? Do you want that? And if Betty found it all too much for her and things got out of hand, well, it'd be a bit embarrassing to sack a neighbour, wouldn't it? It's said of most situations – like with solicitors or doctors – never employ a friend.'

'Well, that does for me where doctoring you lot goes then, doesn't it?' Margaret said with a chuckle.

Betty said in a low voice that she'd beg cuttings and seeds from friends for any special planting she wanted to do. 'Like people did in the old days. I'd keep the costs right down.'

Alex, seasoned chairman of a thousand committee meetings, produced the formula: if Betty found she had taken too much on, well, then she could resign. But he hoped that would not happen. He asked the meeting to sanction the purchase of a suitable mowing machine in due course, and added that tree surgeons would, of course, be called in for any tree work. He put these matters to the vote and they were passed. All present, with the exception of Martin, were in agreement to employing Betty as their gardener. Something sturdy and likable about the quiet woman made them accept her and her needs, and take her skills at her own valuation.

Duncan, Donna and Sam were lying around in Sam's untidy room, drinking the remains of a bottle of wine ('Can Mum spare it?' groaned Sam), talking and listening to music. Or rather, the two eighteen-year-olds were talking about schools and subjects, while Donna, stretched out on Sam's bed, was absorbed in silent study of their male qualities. Duncan was the younger by several months and a year behind in academic terms. He was, Donna noticed, propping herself on her elbow, deferring to Sam who had already proved himself with a place at Exeter to read history. Her brother was generally bossy but all right; not darkly dramatic or anything really sexy, but with the sort of open, reliable face that inspired confidence. Since several of her friends pronounced him fanciable, and most of them preferred to proclaim how loathsome their friends' pimply brothers were, she was able to feel good about him, something she rarely felt about her parents.

In contrast with Duncan's faded jeans and disintegrating pullover, Sam was wearing neat black chinos and a dark red shirt buttoned up to the neck with no tie, a sartorial statement that impressed her as meaningful, though she wasn't sure in what way. He was informing Duncan of his views on Europe and monetary union and managing somehow to combine political, historical and economic aspects with great fluency into his verbal display of scorn. '. . . And then take the language barrier. In America people forced into unemployment by the differing effects of the economic cycle on different areas can move a thousand miles to a new job. But what use is an engineer from the Midlands in Munich or Milan? Our problems have to be solved by Brussels' directives − bureaucracy rather than democracy.' A jerk of his head flicked a wayward lock of hair from his eyes. 'And how concerned are the Germans or the Spanish over the problems of our Midland engineering companies or West Country fishermen? Historically and economically we've always been in competition if not in conflict.' Donna could not be certain he was right, but she did think that his crisp reasoning showed a grasp of interlocking perspectives that was impressive. Excitement filled her at the idea that subjects she had thought of as boxed and separate could be thus combined. She was suddenly within touching distance of a world whose existence she had vaguely suspected and yearned after, but had never encountered in her own family, still less at school; a world where articulate, informed people could communicate and discuss ideas as easily as her mother's friends chattered. She relished Sam's academic style of conversation; intelligence always did turn her on.

She liked his throwaway style of good looks, too, though

she wasn't so convinced of the merits of mere appearance. While she felt uneasy around people who lacked physical charm, experience had taught her that those possessing it in abundance too often turned out to be self-satisfied and exacting. She reserved judgment on Sam; he seemed almost too good to be true. There was something endearing about the way the ends of his hair curled on to his neck and his biceps swelled beneath his sleeve, and she was sure his bony hands looked dramatically artistic. Anyway, she might have a go at drawing those; she liked tackling heads and limbs and hands. She sighed and levered herself to a sitting position on the bed.

Sam rolled over on the carpet to turn his green cat's eyes on her. 'Sorry, we must be boring you.'

'No. Why?' Put out, she glared at him.

A twitch of a dark eyebrow. 'I didn't think politics . . . Well, you might be . . .'

'Half-witted? You don't think a girl would be interested? Sexist, are you?'

'No, no.' Grumpily: 'It was, like, well, we'd got a bit over-serious.' Challenged, he was less articulate.

She must keep him off balance, the condescending male. 'Get real! What's wrong with being serious? What do you know about girls and what they're interested in anyway?'

He grinned suddenly. 'Not much. I wouldn't mind learning, though. Like Duncan says, all-male schools don't help, and I haven't even got a sister.'

Donna stared. 'But you've got a mother . . . I mean, she's a doctor, she's clever, she talks about things, doesn't she?'

'If you mean what I think you mean, not much.' He rolled his eyes. 'Oh, when Dad was around they always disagreed, so he'd be rude and she'd go silent. They even read different newspapers. Which do you read, Donna?'

Donna gave Duncan a despairing look, but he merely shrugged. 'I don't. And don't smirk, Duncan, you don't either. Dad takes *The Times*, but it's sacred to him. We do see the news on telly, though. Mostly.' She closed her eyes to end the conversation.

'You should make your dad divide the paper over break-fast,' Sam told her. 'Get in touch with the world, broaden your mind. Is it true you're not going to school? That you're studying at home?'

'Yeah,' Donna said warily from behind the shut lids, unsure whether admiration or a put-down of this strategy was to be indicated.

'Aren't you finding it bloody difficult?'

Put-down. Bastard. Her eyes flashed open. 'No. Why, should it be?'

He looked at her attentively. 'Well, I didn't find those exams a walkover. Besides, I'm a lazy sod, I needed pushing all the way – particularly in subjects like maths and physics. I got really stressed out, knowing I had to have maths for a university place. I know school's tedious, but I don't think I could have coped with going it alone.'

His remarks came unexpectedly near sympathy and they caught her off balance. She wanted to explain her horror of going to a comprehensive school where her strange late arrival and her different accent would have made her a butt of ridicule, but she could not bring herself to the point, not to him. Such excuses, such justifications would sound shallow and stuck up. Worse, she'd look childish. Her face grew warm as she searched for the right sophisticated, shrugging response; to hide her lack of one she swung her feet to the floor, tossing her hair back.

'Doesn't worry me. I did all right in my mocks at the end of last term and Dad'll help me in history and things. He's a Cambridge man, you know.' And on saying this, she felt for the first time in several weeks that there might be something affirmative, even good, about her father, and she put the thought by for contemplation later. 'And I'm being tutored in French and maths and the sciences.'

'But you don't do much work, Donna,' Duncan said.

'How do you know? You come home from school for one weekend and think you know it all. And you don't.'

'Dad said.'

She turned her back on him, collecting up her shoes from

Sam's rug and pulling them on. She informed Sam, 'Anyway, I don't need to sweat my guts out for fabulous results. I'm not aiming for some stuffy degree, I'm going to art college.'

'Really? You're not joking?'

' 'Course not! Why should l?'

'I never met anyone who did that. You paint? What sort of painting?'

Donna made an evasive gesture. 'People, landscapes.'

'She did some brilliant ones of the snow last month,' Duncan interpolated from the floor. 'On the fields at the back. I wanted one to frame for my room but she hoards them. You can't prise them away from her. She says they aren't good enough but I reckon they're pretty sound. They're better than lots of the stuff you see in art shops and galleries and things.'

'Shut up,' Donna told him. 'You don't know.' She looked at Sam's interested face and felt anguished. He might ask to see some but she wouldn't know what he'd like; she didn't want any boy judging any part of her work and finding it boring and grunting, 'Yeah, great!' at it in the unconvincing way boys had.

'The Judge's wife, Celia Thorne, she's an artist,' Sam pondered. 'And she's successful. You could talk to her about what you're doing, couldn't you? And then she might help you get a good grade.'

'No way,' Donna told him, 'am l going to morph into a Sloaney slimeball.' For days she had been screwing up her courage to show Celia her best pictures with that exact thought in mind, only to withdraw in terror of rebuff. 'Anyhow, she's a botanical artist, quite different. And I've hardly started. Why should she be interested in what I do? Why should she be bothered?'

'Why not?'

'Yes, why not?' Duncan agreed, rasping a spot on his chin with his thumb and supporting his new friend. 'Go on. She's all right.'

Donna dropped back on to Sam's bed and pressed her cheek against his pillow, scenting as she did so the male tang ingrained in the fabric – his scalp, his skin, his aftershave. What did he know? What did Duncan know? Boys had no subtlety, no idea of finer feelings; they were as lacking in perception as exuberant puppies. She felt exceptionally lucid and alone and brave. 'You can say what you like, I'm not going to do it.'

7

Martin went for Betty in the venomous way she hated. It was rare that he lost his temper, but when he did he turned into a different man, one who fixed her with a horrid insulting stare and seemed oblivious to the fact that his words hurt.

He walked from the meeting in a heavy-breathing silence until they reached the west wing, then as she opened the door he grabbed her arm to shove her through, slamming the door behind them so hard that the house shuddered. He put his face up against hers; she could see a pimple beside his nose and that his eyes were bloodshot.

'Did you enjoy making a fool of me in public like that? You must have gone mad if you think I'm going to let you do a dirty labouring job for a few pathetic pounds a week.'

She backed away. He had always disliked gardening, but this verged on the ludicrous. She struggled to keep her voice calm; she had been mortified too. 'I'm not going to be one of your soldiers tidying dusty shrubberies round old barracks, Martin; I'm going to be creating something good, something real. And in a year or two there'll be people visiting it. I could become a somebody round here, look at it like that.'

'Rubbish. Pathetic rubbish. It would take an age to make that scuffed mess of a garden look good. And in the meantime you'd be slaving away and complaining of backache and making people think we're so poor we can't make ends meet. God, do you have to rub it in? I *know* we're broke. Don't you think I feel bad enough already?'

'I know you feel bad, of course I do. But what about me, struggling to make ends meet and aching to do something positive? Now I can help.'

Her words were an affront. In the Army Martin had had power and authority; he had been an officer, his men had saluted him, not simply because they had to, but with respect. Now his own wife was planning to reduce him to the status of those unemployed louts whose women took menial jobs to keep the family fed. 'No. It's humiliating.'

'It's no more humiliating than wearing darned clothes. Think, Martin. The money Alex pencilled in the budget for the gardens' maintenance and the gardener's pay isn't exactly magnificent, but my earnings could be put towards decent clothes, and . . . and the new car we're going to need in a year or two, even a holiday.' She thought with a rushing and pitiful longing of her son. 'Martin, we could visit Adam in America. We haven't seen him for more than a year. We could visit New York, too, that would be something to talk about.'

'We've travelled the world with the Army, you stupid woman; we don't need to impress the locals.'

'Then why worry about me gardening, you stupid man? Besides, most of the local ladies are keen gardeners themselves from what Celia says.'

'But you won't find them doing jobbing gardening. I don't want my wife reduced to that. And that's final.'

Betty turned to leave the room. 'We've bought into Brambourne Manor so in part it's our garden. *Ours*. You've got a warped mind if you think that means jobbing gardening.' She opened the door, but fury and yearning boiled up in her so that she swung back to choke out words she had never imagined saying: 'And what about me? Doesn't what I want count for *anything*? You're mean, Martin, mean. You had your chances and you blew them. Twice. But don't you dare spoil mine. Everybody said how lovely my last garden was. And I'm going to make the manor gardens beautiful too, so

there. And if you don't like it you can damned well do the
other thing.'

The book he threw at her hit the edge of the closing door
and fell to the floor. She spun round, snatched it up and
hurled it back before flinging herself out of the room. 'You
bastard!' The book, a stout history of the origins of the
Second World War, hit him corner-on in the left eye.
Clutching at his eye, Martin collapsed on to a chair, as
shocked as if a mortar shell had exploded in the room.

In the morning Donna was restless. She had had the intention, and even for a while had believed it possible, to study
regularly on her own. But it wasn't happening like that. She
sat before an open book by Jane Austen and the words turned
to dancing black dots. She looked at a page of mathematical
figures and they could have been ancient Egyptian hiero-
glyphics for all the meaning they had. At school, teachers
bounced ideas at their pupils, there were discussions, they
moved from classroom to classroom, the pattern of the days
varied. Here it was all the same – faceless, patternless, dead.
She had a sense of being suspended in nothingness, while
outside Sam was laughing. She had to pass her exams to go
to art school. Did she want to go to art school? What would
she be expected to do there? Would she be good enough?
'Well, find out,' her father had said vaguely. But how? Donna
spread her hands and stared at them.

Celia was placing a last fine touch of blue on an *Iris unguic-
ularis* flower when someone knocked. She drew the brush
steadily down and round, studied the effect and nodded,
then went to the door, brush in hand. Donna was hovering
on the landing, peering at her from beneath lowered brows.

'I wanted . . . I wondered if you would . . .'

'Do you want to borrow something?' Celia asked briskly,
ignoring the scowl which seemed to be standard on this odd
girl.

'No, not that. I just wondered if you had time to look at . . .
well, to talk about . . . my pictures.' Her eyes flickering over

the fine-pointed paintbrush in Celia's hand she jerked out: 'But not if you're working.'

'No,' Celia said, touched by the sight of the battered portfolio the girl was half-pushing at her, 'no, I'm not. I've just finished. Come in.'

From the doorway Donna considered the studio. It was a workroom, untidy, purposeful, its low cupboards and big tables smothered in papers and paints and jars of water and specimens. There were photographs and childish paintings stuck above the cupboards; the photographs were of two small children playing – on beaches, in play-parks, in summery meadows – looking over their shoulders and laughing at whomever had the camera. Celia's grandchildren, she supposed; a lively pair. She drew in her breath at the watercolours of birds hanging on the wall to her left, a heron hunched in a brooding sort of way, a crow with its feathers untidy in the way she'd noticed crows' often were, and a long-eared owl that stared at her with an unfathomable look that was somehow on the edge of caricature. 'I decided to try the bird series by way of a change,' Celia said. They gave Donna a frisson, but it was a chic, modern sort of frisson. 'They're smart,' she told her father later. She wouldn't have minded having that crow and the long-eared owl in her own room, although normally she preferred the sort of semi-abstract paintings her teacher, Mrs Peel, had liked her girls to do – vivid sun-drenched landscapes with animals, or rain-drenched cityscapes with figures, that drew you into their depths with vigorous swirls and dabs of colour, the diametric opposite of the exact and premeditated perfection of the botanical paintings and the birds. Could you like both? Should you like both? Donna circled round to Celia's adjustable work table and gloomed over the still-damp painting, which looked unbearably flawless.

To Celia she looked uncertain and vulnerable, a nervous young cat sniffing at the corners of life. She'd told Hugh that Donna needed a mother in whom to confide, someone sensible to advise her. But Fenella – 'That highly honed bitch!' said Hugh – wasn't that sort of person. And the father, whatever Hugh said, spent too much time feeling sorry for himself.

Donna put out a finger to touch the iris in its jar, then pointed at the painting. 'It's funny, mostly when you look at things you get a blur afterwards, like when you've read a book too fast, but you show how the bits fit.'

'Someone once said I was too meticulous,' Celia observed, 'that I must be positively . . . buttoned up inside to produce such exact paintings.' 'Anal-retentive,' had been Joan's exact wording, to which Celia had responded: 'What shit!' Apposite, she'd thought, but the friendship had waned thereafter.

'Buttoned up? That's silly,' Donna said. 'They're supposed to be exact. They don't look buttoned up to me.' But she was relieved to know that even someone so successful could attract criticism. She chewed her lip, searching for words. 'Anyway, it must be . . . I dunno, sort of restful . . . being held to a definite style,' she produced finally.

Celia nodded as if she understood. 'It is,' she said. 'Very. And for me it's never boring. But you have to experiment first in order to be certain when you think you've found what's right for you.'

'Like you did when you went to that Paris art school,' Donna agreed, pleased with this perception. 'I mean, it must have been horrid, but at least you knew what you *shouldn't* do.'

'Yes. It's difficult at your age, you're lacking the wide thrust of experience and you're so very much on the edge of life – you know who you are, but not what you could be.'

'That's just it,' Donna said fervently, thinking of Sam who did know what he wanted and was smug about it, telling her loftily, 'I intend to be a history don and I shall write politicians' biographies as a sideline.' Donna wanted her life sorted, too, but it had to be a life that couldn't collapse into nothing one day the way her dad's had. She said to Celia: 'Mum says I shouldn't specialise in painting because if it doesn't work and you can't sell it, where do you go from there except teaching? And that pays so badly, unless you're working in a Faculty of Art in a University. She says I should think about doing a degree in illustration or film and animation, perhaps even History of Art, then there'd be more job opportunities. I do like history . . . but then I don't know.' A sigh. 'It's like standing at a crossroads where all the lanes look interesting but you can't choose which to take. Did you feel like that?'

'Of course. It was awful. Come on, show me those paintings.'

Five were proffered. Celia put them on her table and studied them in turn. The first, a watercolour, depicted the naked brown figure of a seated female, big-eyed, elongated, lengthy curving strands of greenish hair balancing the curve of the back; the unexpectedly sturdy line of the thighs anchoring her firmly to some barely visible floor. The second was again a watercolour on thickish paper, this time of a girl's half-turned oval face balanced above a sloping neck, its skin lightest grey, the hair mauve, set against a background of darker pinky mauves – a few strokes, a few dabs, the essence revealed. A touch childish but not amateur. Or was it the other way round? Yes, well, not bad. Unusual, too. Certainly not embarrassing, as they could have been.

The other three took her by surprise as being on quite another level. These were landscapes in acrylic; one was a vista of wintry woodland while the others showed the fields behind the manor house under the snow. Donna had reduced these motionless distant scenes to their essential pattern of curves and straight lines, dramatising them by their relationship to the low folds of the downs and the broad sweep of the pale and moody sky. Shadows enhanced an eerie sense of their cold tranquillity with muted blues, greys and purples, while her almost pointillist technique conveyed the icily glittering texture of the snow in wonderfully assured fashion.

Beside her Donna stirred, a move of impatience, carefully controlled. Unusually, Celia felt protective; was it because the girl had left herself so wide open?

'Those,' she said, pointing her paintbrush at the last two, 'are *good*, especially in the way you are conveying atmosphere and creating a mood.'

Donna had stiffened but now she relaxed and her pale face lost its fierceness. 'Thanks.'

'The others are good, too. You've demonstrated a sense of line in your sketches of the two women, and the colours are zany but fun. I hope you know why you painted those girls in those colours. Experiments at school? Fine. Now, what you want to know is, should you go to art school – in fact, are you good enough? Isn't that it?'

A jerk of the head in response.

'Then yes, clearly. But that's my view, and my view may be out of date.'

A relieved grin. 'My teacher said I'd be fine.'

'Ah, but for what course?'

The scowl reappeared. 'I don't know about that. I don't know what's on offer.'

'Then you'll have to find out between things like fine art and visual art, textile art, history of art and design and so on. Also what you need to win a place on whatever course you do decide to go for.' She looked at Donna's face and added: 'Where your roads have no signposts you need a map. Why don't you telephone around for prospectuses? If you don't know where, then your father could help, surely?'

Fear seeped into Donna. She had thought herself grown up compared with her friends, but now she hesitated, recognising her inadequacies. At school everything was done for you; you were told which subjects you should take, and where and how to find a place. A black hole of ignorance gaped before her; perhaps she wasn't so streetwise after all.

She admitted: 'Art isn't Dad's thing and I wouldn't know where . . .'

Celia groaned inwardly. She and Hugh were due to drive back to Richmond that evening and she had a dozen things she must do before then. But the girl's eyes were imploring. 'All right,' she said to Donna, 'you put the kettle on and while we have our cups of coffee I'll write you a list of the art schools and colleges you should contact. And you could call the Winchester School of Art straight away.'

'I didn't know there was one, but I will. Thanks,' Donna said, her face flushed. 'Thanks very much.'

Martin's black eye was shocking, a real disgrace, Betty told herself as she went to feed her birds in the garden. He must stay in the flat, he couldn't appear in public with that reddened eye and the purple and black bruise beneath it. People would stare and look at them meaningfully. She threw her crumbs in an arc: 'Come on, birds, come along. Lunchtime.' Unexpectedly her body shook with a giggle. Folk would probably say she had thumped him with the rolling pin. Too bad, he shouldn't have been so disagreeable. The birds fluttered down to dart about, peck, peck, peck, and the robin came right up to her foot, cheeky fellow. Martin had started it, *and* he'd been the first to throw the book, landing himself wholly in the wrong.

It was a big change she was demanding for them both. In the Army it had been almost impossible for the wives to work outside the house because their men were moved around the world at such frequent intervals. A few officers had wives who stayed behind in England, building their own careers while their men served abroad. 'We're only like naval wives!' one of them had protested to Betty. Yet this was frowned upon as disloyalty by the other ladies, and she, Betty remembered with discomfort, had agreed with them. Now, for the first time desperate for an interest of her own and its accompanying independence, she understood those women who had refused to move. She had not simply felt disappointment last evening when Martin opposed her, but anger and even hatred. All those years she had been a good Army wife, never complaining of her frustrations, though they had been very real. To comprehend another culture you must *live it*, learn the language, experience the customs of the people. That experience was never available. Life in Army quarters had been life at one remove, forcing her into the role of spectator. For the men it was different; they were stretched and pushed – sometimes to the edge of fear, sometimes to the limit. As in the Falklands or the Gulf.

They had been responsible for their men's lives, enduring experiences that developed them. Betty, behind the scenes, had helped to run Wives' Clubs, advised soldiers and their wives when they were ill or had marital problems, acting effectively as an unpaid social worker. She had put up with mosquito bites and prickly heat, and living in houses that were not her own, stocked with Army-issue furniture she would never have chosen herself, even, on one occasion, with being a sniper's target. (He had missed.) 'But I've had an exciting and interesting life!' she had told a shocked friend. Yet it had been Martin's life, not hers. Then had come the slow failure of the wine business. She had liked furnishing her own house and enjoyed even more creating beauty in its neglected garden, but Martin had deprived her of that in the final débâcle of selling up. All those years she had supported him and listened to his financial worries, and then yesterday, just as a spark of light and colour looked likely to enter her life, he had wanted to extinguish it, extinguish her.

She had thrown all her sadness and resentment at him last night, the only time she had truly berated him in all their years together. 'I supported you in your dreams, Martin,' she had concluded while he undressed as awkwardly as any man would with a cold wet cloth clutched to his eye, 'now I need support in my dreams and you refuse me. You're despicable.'

He had said nothing, simply crawled into the far side of the bed and curled himself up with his back to her, breathing heavily – with resentment she had decided.

'Now listen,' she flung at him finally, 'this isn't a threat, Martin, it's a promise. I'm going to make the manor gardens into something great and I can either live with you here on the spot, or leave you and live in a council bungalow and do it from there. You can tell me in the morning which you want.' Then she had switched off the light to sleep surprisingly well.

Overnight the shocks she had inflicted on him seemed to have changed him. He had not apologised for making her look a fool in the eyes of their neighbours at the meeting, that would have been too much to expect, but after breakfast he had folded the *Telegraph* he'd been hiding behind and told her that if she felt that creating and promoting the gardens of Brambourne Manor was of such importance to her, very well, he would not stand in her way.

'Thank you,' she had replied, herself at her most dignified, 'that was how I hoped you would see it.'

Well, she wouldn't let him go back on his words. Suddenly, the wonder of it all rolled over her and she could have burst into song. She lifted her eyes to look across the wintry garden, seeing it bloom in her mind with shape and colour. She could transform it, she knew she could – and wonder of wonders, make money, her own money, from an interest so enjoyable and creative. She watched the birds flitting round her feet for more food; how comic they were, like small children. As gardener here she could plant berried trees and shrubs for them, encouraging them to build nests and sing on the walls. She'd have buddleias, too, bringing the butterflies into the garden. She could feel the energy of her happiness flooding through her in a tide of ideas.

She heard footsteps on the flagstones and Donna arrived beside her.

'Hiya! Aren't your birds friendly? The robin's almost ready to come on your hand.'

'I'll have him there yet,' she agreed.

Donna was in an exuberant mood to coincide with hers, jigging up and down against the cold. 'Hey, Betty, what've you done to Martin? I called round the west wing to see you and found him with a shocker of a black eye. He said he'd walked into a door, but it didn't look like that to me.'

Betty laughed. 'Maybe he did walk into a door. Robin, cheese crumbs, look! Or maybe he trod on a rake. Or it could be that I threw a book at him.'

Donna blinked. 'Did you?'

Betty countered: 'Why? Does your mother throw things at your father?'

'No,' Donna said sadly, 'she just goes on and on about our

move. So he walks out. Sometimes he gets in the car and goes. Sometimes he just walks. I didn't know other people had rows. Not happy people, I mean.'

Betty looked at her. 'Everyone does some time.'

Donna was watching the birds. 'Have you done your weekend shopping yet?'

'No. I'm planning to go this afternoon. Why?'

'Because I have to cadge a lift into Winchester, please, dear nice Betty. I'd ask Mum, only she's out having lunch with a friend. And she's going to an exhibition in London tomorrow and I need to go now.'

They had been to Winchester together before: 'Since we both like history,' Betty had said when inviting Donna to join her. On that first occasion they had explored the cathedral and the museum, then on another day, captivated, walked up the hill to see the castle hall and the Arthurian round table, the West Gate and the plague monument, and finally spoilt themselves with pastries and cups of rich hot chocolate at an old coffee house in the High Street. Betty had remembered the baby daughter she had lost and had thought longingly that if she had lived she would have liked her to be as lively and interested as this girl. She and Donna were relaxed in each other's company, enjoying the same things, and it was fascinating to glimpse life through her eyes. Someone had once told her that our young were a mirror into our past, a mirror that let us see our one-time selves in them, but Betty could never remember seeing anything of herself in Adam, who from birth had been insistently separate. She could recognise her own past in Donna, though, in the girl's part-formed yearnings and her insecurities, as well as in her pleasures. She wanted to help her before the twisted, pent-up animosity existing between her parents wrenched her life out of joint too.

'Yes, I'll take you,' she said, 'will two o'clock suit? What are you planning to do?'

'I'm going to start sorting out my future,' Donna told her. 'I'm going to find the art school and get its prospectus. I have to know what I'm going to do in life.'

'You're absolutely right,' said Betty. 'You don't want to leave it as late as I've done.'

On her return from Winchester Donna found her father sitting on a sofa with his head bowed, carefully not looking at her mother, who was waiting by the door with the familiar look of bitter patience that troubled Donna, her diary in her hand.

'Well? So what do you want to know?'

'What you are doing next Friday evening, Fenella.'

A shrug. 'I'll be in London with my cousin Holly for part of the weekend, but my visit doesn't necessarily have to include that evening. Why?'

'We're invited to dinner with the Thornes . . .' He broke off, seeing Donna join her mother in the doorway. 'Donna, at last. Where have you been, darling? We were going to go over your modern history essay on women and work during the Great War together, but I couldn't find you anywhere.'

'Betty took me into Winchester and we went to the Art College for their prospectus.'

Her father's and mother's frowns combined both reproach and annoyance.

'Why Betty? I could have taken you yesterday if I'd known you wanted to go,' her mother said. 'I'd have been interested to learn what they're doing at the art college.'

Alex let Donna know by means of disconsolate sighs and shaking head that he was hurt that she had not asked him. 'I would have driven you in, you know I would. We could have had one of our lovely chats and looked over the place together. It would have given me pleasure.'

'But you're always saying you despair of modern art,' Donna objected, 'and Mum doesn't like art students, so what would be the point? Anyway, the college staff told us they only take people round on Open Days and then they concentrate on A level students.'

'That's not very helpful,' Alex exclaimed. 'But then perhaps if I'd been with you I'd have persuaded them otherwise.'

Fenella gave him a derisive look. 'I doubt it.'

'And just what does that mean?' He looked at Donna for sympathy, but she looked away, impatient with their endless connubial disagreements.

'Oh, stop it, you two. What are you getting snarly over now, anyway?'

Her father gave one of his deepest sighs. 'I'm waiting to know whether your mother wishes to accept an invitation for dinner with the Thornes next Friday.'

'Certainly,' Fenella said. 'Provided you don't sigh or shut your eyes with a look of brave suffering every time I speak. It must be almost as annoying to others as it is to me. Do you ever think what a poor light you put yourself in, Alex, with that sort of sour behaviour?'

'Oh, why don't you both drop dead!' said Donna, and left them to it.

Alex, Margaret and Sam were standing together surveying Margaret's battered Peugeot when Donna emerged from the house the following morning and stalked over to join them.

'Christ, what hit you?' she asked, poking at a crushed headlamp. Glass tinkled.

'A tractor on a bend,' Margaret said. 'Straddling the centre of the lane to Litton he was, stupid bastard, no room to avoid him. *And* he swore at me.'

'You should have sworn back,' Donna said with sympathetic indignation.

'Well,' Margaret admitted, grinning, 'I wasn't exactly polite.'

'You'll need,' said Alex, his tone bordering on ghoulish relish, 'to have the bonnet replaced as well as the front panels and that light unit.'

'How long will that take? Two or three days?'

'Weeks, more like. A week is the very minimum.'

'It's the panels that'll take the time, Mum,' Sam told her 'cutting them off and welding new ones back on.' Seeing Donna stomping off kicking a pebble, he strolled nonchalantly after her. 'Hi. You all right?'

'I got a prospectus from the art college yesterday,' she told him. 'There are heaps of good courses I could take. Intellectual. Academic. History of art and stuff.'

'Great, I thought you looked cheerful.'

She gave him a suspicious look. Cheerful wasn't a word used by her friends; it sounded outdated, like those hearty teachers who urged you to work at their useless subject when you were utterly pissed off. For her, anguish was a proposition more worthy of scrutiny. Neither of her parents had paid the least attention to her prospectus last night, each focussing solely on aggravating the other. 'I'm OK,' she shrugged, kicking her pebble and the notion of cheerfulness out of play. Then she relented. 'Show you if you're interested.'

'Yeah, why not? Look, the sun's shining, would you like a walk? We could discuss it. You like walking?'

Donna nodded. 'Walking's good round here. You?'

'Mostly.' A grin. 'It depends where you're going and who you're with.'

After further skirmishing they arranged to meet in ten minutes and walk to Flintpen Ring, a local hill noted for its Iron Age settlement. 'And we'll take something to eat and drink,' Sam called after Donna as she trailed off. 'Um, yeah, and don't forget your prospectus.'

Margaret observed to Alex that Sam would have to sharpen his technique.

'He's all right,' Alex said. 'He's young. Feeling his way's better than feeling a fool.'

'Were you that tentative at that age?'

He shrugged. 'I can't remember.' Was Sam actually sniffing round after his daughter? The boy'd better behave himself. Alex sighed. He'd said he couldn't remember, but he could, only too well. Of course he'd been tentative. A life of boarding schools and no sisters had left him without a clue as to how to tackle the opposite sex. He remembered telling a kindly aunt that it wasn't fair males having to make all the moves. How were they supposed to know whether a female would be receptive or not? And he'd hated being rejected, certain that he'd be the butt of jokes. Women grumbled too

often about life not being fair to them; little did they understand the horrid burdens shouldered by men – and with no
maternity breaks either. What was Margaret saying?

'I liked boys who advanced on me with assurance and
made demands. That was exciting. Made me feel superior
and complimented.' She kicked her damaged car. 'Oh hell,
it's Saturday, I hope the garage is open to collect this and hire
me something reasonable.'

'I'll drive you while it's being repaired,' Alex said. 'For as
long as you need.'

'I can't take up your time. It won't work. I'll hire a car.'

Alex was insistent. Here was an opportunity not to be
missed, unbelievable luck. 'No, you won't, it'll give me
something to do – and besides, I'll enjoy it. I like your company, you see.' Assured, demanding.

Her eyes examined him. She said, 'It would help. But your
wife? Won't she object?'

Fenella had her own car, he told her, and her own life
also. He added, picking up glass from the broken headlamp,
'You could say our lives run in parallel, but not in unison,
not for many years.' She was hesitating, more confidence
was needed. He let the glass slide from his hands onto the
crumpled bonnet, dusted them off and smiied at her. 'You'll
be helping me, Doctor Margaret dear. I'm near death from
boredom. It's a pernicious disease requiring positive action
now.'

'If that's how you feel, then thanks, offer accepted.'

8

The drizzling rain gave a wet sheen to Walton Street, car lights shone and shop windows glittered in the grey light. Celia, sipping her after-lunch coffee by the restaurant window, found the contrasts of lustre and overcast quite beautiful, and sighed with contentment. Brambourne was delightful on bright frosty days, but in wet late February London was infinitely preferable to deepest Hampshire.

That rain in the streets was superior to wintry weather in the country was Celia's considered view. Rain there was dismal stuff, a sordid shroud over dead woodlands and a dirge of drips from the eaves, while country puddles were sprawling dun-coloured nuisances that either sprayed your car with mud or froze to make you skid. Town rain, on the other hand, could largely be ignored as you moved from one warm place to another, and its puddles were friendly affairs reflecting people, bustle, lights that winked at you. In the warmer months, though, the situation was reversed. Better then to be away from the sizzling pavements and the polluted air of London with its never-ending noise. Brambourne would come fully into its own with birdsong and primroses and tiny lambs on the hills. Soon, quite soon now. In the meantime Hugh was attending a judicial criminal seminar for four days at Warwick University and she could take a mid-week break here where things were happening.

She put down her coffee cup and paid her bill. She had spent a useful morning shopping for shirts for Hugh in

Jermyn Street and educational games for her grandchildren
in Harrod's toy department, and now she was ready for the
delights of the Cartier exhibition at the British Museum. A
pity the friend who should have joined her had telephoned,
croaking with laryngitis, to cry off. But Celia could still enjoy
it on her own.

At the entrance to the exhibition she paused; after the
clarity of the light behind her in the Egyptian sculpture
gallery the contents of the darkish room were almost invisible; grey shapes that were people staring into splashes of
unresolved brilliance. She blinked, and slowly the cases of
exhibits took shape.

Her first reaction was one of surprise at how much taste
and style in jewellery had changed since the period from
1900 to the Second World War, and secondly, how insignif-
icant the effect of the art nouveau mode had been on the
Cartier style. These designs were inspired, it seemed, more
by the architectural ornament of the Renaissance and neo-
classical periods; delicate settings of diamonds in
platinum glittering triumphantly up at her in all their intri-
cacy and fine workmanship. Taking in deep breaths of
admiration she moved round to study how the designs pro-
gressed from the original sketches to the presentation
drawings and templates, and finally to the finished commissioned piece. She flushed a little in appreciation of the
colour combinations of turquoise, sapphire and jade, of
emerald, onyx and diamonds. It occurred to her that she
could have worked successfully in this field. She pored
over handsome examples of the Egyptian style, the Persian
style, the Chinese and Japanese styles. Time passed. She
did rather wish she had someone with her to share her
pleasure.

'That's for *you*, Fenny!' a heavy shouldered man a few
feet ahead of Celia exclaimed to the woman with him, flour-
ishing a finger at a piece in a case on the wall. 'It could have
been made with you in mind.'

His companion, sleek and stylish in black, seemed to
catch her breath with pleasure, clutching his arm. 'Oh! I love

it – it's . . . it's the sheer elegance of the design combined with the restraint in colour that's so right.'

Intrigued, Celia joined them to look and saw on a simple black cord a pendant of stunning originality. *Pendant with onyx ring and pearl tassel.* But the description was inadequate, there was a little coral cylinder there too, studded with small diamonds and linking the black ring with the pearls, and it was that note of coral which seemed to Celia to transform an otherwise cool combination of black onyx and diamonds and long tassels of pearls into something exceptional.

'It's fabulous.' She glanced at the dark hair and narrow build of the woman beside her, drew in a breath and added, 'Your friend is right, it would suit you exactly. Well. Hello, Fenella.'

The blood was travelling up into Fenella's face, but she replied with calm: 'Hello, Celia. How extraordinary that we should meet here. Or perhaps not so strange. Great jewellery, great artistry. Um . . . this is Roger Dodson, a friend and a . . . a sort of cousin of mine. Roger, this is Celia Thorne, also from Brambourne Manor. Roger,' she added as an afterthought, 'is a barrister.'

'How do you do. I know dozens of barristers, but I don't think we've met, have we? What sort of practice do you have?'

He shook her hand. 'Don't ask.' A grimace crossed the strong face, then he added, 'Sorry, I know that's not what you meant. I do criminal work, as it happens. I'm here today because a case I'd expected to last four weeks collapsed after only two days in court. No doubt my clerk will conjure up other work shortly, but meanwhile . . . well, I'm grateful to Fenny for keeping me amused.'

'Goodness, yes,' Celia said. 'It's remarkably fine, this exhibition.'

'Roger liked the clocks,' Fenella murmured, smiling. 'Didn't you?'

'I never thought Cartier would be my thing,' the man said bluntly, 'but now I'm glad I came. The clocks were spectacular; I hadn't known about them. Tell me . . . your name's

Thorne. You wouldn't be related to Judge Thorne, would you?'

'I'm his wife.'

'His wife? What a coincidence. I've appeared in front of him on several occasions. Steady chap, none of this chucking volumes of Archbold at counsel stuff, but he won't stand any nonsense. Good with a jury, too. They vary just as individuals do, but he's a knack of getting through to them.'

'So I've been told. He says he picks up each new lot's particular prejudices from their facial expressions, the twitches and blinks at the evidence – or the lack of it.'

'Yes, he has a real grip of what's happening in his court.' A flash of amusement. 'You'll know that though. Look, Fenny and I were going to have tea after we'd looked at these last few things. How about joining us?'

Celia agreed, but as they sat down at a table she wondered just what she thought she was doing. The two of them were clearly involved in an affair; this was the sort of equivocal situation she would normally find any excuse to avoid, rejecting embarrassing involvements. She was thankful she hadn't known about it when Alex and Fenella had come to dinner recently. It had not been an easy meal as it was; she'd found them an uptight pair, Alex dull and over-deferential to Hugh when he wasn't struggling to repress his wife on the topic of their move to the Hampshire countryside: 'Sheer hell – except that hell might be better, being at least hot!' Hugh's comment afterwards had been, 'Never again. Whatever could have induced Alex to marry that sour female?' Celia wondered whether Alex knew about Roger Dodson and if this was a further cause of strain.

Over tea their talk was kept carefully light. Roger had been intrigued by the Indian-style jewellery and the pictures of the Indian princes who had commissioned Cartier, teasing Fenella that she'd pass any Englishman over for the maharajah with his turban and his chest festooned with rope after rope of pearls. He gestured largely over his own chest.

Fenella laughed back at him. 'No, no, it was the black moustaches and the hot brown eyes that ravished me.'

'But you thought the pearls made him look magnificent.'

'Well, they didn't detract from his masculinity. Or not in my eyes, no more than the stars of those Orders he was wearing. Oriental splendour. What do you think, Celia?'

Celia smiled without replying. What she found disconcerting was the gaiety of a neighbour she had barely seen smile before. If Fenella was embarrassed there was no sign of it; on the contrary, she seemed as agreeably pleased to see her as if nothing could possibly be wrong. Presumably that was the impression she intended to convey, Celia concluded cynically as she toyed with a pastry concoction and drank her tea.

Roger turned to her. 'I'm puzzled, Celia. As Hugh Thorne's wife, how can you be living in Hampshire?'

She put her cup down and explained that Hugh was now sitting in Winchester Crown Court.

'Is he? I hadn't caught up with that move. How's he finding it?'

'He thinks it's great. It was a move he wanted.'

'And what are your views?'

'I was cross at first over the upheaval, but now I'm enjoying both country and town – we kept on our Richmond house, you see.'

Murmuring something about retrieving her coat from the cloakroom, Fenella left them.

Roger nodded. He shut his eyes for a second as if he were tired, then opened them to say: 'I'm glad it's good for you. It's not so for Fenny, as you may have gathered. She's the sort who isn't happy unless she has a pavement beneath her feet. She's not just fed up, she's in a crisis. I'm not surprised. Alex claims to love the Hampshire countryside, but he can't know much about it. He's a suburban man by instinct. And how's he going to find his sort of work down there? Oh, he says he could drive to places like Winchester, Basingstoke, Southampton or even Portsmouth and that he's desperate to find something. But I don't see it. Do you? I suspect a cop-out. And it's hell for Fenny, stuck among dripping empty woods and fields and with him underfoot all day, self-pitying and glum.'

To avoid a silence Celia uttered a non-committal, 'It can't be the best of situations.'

He gave her a thoughtful look. 'I'm sorry. I shouldn't have spoken. Embarrassing. You won't know them well enough yet, I don't imagine.' A pause. He sighed. 'I just wish Alex'd show her some sympathy, some generosity of spirit. She's a damned generous sort herself. She deserves better.'

Celia trod carefully. 'I gather she regrets leaving their previous house.'

'She had friends there, she had a life. She's lost that with this move. Alex thinks he's the only one who's suffered, but Fenny was helping a friend run a charity shop for the British Heart Foundation – she had a sister who died of a heart defect at the age of four, and she's never forgotten her. She hated giving up that work.' A short laugh. 'Alex used to speak of it as if she was playing at good works, pretending. He has a mean streak, that man.'

Disconcerted by a vision so different from her own concept of Alex and Fenella, Celia was silent. Had she and Hugh been wrong about the woman? Was she a hurt and angry victim rather than the highly honed bitch Hugh had dubbed her? She had a mental picture of Alex driving Margaret Jessop from patient to patient as he'd been doing recently while the doctor's elderly car underwent its repairs; she recollected Donna's grouchiness. It's not unheard of for victims to bitch. Celia knew herself that she could never have made a social worker or a probation officer, she was not sufficiently interested in people, but this contradictory situation caught at her attention; more, she was intrigued. When Hugh returned from his judicial seminar he must tell her all he knew of Roger.

As Fenella reappeared with her coat Roger rose to envelop her in its cashmere folds with hands that lingered on her shoulders. He was on the broadish side and muscular; Celia glanced at his rather heavy face, his strong, almost coarse nose, his wide, full mouth, and she saw a man with more to him than Alex Lindridge, in personality as well as physical presence. Not bad. A likable sort. She itched to discover whether he was married, but tact combined with embarrassment kept her silent.

Outside the museum, after Roger had left them with a swiftly brushing kiss on Fenella's lips, Celia did, however, put one dry question to her.

'I take it I shouldn't mention Roger to Alex in connection with our meeting here?'

'Take it as you like,' Fenella shrugged, huddling into her coat and pushing up its collar as if a cold wind had hit her.

'Then I shan't,' Celia decided.

'That's OK then!' Fenella said with an unexpected snort of amusement. 'And I take it you have your own car, so I can't offer you a lift? Right, 'bye then. Glad we met.' She swung round and was gone in a flurry of clacking heels.

Time was passing quietly for Alex. He occupied himself in desultory fashion; his destiny seemed to be held in suspense, yet he was less discontented, rather than more. He drove Margaret; he discussed Donna's history and English assignments from the tutorial college with her; he studied the employment pages of the papers in company with Martin, shrugging his shoulders when they held no hope for either of them; when the weather permitted he joined Todd Steele on relaxing downland walks, liking the companionable silences of the dry old teacher. Todd had taken over Donna' s mathematics coaching after she appealed to Alex for help one evening and he'd had to confess that he hadn't a clue. 'The chap who's teaching her isn't getting through, I'll have a go if you like,' Todd grunted, 'it'll give me something to do.' Donna said he was great.

Alex was certain his sense of calm came from driving Margaret, and he was determined it should continue even when her elderly car was back on the road – unless his recent interview produced the job he craved, please God, please God. In the meantime helping her to deal with her work in an area of Hampshire that was still strange to them both gave him a sense of being needed, and for the first time since the blow of his impending retirement had struck he became aware of something approaching wellbeing. Margaret rarely spoke of her own problems and she was short when he spoke of his. 'Leave it out, Alex. I'm a doctor, not a counsellor from Relate or an employment consultant, nor do I run an agony column.'

Griping was banned on their journeys, she decreed. It was a pain, no, a virus, a modern infection that was growing to epidemic proportions and she refused to countenance it in any part of her life. Instead they discussed whether her practice should combine with another local two-doctor rural practice, or how the big firm of solicitors in Southampton couldn't possibly turn him down for their post of administrator after his perfect interview. This he recognised as good therapy. He told himself that Dr Jessop was a wise woman.

We are looking for an experienced administrator with detailed knowledge of the legal system . . .

Alex had sat in Margaret's car reading first the advertisement, then, two days later, the job description. Hugh Thorne had drawn it to his attention, and it was him, exactly him. *The successful candidate will need to have strong analytical ability, good communication skills, and the capacity to work as part of a team, together with high computer literacy . . .* He had filled in the application form while Margaret coped with an asthmatic child in a stuffy dirty cottage, written a letter: 'I have a Cambridge First in History . . . many years of experience in your field . . . the Court Service . . . a high level of computer literacy . . .' Then had come the interview, a week ago now. He had to get that post, he had to impress her. But how long, oh Lord, how long?

There were times when Margaret returned to the car after the last patient of the day, sliding into the seat beside him with a sigh and a smile, when he thought that he should immediately drive her to some remote spot and pull her into his arms. Yet even as he took a preliminary breath and switched on the engine, she would disconcert him by speaking of this man's terminal illness or that child's allergies, debating aloud with herself alternative treatments and making him aware of his own ignorance in a way that seemed both cold and ungrateful.

He would not let himself mind though. He knew from what she let fall in unguarded moments that her husband had put her through hell, particularly in the last months of their marriage, and with Fenella still so evident in his life he was fearful that Margaret might despise him for fastening upon her as her husband had upon so many women. He would leave it to her. At the first hint that she might be receptive, well, that would be different. Besides, he had nothing to offer her – yet. A furtive affair of snatched moments of lust was not what he wanted. He aspired to be her friend as well as her lover and he needed her to trust him.

Had he had any extra-marital affairs? she had once asked him, and he had replied with the truth, yes, but only the one and that with a secretary who had shown a weakness for him, and a blithe penchant for sex in odd places, under his desk or behind the filing cabinets. It had lasted but four or five months. Propinquity had been the trigger – her habit of hanging over him at his desk with her bra-less breasts clearly visible; lack of time or place to pursue it the cause of its early demise, together with his very real fear for his professional position. No, Fenella had known nothing, and no, he had not done it in secret glee to score over her. It had just happened.

'Hmm,' Margaret said, and enquired no further. She had already told him she'd never been unfaithful to Boyd. 'It amazes me how people find the time. With a busy work schedule and a son and a house to look after, I never could. Besides, for years I was fool enough to think we had a good marriage. I never gave off signals to other men, I never looked elsewhere. I valued fidelity.'

When Hugh returned from his seminar, Celia asked him if he knew Roger Dodson.

Hugh nodded. 'Yes, I do. He's appeared before me several times.'

'What do you think of him?'

'As a person or a barrister?'

'Both, I suppose.'

Hugh massaged his chin, frowning a little, before pro-
nouncing judicially: 'Roger? Well, as an advocate he's
competent, certainly. Perhaps something more than that. Not
brilliant, I wouldn't say, but better than average. There are
some you have to watch all the time, who attempt every trick
known to confuse a jury, but he's not like that. As a person I
don't know him well, but I'd say a decent sort.'

'Is he likely to take silk or be appointed a judge?'

'I can't see him making silk as a criminal practitioner. The
competition's fierce, he's on the oldish side and he's not in a
first eleven chambers. Good second eleven, but from that
level you have to be either startlingly brilliant or very lucky
to achieve silk. He might make circuit judge, but then he'd
need to become an assistant recorder in the very near future.

'Is he married?'

Hugh grimaced. 'Divorce pending, somewhat notoriously.'

'Why's that?' Celia demanded, wondering if Fenella might
be involved in a scandal, having a sudden horrid vision of
hordes of journalists besieging the manor house.

'His wife's a barrister, does matrimonial work. No children. She's ambitious and something of a tigress in fighting
her cases. Not long ago she was junior to a well-known QC in
a longish case and they got stuck in one of the court lifts
together. On release they were revealed locked in lust. The
Bar's been chortling over it for months.' He laughed himself.

'Except for poor Roger,' Celia said crossly. 'How hideous
for him. How can you men be so crude and horrible?' She
visualised Roger cringing at false sympathy from those he'd
thought were his friends, at half-smothered guffaws as he
left robing rooms, at nudges among the clerks. So he was a
cuckold, poor miserable man. Had he turned to Fenella for
comfort? And she to him? After all, Fenella had mortifica-
tions of her own. Alex Lindridge, whom Hugh thought so
reliable and steady, had his tongue lolling out after Margaret
Jessop. Whether Fenella loved Alex or loathed him, it could

hardly be agreeable for her to have their new neighbours watching and grinning and speculating over whether they were or they weren't. She felt a spasm of female solidarity.

'Why do you want to know?' Hugh asked, his face serious now. 'You haven't met him, have you?'

'We met at the Cartier exhibition when I bumped into Fenella. He was with her. They spoke of being distant cousins but the relationship didn't appear that distant to me.'

'I don't believe it,' Hugh exclaimed. 'Poor Roger. What a horror story. From the claws of the ravening tigress to the jaws of the snarling bitch.'

Celia was still cross. She ran a hand through her white hair so that it stood up like the fur on a bristling cat. 'Don't jump to conclusions about the bitch. Fenella was quite different in his company. Almost unrecognisable from the angry female we know here. At one point she suddenly told me she knew she'd blown it with us all at the manor that first day with her snappiness, but that she'd been so seething with fury over the move she hadn't cared. I *think* she meant it as some sort of apology.'

As Donna opened the front door to collect her family's milk, a blue tit rose in a flurry of wings from the Thorne's bottle of semi-skimmed, leaving a well-pecked silver and red foil top behind. Donna decided she must take the bottle to Celia, before the bird helped itself further.

'It's one of those mornings!' Celia said, regarding the bottle with disgust. 'And why *my* milk? It isn't the lovely full-cream stuff tits generally go for.'

'Maybe it's on a low-fat diet,' Donna said. 'Everyone else is. What is wrong?'

'Hugh says his morning's ruined because I left his special coffee beans in Richmond and he hates tea. And Margaret's plumbing is leaking water through the ceiling, and who'll have to deal with it? Me. Beastly plumbers and decorators, not to mention the insurance aspect. Hell!' She drew Donna into her hall and pointed to a large grey patch on the ceiling.

'That's bad. Does Margaret know? She and Dad'll be off in two minutes. Shall I tell her?' Donna wanted to be on good terms with Sam's mother. She really liked Sam.

Margaret looked revolted at the tale of the leak. She dashed to the bathroom and Donna heard her groan, 'Oh hell, no, not my poor carpet! Look at this nasty stain creeping from under the bath, will you?' She tugged a panel away at the side. 'Everything's sodden.'

Donna joined her, lying on the floor and peering. 'It's from the bath, not the pipes going to the taps.' She knelt back on her heels. 'The developer's plumber didn't seal it off properly.'

Alex was knocking at Margaret's open front door. 'Margaret, are you ready?'

'No,' she called back in a voice of tragedy. 'I've a flood in the bathroom and it's gone through to Celia's hall ceiling. So embarrassing. And now I'll have to find a plumber and deal with insurance and God knows what else. That useless developer.'

Alex came in, tall and thin, and startled at seeing Donna there. He glanced at the dampness oozing from beneath the bath, saying with an air of satisfied gloom: 'I'm surprised we haven't had more of this. Inevitable with builders – it's their trade mark. Don't worry, I'll find you a plumber and get estimates for Celia's redecorating work. But first we have to get you to the surgery. Come on.' He considered Donna, still crouched on the floor. 'Darling, if Margaret gave you a cloth you could mop the worst of the water up, couldn't you?'

'Yup,' said Donna, relishing a good excuse to be late for her biology coaching. 'Sure. No problem.' Her mother would be annoyed, but then she didn't know about Sam.

Margaret laid a warm hand on her shoulder. 'Thanks. You and your father are very kind. I can hardly believe my luck in finding such good neighbours. It's incredible.'

Donna was pleased. Wholehearted approval was not always apparent in her life.

Mid Friday morning Alex put his hand out for Margaret's car

phone, withdrew it, then snatched the thing up again. She'd be some minutes yet with her elderly patient and he must know, he couldn't bear another whole weekend without knowing. A receptionist answered, irritatingly smooth: 'Rider, Gee and Fox, how may I help you?'

By telling me I've got the job, damn you. 'I'd like to speak to Mr Fox, please.'

'I'm afraid Mr Fox is engaged at present.'

'When will he be free?'

'I'm afraid I couldn't say. You could speak to his secretary if it's urgent.'

Alex considered it desperate. 'Hello? I'm calling in connection with the post of administrator, my name is Lindridge—'

The secretary's impatient voice broke in: 'You're far too late to apply for that. The successful candidate is already in post . . .'

He could hardly believe his ears. His stomach heaved. He'd been encouraged to hope. 'Hold on, I was one of those interviewed but I've had no letter . . .'

'Mr Fox always tells candidates for posts here that the successful person will be informed within three days. That's well past.'

Anger shuddered through him. 'You don't let the other candidates know? You can't be serious!'

'Mr Lindridge, did you say? Oh yes, the ex-civil servant . . .'

Was that what had done for him? The stereotyped view of the hidebound civil servant clinging to outmoded methods of working? What was she saying?

'. . . afraid I can't discuss the matter any further. We're a busy commercial partnership here. Goodbye.' Click.

He couldn't even yell his opinion of her foul boss at her. Hate ran through his veins like molten metal. Then the thought of telling Margaret of his failure welled up in him. He'd been so sure. He put his head in his hands. His eyes stung, then his nose, and suddenly he was sobbing, gulping and gasping for air, struggling to control himself before

Margaret returned from the dilapidated cottage only a few feet away. Fool, fool, you fool, get a grip on yourself. He felt in his pocket for a handkerchief, battled to dam the flow of tears and snot, but still the weeping went on, mourning his loss of work and status. He hadn't cried like this since his parents had parted, all those years ago. He wanted to die.

The robin had fed from Betty's palm for the second time, his tiny beak pecking confidently. She was dusting off her chilly hands in triumph when she heard a voice calling to her.

'Betty! Hello, Betty! Care for a cup of coffee? I'm about to make one for myself.'

She turned to observe Fenella, an anachronistic figure at the far side of the terrace in her sleek grey wool dress, cashmere cardigan and elegant Ferragamo shoes, her arms wrapped around herself.

'Heavens, how can you bear it out here? Brrr!' Fenella shivered dramatically. 'Come inside and warm up, do! You won't transform the gardens if you're frozen into a pillar of ice!'

It was a cold morning, just short of glacial, and Martin hadn't brought Betty any coffee; he seldom did, the sulky brute. And since going indoors involved tugging off dirty wellies and much hand-washing, Betty rarely bothered with it, telling herself that brisk digging would sustain her body warmth. But today, standing like a statue to feed the robin in a penetrating east wind had left her stiff with cold. It was thoughtful of Fenella. Betty was beginning to revise her original assessment of Fenella; more than once Martin's disparaging remarks about his wife's strange passion for gardening had held nasty similarities with the way Alex spoke of Fenella, and a certain sympathy for Fenella's curtness had crept into Betty's reflections. Besides, Alex spent a deal of time in the west wing with Martin and she found the theatricality of their mutual self-pity was becoming boring. Two men, who for the better part of their lives had done well, had come up against the intractable problem of failure and couldn't cope without whining, worse, without taking their disappointments out on their wives. She was exasperated with them both.

'Goodness, yes, I'd love some coffee – if you don't mind my dirt,' she called back.

'We'll drink it in the kitchen,' Fenella said. 'No problem. Come on!'

In her wonderfully warm kitchen they sat for some time drinking hot coffee, chatting over their husbands' troubles. Betty wanted to know whether Alex had heard yet about his much-coveted administrative post with the solicitors in Southampton.

'Told you of that, did he? No, he hasn't, and he's seething with impatience. He swore he'd telephone if he didn't have a letter today. Probably already has. The silence is ominous. So I live in trepidation of lunchtime. He'll be unspeakably doleful if he hasn't got it.'

'Martin seems to treat being doleful as a full-time occupation anyway. Thank God they have one another,' Betty said. 'When Alex isn't driving Doctor Margaret around they're in my sitting-room reading the editorials or the letter pages of their newspapers to one another, agreeing with grumpy relish how greatly Britain has deteriorated over the last decade and how much worse this government is than any government they've known. Not to mention their howls of enjoyable outrage over journalistic inaccuracies and lack of knowledge whenever the armed forces or legal matters are involved. Mm, lovely coffee. So comforting for the men, don't you think, to be able to preen themselves over how much more knowing they are than the general run of cretins?'

Fenella, half-laughing, half-sighing, said, 'I think it's you who's the knowing one.'

'And then each time one is turned down for some post the other can sympathise while secretly feeling better about his own failures. So much better than standing it on their own.'

'I didn't know you were such a cynic, Betty.'

'Oh, that's not cynicism,' Betty said ruefully, 'that's human nature. Of course, they're at their lowest when it comes to the appointments pages, and there's nothing there for the poor brutes. I encourage them to take themselves and their papers to the pub on those days. At least by the time Martin gets back he's mellowed a touch.'

'And Alex claims his consolation from the doctor, I don't doubt,' Fenella muttered.

Betty shook her head. 'If you mean what I think you mean, I don't think that's happening, not from what Martin's said. After the bad time Margaret's husband gave her, I have a feeling she's comprehensively distrustful of men and their motives.'

'Aren't we all?' Fenella exclaimed.

'They do have their off moments, don't they?' Betty said. 'But don't you worry overmuch about Margaret.'

'Oh, I don't,' Fenella told her. 'Except that I fret about it going on under Donna's nose. I hate to think how she might react.'

On Saturday morning Sam and Donna went for a walk along the river. Donna liked the times when Sam came back from his scaffolding erecting prepared to give her his attention; she had the emotions of a potholer stuck in a tight place who sees a face peering in with friendly concern. He couldn't get her away, but at least he was sane and you could talk to him. Like Mrs Peel at school. Sam and Donna even shared the bickering-parents syndrome. 'At least yours have given up fighting and parted,' she pointed out, 'mine just go on and on. They're childish and beastly! And Dad's in the pits of despair because he can't get a job. The drama he makes you'd think he was dying of cancer – and it was Mum who'd caused it.'

She went into the Abbotsbridge post-office stores to buy Cokes and chocolate bars while Sam sat in the sunshine out-side. Donna had made the acquaintance of Mrs Chubb and her husband who ran the stores, some weeks ago. Les was dour and most people kept out of his way, but Nancy was plump and insistently jolly, with a wrinkled baked-apple face and a steadfast determination to be at the centre controlling and radiating all local news.

'Good to see you, dear,' she said now, as Donna arrived at the checkout. 'Going for a walk with that young man, are you? Isn't he the new doctor's son?'

Donna fished in her jeans' pocket for money. 'Sam? Yeah, they live at the manor too.'

'Tall and handsome, that's lucky for you, isn't it?'

Donna looked revolted. 'He's just a friend. How much?'

'That'll be two pound twenty, dear, and I'll put them in a bag. There. That's a friendly crowd you've got at the manor, isn't it? Yes, I was saying to my Les, very friendly the way your dad drives the new lady doctor about. We see them together every day.' She folded her arms beneath her ample bosom and shot Donna a sideways glance. 'Smart lady, your mum, very. Knows what's what, you'd think. Kind too, though, letting your dad spend all day with the doctor when there must be plenty still to sort out at home.'

Donna, who had been feeling unusually contented, now tensed at this oblique offensive and regarded Nancy with distaste. She surfed through a mental range of snubbing responses and discarded the lot. She might be stressed out by her parents because they were so stupid and *sad*, but she wouldn't have any nosy outsider getting satisfaction from riling her. Instead she gave Nancy her most saccharine smile and told her, 'Oh yes, my parents are the kindest people in the world. Pity there aren't more like them.'

Outside she muttered to the somnolent Sam, 'Witch, bitch, witch!'

'Sorry?' said Sam, alarmed.

'That stupid smirking woman in there. Going on about my dad driving *the new lady doctor*, as she calls her, round the villages. Disgusting. If you'd done that bit of shopping, Sam, you'd have heard her and you'd know what I mean. But, typical male, you had to laze in the sun.' She marched off down the lane towards the hump-backed bridge and the river.

'What the hell are you talking about?' he demanded, following her.

'Your mum making use of my dad.'

Sam gave her a look of understanding and comprehensive

cynicism. 'Oh that. What do you expect? He's OK I suppose, but he's always sniffing around.'

'He's bored. He's looking for something to do.'

'Or someone to do!' Sam cracked. He picked up a flat pebble and skimmed it across the river – bounce, bounce, bounce.

Donna couldn't imagine her father . . . well, not her own father, not at his age. 'Shut up trying to be smart. You're as disgusting as Nancy Chubb. Dad's not like that. He's being helpful.'

'Hopeful!'

They bickered along the river path for two miles and bickered their way back again. The snog they'd enjoyed on the last walk had no chance of reoccurring.

As Donna stalked back into the flat shortly before lunch, she told herself she was in the depths of despair. She knew, she just *knew* Sam had been sneering at her for being naive over her father and Margaret. Was it true what Nancy and Sam inferred? If so, where did they do it? In his mother's bed? In her parents' bed? And when? It was all stupid and sordid and treacherous, and she couldn't begin to visualise how Fenella would deal with Nancy's insinuations if she heard. Her mother was so tense and brittle these days that Donna could imagine her cracking apart like flawed glass, pierced and livid with pain. Would she walk out? She'd clearly had more than enough as it was. Donna was fed up with her nagging over homework, but she'd never want her to go. As mums went, she rated OK most of the time and like herself, she'd really been bleak over the move. Dad never gave *her* credit for feeling bad over his troubles, never gave her credit for anything.

Her mind reverted to the sex thing. Perhaps it wasn't true. Perhaps Sam was just being a show-off and foul-minded. Boys were like that. Donna rather liked Margaret, who dealt with her doctoring work in a brisk fashion and never fussed about what Sam was wearing and when he'd be back for meals, like her parents did with her. But she didn't want to think that Margaret could move in on her father like that, not at their ages. The prospect of growing older than twenty-five was grim anyway, but at forty-five or fifty? Were people actually still doing it when they were that old? Why did people teach you so little about the most important thing in life? She needed to know much more. Now.

What must Sam think of her? The awful possibilities of his scorn and mockery made her cringe. She'd dreamed of him as a real sexy boyfriend she could boast about, adult and interesting and way ahead of the dim spotty sorts who buzzed round girls yakking of football – but now she'd spoilt it. She'd been childish and petulant, and she'd probably never find anyone halfway decent again, and the whole world would think she had bad breath or lesbian leanings and despise her.

In the kitchen her parents were arguing in the ultra-flat voices that struck Donna as a warped refinement of cruelty in their lack of feeling. Theirs was never a straightforward anger but a cold and deep dislike. She hated the way they sniped and sneered and scored points. She wished they would bellow like her friend Georgia's mum and stepdad – it might take the tensions out of their systems. Georgia's pair hugged and made up; Donna couldn't remember ever seeing her parents hugging.

'Just occasionally, don't you think we could do something together as a family?' she heard Fenella asking. 'Or do you see that as impossible?'

'No,' her father said with one of his most pointed sighs, 'not if you think you could agree to something that doesn't involve driving to some crowded and polluted city centre and tagging round some awful pretentious exhibition. But why this sudden interest in doing things together? We haven't for years. Why change now?'

'Because before we moved here Duncan and Donna had plenty of their own friends around them. Now they've lost that I feel we should be giving them support. Don't you?'

'Naturally,' Alex said. 'That's why I've invited Donna and Duncan's friend Sam and his mother to the point-to-point at Easter.'

'Something you know I've no knowledge of or interest in. All right, go with your darling doctor to that. But Donna wants to see next month's exhibition at Southampton City Art Gallery. It's called Art for the Millennium, I believe. A demonstration of today's vision. We could go together to that – and invite Sam, too. That'd be supporting Donna's interests.'

'You mean your interests. Appalling outsize daubs they say are expressive of some profound experience or spiritual emotion, or . . . or that they're form and colour articulated into a vernacular of symbolic discourse, or some similar crap. Or dead cows or elephant dung or filthy beds. I don't want to contemplate the vomitus of their self-immersed, self-advertising souls. Neither does Donna.'

'Don't you invent what I want,' Donna said furiously, appearing in the doorway. 'You don't know anything about it and you're talking rubbish. I do want to go and what's more it was my idea. And it was praised in *The Times*. You should come, Dad. In fact you've got to come. Learn something instead of spending your time being nasty to Mum and whingeing to Margaret about the waste of your mind in not working.' She gave Alex a long, cold, measuring look. She was going to watch him from now on, find out what was going on between him and Margaret. If it was there to be found and the pricking of her skin told her it was. She wasn't going to be caught looking stupid again.

9

His Honour Judge Hugh Thorne had a morning of pleas and directions hearings. When he went into court at ten-thirty he had already spent a considerable time reading the papers, going through the case summaries, noting particular points, checking and highlighting. There were ten or twelve barristers in counsels' rows. A nodding bow and Hugh sat down, glanced at his list. First on was a rape case, the complainant a girl of fourteen.

Counsel for the prosecution – Roger Dodson. Dodson . . . what had Hugh heard of him recently? Ah, yes, divorce from his notorious wife, Annie, and then Celia's talk of his being entangled with Fenella Lindridge. Fenella? The man must be mad or given to masochism. He shook his head in rejection of such imbecility. Leave that, get on with the case of Jenkyns.

'Yes, Mr Dodson.'

Roger rose and said: 'Yes – Your Honour. May the indictment be put?'

The engine of justice ground into gear. As the clerk arraigned the defendant, Hugh watched Gary Jenkyns, his attention focussed on the undoubted ordinariness of the man's appearance. A round, reddish face; bristly dark hair cut close to the solid scalp; ears, eyes and nose bog-standard, unremarkable. Not the sort to arouse antipathy in jurors – or underage girls. You could see a dozen of him in any street. He could have been a barman, a postman, a security guard.

Only he wasn't. As judge in this matter Hugh had seen the defendant's previous record and was sharply aware that the man had started his career in crime at the age of nine, accelerating from petty theft and criminal damage to robbery with violence and rape. He was now twenty-nine.

Over the years Hugh had observed many defendants. Some radiated resentment, some anger or a tension so intense that you could feel its vibrations. Others looked resigned or quietly sullen. But Gary Jenkyns was indifferent. He could have been a gallery onlooker from the detached way he glanced about himself. A dangerous man. Hugh shifted his body in his chair. It occurred to him, not for the first time, that Walt Disney had done justice no favours by presenting his evil characters as caricatures of menace and horror, since many ordinary men and women had a struggle to believe that other apparently ordinary people could commit horrendous crimes without that evil being vividly painted on their faces. He did not envy Roger Dodson his job. This was an exceptionally difficult case, and deadly serious, since the offence on which Jenkyns was being arraigned reflected the two previous attacks of which he'd been convicted: the use of a vehicle to take an underage girl to the depths of a wood at night for violent and repeated rapes. Nor did Hugh like his own position. As judge he must be neutral, yet weighing on him at every moment was his deep concern for the protection of the public.

The length of the trial, it was determined, would be five days. 'And I am reserving this case to myself,' he stated. 'Now, is there an application for the matter to be heard on video-link?'

There would be two children giving evidence, Roger Dodson told him, his fingers shifting among his papers. There was a video of the complainant's evidence, to be used as evidence-in-chief, while her sister would give her evidence over video-link. There was not yet a transcript of the complainant's video, but one was being prepared.

'Very well,' Hugh said, 'I will give you fourteen days to produce the transcript, seven days thereafter to agree it. The same applies to the taped interview of the defendant. Now the date. It will have to be a fixed date because of the doctor's evidence and the video-link. And witness orders . . .'

Finally he stated that the case would be allocated for the last full week before Easter. The clerk confirmed this as commencing on the ninth of April, Easter being late this year.

'Thank you, Mr Dodson.'

Roger had lost weight, the skin on his face sagging from the lack of flesh and making him look tired and much older. He'd had, too, a defensive appearance as he stood in court and looked quickly around, as if enemies might lurk among the padded leather seats. Hugh hoped that his mind in April would be wholly occupied with the case, putting aside the complexities of his relationships with those two difficult women, his ex-wife and Fenella Lindridge. There would be no room for mistakes here, not even a second's slip. It occurred to Hugh, not for the first time, that he had himself been in a privileged class where marriage went. And sexually. People like Roger and Alex were like sad ghosts at a feast, living with a deprivation of affection and sexual warmth it hurt Hugh to contemplate even for a few moments. Intolerable. Was it true, as he'd heard, that Roger's career had been adversely affected by his wife's behaviour? Recent gossip said he was going downhill; who had started that? Whether it was true or not, Hugh would shortly be able to judge.

The next case was of robbery – banditry some might call it – in a petrol station.

'Yes, Mr Stead,' he said, focussing razor-sharp attention upon it.

Betty Upcott met Brozie Hamilton in the Abbotsbridge post-office stores. Betty had not called at the stores more than twice before Nancy Chubb, poised at her checkout, pointed out that she was a new face, adding, 'Nice to see new people. Moved into the manor at Brambourne, haven't you? Didn't I see you digging the garden when I called with the groceries for the smart lady, Mrs Lindridge, and the new lady doctor?

We do deliveries Fridays, giving a service to our little community. We believe in that, my husband, Les, and me. Just drop your list in and we'll be happy to help.'

'Thank you,' Betty had responded, unloading her wire basket. 'Very useful. Oh, I almost forgot – sultanas?'

'Sultanas? Centre aisle, left-hand side. Got some lovely dried apricots there too. You should try them. That's it.' Settling herself more amply into her swivel chair, her fingers flashing over the till keys, she invited confidences. 'How do you like the manor, then? Made those flats comfortable, the developer, did he? I'm glad to hear it. Made a mess of the gardens, though. Cement mixers and planks and men in boots all over it. No one liked to see that; keen on our gardens we are here. Some of them open to the public, too, just a day a year, but really lovely, Abbotsbridge House, the Rectory and Walnut Tree Cottage for instance, you want to see them. Gardener yourself, are you? Restoring those old gardens? Ah, that's nice. Lavender and roses and peaches growing up the walls again, that's what's wanted. Twenty-four pound seventy then, dear.'

It was on a blowy March morning, when Betty was again at the checkout packing her purchases, that a lanky middle-aged lady entering the shop caught her attention. It was not the nondescript brown coat that amazed her, but its combination with green wellies and an amazing hat – a claret-coloured, yellow-feathered, Harris tweed hat placed at a rakish angle on the greying head that gave the woman a jokily aristocratic look.

'Good morning, Nancy,' said a contralto voice and the hat nodded towards Betty. 'Fresh outside, isn't it?'

Nancy insisted on introducing them. 'Mrs Hamilton runs our local horticultural society *and* the flower rota in the church *and* she delivers the parish magazine,' she told Betty, 'and we couldn't do without her. And,' to the hatted woman, 'this is one of the new people at Brambourne Manor and she's trying to put those poor gardens to rights.'

'Betty Upcott,' Betty said, shaking hands.

'Brozie Hamilton. Welcome to the villages,' the other said.

She was in her late fifties, sallow-skinned and with curiously speckled blue-green eyes that gave Betty an assessing look before the plain face broke into a smile. 'A gardener, are you? That's what's needed at the Manor. When I came here, a quarter of a century ago, Brambourne Manor gardens were something to behold, but the folk who ran the place as a nursing home for fifteen years neglected them shamefully. They did little more than cut the lawns. It was a shabby thing.'

'You'll want to grab Mrs Upcott for the horticultural society,' Nancy Chubb told her bossily, 'and you could tell her what to grow at the manor, too, I daresay.'

Brozie Hamilton counted coins on to the counter, said, 'Just the *Hampshire Chronicle* this morning, thank you, Nancy!', grabbed one, seized Betty's elbow and almost dragged her from the stores, pushing its door firmly shut. 'Walking back to Brambourne, are you? Oh good, I go that way. I'll be fascinated to hear of your plans for the garden, but not with Nancy listening. She's all right basically – very basically – but a dreadful gossip.' A large black Labrador greeted her with yelps and lunges of affection as she released his lead from a hook on the shop wall. 'Quiet, Cerberus. Don't mind dogs, do you, Betty? Good. Let's go, then.'

The name Brozie, Betty discovered as they walked, was short for Ambrosine. 'My father wanted a son he could name Ambrose after his father, hence the awful result which I shortened to Brozie.' She walked and talked with energy, reaching into the hedgerow for sticks to hurl for the dog. She told Betty that the village flower show was one of the county's best, that the church needed another flower lady, and that the rector, 'A lovely man!' was also a dedicated gardener. 'His arched rose walk is a miracle of beauty and scent in June.' She clutched her hat against a sportive gust of wind. 'Not June now, though.' Their footsteps echoed against old cottage walls. The wind pushed them up the village street, bringing the cries of the school playground and the sheep in the meadows beyond around and about them. 'Tell me of your plans for the manor-house gardens,' Brozie requested.

Betty explained the themes she had in mind for the different areas and the ideas behind them with a strong feeling of talking to someone of genuine interest and understanding. 'And I felt I should make sure that different groups could sit at peace in separate areas.'

'I know,' Brozie agreed, raising her eyes heavenwards in sympathy. 'While the middle-aged yearn for peaceful teatime conversations amid the scent of roses, teenagers demand the right to tan themselves to loud music, and other people's grandchildren want to rush around and scream and throw balls into your most cherished borders. And they all choose the same spot to do whichever it is.'

'You've hit it! But I think my plans will cope with such problems.'

'Oh yes. You've room enough. And I love your perception of how it should be – not a pastiche of the past, yet in keeping with the old house. That's absolutely right.'

They passed the avenue of lime trees leading to Abbotsbridge House; the sun lit briefly its three-storeyed Palladian symmetry, and played across the Ionic pillars of its portico. It was breathtaking. Betty longed to see inside it, but doubted she'd ever be invited, not the wife of an unemployed ex-Army officer. She asked who owned it.

Brozie told her of the Manningford family, its owners for almost three hundred years, still going strong, still keeping the estate together. 'Amazing when you think how many of these places have been sold up and developed into those appalling conference venues or themed hotels with plastic stags' heads in the hall. But then these are good people, well endowed with the genes for competence and common sense.' A sudden grin. 'What our grandparents called good breeding. The present Mr Manningford farms the estate and his wife, Arabella, manages the house and the garden and their four children, as well as sitting on the local Bench and running the WI *and* an antiques business. She does have help, of course.'

'Even so,' Betty said, discomfited by the contrast of such achievements with her own mundane life, 'it's impressive.'

Clouds scudded, rooks cawed. The Labrador flushed a cock pheasant from a field gateway in an explosion of feathers and was called to heel. 'Cerberus, no!'

Striding on, Brozie asked about Betty – had she a family, had she worked? Betty explained about her years as an Army wife and the constant moves. 'It limits you, it makes a career virtually impossible. Still, I did enjoy the life. I saw so many different countries and experienced their cultures.' She passed over her frustrations. She mentioned Adam, her one achievement, and her sadness that he lived and worked in America, but she refused pathos. 'He's doing remarkably well,' she said.

In turn she discovered that Brozie was a widow and childless. 'Not even a son in America; I married too late,' she said gruffly. It was after her husband Hubert's death from cancer that Brozie's real life had started, and for six years now she had flourished as the day-to-day manager of Arabella Manningford's antique business. Her father and her husband had been antique dealers, she said. A wry look: 'In fact Hubert, whom Dad brought in to help him as he slowed down, acquired the business through marrying me. And although neither of those old-fashioned men ever involved me in it, I loved the shop and somehow sucked in the knowledge I'm using now. It enabled me to claim ownership of my fate when I was already over fifty – and now,' she said triumphantly, 'I'm happier and more myself than I've ever been.'

'You've acquired what I'm after,' Betty exclaimed, 'something to establish my own sense of worth. And my something is going to be making Brambourne Manor's gardens special once more.' Let Martin be grumpy, silly man, it didn't matter. She was stimulated by Brozie's tale of middle-aged success. She wanted her own vital energies to be engaged, so that she could become equally vigorous and positive . . . and creative.

Brozie held her hat down against the wind. 'Here,' she said, indicating a Victorian cottage perched on a bank above the road, the last house in the village, 'this is my place. Come in for a coffee and I'll tell you about our local gardens and

gardeners – and give you the bumf on the horticultural society. It meets next on Tuesday. We're having a lecture on old
roses and I can introduce you to all sorts of useful people –
Mrs Manningford for a start. And we've real plantsmen in
both villages who'll be happy to give you cuttings and help.
Do come.' She pushed open an aged wooden gate.

'I'd love to,' Betty said, following her up a flagstone path
between clumps of purple and white hellebores and *Tête-à-
tête* narcissus, and admiring the myriad tiny white blossoms
of an early-flowering Prunus tree that were sparkling frostily
against their background of yews. Introductions, friends,
plantsmen; she breathed the cold energising air into her
lungs and glowed at the thought that she was breaking into a
new world – the tight-knit community of the villages – and
might even get to see Abbotsbridge House. Brozie was the
sort of person she liked; more importantly, the sort of person
with whom she would have a great deal in common. One
glance at her enchanting garden was enough to tell her that.

Meeting Celia in the front hall mid-week, Fenella spoke in
her abrupt way. 'Alex is running Margaret round as usual
and he won't be in to lunch. Why don't you join me? Donna's
gone to her coaching and she'll eat in Winchester, so we'll be
on our own.'

Celia was touched. Was Fenella going to tell her all and
swear her to secrecy? Or could she want advice on Donna' s
projected career in the art world? Or was she simply lonely?
Whatever her motive, it could prove interesting. Besides,
Celia had liked the alternative Fenella of the British Museum
and she wasn't going to accept Hugh's condemnation without discovering more. 'Yes, that sounds good. Half past
twelve? Thank you.'

Monkfish and scallops in burgundy with roasted vegetables was more than Celia would normally bother with, while
the fish had turned purple and looked menacing, the flavour
she discovered, was tremendous. The dish that followed was
equally delightful: a compote of red fruits tucked in a filo
basket with crème fraîche. Fenella's tongue might be sharp

but her food was smooth. Over coffee Celia commented on the Cartier exhibition. 'Unusually good, wasn't it?'

Fenella smiled. 'I thought so. Consummate design coupled with brilliant frivolity. Roger suggested it. He's always perceptive of what I'll enjoy.'

Celia composed her face to bland neutrality: so she did want to talk of him. 'You said Roger was a sort of cousin. Have you always known him?'

A hesitation. 'Mainly by hearsay. I'd only met him intermittently at family weddings and christenings before . . . before we became close. The first time was many, many years ago, we liked each other, we flirted and that was it . . .' She reminisced to Celia of a man bursting with virility and potential, who had manoeuvred her into a corner to exchange nonsense, laughing with her at the bride's father's furtive leers down the bridesmaids' cleavages and the groom's purple damask waistcoat and over-tight trousers, their faces bright with champagne and delectable mild malice. He had confided his ambitions for his career at the Bar, where he had just started in practice; she had said she'd love to hear him in court. 'Why not?' he had returned. But then, the reception over, her father had called, 'Fenella, let's go.' In the car the glow had vanished. Roger hadn't asked for her telephone number. She had gripped the seat as the Jaguar swerved round corners, shutting her eyes to Daddy's drunken driving. Why should a smart young barrister like him bother with her? She was no intellectual, she hadn't a keen mind, she was shallow and frivolous. She despised herself and it was a painful emotion, the more so because she was unused to self-judgment. It was at this time that Alex had come into her life and Roger had not reappeared. Yet the memory had lingered.

'How did you . . . then how did your present relationship arise?'

'We met at the theatre. In a party organised by our mutual cousin, Holly.'

Encouraged by Celia's nods of interest, she drew a word picture of that event also, so that a view of the foyer of a

theatre Celia knew well appeared in her mind and she saw
its pillars, its curving stairs and crimson carpets, and the
party of friends chatting prior to leaving, with Fenella to one
side and one stair up listening to her cousin, Holly, as always
certain that she had grasped points about the play the others
had missed, showing off to them all: 'Conceptually daring,'
she had proclaimed it, 'and brilliantly perceptive of the
female condition at the end of the second millennium. *And*
compelling narrative drive, don't you think?' There had been
nodding heads and lips thinly shaping agreement while their
eyebrows signalled ridicule, and Fenella had taken a deep
breath – and then Roger's eye had caught hers with a wink.
She'd suppressed the remark quivering on her tongue in
choking back laughter, and in seconds he had joined her on
the stairs to kiss her cheek and remind her that it was four
years since they had last met and that was too long. 'You
think so too? Oh good. I've been wanting to speak to you all
evening, but there are too many of us in this party. Typical
Holly.' Then with a shrug, 'Compelling, our evening's offering? You don't think so, do you?' Smiling, she had returned,
'That pretentious stuff? No. But it's been worth it to see you
again.' There had been light-hearted talk, and then Holly had
suggested they should join her next morning at a gallery off
Piccadilly to see an exhibition of paintings by an artist friend
of hers, Gregory Meade.

'I was convinced Roger wouldn't turn up, but there he
was, peering at the pictures as I came through the glass door
with Holly.'

Again Fenella made the occasion come alive. Celia could
see Roger swinging round as she described, advancing on
them with smacking kisses, then flinging out an arm – he
was given to ample gestures – to indicate the works around
them. 'Interesting,' he said, and Fenella understood that he
was using the word in its genuine sense rather than as a
caustic comment indicating the opposite, as Alex would
have done. Roger, though denying any particular knowledge
of modern art the previous evening, appeared open to new
impressions and ideas. Was this genuine or designed to

ingratiate? No matter, both were positive. She had told him she owned one of Gregory's paintings. 'I love it,' she said now. 'It's a portrait of a woman and it hangs over my bed.'

She'd visited that earlier exhibition at Holly's insistence that the artist was a really sweet and *brilliant* man, the partner of one of her greatest friends, and they *must* support him. Fenella had liked the way his subjects had been simplified to an almost abstract pattern of lines and curves while still retaining a strong sense of reality. But it was the uncanny familiarity of *Woman with a Lemon* that had caused her sense of déjà vu. She knew the emotions stamped on those twisted features, but from where? Or when? Holly had opened wide her black-fringed eyes and said, 'God, Fenny, she could be you.'

Gregory, dragged over, had told of a woman bleeding inside as she freed herself and her child from a bad relationship, and explained how he had veered towards abstraction to reflect in the distorted intersecting planes of her face something of the disillusionment that for years had distorted her life. Fellow feeling had surged over Fenella. Here was someone she could connect with. And she liked the symbol of the acid lemon. She had bought it. As a friend. On this occasion neither had bought, but they had talked and talked.

On leaving the gallery Roger had insisted Chez Gerard must be their place for lunch. 'You look in need of some good red meat – how about a Chateaubriand?' He'd told her of the recent collapse of his marriage: 'Annie's gone off with a fellow in my Chambers who earns considerably more than I do, so who could wonder at it?' Later he made a theatre date with her: 'If your marriage is on the rocks, as Holly has inferred, then we should console one another.' His confidences, mingling hurt with self-deprecating humour, had made Fenella feel needed. She was at once elated and uncertain. Could he genuinely like her? Or was this interest in her a ploy to insert himself into her comforting bed? If so, did it matter? And so it had started.

Defensively she told Celia, 'Sex with Alex has been minimal for years. I may be too skinny for his taste, but why make me feel bad about my body? It's pretty good for my age and my breasts don't sag. Margaret Jessop's do. Not much, but you can see it – and she must be ten years younger than I am. Roger likes my body as it is.'

It was his warmth afterwards that had so impressed her, the way he had hugged her and murmured affectionate nonsense in her ear and called her his dear, gorgeous Fenny. Later, propping himself on one elbow, he had run his fingers along her collarbone, remarking that her finely built bone-structure was terrific. 'Chic. You're part bird, part vixen and wholly sexy.'

'He's so warm. He makes me feel good – and then I want to be kind and good, too. The opposite effect from Alex.' She shook her head. 'Roger and I telephone each other every day – when Alex is out. Sometimes I seem to see his grey face appear beyond the window while we're chatting, as if it's floating in the wet air outside, the eyes staring. Aaah, the relief when it's not Alex, just Nancy Chubb pushing back the lank hair from her face while she knocks in the hope – so she excuses herself – that I'll take in someone's grocery order.'

'I know,' Celia murmured, sipping her coffee.

'And then I think, no, Alex isn't here to peer, he's miles away driving Doctor Margaret around her flu-ridden patients. So helpful of him while her car's being serviced, people say. Or is it Margaret who needs the servicing? He cares about her, I see that. He never cared about me. I ask myself why he married me. Was my money the lure? Of course, to the junior civil servant he was then, our place at Wimbledon, suburban palace or not, had to be preferable to a nasty little box on a very big mortgage, didn't it?'

'Ever thought of asking him?'

'What good would that do? The truth would be bad, pre-varication worse. Hypocrisy's hateful.' She lowered her head. 'Oh, I don't know; I don't understand him. All the snubbing and the coldness and the flat voice of uninterest – why? I cared about him once. I wanted us to be close but he'd decided I was shallow, snobbish and money-mad like my parents. How could someone like me share his interests? How could I appreciate Beethoven's symphonies without understanding the cultural context in which he worked, or *A Man for All Seasons* without being a historian? Wasn't he the snob, for culture rather than currency? So subtle, his belittling, yet I smarted just the same. My life and my parents' life was all the experience I'd had and he hurt me when he despised it as futile. He could have taught me better if he'd wanted, but he chose not to. Now it's me who hurts him – I'm sharp-tongued and mean-minded, living up to what he thinks of me. Nasty: I've heard myself; I know it. I was dreadful over the move in particular; I know everyone here thought me a hard-hearted bitch, but I didn't dare sympathise with Donna because I had to keep her brisked up to propel her into doing any sort of study. And I was in such a temper! But this freakish retreat to a country village was the last straw.'

'Strange, that,' Celia said. 'Wouldn't employment be more difficult for Alex to find here?'

A shrug. 'Maybe that's why – an advance excuse for failure. Or perhaps he hoped I'd leave him, knowing that the rural idyll bores me rigid. To be fair, I suspect that fundamentally he was yearning for an idealised version of the Georgian heyday of pastoral charm and the simple life. And by having the flat on the ground floor he might delude visitors into thinking that we owned the entire place! I fought against coming here, oh, I fought it, but he was immovable. And our marriage was as fragile as a house of cards. This . . . thing . . . with Roger had barely started, I didn't know where I was, and in any case I couldn't break up the family with Duncan and Donna's exams looming. Alex talks proudly of being a Cambridge man, but it's been me who chased them off to their homework, me who runs Donna to her tutorials now.' She stared down at the coffee cup she was cradling between her hands. 'What I resent most, though, is how everyone's been encouraged to despise me over the years. Am I truly such a crass person?'

Celia blinked, replied calmly, 'Roger doesn't think so. He called you a generous soul.'

Fenella looked up and her tired eyes brightened. 'Did he? How lovely of him. He worries about me being in "bad thoughts mode", as he calls it, when I'm riddled with rage and depression. He says he'll teach me his technique of blocking out those thoughts. I asked him if that was what he did. He looked at me and said, "Oh yes, with my marital difficulties and my fading career, how else do you think I survive?" But Celia, I don't know what's wrong. Why should his career be withering? I ask him and he edges away from anything more than, well, everyone has bad spots from time to time at the Bar. But I know there's something more, I just know it.'

'His wife did make him look a fool,' Celia remarked dryly.

Fenella jerked to attention. 'You mean – apart from the affair?'

Oh hell, dare Celia pass on Hugh's confidences? Yes, why not? It was, it seemed, public knowledge. 'She and her lover were caught being randy to the hilt in a lift at the Law Courts. The Bar was exceedingly amused.'

'It's unbelievable.' Her voice mourned. 'Poor Roger, he should have told me. No wonder he's down, he must be squirming. That crude show-off. Holly never did trust Annie, and she was right, too. But then, hold on, solicitors who brief counsel pick up on their gossip and there would have been plenty around. They'd have spread the word among their number and the ripples of salacious laughter would have spread ever wider.' She thumped her coffee cup down on a glass-topped table so ferociously that Celia jumped, afraid both would break. 'No one wants to brief a laughing stock. Oh, it makes me so cross. It's so unfair on Roger. But what can I do?'

'Calm down,' Celia said, fascinated to note that Fenella was more annoyed over Roger's betrayal by his wife than over her own by Alex – presuming, of course, that Alex *was* being unfaithful. 'What can you do? Well, he certainly needs your support.'

'But how? He wants me to leave Alex and live with him, he's said so. I see now why he's so desperate for my comfort.

But he's in a cramped studio flat over a friend's garage in Putney because that cow kept the matrimonial home. There wouldn't be room for us both. And I can't walk out, because of Donna and Duncan. I'm stuck and powerless, aren't I?'

'Not necessarily,' Celia said. 'Couldn't you and Roger find a place near your old friends in Wimbledon, get you back to your interests there, like the British Heart Foundation? Donna and Duncan could visit you easily enough – or live with you. No, forget it, I can't interfere. In any case, I must thank you for the delicious lunch and go and clear my muck heap of a studio. But before I leave I'd love to see your other pictures. I see you've hung that large Keith New landscape in the hall. I love those distant cooling towers seen through the jagged gaps of a castle ruin. Peaceful in a strange sort of way, but powerful too – almost abstract, yet never letting go of a sense of place. I have a feeling I see his influence in some of Donna's work, which, by the way, I think is remarkably mature for her age.' She turned her head. 'And these two paintings in here appeal to me strongly, too. William Fowler, aren't they? Most of all I want to see that one in your bedroom which you feel has something of yourself about it.'

10

Yet another day. The sun came out and mocked Alex. In the morning he was woken by the dawn chorus, jubilant birds everywhere, in the bushes and the trees and on the fences, singing rhapsodies for spring; he breathed in the freshness of the dew-sprinkled grass and the first sweetness of Betty's spring flowers and noticed none of it. He lay in the hated marital bed, white-faced, his eyes black-circled, and all he could smell was *Poison* and *her*, and the trap of failure gripped him in its jaws. He gazed at the too bright rectangle that was the sash window so long that it hurt. He thought of his grey life, of Margaret holding him at arm's length, of Donna's scowls and Fenella's scorn, and a great weight lay on him. Groaning, he dragged himself from the bed. He had to keep going; he had to present an assured face to the world.

In the front hall, trudging out to the car and his work as unpaid chauffeur, he encountered Hugh Thorne.

'Ah, Alex,' the Judge said. 'Good morning. Tell me – I haven't heard how you fared with those solicitors in Southampton. Did they give you the post?'

'No,' Alex said flatly and swallowed. 'No, they didn't.'

'Oh, I'm sorry,' Hugh said with ready sympathy. 'More fools they. I told that strutting fellow Peter Fox you'd be the best candidate they were likely to see.'

'It was kind of you.' Raising his spirits only to dash his hopes.

'There'll be other posts coming up. I'm keeping an ear

open, but I don't hear of much, I'm afraid.' Hugh rubbed his well-shaven jaw thoughtfully. 'Have you met many people in the area? You have to network – revolting expression.'

'Yes, but with whom? Any network I'd have would be civil-service based and that's of little use here.' He was little use for anything anywhere.

'I'll introduce you to my cousin James at Abbotsbridge House, see what else I can do. Come to think of it, Arabella's having one of her drinks parties next Sunday morning, I'll ask her if I can bring you and your wife. He's a good chap, James, and he knows half the world.'

A chink of hope? Alex doubted it. Still . . . He took a breath, 'It's kind of you,' he said again.

Over his pre-prandial drink that night Hugh remarked to Celia that he felt distinctly uncomfortable about his role in Alex's recent job interview with the solicitors in Southampton.

'I'd heard they were looking for a good administrator, so I suggested he should apply and said I'd back him, which I did – told them he was damned good. But they turned him down, stupid people, and when I saw him this morning I thought he was looking pretty rotten about it. Awful to be him, made redundant through no fault of his own and then made to go through the hoops by people like Stuart Fox, only to fail again.'

'You couldn't help that,' Celia said.

'Ah, but that's my problem,' Hugh said regretfully, 'I think I could. Or rather, I couldn't, but sod's law intervened for the worse, as it so often does when one tries to do the right thing.'

'Darling, you're talking in riddles. Explain yourself, will you?'

'Fact is, just the day before his interview I made a wasted-costs order against Fox and counsel in a case, and it was a big one. Probably a five figure sum.'

'Ah! Now I see what you mean. Why so much?'

'They'd made no real effort to get their witnesses to the

trial and it had to be aborted after six days. Those particular
solicitors aren't usually that bad, but nevertheless there was
no way I could let them get away with such a waste of public
funds. So I don't suppose my recommendation would have
done much for poor Alex.'

Mid-morning two days later, Alex joined Martin at Betty's
suggestion in walking down to The Bull at Abbotsbridge to
mull over the latest appointments columns of *The Times* and
the *Telegraph,* their mutual irritability at failing to find anything remotely suitable to their requirements only marginally
assuaged by pints of excellent local ale.

'It's all sales and accounts and marketing,' Martin grumbled. 'And they're all so hearty farty. Listen to this, will you?
"People developers for a developing enterprise . . .",
"Creative applications only required . . .", "Join a business
that's a hundred years young and still growing!"'

'Don't tell me,' Alex groaned. 'I'm a hundred years old
and shrinking.'

'Not with the lovely Margaret, I hope,' Martin commented
with acid humour.

'It's not like that.'

'Don't tell me she still hasn't let you in? Not when the
world thinks you're getting it hot and strong? I'll tell you
something, Alex, she's having you on, making use of you.'

'She's had a bad time with her ex-husband – still is
having. She's not ready for another relationship.'

Martin drew in his breath noisily. 'Alex, she can't be feeding you that, it's a pathetic cliché. Tell you something, either
she does really like you or she's making use of you. So put it
to the test, why not? Make mad passionate love to her, not
next week or next month, now!'

'Shut up or I'll thump you. She's a serious sort of woman
and the whole situation's impossible. And what can I give
her? I've Fenella on my back, my career's smashed, my
income's pathetic, I've two kids in education and I'm going
precisely nowhere. Besides, I thought you were the upright
sort who disapproved of adultery. And you aren't doing so

well in your own little love nest, are you? Doing the hoovering over the weekend, weren't you, Major Upcott? You know how it feels, all of it.'

Martin was silent, his moment of sly rancour over. Alex had confided that during the terrifying time of the reorganisation of the Lord Chancellor's Department he had felt like a puppet manipulated by unseen hands: each time he attempted a move the strings jerked and he was rendered limp and ineffectual, his strategy blocked. For Martin, it was more a nightmare. It wasn't other hands that were intervening, it was he who was groping in a mist on ground that was shuddering. Betty had drawn up plans for the manor gardens with a decisiveness that confounded him, acquiring in the process innumerable exasperating gardening acquaintances, who interrupted him in the important task of crafting job-application letters by appearing at his door with offers of cuttings or pots of strange plants, all accompanied by mouthfuls of Latin names and raised eyebrows at his incomprehension. Idiots. Show-offs. What did they know of the logistics of transporting tanks? Or running a wine business, damn it. But he wasn't an officer or a businessman now; he was a nothing, a nonentity with no reason for being. Small wonder these people shrugged at him. And he was losing Betty in the mists.

He finished his second pint and said, 'I feel as if I'm lost in a nightmare place, in a land where I don't belong. Not having any work to go to is terrible. With Betty working in the gardens every day, digging madly and shifting clumps of bulbs around and putting in the plants these gardeners keep bringing round, I'm expected to help in the house – like you said, that bloody hoovering. I loathe it. It's boring and it's not my scene. I know that's politically incorrect, but it's how I was made. My mother thought no man should even make his own bed and in the Army I had a batman. But Betty's like someone possessed when there's a spade in the vicinity. I hardly see her, and when I do she isn't with me in spirit, she's wafting through one of the magical gardens in the books her new friends lend her. She's changed. She keeps telling me men and women don't spend their working lives in a single enterprise now, that's a scene that's gone. Instead they move from one field of employment to another as new concepts and technologies present new opportunities. A door shuts, a door opens. Retrain, Betty says. Upskilling, the university of the third age to keep my mind alive, all that crap. I've to get off my backside, anyway. She never used to be like this.'

'Perhaps my wife's rancid tongue is infecting her,' Alex commented, crumpling up *The Times* in disgust.

Martin went on as if he hadn't noticed: 'I don't *want* to retrain. I wish I were back in the Army, or at least had an adequate pension so that we could travel a bit and do things to relieve the tedium of retirement. Driving Margaret round her patients at least gives you something to do, Alex. Betty says I should help her dig, but that's a worse tedium.'

This Betty wasn't his gentle quiet wife, this was a new woman. He was, as he had told Alex, disoriented. And changes in the steady passage he had expected through life ran counter to his strongest cultural values, values that were very English and deep-rooted in his personality. He needed Betty to bolster him, not toss him a look of scorn along with a shopping list before striding out to her own rapidly developing new life. Only last night she'd accepted a telephoned invitation to pre-lunch drinks on Sunday at Abbotsbridge House with him barely tagged on as an afterthought. He didn't want a gender earthquake in his house, it triggered his deepest inchoate fears of deterioration and subordination. He had been an officer, he had always been in command. He required the respect due to the dominant male that nature had ordained before he could tackle his own redevelopment, his own progression.

He confided something of this to Alex, who said he felt the same. 'Yet you have to admit it, men like us haven't the most flexible of personalities, have we? But work this one out: if you hadn't done what you did as a career, what could you have done?'

Martin pushed away his glass, then shook his head. 'God

knows. As long as I can remember, it was the Army for me – it meant comradeship, seeing the world, excitement, in fact a great life. I suppose, if it hadn't come off, well, I could have coped with some sort of teaching. I trained the RCT Junior Leaders' Regiment at one time. I did enjoy dealing with those young lads, pointing them in the right direction, firing them up with enthusiasm, seeing them settle into confident adult personalities. But I'm too old for that now. What about you?'

'I wish I'd studied medicine,' Alex said with a dry laugh. 'Like any doctor, Margaret will never be redundant. Under pressure, yes, but always needed. And people are grateful for their GP's care. Incontestably useful work within a community that knows you and *needs* you, that's what I'd choose if I had my time again. Only I haven't. Now I'd take almost anything. I want to move on, not stand still and scream inside.'

Move on. The words echoed inside Alex's head, over and over, each time in a different context. Get up and go for it, they said. *Move on* in finding a job; be creative with your history rather than civil-service exact, rejigging each application letter and your CV according to the potential employer's needs. Make flourishes. (These had been Margaret's suggestions.) *Move on* in edging Fenella out: when she complains yet again of the dull and dripping rural scene suggest a visit to her rich Wimbledon friends, a fortnight's shopping with the awful cousin Holly, a cruise in the southern Mediterranean for a month . . . hey, yes, of course, with the unknown lover. Then maybe she won't want to come back. (This was Martin's advice; he didn't like Fenella.) *Move on* with Margaret. For weeks Alex had dreamed achingly of how it would feel to kiss that soft shadowy throat and those full breasts, pictured the joys of exploring the hidden profundities between her long legs, visualised with shortened breath the fervent embraces that would imbue her with his own wonderland of passion. Now he shifted from such adolescent fantasies to precise plans for the how, when and where of the all-important encounter, the encounter of his penis with the

deeps of her body, he leading her, taking her in tender steps to
a mutual consummation, losing themselves in rapturous love.
It must be in her flat, on a day when Sam was away, in the
bed with the pretty caned bedhead he had helped her buy in
an antique shop in Stockbridge. Late afternoon would be the
best time. He throbbed with anticipation. When?

Donna was talking to Betty in the garden. She liked her a lot.
Betty knew what she meant by things even if she couldn't
quite explain them, not even to herself. Like what she felt
about losing Mrs Peel for art, or having to sit for hours in her
room learning pointless stuff like maths – and then about
Sam. Sam was sometimes tremendously understanding and
other times elusive and aloof, as if she were too young and
silly to understand him. She had to talk things over with
someone and her parents were in such odd moods these
days – as if they were living on different planets where
things were, well, different. She couldn't talk to them. In
fact no real conversation ever took place in the flat, so that if
she started up the sounds seemed to echo back off the walls,
so deep was the silence. And then she became embarrassed
because of the way they were staring, and she coughed or she
swallowed and that echoed too.
    When they'd moved to Brambourne Dad had talked about
their doing things together with Sam and his mother; going
for walks, or to the races, the theatre, concerts. But it wasn't
happening much. Margaret was too busy, or it was raining, or
there was only boring stuff on. Besides, not only was Sam
away all week, but sometimes weekends too, seeing his dad,
or disappearing with friends. Just once they had been to a
candlelit concert at Winchester Cathedral – Handel and Bach.
She and Sam had enjoyed the thundering music filling the
nave and soaring up to the great shadowed arches of the roof,
but afterwards the adults had decided in righteous voices
that they shouldn't go for drinks in a well-known local pub
because Donna was under age, making her feel so juvenile in
front of Sam that she could have murdered them, the stupid
geriatrics. And that on top of her despicable parents getting at

each other all evening in that poisonous silent way they had. It was unbelievable how much hate you could express without a word being said; vile and loathsome. She wasn't ever going to get married if that was what you had to put up with, that and their stupid infidelities. Next day Sam had lent her a novel he said everyone was reading and she should too. Donna had realised that she was intended to grasp that it was deeply meaningful, and to be impressed. And she was impressed, because the couple whose declining relationship it depicted were so articulate. They never stopped talking. They talked about their susceptibilities and their longings, they explained how each had hurt the other's self-esteem and what it implied about their inner derangements. And in the end, the couple saw that they must part, but because they had done all that talking they did it with beautiful restraint. Huh! Her parents used restraint but it wasn't beautiful, just obvious. What the hell, she ruminated, stamping on a spider that was running across the soil towards her trainers, was wrong with talking? Maybe her parents wouldn't part, maybe they could sort it out. Lots of her friends at school had had divorced parents but Donna thought that was hateful. Her parents were OK – individually, that is – and she didn't want either of them to vanish off the scene. The trouble was they were so awful together. Trying to cope with the putrid atmosphere in the flat made the prospect of growing up seem more than usually complicated and all she could be certain about was that her parents and most of their acquaintances had mucked it up, judging by where they were at now and how pissed off they were. Celia and Hugh were the only ones she knew who were satisfied with their lives, and he was a judge and she was a bit terrifying, too.

'Talk to me any time. It seems a bit odd,' Betty said, plunging her spade deep into the dark soil of the long border, 'but we've got the same sorts of predicaments. People problems and life problems. You're planning for your adulthood and I'm planning for my second adulthood, as you might say – and Martin can't make head nor tail of it. We'll help each other.'

Donna appreciated that, it made her feel full grown. She remembered Betty marching into Waterstones' bookshop in Winchester to ask for a book about tackling the later years with zest and how the girl had laughed and asked did she mean growing old disgracefully rather than gracefully? 'Yes!' had said Betty, laughing too. Donna had looked at her with new eyes. She'd thought her father must have gone senile if he was chasing after Margaret Jessop, seeing that both of them were well on the wrinkly side, but now here was Betty actually reading a book called *Red Hot Mummas* and planning for her fifties and sixties and even her seventies as if they had significance. Yesterday she had telephoned for a prospectus on part-time courses in horticulture at Sparsholt College nearby. It was weird at that age, but it did make you see that vigorous life went on much longer than you'd thought.

'Men and women now have probably twenty or thirty years to fill after they've retired,' Betty said, disconcerting Donna by seeming to know what she was thinking, 'and that means they need to invest their energy in doing something from the start – something that'll fill those great empty spaces of the years. And you must think about that too, Donna. The long-term matters. You're right to study your art college prospectuses well ahead of time, so you can organise your ideas before the pressure's on to make a decision.' She broke up a clod of earth vigorously with her spade. 'The more you know, the more interesting life is. For me it's been, well, knowing about plants and gardening. I'm never bored while I'm digging because my head's busy planning how to plant up these gardens.'

'You think about that a lot, don't you?'

'Oh, all the time. And in bed at night I study how famous gardeners put certain sorts of plants together to produce subtle colour effects or contrasting shapes, and then terrific ideas wake me in the morning.' She laughed and waved her spade aloft. 'Subconscious cerebration, you could call it. At dawn today my idea was to invest in some really dramatically big pots, fill them with things like purple sage and rosemary and silver thymes – that's a rosemary beyond you, there – and put them beside the seats in the herb garden, so their scents will waft over us as we sip pre-dinner drinks on those handsome flagstones Todd helped me put down last week.'

'You do say nice things, Betty.'

'I'm happy. So should you be with your planning. How's it going?'

Donna gave her a sideways look and nudged a fat wriggling worm with the toes of her trainers. 'It's amazing what those art school prospectuses say you can do. I mean, if you take a BA in Fine Art or History of Art you get study visits and even work placements in Europe in your second year. In places like Paris and Florence and Rome and Vienna. That'd be great.' It would give her the conversational advantages she was so conscious of lacking – *Italy? Yeah, well, I've lived in Florence, so naturally I know it's fabulous.* More prosaically she added: 'Dad's always on at me to aim for academic credentials because he says I'm bright and it would be wrong not to, and Mum's always said I must have proper qualifications so's to hold down a good job if I had kids and my partner walked out on me – or lost his job. You know the sort of thing, well, of course you do.'

'They're right,' Betty said gruffly, easing docks and dandelions from the loosened soil and flinging them on her weed pile. 'Both of them. Wish I'd learnt more.'

'And Sam says so. He says . . . he says it's like intelligence is an aphrodisiac, that sharp girls attract men like him. You can discuss things and argue with them and that's stimulating.'

'The old idea that beauty and brains can't exist together has been chucked out of the window,' Betty agreed. 'Grey-matter chic doesn't threaten men these days, it appeals to them, or so my son Adam says. Do you like Sam? A lot, I mean?'

Donna produced a world-weary shrug. 'Dunno. Sometimes he's around, sometimes he's not. He's got this scaffolding erecting job and he sees his dad.' Three times he'd snogged her. The first time in his room when he'd barely landed a smack on her mouth before his mother

turned up and he'd stopped, and then when she'd left (after
tactlessly asking about Donna's GCSE's and making her
sound like a kid) he'd gone all cool and poised adult, and
said he had to ring a friend and he'd see her sometime. The
second time they had been walking and laughing in the
woods behind the village and he'd pushed her against a tree
and kissed her properly – and then some lumbering berk
calling his dog had interrupted and that had been that. Still,
the next weekend they'd had a real kissing session and he'd
touched her breasts and everything. Yet then, oh hell, she
had fucked up by flying into a temper over Nancy Chubb's
suggestive looks and words. Getting to be a woman was very
difficult, other problems kept barging in the way.

   She kicked the stupid worm aside and wondered if all
this anguish meant she was falling in love, but she couldn't
be sure. Her mother once said the emotion was greatly overrated; in her view what was called love was a dubious mix of
dread of being alone and unwanted, and a wild faith that
once you grabbed the man who spoke of it you'd never face
that shame. And *real* love? Five per cent could be lucky,
Fenella had reluctantly conceded. Donna concluded love
had to exist, even if everyone couldn't win it. Like the lottery. And Sam, even with his mood switches and his bouts of
condescension, was far more attractive than any of her
friends' boyfriends or their brothers. She listed his charms to
herself. He was tall and his hair flopped sort of sexily, while
his bony hands and his deep voice definitely did something
to her blood. Then there was a pleasing solidity about his
personality: he knew a lot and he could take charge. Her
friends' brothers all had stutters or two left feet and there
was nothing sexy about *their* greasy hair. Sophie and
Georgia, her closest friends, had already lost their virginity.
They confided that sex was great once you got past the first
time or two. She thought she wouldn't mind losing her virginity to Sam; it was about time she did it. Like with an
examination – once you'd passed it, you could move on to
the next step in life.

   Frowning, she added to Betty: 'I expect I'm a bit young for

him. And I don't know about the theatre and music and history like he does. Well, not as much, anyway.'

'You haven't had the chance yet. But do you want to?'

'Yeah. Sam makes it sound good. Properly interesting, you
know. And I don't want to be the sad sort. He gets the hump
if I can't keep up with him. But I like to hear him talk.'

Her father made professional qualifications sound plodding and earnest and grey; to her disgust he had even yakked
about the importance of a good pension. A pension! Mum
was better, even if she was rude about art students, but then,
as Dad said, how could she know anything about the world
of work? She'd never done it, never been involved. Sam was
different, he made achieving a good degree come alive as
something impressive which would lead to equally impressive, even glamorous job offers. 'That's if you happen to see
glamour in a more intellectual way,' he'd added, stretching
and looking down his nose at her, 'like writing the biographies of distinguished politicians and meeting their famous
colleagues and friends; being in the know and being known.'

Anyway, she was moving on in mapping out her life. She
wasn't sure about its final shape, but at least, like dear old
Betty and unlike her father, she'd agreeable possibilities to
consider. Aloud she told Betty, 'Yes, I'm pretty much settled
on a degree course. With the Fine Art one you can combine
studio practice with history of art according to how much
you want to do of each. I've time to decide, anyway.' She
remembered suddenly Sam saying he wouldn't mind going
to an art exhibition or two, seeing it was something he
should know about. Right, she'd make sure he came to the
Art for the Millennium thing at the Southampton gallery,
and then, better still, Fenella could take them both to the
Summer Exhibition at the Royal Academy, and then to the
Ruskin, Turner and the Pre-Raphaelites at the Tate. She'd
make sure she read up on those artists thoroughly and then
she might even impress Sam.

Hugh Thorne walked into his flat at the end of a hard day to
find young Donna ensconced at the kitchen table with

Celia, both drinking tea and eating hot-buttered toast with honey.

'Hello,' he said, kissing his wife's neck. 'That toast looks yummy. Any chance of my having any? My lunch was dreary in the extreme.'

Celia put a fresh slice of granary bread in the toaster, pushed the butter dish and the honey towards him and said, 'The tea's still fresh. Find a plate and whatever and pull up a chair.'

Hugh did so, wedging himself between her and Donna. 'This is good,' he said with relish. 'I've had a heavy day. Pleas and directions, and also sentencing. I had to send six people to prison today. So I need sustenance.'

Donna looked at him, shocked. 'Six? What had they all done?'

Hugh thought. 'Two, no three of them were caught doing residential burglaries. Two others had been involved in serious violence, while the sixth, a woman, was sentenced for defrauding an old people's home of which she'd been matron – a nasty breach of trust.'

'How horrid.'

Hugh looked back. 'Yes, the people I sentence are horrid. Repeatedly, persistently so, most of them. That's what many people don't understand – until they become victims of their crimes.' He began to butter the toast that Celia had placed before him. 'Never mind about that, what have you been doing today, Donna? Studying? Painting?'

'Tutorial college this morning. After lunch I wrote up my biology notes. Then a walk with Celia down by the river, looking for the early wild flowers to see if she could maybe build up a series of those. We went over into the woods a bit, too.'

'Did you find any that were suitable?'

'Yes, we did,' Celia said. 'Quite a few.'

'Marsh marigolds coming into flower along the river,' Donna said happily, 'great patches of them, and wood anemones and sweet violets at the edges of the woods. Celia says the sweet violets' fragrance has been the scent of love for thousands of years – that in fact they're the flower of Aphrodite, the goddess of love. They're exquisite. And we saw speedwells and other things too. I never knew how much there was to see in the country before. And we saw pied wagtails *and* a yellow wagtail, too, which Celia says is unusual, because they're so shy.'

'You're enjoying living here then?' Hugh asked, amused by her enthusiasm.

'Oh yes. I thought the country would be boring, but it's not. It's just that it's different. Betty was horrified how few birds' names I knew at first – I hardly knew any of the ones she feeds – so she's taught me them and about their different habits and their calls, *and* about all her plants, so between her and Celia I'm becoming pretty knowledgeable. It's fascinating, once you get going. Quite different from anything you learn at school, and yet it, like, fits in with it.'

Alex woke to the sun again. It peered into the bedroom, and shone on his pillow, and when he left the bed and padded to the window he saw a sky of clear blue depths and the dew on Betty's clusters of new plants radiating sparkles of jewel-like light. Clumps of crocuses and early daffodils flaunted their colours along the margins of the lawn. Strange that he hadn't seen their beauty before.

Today the light and the colours of Spring filled him with a sense of anticipation. Last night there had come an invitation to drinks with the Manningfords at Abbotsbridge House. They might well be able to do something for him, Hugh Thorne had said. And Margaret had been particularly buoyant in spirit when they were together yesterday, as though she knew of good things to come. Alex felt a tingling in his temples and the back of his head at the neck, a tingling he had known as a boy when someone was unexpectedly kind to him. He was restless. He needed to get away from this flat, so steeped in all his days and nights of misery, away from Fenella's tight lips and Donna's scowls. He shaved and dressed, careful not to wake Fenella, and the strange excitement grew in him. Perhaps today there would be

Margaret . . . perhaps today. He strode into the kitchen to
cook himself bacon and eggs: the bacon was deliciously crisp
and the eggs were golden and runny inside. He ate, alone
with his titillating thoughts. Afterwards he walked out into
the garden and felt sure of himself, that the day would be
auspicious.

Morning surgery went swiftly and there were few calls to be
made.

'Free until evening surgery,' Alex said triumphantly to
Margaret as she dumped her bag in the back for the last time
and climbed in beside him. 'You've been quick. Well done.'

'The sick sense themselves improving when the sun
shines,' she returned with cheerful cynicism as he drove off.
'Nothing to do with my diagnostic skills or any pills. It's the
thought of spring making the sap and the spirits rise. In me,
too.'

Flushed and smiling, she appeared to him the incarna-
tion of the day's warmth and beauty. 'Blissful, isn't it?'

She sighed happily. 'That and the thought of Jane and me
having new partners and a new surgery. It's moving on so
fast — Alex, it's signed, sealed and settled. Last night. I
couldn't tell you before because I was superstitious about
things going wrong. But they haven't.'

'That's tremendous news.'

'It's the stuff of my dreams, the four of us doctors working
together rather than two against two. We'll support one
another with our different skills and expertise, *and* we'll
each be able to attend courses or take holidays without worries as to the pressures on the single partner left behind. It'll
be excellent, really positive. And then there's the new surgery in that old Victorian house. I love the conversion plans.
They're futuristic, but right. We'll be dispensing still, out in
the country as we are, but with the prescriptions entered
straight on to the computer the dispensary will be superbly
slick. The patients' medication will be packaged and awaiting them on the way out. No plod to the chemist, no hanging
about.' Her voice flowed on, fluently, happily, in a discursive

stream over primary care groups, and the provision for surgery nurses and regular clinics, and the importance of preventive medicine. Alex listened, feeling his whole self become amused and invigorated by her enthusiasm.

'I'm so pleased for you,' he said.

He loved her. His Margaret, his Maggy, Meggy, Megs. Her reply to his mention of the bliss of spring had been woefully prosaic, but it was packed with thoughts for helping others, and that to him was adorable. She was never satisfied simply to grind through her day's work, often a heavy load; instead she persistently directed her mind towards improvements in patient care. She was kind, tolerant and good. Not once had he had to wince for her as he did for Fenella, not once cringe at the crassness of her views. With Margaret he was tuned into perfection.

'How about a celebratory drink at The Bull?'

She stared ahead up the old road, smiling a little enigmatic smile. Rooks were flying around their untidy nests in the lime trees leading to Abbotsbridge House, blackbirds were flitting in and out of the hedgerows, and on the grassy banks there were celandines and aconites, spots of gold among the new green.

'No,' she said. 'It's spring today, with the world all special and new. I want to stop and enjoy it. Do springtime things. Let's drive along that old farm lane, look, up there on the right. We'll have lunch at The Bull later, if you like, celebrate then.'

'Yes.' He remembered that Fenella was taking Donna to some London art exhibition, (Jackson Pollock, was it? Someone idiotic!), that he and Margaret could pass many hours together without comment. 'Yes, we'll do that.' Alight with inward glee he braked and turned on to a rutted chalky track, bumping the car along between tangled streaky hedges until the rise gave way to a dip and they could look down over pastures towards the young wheat fields on the further sunlit slope and on to the smoky-blue hills.

He braked and switched off the engine. He rolled down his window and the sweet air rushed in, together with the sounds of larks spiralling way above them in the blue heights

of the sky. A wood pigeon flew past to land in a sapling, followed by its mate. They bustled together, the male cooing
and bowing. Above the rising grass of spring, insects were
dancing in intricate patterns. Beside him, Margaret stretched
and breathed out a long deep sigh.

Alex unbuckled his seatbelt, turning his head to look at
her, tantalised and confused, distracted between the entice-
ment of her warm body, the breasts rising and falling with
each breath, and the impediments that stood between him
and the achievement of his desires. 'Such peace,' he managed on a faint gasp as he leaned towards her.

'Yes.' She lifted her hands to push them through her hair,
then abruptly transferred the hands to his shoulders, his
neck, tugging him close until her mouth was full against his
and hot waves of desire swept through him, so that he kissed
her back in fiery intensity for a long time, until the need to
draw breath overcame them.

'God,' he said, entranced by her response. 'Tell me this is
real.'

'What else? Did I force you against your will?'

'Never, never,' he said fervently. 'But now I want more.'

'What, more?' She laughed lazily, sensuously, in small
puffs of breath.

A series of kisses, then his fingers unbuttoned her coat and
reached beneath a pullover to unhook her bra and caress a
breast, triumphant at feeling its fullness and weight, so different from his wife's vestigial flesh. A half-smile on
Margaret's face seemed to tease him and he was fired again
into small explosions of desire, kissing her nipples, her neck
and her cheeks, all flushed and heated from the sun that was
pouring into the car. 'This more. Dearest, dearest, I've been
wanting to do this . . .' Kiss. 'I have to love you . . .' Kiss.
'We'll go back to your flat . . . there'll be no one about.'

'No,' she said, in her softest, most determined fashion.
'No, here will be better. Now. Away from home, ourselves
alone, here in the sun and the air.' She gestured at the trees
beyond them, their trunks speckled with gently moving
light.

'We've nothing to lie on. Besides – be careful . . . your reputation . . .'

'No one comes here. And there's a rug in the boot.' She made an outward gesture with her hands, palms up, gently mocking. 'So pleasure me.'

It seemed unreal to him, unreal but wonderful. Things like this didn't happen to him. 'This morning I was having dreams of seducing you. But now it seems you're seducing me.'

'Mutual delights.'

She slid from the car, grabbed the rug to shake it out beneath the trees, and then she was in his arms and they were kneeling and struggling with each other's clothes, eagerly, recklessly, abandoning all caution. He was startled at how much he had forgotten of the urgency and fervour of such occasions, of the elation of wanting a woman who craved him as much in return.

'Oh God,' he said, laughing breathlessly as she fell backwards on to the rug, pulling him on top of her as she went, 'you're marvellous, marvellous.'

But as she moaned and thrashed beneath his body, violent needs conflicted within him. She had to come quickly, she must. But in seconds control was beyond him, co-ordination impossible, and his body shuddered with the violence of his spasms.

'No, don't stop, keep going, please! Pound me and I'll be there!'

Her voice was desperate but he couldn't do it. He was done for, past it, collapsed. 'I'm sorry. I couldn't – I meant it to be perfect. Hell.'

Silence. He rolled off her, took her hand. 'Oh Margaret . . .'

'Yes, I know. Doesn't matter.'

But he knew it did. 'I'll do better next time,' he said. And prayed.

11

As the ebonised bracket clock in her drawing-room struck
nine o'clock on Friday morning Celia was not in her studio
ready to start work, but in her kitchen compiling a shopping
list. This was unusual, but then her life on this All Fools'
Day was being disrupted by a multitude of factors. For a
start, the social life that she and Hugh always had under
control in the past was getting out of hand. Throughout their
married life an engagement calendar in their Richmond
kitchen had informed them which dinner parties, drinks parties, concerts, meetings or whatever were due to occur, and
they had consulted together regularly. There had been no
hitches, no clashes of dates. But with living in two places the
calendar had acquired a reproachful life of its own, con-
fronting Celia with an excess of engagements. Tiresome.
Awkward. A fellow judge and his wife had invited them to
dinner tonight in Winchester, but since she and Hugh were
themselves giving a dinner party for ten the following night
in Richmond, they ought, sensibly speaking, to be back there
this evening. Tonight's pleasure would make tomorrow
hectic, and worse, Hugh's cousin, James, had invited them to
a drinks party at Abbotsbridge House on Sunday morning
and Hugh had accepted without consulting her first. The
clearing up from the previous night's party could hardly be
left for the cleaning woman's ministrations three days later,
and they'd be too exhausted themselves to do it that night.
So, no Sunday morning laze in bed with the papers, but

instead dawn hassles with the dishwasher followed by a sixty-mile dash back down the M3. And she needed to talk to her printers in Italy; she was in the run-up to the Chelsea Flower Show now, the busiest time in her year. Celia groaned.

From the kitchen window she could see ominous dark clouds piling up over the hills, pierced here and there by low shafts of sunlight against which she glimpsed driving rain. She averted her eyes from the erratic April weather, wrote, *avocados*, *veal*, *tomatoes*, *lemon*, on her list, and struggled to remember what was in her fridge-freezer in Richmond. Not much, she suspected. Shop early or work early and shop later? Whichever she did it would be at a rush. Being over-stretched was a menace. In addition she had a feeling that she was becoming over-involved with the other people at Brambourne Manor. Celia prided herself on her independent and detached personality. She was happy working alone in her studio, Hugh was her greatest friend and she was fond of her children and grandchildren, but she had never been one of those women who needed intense connections with a net-work of friends in order to pour out the minutiae of their own supposed perplexities. Why then was she bothering with her neighbours, Betty, Donna and Fenella?

Even now she could hear sounds of conflict coming from the flat below: Alex and Fenella sniping in sharp cracks. She sighed. The relationship once characterised by cool-ness and shrugs was growing stormy. Fenella looked ever more brittle and exasperated, and not without cause: Margaret's repaired car was back in its garage in the old stables, had been for some time, but still Alex was driving her everywhere. For some reason Fenella's troubles had gen-erated real sympathy in Celia − maybe because almost everyone in the manor house, including Hugh, seemed determined to cast her as some sort of monster. So when Fenella invited her to lunch again Celia had accepted on a surge of concern. She wouldn't have put up with Alex's sneering superiority for five minutes herself. Perhaps Fenella's tight-lipped mask was cracking at last. Celia

applauded that; in her view suppression of anger led to
long-term resentments, worse, to psyches damaged from
trauma. Shove it all out in the open was her view.

Hoping no one else could hear the Lindridges she turned
back to her list: what the hell was it Lena the cleaner had
demanded she buy for her use? Oh yes, window polish and
limescale remover. Lena admired Mrs Lindridge, so she told
Celia. 'Always smart, she is, very different from you. Of
course, you're an artist, I know, but she give me some lovely
blouses she'd finished with, Mrs L did, and a jacket to really
make the men open their eyes down the pub. Designer, it is,
you should see it. She's a kind lady.'

Celia decided to shop early to save time. She flung on a
coat, grabbed list, bag and umbrella, and was halfway down
the stairs before she realised that the Lindridges' flat door
was open with Fenella on her way out and still trading shots
with Alex over her shoulder. Celia paused in the shadows of
the carved oak staircase. Fenella was visibly shaking, while
above the impeccable black coat Celia caught glimpses of a
wild white profile and glaring eye.

'And Duncan and Donna, don't they come into this at all?'

Alex's blast in return reverberated from inside the flat,
'I've told you and I'll go on telling you, Margaret and I have
not been having an affair. Given your running tally of
boyfriends I suppose you can't believe that, you stupid
woman, but it happens to be true.'

'You're the stupid one!' Fenella faced back into the flat
and her voice was low now but deadly. 'In all your self-
righteousness you're missing the point. You are hurting your
children. How do you imagine they feel while you're leering
around after Margaret?'

The wind threw rain against the hall window. 'God, you're
disgusting. If they're misled it's because you with your
grubby little mind deliberately put the thought in their
heads.'

'No, not me – they can see it for themselves. Besides, Sam
made snide remarks about you to Donna and she's furious.'

Outside someone slammed a car door.

'You're inventing it.'

'Oh no.' A voice of scorn. 'You're always with Margaret, so obvious in your doting. Even at Easter you're taking Donna and Duncan to the races with *her*, leaving me out. I won't fit in, you say.'

'I try to give them fun with friends,' Alex hissed back. 'A relief from your meanness. Why would they want to be with you?'

He really was reptilian, Celia decided. He oozed charm around Hugh but spat poison at his wife.

A dull colour was rising in Fenella's face. 'Listen to your-self, will you? If anyone's mean, it's you. You must know that in these villages everyone knows everybody else's business – and if they don't then Nancy Chubb updates them at the Abbotsbridge post-office stores. With embellishments. So Duncan and Donna squirm.' Her head jerked and Celia saw tears glistening on the flushed cheeks. 'You've always said how you hated the sniggers over your mother's affairs when you were a boy. You loathed that and you loathed her, didn't you? How can you be such a hypocrite now?'

'Get it into your foul mind – *this isn't the same!*'

'But the effect is,' she fired back. 'They're suffering and you're too bloody self-centred to admit it. God, I'm wasting my time, aren't I? You can't see any further than yourself and your own needs. No wonder if Doctor Margaret won't have you!'

She swivelled round, slamming the flat door with such force that the whole house shook, dashed to the front door and was out, shutting it with equal force. Bang!

Celia rocked back on her heels, feeling shattered. She hated the way those two were destroying themselves. Did they never discuss anything cordially or positively? If so, she'd never heard them. Even their living here she knew had been a cause of endless friction. And as for their unfortunate offspring – well, she despaired for them. She ran down the rest of the stairs and advanced on the front door only to find herself almost knocked off her feet by Fenella hurtling back in again, her face distorted.

'What on earth . . .?'

'That beastly man, Todd,' Fenella gasped. 'My car was blocking his . . . He flew at me . . . I didn't know . . .' She stopped, choking.

Celia put an arm round her shoulders. 'Steady on. Right. Now take a deep breath and tell me, slowly.'

'I backed the car out of the garage to do the weekend shopping, but it's starting to rain so I dashed back inside for an umbrella . . . and then . . . then I was held up by Alex. Only for a minute or two, Celia, but when I went back to the car Todd was waiting and he went for me . . . really shouting. He was so horrible . . .'

'What did he say?'

'That I was a thoughtless miserable bitch for obstructing his car and it wasn't surprising that nobody here liked me . . . He was vile . . .' She choked back tears again, then managed, 'I'm sorry, I'm being stupid, I must pull myself together.'

'It's the shock. Look,' Celia said, taking a grip on the situation, 'come upstairs and I'll give you a drink and you can tell me. Then I'll give that silly man Todd what for, and then we'll do our weekend shopping together, if you like.' She hadn't the time, but Fenella looked awful, sweaty and sick, almost at breakdown point. Well, she would make time. She led the way back up to her flat and made Fenella sit down.

'You won't be able to speak to Todd till he comes back,' Fenella muttered. 'As soon as my car cleared his garage door he shot out in his old Renault and was away.'

Celia poured her a brandy and water. 'I'll see to him later, then. Here, sip this.'

Faced with a reproachful Celia two hours later, Todd grimaced and agreed that he could have been rude. 'But you have to admit Fenella has no more sense in her than a lobotomised black beetle. *She* might know she's only rushed off for an umbrella, but her victims don't. She blocked Margaret Jessop in the other day when she had an emergency call to a miscarrying mother – yes, she was back in two minutes then, too, but it was the panic she caused that mattered. She really is an awful woman.'

'She's under pressure,' Celia said coldly, while the thought passed through her head that Fenella might have done that one on purpose. 'And what caused you to panic and be so unpleasant?'

Todd's cadaverous face broke into a grin. 'A job interview. I'm older than Alex and Martin, and yes, I've formally retired, but I'm bored with doing nothing too, and I didn't need that female making me late.'

Celia relented slightly. 'And did you get the post?'

'Yes, thank you, I did. Through Donna, bless the girl. The mathematics tutor at her tutorial college wasn't up to standard, so I gave her a bit of help and next thing I know she informs me the fellow's leaving and they're searching for a replacement – and she's telling them that I'm brilliant. I'm to do three days a week, teaching on a one-to-one basis – suits me down to the ground.' He bounced on the balls of his feet.

'Good. Congratulations. And now perhaps you could think about apologising to Fenella? Yes, she was in the wrong, but so were you. She was very upset.'

Todd sighed and said he would consider it, but he added that Fenella had a poor reputation around the manor house, and whose fault was that?

Celia wondered out aloud. 'Whose indeed? Has she ever actually been directly offensive to you? No, nor me neither, not at all. I find her perfectly pleasant. Unhappy, yes, and inclined to keep to herself. But then she's having a bad time. Perhaps her reputation is unfair to her. You know as a teacher, I imagine, that it's easy to downgrade people, to destroy their confidence and turn them bitter, even aggressive.'

'Surely.'

'Yes.' Celia looked back in time and bands of old anger tensed across her chest: 'I remember a popular girl at my old school – too popular for some – who was turned on by her best friend. From jealousy? I don't know. But slowly, subtly, she destroyed Penny's popularity. She sighed, she shook her head. She spoke of boastfulness and bossiness. And, she murmured, she'd heard her saying really nasty things about some of the girls – of course she wouldn't say who or what – but wasn't that horrid behind their backs? That girl put Penny through hell. Her friends turned away from her, no one wanted to sit beside her – and she'd no idea why. "What have I done?" she kept asking. "Why is everyone against me?"'

Todd's sharp eyes were fixed on her. 'So?'

'Alex is subtle, too. It's the sighs, the lowered eyes with the shake of the head, the muttered throwaway remark. Nothing one can quite come to grips with, yet it undermines her. I've come to know Fenella in the last few weeks. She's a deeply angry and hurt woman, hence the tight lips and the snaps. She never wanted this move to the country – a strange one for Alex whose work needs, one would imagine, would be better served in London – but she gave in because Duncan and Donna were at a fragile time in their young lives. Alex talks a lot about his darling daughter Donna, but it's Fenella who watches over her studies these days and ferries her to her coaching, leaving him free to help Doctor Margaret – for hours on end. A kind man, or unkind? I don't believe matters are as simple as first appearances might lead us to believe.'

She stopped, considering Todd with her white head on one side. 'Enough. I must get on with my work. I'm glad about the job, Todd.' She turned away.

'Thanks,' he called after her. 'And yes, I will have a word with Fenella. I don't want to be unfair.'

Abbotsbridge House surpassed any house in private ownership that Martin had ever visited, the untouched perfection of its architecture reducing Brambourne Manor, with its eccentric accretions over the centuries, to the comparative status of a country bumpkin, while everything around him in the handsome drawing-room, the portraits, the Chippendale and Sheraton furniture, the silver, the family and their friends laughing and talking in their strong well-bred voices, gave out statements of wealth and security, that solid assurance which the loss of his own position had stolen from him. More than ever, here he felt the undercurrent of his missing status dragging him down. He stood apart from the people around him and drank the Manningfords' remarkably fine wine and his thoughts were in the depths. He was haunted by the fear that some jovial busybody would enquire what he did, and that he would be forced into the shame of confessing that he did nothing these days and that he was nothing, nothing at all. How do you cope with disappointment in yourself? Most disappointments you could blame on other people, but not this one. It was changing him, damaging him, reducing him. He had a tic in his cheek, he cleared his throat and fell silent where once he would have spoken with confidence, he fussed with his tie, he caught himself surreptitiously polishing the toes of his ageing shoes on the backs of his trousers; he was always tired. He was even tired of being a man. He didn't want the responsibility of it. Men's egos are more seriously damaged by loss of status than women's, he thought, in spite of all these decades of feminism. Why couldn't he be like Betty, noticeably blooming as she rose in status through immersing herself in what for any professional man would be a 'nothing' job? Today's world, he decided crossly, was full of inconsistencies and paradoxes that he would never understand, not if he lived to be a hundred.

Look at Betty now, surrounded by what he supposed must be the cream of their local society, chatting away nineteen to the dozen. Nothing wrong with these people, of course; James and Arabella Manningford had been welcoming and friendly, while everyone seemed anxious to make him and Betty feel a part of the community, especially her. There was the rub. It was Betty they were interested in, not him, not since he'd told them he knew nothing of plants. Hardly an Army officer's scene, he'd pointed out. Yet all the gardening fanatics, that strange woman Brozie Hamilton, the rector, a woman called Louise something-or-other who lived in Walnut Tree Cottage and opened its garden for charity functions, even Arabella herself, had been anxious to discuss

how talented and inventive Betty was, and what an asset for
dear old Brambourne Manor. That plan of her's, they
enthused, so cleverly structured that anywhere in the garden
you might choose to sit there would either be a vista or an
enclosed space of tranquillity – heavenly. And then her idea
for an old-fashioned herb garden combining the herbs with
beneficial plants to make it both aromatic and colourful – so
utterly right for the old manor house, didn't he agree? And
her thought of using reclaimed old bricks for raised beds,
quite brilliant . . . and her energy . . . and her artistry . . . and
her knowledge. Blah-de-blah-de-blah. It's a tremendous
task for one person, they concurred with nodding heads; in
the old days there'd have been two or three gardeners
employed . . . but then Betty's phenomenal, so focussed. But
not on him, not on her husband; he hardly existed for her. He
felt put out and put down.

Another couple arrived to a stir of interest. He and Betty
were introduced by Arabella to Candida and Bernard Gough
from Chilbourne House, some miles to the west of them.
Bernard was clearly a person of substance, in all senses of
the word. He was of the same height as Martin but perhaps
ten years older, a well-padded man with a large face
sheened by good living, a jutting strong nose and grey eyes
that were sharply observant. His wife Candida was long and
lean and younger, an elegant and well-preserved sample,
Martin judged, of the same breed as their hostess. Both
ladies were in their early forties, both possessed the same air
of spirit as mettlesome mares, and he betted they both
hunted, too. Martin was sure he'd seen the Goughs somewhere before, but the context eluded him. What was
Candida saying to Betty?

'My dear, Arabella's been telling me of your ideas for
restoring the gardens at Brambourne Manor. I'm so glad
someone like you is living there. I knew it when old Mrs
Waterton was alive and I could have wept to see the house
and gardens deteriorate. Didn't Arabella say you intended to
create a herb garden along seventeenth-century lines, and a
little wild-flower meadow in the old orchard? Lovely. You

must come and see my wild garden – a cross fertilisation of ideas, as it were. I'll boast a little and tell you it's going to look stupendous for the next few weeks – it's narcissus and *Anemone blanda* and fritillaries time, that's why.'

'Of course,' Betty exclaimed, nearly choking over her drink. 'Candida Gough, the garden designer! I knew the name was familiar. I've seen articles in magazines about the gardens you've created and your own gardens at Chilbourne – yes, and I saw a photograph of the wild garden last spring. It was inspirational. Goodness, it's an honour to meet you. Could I visit it, seriously?'

'Well, certainly, that's what I'm saying. Arabella's coming over for lunch on Tuesday week, why don't you come with her? And bring your plans – I'd be fascinated to see them.'

'I'd be embarrassed,' Betty said with what Martin thought was horrid candour. 'I'm no professional draughtsman. But I'd welcome your views and ideas. I've just this week written to the Hampshire county organiser of the private gardens open for charities, you know, the National Gardens Scheme. I want to make sure Brambourne Manor gardens will be along the right lines – but of course your garden must be in their Yellow Book . . . I can't wait to visit you.'

'Are you a gardener?' Bernard Gough enquired of Martin in a paint-scraping sort of voice.

The skin on Martin's scalp tightened. 'No,' he said with irritable frankness. 'I'm no sort of gardener. I hardly know the names of the most obvious plants.'

'Neither do I,' said Bernard. 'Here, let's take ourselves over by the window.'

Following the big shoulders in their immaculate tailoring across the room Martin suddenly knew who he was, too. No mere commonplace Bernard, but Sir Bernard Gough the industrialist, chairman of the Gough Group, wealthy, highly influential, one of Britain's powerful people. For a moment Martin indulged in a fantasy of impressing Sir Bernard to such an extent that he would recommend his personnel people to find him a job, but then sanity and a rueful glimmer of humour showed him the unlikelihood in an entire millennium of any such luck. He shook his head and stared out of the window, sipping his wine.

'Now that's a fine garden,' he said. 'I understand that.'

The long sash window overlooked Arabella's great walled garden at the rear of Abbotsbridge House, a view that Martin immediately acknowledged as something special, even to him. For a start the plan of the beds was symmetrical and he approved of symmetry and proportion. Betty had commented of this garden that nothing but such balance could possibly have been successful in combination with the Palladian perfection of the house and he acknowledged that she was right. He appreciated too the orderliness of the low hedges of box in their sober green, the contrast with the little silvery plants within their confines, the niceties of the clipped balls at the corners where the wide paths met, the stone obelisks arising from golden pools of daffodils. It had for him the same feeling of utter rightness as a military parade. He could almost hear the trumpets sounding.

'She knows what she's doing, Arabella, you must admit,' his companion growled.

'Precision, harmony and style,' Martin agreed. As his eyes moved to the far end of the garden he noticed a formal lily pond adorned to one side by the sculptured tall grey figure of a heron. Beyond it was a classical temple flanked by handsome shrubs. Perfect. Then he blinked. Was he seeing things? Had the heron moved? Yes! The beak flashed down in a stab and back up, holding something that wriggled furiously. That was no statue but a live bird gulping the gleaming fish it had caught. Two seconds later it resumed the immobility that had deceived him.

'See that?' Sir Bernard muttered. 'Damned herons. Come over from the Test, of course, scenting an easy feast. Candida has the same trouble – perpetually having to replenish her fish. I tell her she should fix wire netting over the pool but she says nothing would persuade her to do anything so hideous. Yet still she complains of those birds. Ridiculous.'

'It is, isn't it? I'd have a net – or do without the fish.'

'Sensible man.'

Sir Bernard turned towards him and Martin's hand went automatically to the knot of his tie, then, becoming aware of this, he let it fall. The hard grey eyes examined him. 'Ex-Army?' came from the heavy jaw.

Another time he'd wear a different tie. 'Yes.' Martin braced himself for the inevitable mixture of pity and scorn.

'What rank did you achieve?'

'Major. I'd hopes of making colonel but the Army contracted.'

'Lots like you about. Recently retired, I take it. Found anything worth doing, have you? Or are you simply making yourself useful in the community?'

'Neither, as yet. Not much around and we only moved to the area a couple of months or so ago.'

'Two months?' A sharp look. 'Then your wife's gained her renown in a remarkably short time.'

The man missed nothing.

'Betty's determined and she moves at speed. Three and a half months, to be exact.'

'Hmm. Did you enjoy Army life?'

'Very much so.'

'Good. So did I. In my day we had to do national service, as you'll know, but I turned that into a short-service commission. In the Sappers, post university. I've never believed in wasting opportunities. Those three years taught me a great deal about handling men in difficult circumstances and anticipating their reactions. They also gave me a solid grounding in administration – as well as in handling senior officers and explaining to them both the potential of our technology of those days and its limitations. Then, too, I served two of my three years in Germany and made sure I learned the language. For someone working in the areas I've been in, engineering, chemicals, electricals and so forth, that's been invaluable. So were the opportunities I made to visit factories, engineering works, chemical plants and so forth.' A nod of satisfaction. 'I was also able to buy a damned good car free from the high purchase tax of those days. It's a long time ago now, but I remember the Army with gratitude, as many do. I assume at your age you'd want to work, but I imagine you must be finding it hard to obtain anything worthwhile. The world today views the services as a part of yesterday. Too many films of men in battledress around.'

'You put it exactly.' Sensing understanding, Martin relaxed.

He nodded. 'Times haven't changed in that area, even now. I remember some years ago a Major-General I knew, very bright, very capable, being turned down out of hand for a position well within his capabilities because the idiots interviewing him said he wouldn't be able to cope with the trades unions. He'd bark at them, they said. I was to some extent involved. I told them that a Major-General was hardly of the same ilk as a Sergeant-Major, but they didn't want to know. They preferred a lesser man whose background they could understand and connect with. Despite my friend being the best candidate by far he was rejected.'

'It's no different today,' Martin told him. 'Service officers do a different job every two to three years, alternating the command of troops with an administrative post in a wholly different environment. I know I'm a good administrator and I've proved I'm capable of devising highly complex computer programmes, all that sort of thing, but I fail to convince employers. They see me as too different – and too old. Ageism's another problem.'

'Stupid,' Bernard grunted, swallowing wine. 'It's people's skills and abilities that should determine their employability, not the hue of their hair or the number of their wrinkles. My wife, Candida, is Chairman of the Governors at a local preparatory school, Hamlins, where they're currently seeking a new bursar. Last one's retiring now at sixty-eight. Very good, very efficient, he's been – and innovative. He was ex-Navy and I've advised her they should go for the same ex-services sort again, never mind about the age. They'll be of the healthy energetic persuasion, capable of adapting, and completely up to date with all the latest management techniques and the use of technology.'

Martin's stomach churned with excitement. 'You know, Sir Bernard,' he said, trying to keep his voice under control, 'I'd be interested in a job like that myself.'

'Would you? Why?'

He took a breath, marshalling his thoughts. 'I like the young. I trained the RCT Junior Leaders' Regiment at one time. I'd even had earlier thoughts of becoming a teacher . . .'

'What changed your mind?'

Martin pushed himself on, adopting the other man's brevity: 'I started going to cadet camp. That changed my ideas for my future. The Army presented itself as more exciting. And better paid. Besides, it was more intellectually stimulating.'

A nod. 'I can see that. And now?'

'Now the organisation and administration of a school would have the greater appeal. I've had the opportunity to see a fair part of the world and to assess the way it's been changing over recent decades, I've had a stimulating and colourful life, that's what I'd wanted, but now I'm happy to be settled back in Hampshire, and to work for one of England's older institutions such as a prep school would be something to invest my mind in, something I'd relish. More importantly, I believe I could make a valuable contribution. A school, like any squadron or battalion in the Army, is controlled and run by team effort – as indeed you'll know – and that's my forte.'

Martin allowed himself a brief smile and a sip of his wine. Had he said enough? Had he said too much? This was a drinks party, damn it, and he'd always thought that networking at social gatherings was the pits. He felt the tic in his cheek start up again and tightened his lips to control it.

Sir Bernard was turning his head and frowning. Martin looked round to see James Manningford and Hugh Thorne advancing upon them with Alex in tow, while from the group talking on their left Arabella was approaching with Fenella. It would be Sir Bernard who interested them, not him. He was about to move tactfully away when a heavy hand descended upon his right shoulder.

'You're Martin Upcott, and you're living at Brambourne Manor.' Sir Bernard nodded. 'Right. I shall let my wife know of your interest in the bursar's appointment, but you should also telephone the school secretary for the details.'

'Thank you.' His fantasy could have a chance of coming true, despite his doubts. Martin straightened his shoulders. He had no promises but at least Sir Bernard had not despised him.

Alex was struggling with irritation. He had been introduced to James Manningford, a big and bulky man who, according to Hugh, knew everybody worth knowing in the area, and now to Sir Bernard Gough, and he needed the opportunity to impress them with his alert mind and his capabilities, yet here was Arabella swanning up with Fenella and actually interrupting the start of a vital conversation in order to tell Alex what a lovely cultured wife he had, something so farcical that the breath was almost knocked from his body. He wished, oh how he wished Fenella out of existence.

'It's good to meet someone so knowledgeable,' Arabella persisted, laughing as his eyebrows shot upwards, her slim hand indicating the pictures lining the walls around them. 'You must be very proud of her. D'you know, she identified the artists who painted all these old Manningford portraits almost without pause for thought? Fenella, this is Bernard Gough, Candida's husband, you know. Bernard, meet Fenella Lindridge, who's remarkably knowledgeable about pictures.'

'No, no, a mild interest is all I can claim,' Fenella protested, smiling as they shook hands. 'I'm no more than a dilettante, a hobbyist.'

Arabella shook her glossy chestnut head with vigour. 'You shouldn't be so modest. I can tell you Louise Fennell was impressed – and she certainly is an expert. She used to work at the Holbrooke Collection and give the most erudite lectures on its furniture and porcelains and its pictures. But listen, most people can have a stab at identifying a Lawrence or a Reynolds or his rival, Gainsborough, but Fenella even identified the Tom van Oss painting of old Uncle Laurence in

the Third Corps in 1940, and that's another matter altogether.'

'Pure chance,' Fenella said. 'An old friend of mine has
just such a portrait of her father as a major at roughly the
same period. One couldn't miss the likeness in style.'

Bernard Gough bent his eyebrows upon her. 'What a
remarkable coincidence. I have one of my father at that rank
and painted at about that time by Tom van Oss. It's hung in
my study. One can almost feel the accursed nature of the
khaki. They tell me his work is well-considered these days
and gaining in value . . .'

Alex's irritation was developing into near fury. Fenella
was so scheming in the way she displayed her pathetic
pieces of knowledge to give the pretence of expertise, so glib
with her false modesty. God knew she had a great deal to be
modest about! She had no academic qualifications, no train-
ing in anything; her only assets were the ragbag scraps of
information she had somehow acquired from those glossy
art books she read, rather as her silly friends read modern
novels. Coffee-table trash. Anyone who knew anything about
the subject would see through her in a second. Why
wouldn't she simply go away, fade from the scene? She had
played a large part in his failure; he was positive she derided
him behind his back. Besides, a man needed to be confident
to be certain of success but her sharp voice and her vulgari-
ties drained him of confidence everywhere they went,
depressing him endlessly. He averted his eyes from the silly
asymmetrically draped dress she was wearing. Sir Bernard
Gough was being polite. How could he possibly be interested
in a woman like her in preference to him, Alex? He was certain that if Bernard had taken it on board that Fenella was his
wife he would despise him for such a choice. How could he
tell him that it was she who had chosen him? Latched on to
him like a leech, sucking his life's blood from him.

He held out his glass for one of James Manningford's sons
to replenish. A pleasant, well-mannered pair, those boys,
something near Duncan's age perhaps. He must make sure
they were introduced, and Donna, too, and to the two pretty

daughters who had been politely circulating with spicy bits of food they had concocted. His children needed friends with a background like theirs. Fenella would never think of contriving such opportunities herself. What was James saying?

'My cousin Hugh was telling me that you, like Martin Upcott, have been affected by the government's policy of reducing manpower in all areas and departments. It must be very hard. But we're delighted to have people of your sort moving into the area. Exactly what we need in the villages. Of course, Arabella will certainly be seizing upon you and Fenella to do useful works and God knows she does plenty herself, but there's no need to be steamrollered. There are other things in life beside the local Bench and the W.I. and the village school and its nursery group. But what would you say were your strengths, Alex? Seriously?'

A tactful man, James. A listener would be none the wiser as to Alex's blistering need for an appointment of reasonable, of acceptable status, a position by which he could define himself. They could have been discussing whether he should become a parish councillor.

'I've spent my life in the Lord Chancellor's Department doing administrative work, sitting on committees, often chairing them, moving things forward, facilitating changes – and there have been plenty of those of recent years. And I've been dealing with the staff who work in the courts, too, including the judges. So I'm accustomed to working with all sorts of people at every level, timetabling the changes they've had to implement.' He sipped his wine, trying to keep casual.

'Timetabling. Ah yes. You've given me to think, Alex. I'll pass your name on to someone who might, just might, be interested in what you have to offer . . .' He turned as Celia Thorne joined them. 'Celia, how nice. We've hardly spoken this morning. But then that's the trouble with being the host, one can never spend the time one would wish with each of one's guests.'

'Never mind, James dear,' Celia said, 'we've all been enjoying ourselves immensely, chatting to all sorts of local people, and making new acquaintances. And your wife, Alex, has been a great success. She's so witty and elegant.'

'And knowledgeable,' James said. 'I admire that. I only possess the sort of surface knowledge of art that everyone has.'

Alex gently shook his head in an effort to control his irritation and gratify James Manningford. He managed to say: 'Oh, I don't suppose Fenella could approach your knowledge on the subject. After all, you've always lived with the works of great artists.'

'Whose work she identified without hesitation.'

'And,' said Celia, giving Alex a cold look, 'she has a good eye for modern work, too. Perhaps you don't appreciate her wide-ranging tastes.'

Alex felt snubbed and registered another bad mark to Fenella. He was convinced now that she had been making denigratory remarks about him to Celia at those lunches they'd had together. He had recently been aware of a coolness towards him from Hugh Thorne's wife, and he didn't want any upset in his position with the judge, not at any cost. If only he could be rid of Fenella. He must redouble his efforts there. With his dear gorgeous Margaret beside him everything would be different. To hear Fenella compare his relationship with Margaret to his mother's with her wretched selection of men filled him with fury. She was disgusting, evil, incapable of seeing beauty in any of its manifestations. It filled him with horror that the woman who had borne his children should have a mind so low.

12

On the following Saturday morning Betty was tugging tough strands of ivy from the far corner of the walled garden when Martin appeared to ask if she'd like a cup of coffee. Surprised, she straightened herself and turned to him.

'Thanks, I would indeed.' She wiped her forehead with the back of a hand. 'This work makes me thirsty.'

Martin stated flatly: 'Well, it's heavy work, men's work.'

Annoyed, Betty pretended to take this censorious comment for sympathy while knowing full well that it was not. 'You're right,' she said, stripping off her heavy-duty gardening gloves. 'It's too tough for me. Here, you could dig out those big ivy roots while I make the coffee, couldn't you? These gloves should fit you.'

He stepped back, frowning at his blunder. 'It's you who's paid to do it, Betty, not me. Besides Alex is at our place with *The Times* and I can't just leave him there.'

'Oh dear!' Betty exclaimed. 'And I truly thought you were offering your manly help!'

Martin glimpsed Donna slouching across the lawn towards them in her purple jeans and tight purple mohair top, a mug in either hand, and affected not to have heard this. 'Ah, it seems Donna's bringing you coffee so my offer won't be needed.'

'Good for her. She's such a thoughtful girl. Hello, Donna.'

'Hi, Betty. Hi, Martin.' She looked him up and down. 'We don't often see you out here. How are you?'

'Fine, thank you. And you?' He disliked Donna, who he considered personified in her disrespectful stares all that was most reprehensible in adolescents. Besides, the sight of her stunning hair and those breasts beneath the tight top produced unwanted reactions in his groin. He had no wish for such responses to occur in a public place in broad daylight, still less to be stimulated by his friend's barbarous daughter. He clasped his hands in front of himself. Horrible girl. Had no one explained to her the reflex nature of men's arousal? He wouldn't be surprised if someone raped her. Coldly he added, 'How are the studies going? Come to think of it, shouldn't you be studying now?'

'On a Saturday?' Donna regarded him with equal antipathy. 'You have to be joking. Except that you've probably forgotten what day it is because of never working. Like Dad says, the mind goes rusty from lack of use.' She added in saccharine tones, 'Have you come out to help Betty? That's kind.'

Betty considered Donna's comebacks good, punishing, below-the-belt stuff. She was not in the least sorry for Martin, still grudging over her gardening work. True, since last Sunday at Abbotsbridge House when everyone had fussed over her, he had struggled to utter the occasional agreeable remark himself, only to sound condescending. Now her heart thumped dully with resentment. Why couldn't he help her for five minutes? Why the continuing disapproval? She'd been his attentive audience for years, giving him her interest each evening along with a glass of his latest great wine: all he gave her was a hard time. 'You're late in. When in God's name are we expected to eat?' To hell with him, it was her friends' judgments she valued – Arabella Manningford and Candida Gough, and dear old Brozie. But was it too much to ask, that just occasionally her husband should focus on her?

'Here, take your coffee,' Donna ordered Betty as Martin muttered something and stomped off.

'Hold on a minute,' Betty said.

She wanted the job done before she could relax with her coffee. Unfinished chores were as irritating as whining mosquitoes and had to be eliminated. She tugged the last of the ivy from the wall, dug for the tough root. Some ivies she regarded as beautiful, particularly those whose leaves were spattered with gold or silver, giving the impression of dappled sunlight in dark corners, but this ivy had no pretensions to beauty. Not only were its leaves mottled with some unpleasant disease, but it had been invaded by scores of spiders, who had spun among the leaves those thick and tacky webs which attract dust and dead things in inordinate amounts. Worse, the whole mess had formed a thick cover behind which fat snails had clustered in sticky layers three or four deep, heaving themselves over each others' shells in shock as she disturbed them.

'Yuck!' Donna said, gazing in disgust as Betty flung down a final gnarled root. 'Those snails, I can't believe it. Dozens. Whatever will you do with them?'

'Knock them off and put them to death for chewing my new plants.'

'Kill them? How?'

'Scrunch them beneath my wellies,' Betty said with relish. It would be an outlet for her exasperation with Martin.

'No, you couldn't,' Donna protested, backing away from the horrid thought.

'More merciful than poisoning them with pellets,' Betty pointed out. 'A garden may be a lovesome thing but you have to be callous to keep it that way. Half nature's against me. Greenfly, blackfly, whitefly, and a hundred and one creepy-crawly things all must perish. Pass me the bucket, will you? I'll knock them into that. Thanks.' With the task completed, the roots dug out, Betty took the proffered coffee mug and said, 'Let's sit down on my old bench here. I need a rest. How's the studying, truly?'

'Fine. Todd's sorted my maths. In fact he says I could get an A grade, I've improved so much. It's him who did it, though.'

'And you got him his work at the tutorial college. Martin's put out that Todd's found a job before him.' Her maddening husband had been drinking too much of recent

days, stomping around the west wing in a sodden speechless rage of frustration and tedium. Betty had ignored him,
escaping to the garden each day until it was too dark to see
where the borders ended and the lawns began. Thank God
a letter had come to steady him this morning.

'Why should he care about Todd?' Donna asked. 'All right,
it's boring doing nothing, but to my mind teaching's worse.
Half the kids at my college are the failed sort who don't see
the point of studying only they're forced by their parents,
and the rest are thick anyway. They'd be even worse to
teach.' She paused, thoughtful. 'On holiday in Spain once we
met a teacher from a special school. Dad said what a wonderful job it must be, so rewarding when you reach through
to their minds. But she said he had to be joking, that mostly
you didn't. She said it was more like the labours of Sisyphus
and she couldn't wait to give it up. Sisyphus,' she added
kindly for Betty's benefit, 'was the dubious Greek god who
got ordered by the Judges of the Dead to roll a great boulder
up to the top of a hill as a punishment for his tricks, only he
couldn't do it without stopping for breath and then the
beastly boulder bounced back down to the bottom and he
had to start again, over and over to eternity.'

'Thank you, Donna.'

'Did you know that one? Sorry.' Donna gulped her coffee
noisily. 'Anyway, Martin shouldn't brood over Todd's bit of
teaching. Not worth it. How's his job search going though?
Anything about?'

Betty lashed out with her foot at a particularly speedy
snail lipping the top of the bucket, tumbling it back down
inside. 'Martin? Don't tell anyone, Donna, really not, but he
does have an interview coming up this week. And he thinks
he *might* have a chance.'

'I'll keep my fingers crossed,' Donna said without enthusiasm. 'Dad has one, too. On Tuesday. He keeps going on
about how it's absolutely crucial. It's been six months now
and he reckons if he doesn't start a normal working life
again soon, then he never will. He says employers won't
look at the long-term unemployed. So he's hardly sleeping,

he's so frantic. Funny, after what I was saying about schools, that this one's in a school. Not teaching though.'

Betty stiffened. 'Oh my God, don't tell me it's the bursar's post at the prep school . . . what's it called? Hamlins? Just don't.'

Donna groaned. 'But it *is*! Hell, that's bad! They'll make mean rivals, won't they? Better neither of them makes it than one pushing out the other. Can't you just see it? The rejected one standing with a smile stitched on his face and hatred in his guts.'

'And then forced to buy the pub round to celebrate the other grabbing the job he thinks should be his.'

Donna looked at the heaving snails and shuddered. 'Do you think they know? I mean about each other having an interview?'

Betty shook her head. 'I'd say not. We'd each better warn our own not to let it out and others who might know something . . .'

'It was Hugh who worked Dad's interview, I think.'

'I'll murmur something tactful to Celia . . . Anything to reduce their agonisings.'

'They do go on, don't they?' Donna commented bluntly, 'but this would be a grievance too far.' She stood up, stretched and told Betty she would dump the snails in the meadow behind the old thatched cottages opposite. 'So you won't have to stamp on them.'

'Fine,' said Betty, rising in turn. 'The cows'll probably munch them along with their grass, but you'll have given them a chance.' She piled her ivy branches into the wheelbarrow. 'What are you doing this weekend, Donna? Anything interesting?'

She shrugged. 'I'm going for a walk this afternoon with Sam. I'll probably spend the evening at their place, too. Sam said he might cook for me, though he doesn't know what yet. Depends whether his mother's done any shopping, and what's around. She's a bit vague about food, Sam says. Often they go for a pub meal because she's been too busy to shop or she can't face cooking. Mum doesn't do that. She's out a lot, too, but she makes our meals first so we only have to microwave them. They're good.'

'What about Duncan?' Betty asked. 'Isn't he due home for Easter soon?'

'He's with friends in Wimbledon, where we used to live. He'll be back next weekend.'

Betty looked across the walled garden and up at the sky. A fine thin cloud had blown between them and the sun and behind it bigger clouds were crowding up. She tutted as a gust of wind tried to tug the hair from her untidy bun, pushing it back with her fingers. 'I doubt you and Sam will get your walk, there's rain coming.'

'It's not going to matter that much.' Donna flashed her a glance of amusement. 'I expect we can find indoors things to do.' And she went off with her jaunty stride, swinging the bucket of snails.

Betty stared after her. And what might Donna find to do indoors with Sam? It wasn't hard to conjecture. She thought both Fenella and Margaret should take closer notice of their adolescent offsprings' doings, but would never dream of telling them so. Lucky Sam and Donna, bursting with health, energy and raw imagination, she reflected as she trundled her barrow to the bonfire site in a corner of the old orchard. Did they realise how blessed they were? She saw them as standing on a high hill, surveying a wide sunlit landscape; so many ways to go, so many opportunities. As you grew older though, horizons narrowed, opportunities dwindled, until finally there was nowhere further to go. That was Martin's insistent depiction of his own condition in an unjust world: 'I feel futile – old, broke, humiliated. Where can I go now but down?' Betty had stopped trying to minimalise his grievances, abandoned sympathy. Sometimes when she was tired and he was being particularly peevish it was difficult not to feel bitter herself, not to dwell on the injustice of Adam working so far away in America, or the social blight of a husband who did nothing but moan.

The rising wind pushed at her barrow, almost overturning

it. She slowed, bracing herself, balancing her load. She mustn't allow herself negative thoughts; she must be positive at every level of her internal existence. Adam was happy and successful where he was; Martin's position bore no relationship to hers, and please God, he could soon have the appointment he craved so desperately. And she had Brambourne Manor gardens to develop, an act of creation that was already visibly taking on shape and colour; her little paradise. She tipped the dusty mass of ivy on to the ashes of previous fires, remembering them with affection. She liked bonfires, their leaping cleansing flames and the sweet-smelling smoke that drifted in curls across the gardens and the meadows beyond. But the bad thoughts persisted: there would be none of those pleasures today, not with the coming rain. She could feel the first spots now. Instead, she would be shut in the west wing with Martin and quite possibly Alex. Alex, whose wife would be elsewhere, as she so often was. From her early mistrust of Fenella, Betty had veered to definite sympathy. No doubt she felt as Betty did, discouraged and constricted by her exacting husband's moodiness. And Fenella had no work to occupy her, nor any rural interests whatever; only two nearly grown-up children, whose need for her was dwindling by the day. Worse there was Alex's over-eager friendship with Margaret Jessop. It was embarrassing, and so bad for those unfortunate adolescents of his. Particularly for her dear young friend, Donna, who was unable – as they all were – to avoid noticing it.

Betty's old friend the robin fluttered into a nearby apple tree, hopping from twig to twig to catch her attention.

'I see you, boy,' she said. 'Been deserting me recently, haven't you? Concerns elsewhere, other charms than my crumbs? A girlfriend, that's what. Unfaithful one!'

The robin burst into his high sweet song as if to reassure her of his continued friendship and for a moment the spitting rain held off. Comforted, leaning on her garden fork, she listened, and then out of the corner of her eye she caught movements by the orchard wall. From a bramble tangle Betty had marked for clearance emerged the robin's mate, flitting to the top of the wall to study her, head on one side.

'So that's where your nest is,' Betty breathed. 'All right, I shan't touch it. Trust me.'

She backed her wheelbarrow away with care not to alarm the little birds. For a moment the sun shone down on the untidy grass and then as she returned the wheelbarrow to its shed, the male hopped and flew alongside her, his red breast vivid in the watery light. She thought how companionable birds could be. Not that she minded working alone. Neighbours and friends popped in and out to exchange a few words, offer a new plant, but even when no one was about the quietness never troubled her, nor boredom. How could it when her mind played daily with fresh visions? As she had once said to Donna, a garden is for ever a work in progress, changing and evolving as plants grow, reach maturity and fade, to be replaced by other fancies, bringing a changed beauty. She was part of another world now, the world of work, where her days were brimful with the mingled fascination and pleasure of accomplishment. Tiredness could be a problem, distasteful tasks had to be tackled, but the fascination overrode the drawbacks. She did not see that it was exactly the absence of these factors, the intriguing variables of planning and strategies, the relish of claiming success in the face of challenge, that led to her husband's anguish of boredom, to his angry regrets and resentments. It did not occur to her to see her little world as in any way comparable with the professional world of work from which he had been ejected. He had enjoyed success for many years, not vast, perhaps, but not paltry either, and he had served in many interesting parts of the world. Why could he not look back with satisfaction on the achievements of his Army days, relax, and take life as it came? She did not understand the level of affliction which he and Alex continually nurtured in one another.

The rain lashed noisily against the windows of Margaret's flat, flowing down the panes in curtains of water that gave

Donna the comfortable fancy of being hidden from the outside world. She prowled around the sitting-room, picking up Margaret's Victorian dolls to stare at their primly pretty porcelain faces and then tossing them down again, switching on table lamps to banish the shadows, not looking at Sam, the undercurrent of sexual excitement between them engendering a restlessness in her. She didn't know what to do with herself here. In her parents' flat she could have taken charge, lost her uncertainties in making lunch, confident in the familiar kitchen. But she'd never thought of inviting Sam there; her parents might be around, fighting, and that would be mortifying.

In Margaret's kitchen they discovered that food shopping had not made a part of her morning's activities, but in the depths of the fridge they did find eggs, cheese, and the makings of a salad from faintly tired-looking lettuce, cucumber and celery.

'That's OK then,' said Sam, breaking off a piece of celery to scrunch it, unwashed. 'We'll share a cheese omelette.'

'Will we?' said Donna, challenging him. 'Who makes it? Not me, I hope.'

'Me,' said Sam, picking a bit of grit from the celery from his tongue. 'I can cook.' And he could and did, rinsing the salad on Donna's instructions and dressing it, while she grated the cheese. Then he whipped up the egg whites until they were stiff, deftly blended in the yolks and poured the mixture into the buttery hot pan. 'A soufflé omelette,' he said. 'Butter us some bread, will you?' Finally he poured two glasses of a white wine, handing her one with an offhand kiss.

'It's a good omelette,' Donna said, trying it, and then they ate side by side in silence, looking at each other and away, half smiling, half serious. She felt at once very adult and very young. They were only inches apart so that she was deeply conscious of his body warmth, of his bony hands and the hairs on his forearm and his long strong back – the sheer facts of his maleness. She sipped her wine uncertainly. Males were so different from females. How were you expected to understand them and know how to treat them when you'd so little knowledge of them? Having a brother didn't help. Brothers rarely talked about their inner feelings, she'd discovered, and never about sex, not to their sisters. And older brothers, particularly hers, didn't take much notice of you at all, except to tease and jeer. This time over lunch was all she had to make some crucial decisions.

His bony male hand removed her plate, offered her the fruit bowl. 'The apples are good,' he said.

She shook her head; Duncan said she scrunched like a horse when she ate apples, and whatever your views on horses, that wasn't alluring. She pulled a banana from a bunch and Sam did the same. The rain pattered.

He zipped open his banana slowly, his eyes upon her in frank appraisal of her rich untidy hair, her full lips, her startlingly mature breasts under the tight top. Donna undid her own banana and felt herself grow unaccountably hot. She took a bite by way of distraction and immediately thought how unattractive the action of chewing was, but his eyes were still focussed beneath that level.

'God, your breasts are great.' He put his free hand over one, warmly, possessively. 'Perfect.'

She had the sensation of standing on the edge of a cliff with a great empty space beneath her, dizzily stirring and hazardous. Her insides turned over. She cleared her throat.

He relinquished her breast to finish his banana and drink the last of his wine, then he stood up, looking with disfavour at the messy kitchen table, all crumbs and banana skins and smeared glasses. 'We can't stay here. We'll go to my room.' He crossed the kitchen to switch on the kettle. 'Coffee?'

Donna nodded. Her breast was cold without his warm hand over it.

'We'll take our mugs with us and listen to music,' Sam said, 'and talk and things. There's no hope of getting outside in this lousy weather when we haven't got a car.'

Donna agreed. She was going to demand driving lessons as her next birthday present and told him so. 'Not being mobile is a pain,' she said grandly.

'Yeah,' Sam said, pouring steaming water into the coffee mugs. 'I'm taking my test in ten days time and I intend to pass. It'll make a big difference. I'll be able to have mum's car at the weekends.'

'If she lets you,' Donna said.

'Well, she hardly uses it, does she?' Sam pointed out and his lips twitched at the look on her face. 'You don't know what to think about Alex and her, do you? Little innocent.'

'I'm not.'

'Really?' He carried the mugs through to his room, tossing over his shoulder: 'Then why did your father say to look after you, because you were a virgin? Warned off, you could say. "Just a few brief words, young Sam." And all that. And you are, aren't you?' He dumped the mugs down on the chest beside his bed.

'Are what?' Donna fenced, scowling at this mortifying assumption.

'Like he said, a virgin.'

Donna flung herself full-length on his bed. 'So what if I am? It's something I want to stop being.'

Sam stared down at her.

'Well,' she said irritably, 'are you up to it?'

'Yeah, of course. Are you sure? I mean, what, here and now?'

'Why not? You're not a virgin, are you?'

Sam looked offended, then grunted out an unexpected laugh. 'No, certainly not. If you want to know, I had my first sex with a friend's au pair girl when I was staying with his family in the holidays. Well, she wasn't Ben's au pair, of course, but his little-mistake five-year-old sister's. Marie-Chantal, she was amazing, she seduced me.'

Donna wriggled herself across his bed, making room for him beside her. 'What do you mean, she seduced you? Why not you her?'

He sipped his coffee, grinning, remembering. 'She was about twenty, I was only fifteen – it never occurred to me she would . . .'

'Be interested in a schoolboy?' Donna made a sinuous

movement of her body against him, and gave him a teasing smile. 'So did she leap on you? Tell me what happened.'

He put his mug down and turned to lie half on top of her, pulling up her skimpy purple top, his hands reaching round her back to undo the hooks of her bra. 'She was a nymphomaniac if ever I met one . . .' He thrust Donna's bra upwards and lowered his head to kiss her nipples. 'Mmm. You're lovely. I'll tell you this, her breasts were nothing to yours. She was a skinny little thing.' Another kiss. 'On my first night there I woke up thirsty at about one and crept downstairs for a glass of water. I heard sounds, saw a streak of light round the kitchen door but simply assumed someone else was thirsty, too. But when I opened the door there they were, Ben's father and little Marie-Chantal going at it full pelt on the kitchen table. I stood frozen and gawping until she jerked her head sideways and winked – and then I backed out, so embarrassed I nearly fell over my own feet.'

Donna let out a staccato burst of mirth, 'And without your drink of water! So then what?'

He shrugged. 'I kept quiet, didn't say a thing to a soul, how could I? Though I did feel awful knowing things about Ben's dad that I thought Ben didn't. Then around midnight the next night that little French girl came sidling into my room and my bed – to give me my reward, she said, for having kept silent. There were several rewards over the week. I felt like I'd won the lottery.' He paused, frowning. 'Except . . . she didn't want kisses or cuddles, just sex, no holds barred and keep going. Later on, Ben said she was letting him have it, too. She taught me a lot, but I didn't like it, that detachment.'

Donna gave him a look of laughter that seemed to veer for some moments between mockery and disparagement. 'How weird. You'd think that would be any boy's dream, sex on offer without any demands or commitment.'

'No, I hankered for a girl who was a friend, not just a sexual-release mechanism. I did wonder, when I overheard my dad taunting Mum with all his brief affairs and one-night stands, whether I'd get to be like him. I mean, wanting sex does plague you the whole time, but when it was offered to me so casually, well, it didn't feel right. Sex for me isn't a matter of scoring, it's all tied up with other things like affection and being able to talk together.'

'Yeah,' she said, thinking about it. 'Sounds like I feel.'

She wondered if he was implying what she thought he was, decided that appearances showed he must be and pressed her body with a flutter of pleasure still closer to his. She closed her eyes, signalling an end to conversation. Their mouths met in long greedy kisses. The world narrowed and became instinctive; all was touch and breath. 'Like this? And this?' 'Mmm, yes, yes.' She became tense, wanting to get on with it, to do it and know it. 'Take my clothes off,' she gasped, and shakily, wriggling and tugging and laughing, they removed the restraining garments from each other's bodies, tossing them on the floor. Rain pattered coldly at the window, but clutched together again they generated a focus of warmth, a rising heat. Briefly, he pulled away, sat up. She shut her eyes and kept them shut. Then his mouth was murmuring against hers once more.

'Hold me,' he said, then, 'You all right? Sure?'

'Yes, yes,' she managed, her eyes shut. 'Go on.' And she struggled to relax her tense body sufficiently to encompass him within her.

Afterwards they both lay silent, a sheen of sweat drying, hearts thumping, breath still short. Beyond them on the windowpanes the rain was pattering as steadily as before. It struck Donna as odd. She had been through this momentous experience – yet only a few minutes had passed and nothing seemed changed. She considered it. Yes, nothing external had changed, but in some hidden recess of her self she had moved on. There had been pain and at first she had felt embarrassingly awkward, but then those feelings had passed and new sensations begun. They would be explored in the future. In the meantime she had changed status, moved to full womanhood; she was one of them, the adults. She knew.

Sam's hand felt for hers and gave it a squeeze. She waited perhaps a minute, then withdrew her hand and sat up in the narrow bed. Her body was too hot, her heart still beating double time.

'I need a bath,' she announced. 'I'm all sticky.' She scrambled from the bed and stood up, looking back at him, imprinting an image in her head.

'You were all right, you know,' he said, smiling lazily, pleasedly, up at her, 'but God, were you tight at the start. You really were a virgin, weren't you?'

'Yes,' she said, cross at this, 'and it hurt.'

He levered himself to a sitting position. 'Sorry, I was as gentle as I could be.' Then he stared at the duvet cover, uttered, 'Oh, my God!' and pointed. 'Blood! What the hell do we do about that?' Then he blinked and added: 'You OK?'

The stain looked dramatic. She told him she was fine, hoping it was true. 'You stick the cover in the washing machine, of course.' She added tartly, 'We can have it dry before your mother returns – hide the evidence if that's what's worrying you.'

He grinned. 'Well, it would save embarrassment. But I can't work the stupid machine. We bought this one when we came here and Mum does my stuff.'

Not the machine that was stupid, but him. She relaxed, meeting his apologetic eyes with an amused lift of her eyebrows. 'I can work it. I'll deal with it. No problem.'

In bed he had been the leader, the knowledgeable one; now she'd take charge. She sensed the youthful awkwardness that had been haunting her lift and dissipate like the early mists from the meadows. She was different now, part of the adult world. She drew herself up, gave the body and the breasts he had admired and lusted after a slow smiling appraisal, arching, even preening herself. 'But first I'm going to have a long soak in the bath, and you can wash my back.'

13

He ran the bath for her, sending the water cascading down from the taps on to generous dollops of his mother's Badedas, swirling up the foaming green water.

'There,' he said.

'Great.' She stood beside the bath casually tipping back her head and combing her hair with her fingers until it cascaded in one long thick mass down her spine. Watching him from beneath her lashes she grasped the mass in her hands, twisted it round and lifted it up on her head, clipping it there. She liked the look on his face as her actions raised her breasts and tightened the muscles of her stomach. The girls at her school had admitted her figure to be good, his hungry eyes, so soon after sex, assured her it was something more.

'You're so gorgeous,' he murmured, pulling her hard against himself, his hands caressing her buttocks. 'I could do it again right now!'

Donna freed herself, a touch overwhelmed. She stepped back to feel the water, staring at his naked body, mesmerised by the sight of his masculinity. He was . . . impressive. Six foot tall, finely sculpted with no superfluous flesh, yet his shoulder muscles were heavy and his biceps swelled as biceps should – all that heaving of scaffolding poles, she supposed. The hair on his chest was dark, spreading to halfway across the breast area and there was more lower down . . .

'What are you thinking?' he demanded.

'Nothing you need to know about—'

'Checking me over? Do I pass?'

A flicker of insecurity? He had a way of appearing casual but very much in control, with no adolescent rough edges. She remembered how his skill with words and ideas had impressed her at their first meetings; she remembered also the slow development of their relationship, his offhand airs that had left her with a gnawing sense of let-down and the barely admitted fear that he would, when he chose, turn to some older, smarter girl. Now he was fishing for admiration, for reassurance.

She stood up, casual herself. 'You pass,' she said with a flicker of a teasing smile. 'You're OK.'

She lay down in the bath, stretching her body languorously beneath the scented foam, her legs and feet floating. 'Mmm. Lovely.'

Sam ran a fingernail the length of her body. 'I'm joining you. I can wash your back – and other parts – better if I'm in there with you.'

Share her bath? Her parents, to her knowledge, had never shared a bath. But he was laughing and suddenly she wanted him in there with her, his attention wholly hers.

'All right,' she said, half raising herself. 'Take the taps end. Hey, but Sam, when's your mother due back? You may not care, but I don't propose to be caught like this. Where is she?'

His eyebrows shot upwards. 'Don't you know? You should, because it's your father she's gone off with – I don't know where.' He lifted his long legs over the side and sat down with a bump, sending a smacking wave of water down the bath, almost swamping her.

She clutched the rim of the bath. 'Oh, Sam, stop it! And get off my foot. No, she couldn't have. Dad's with Martin. They go for a pub lunch, Saturdays. Often.' But her breath was already short with fury at her blind trust.

'Really? Not today.' He picked up one of her feet and began a gentle soapy massage, frowning. 'And your mum? Where's she? She's involved with someone, too, isn't she?'

'What do you mean?' But the spasm in her guts warned her he could be right.

'She's always out. Away weekends. I saw her drive off with her bags this morning . . .' He let her foot slide back beneath the water, his eyes averted.

'She stays with friends. She doesn't like it here.' It was obvious, now she thought about it. Then why hadn't she known before? Because no one would ever imagine their black-clad and cranky mother in her fifties naked in bed with some strange man. Nor would she ever have connected her mother with love, Donna thought, her anger intensifying because she had never seen any affectionate contact between her parents, never seen Alex kiss her mother, not even on her birthday. Hell, that was awful. She scowled. Would anyone fancy her mother, so despised and denigrated by her father? Yet there were telephone calls . . . a lot of calls.

She kicked at his thigh. 'So come clean, Sam, just what do you know?'

He shrugged. 'Only something I heard your dad say to my mother.'

'*What*?' she insisted.

'That he reckoned your mum had someone . . . Nothing else.'

Donna clenched her teeth. She told herself that it wasn't so much that she minded what her mother did, as not being told a thing about it, worse, not having seen it for herself.

Sam said, 'Be glad they're having fun. At that age you need all you can get.' He tugged at her. 'Turn round, and I'll do your back. You do still want it washed?'

She nodded, half scrambling to her feet, turning, then crouching between his legs. He washed her back with long strong strokes, as though she were a bristling cat which needed to be soothed. Donna clasped her arms around her knees, thankful he couldn't see her expression of outrage. If either of her parents had come into the room she would have stood up and hit them, naked and soapy as she was. She hankered to hit Margaret, too. They were a foul rotten lot; worse, they were pathetic.

The truth was that she had visualised those men and women who involved themselves in covert love affairs as being suave individuals of impressive glamour, who threw parties of scintillating splendour and were involved in passions of an intensity unknown to the ordinary boring sorts her parents were. And not with the most titanic mental effort could Donna ever have placed either her parents or the diligent Doctor Margaret in the category of glamorous. The thought was ludicrous! But if people like them were involved in hidden passion, then that dissipated all its splendours. She looked with a jaundiced inner eye at Alex and Fenella and denounced them to the patient Sam, now rinsing her back.

'You wouldn't believe they could be doing it all round the place like that, would you? They're so awful – and they sag everywhere they shouldn't!' You heard of other people's sad parents going off with new partners, but not your own ancient originators.

'Oh, I dunno,' Sam said, 'perhaps they don't think that sagginess matters. After all, they've had years to get used to it, haven't they? I couldn't believe it when I heard about my dad and his women – they weren't all young, either. Mum said it would have been better for her pride if they had been, but I don't think he was that bothered. He just said Mum made him feel inferior – and having a fun time with women who fancied him – ' a shrug ' – well, it put the balance right between them. And made him feel great.' His bony hands soaped her breasts, lingering over the nipples. 'Sex isn't only for the young, you know . . .'

She exploded, suddenly beside herself, 'I've worked that one out for myself, thank you, Sam. Don't be so bloody condescending. And take your hands off my boobs.' Her eyes were stinging and she wanted to howl and she couldn't think why. She stood up and stepped out of the bath to stand dripping and shivering and glaring at the towel rail. 'Which towel am I supposed to use, then?'

Sam heaved himself out and passed her the largest. 'Sorry. Here, take this, I've only used it once.' He wrapped it around

her, then looked at her with a glint of humour. 'Hey, stop
being cross and think about where they're at, our parents, I
mean, middle-aged and knowing they're going downhill –
marriages collapsing and their jobs boring them, or worse,
not having one like your dad and Martin, and feeling down-
graded. It must be awful. They need someone around who
matters to them, who thinks they matter, too. So getting tangled with a new love must liven them up, mustn't it? And
why not? Like the grasshoppers, they want to sing a bit
before the winter of their lives really sets in.'

Donna, while inwardly deploring this repellent analysis,
accepted that he might be right. Still, that was no reason
why she should treat Alex and Fenella as anything but
regrettable and give them hell for it. It wasn't that she was an
idealist, she told herself, but she did think that her own parents, after moralising to her for years, should at least behave
reasonably to each other instead of conducting their endless
sneering, sniping guerrilla war *plus* leaping into other
people's beds. They were such hypocrites.

Clutching the damp towel about her, she trailed into Sam's
bedroom and began to put on her clothes. The room was
shadowy and quiet; there was only the endless drip, drip,
drip of the rain. Sam came in, discarded the towel tucked
around his waist, pulled on his Y-fronts, then squatted down
on his haunches to retrieve a sock from beneath his bed. A
worrying thought nudged at Donna's mind. She paused in
tugging up her purple jeans.

'You have got rid of the condom so your mother won't see
it, haven't you?'

He looked up. 'What condom?'

It was as though the room held its breath. 'You used one –
didn't you?'

He straightened himself. 'No.' Defensively, the sock dan-
gling from his hand, he added, 'I asked if you were all right,
you know I did. Yes, yes, you said.'

A frown of unbelief as she recalled this. 'I thought you
meant was it OK for you to go on, was I sure about doing it.'

He licked his lips. Down the lane a tractor rumbled.

Persisting, she said, 'But you were fiddling with your thing for ages.'

'Lubrication, not to hurt you. You must have seen.'

'I'd my eyes shut.' Psyching herself up for the great event, though she'd never admit that to him. A fearful and dragging ache seemed to tug, wound-like, at her guts. She collapsed backwards on to his bed. 'Oh Christ, now what do we do?'

He said without conviction, 'The bath should have washed it all out.' He pulled the sock on, reached for its brother. 'Anyway, I thought all girls were on the pill now.'

'Not me, not as a virgin.' Grimly she said, 'I suppose I'll have to get hold of a morning-after pill, God knows how. Pregnancy is the last thing I need.'

'It's highly unlikely anything will happen,' he said, trying to sound confident. 'Some couples try for years without success.'

'I can't risk that. Oh, hell, you are the ultimate idiot, Sam.'

Betty was relaxing on her sofa, her feet up, an Albinoni oboe concerto on Classic FM, a book on restoring period gardens in her hand. She was alone, Martin having unexpectedly driven off at midday for a pub lunch in Winchester with an old Army colleague he'd discovered lived in nearby Stockbridge, a Green Jackets man. 'Thought I'd told you,' he'd said. Betty had considered giving him a tongue-lashing, then abandoned the notion. Better to be by herself than to share the sitting-room with a bellyaching grouch who zapped the television non-stop, while sourly dismissing any prospect of locating anything worthwhile. Martin maintained that since the supply of quality programmes was constant at barely above zero, while the number of channels was heading for infinity, the likelihood of finding anything other than trash was infinitesimal. 'Why bother, then?' Betty would sigh, to which his unanswerable response was: 'I've bought the thing, I've paid for the licence, I'm damned well going to watch it!'

Now the front door bell was ringing. Who on earth . . .?

Donna. 'Hello, Donna. I thought you were with Sam this afternoon.'

'I was,' Donna told her, standing rigidly stiff. 'But . . . Thing is, dear Betty, I need to go to Winchester. Urgently. Please, *please*, would you take me there?'

'Sorry, but I can't,' Betty said. 'Blasted Martin's gone off in the car to Stockbridge.' Once they'd had two cars, but not these days. She surveyed Donna, who was looking and sounding unusually fraught, her face pale, her eyes evasive. 'What's wrong? Come on in, you'd better tell me. Row with Sam?'

She walked back into her sitting-room and Donna followed, her feet dragging.

'Not exactly. Should've been.' Her voice was husky. 'Men are so stupid.'

'Are they?' Betty widened her eyes in a comical look of surprise. 'Do you know, now I come to think of it, yes, you could be right.'

Donna let out a faint snort of what could have been amusement before her face reverted to despair. 'I thought he was sensible. I thought he knew about things. Stupid prat.'

'Are you talking about drugs?' Betty demanded to know. 'Cannabis?' If Donna wanted it dragged out of her, she might as well start there. Adam's shrugged-shoulders attitude had appalled her not so long ago, and he had been far less habitually hopeless than many of his friends: lethally fast driving in their parents' cars, shoplifting, promiscuous sex, drugs, persistent lying. She had asked one boy after his second conviction for possession if he wasn't concerned about the difficulties of finding worthwhile employment. A blank look: who'd tell his prospective employers? 'Application forms ask about convictions,' she'd informed him and he had actually cackled at this unwitting humour. No one tells the truth on forms, he said, they like you to be creative. Anyway, cannabis didn't count.

Donna was shaking her head impatiently. 'No! We wouldn't mess with that!'

Betty gathered that only complete idiots did drugs these

days. It was boring, Donna told her, a cop-out from reality that didn't get you anywhere. She and her friends wanted to be in control. An angry sigh.

'So what is the problem?' Betty said, catching her eyes and holding them.

Donna blinked, on the verge of tears. 'Sex. Unprotected.'

'What a fool. Well, it's a bit late to go to the chemists' for condoms now, isn't it?'

'Not that, Betty! I need a morning-after pill. A baby would wreck my life, and anyway I couldn't possibly have it. Not with my parents like they are.'

'Ah, yes. Are your parents out – or don't you want them to know?'

'Out. And no, I don't.'

Naturally. 'Right, let me think . . . Celia could be in – I seem to remember her saying that she and Hugh had some formal dinner tonight.'

'But she won't take me unless I explain why. Especially in all this rain, who would? And she's . . . I mean, for all her niceness she's pretty tough.'

Betty would have thought Donna afraid of nothing and no one, but it appeared not. She looked at the girl's distraught face; the brown eyes seemed woefully large and lost. It struck her that despite whatever sexual experiences Donna might have had she was still a child. Oh Lord. Donna was not her responsibility, but she couldn't turn her back on the panicking girl. 'You mean you want me to go to the Thornes' with you and help explain your predicament to them? Right, then.'

'Not them, her!' Donna protested, looking horrified at the thought of the Judge knowing. He was considerably more terrifying than Celia, and besides, he'd probably think keeping a secret was unethical or something and inform her parents.

Betty nodded her acceptance of this protest. 'All right. Come on then.'

It was Celia who came to the door, to their mutual relief; Celia who tactfully closed her studio door to listen to the problem, she who pointed out the obstacle to their plan.

'But the morning-after pill is available only on prescription. You'll need a doctor first, Donna, and I doubt you'll find any doctor holding a Saturday evening surgery.'

The relief of finding Celia ready to listen without reproaches had given Donna some composure, but this information shattered it. 'Oh no, I don't believe this. And I suppose there won't be any doctors or chemists about on a Sunday, either.'

'Just for idiots like you?' Celia said dryly. 'No, don't fly off into a frenzy. You can always go to Margaret Jessop. There's a dispensary at her surgery.'

The wind blew the rain drumming across the windows.

Donna looked still more horrified. 'No, not her. Never!'

Celia gave her a sardonic smile. 'So that's the way it is. How horribly complicated matters are becoming in this house. Well, let me say this, Donna, she'd be better as a last resort than nothing. In the meantime, however, sit yourselves down and I'll do some telephone research.'

'That's very kind,' Betty said, perching herself on a stool and giving Donna a meaningful look.

'Yeah, thanks,' Donna managed, sniffing.

At the conclusion of a brisk call Celia told them there were two doctors who held emergency surgeries on Sunday mornings, she had a note of their names, numbers and times, and yes, a requirement for the morning-after pill did count as an emergency – remarkable but reassuring. Also, Donna would be glad to know, there was a Winchester chemist open from midday to one. She'd better buy young Sam a pack of condoms at the same time, hadn't she? And tell him his mother should have taught him to be more careful.

With a tempestuous change from terror to relief Donna leapt from her stool to hug Celia. 'Thanks, Celia. That's great. God, the relief. And Betty, too. l don't know what I'd have done without you two.' She embraced Betty and fled the room.

She was back down the stairs and opening the door into the ground-floor flat when she heard Sam's voice calling her from above, softly at first, then more emphatically. 'Donna!'

She looked upward to see him leaning over the banisters on the top floor, his floppy hair hanging over his forehead. 'You OK?'

'Yeah,' she said, rather crossly. 'Small thanks to you.'

She made to withdraw into the flat, but he stopped her, calling, 'Wait, I'm coming!' and running quickly down he muttered on a deep and difficult breath: 'Look, I'm sorry.'

The words were sufficient to release all her pent-up emotions. She fought to restrain tears, snapping, 'So you bloody should be!' and marched off into the flat, but he persisted, shutting the door behind them and catching at her arm to pull her round and hold her against himself.

'Don't!' he said. 'Don't! It was stupid of me. You always seem so adult and sure of yourself I didn't think, and I should have done. Of course I should.' His arms tightened.

Mollified, she gulped, sniffed, and struggled for composure. 'You don't have to worry, Sam, Celia and Betty sorted it. I'm going to get a pill tomorrow morning.' She added, unable to resist a last swipe, 'Celia said your mother should have taught you to be more careful.'

'Oh, hell, it wasn't her fault or yours, it was mine. You were so great, so lovely and sexy, I got carried away.'

His readiness to carry the burden of guilt struck her as quite impressive and the corroding conviction that she had made herself appear a juvenile idiot in everyone's eyes began to abate. 'Yeah, well . . .' She leaned her head on his shoulder, suddenly tired. 'So what now? I mean, it's only halfway through the afternoon.'

Sam looked over her head to the window to see the rain retreating across the ploughed fields to the hills while a struggling sun lit the last fingers of cloud. 'We could curl up together on my bed and listen to music or we could pull on our wellies and walk along the river. The rain's stopped. Or perhaps we should head for the Abbotsbridge stores and buy ourselves food for tonight. I don't know what Mum thinks we're going to eat.'

'The stores?' Donna said in total horror. 'Oh no, imagine Nancy Chubb — those laser eyes would see *sex* in a second, and then she'd radio it round the villages. Better we stay here and chill out on *my* bed to *my* music and then I'll cook *you* a meal. There's always food here.'

She wanted him to stay with her, in her place, not his – and on her terms. Worries became snarled up in your mind after bad experiences, worse than the real event. They nagged at you all day, then woke you in the small hours to goad you with being stupid, so you despised yourself and wished, desperately, that you could wipe that time out, only you couldn't. But if Sam stayed, it would prove, wouldn't it, that she wasn't so adolescent and hopeless as she'd looked? His apology had made a big difference, but she needed more than that. She needed to know that he hadn't only wanted her for sex.

Her suggestion sounded fine to Sam. He too needed to chill out. He had been heavily shaken by his own bungling confusion and he needed time to recover his sang-froid. The obstacles males must overcome to present a resourceful and assured self to the world loomed larger than ever. He had constructed for himself a sardonic, clever and capricious persona, predestined to be an insightful lover of women – in serial monogamy, naturally, unlike that lethally randy father of his – someone unequivocally cool and competent, but now he wondered how any girl could fancy such a dismal pillock. At least Donna had offered to cook him a meal. She must still like him a bit. And she hadn't jeered at him. Some girls he'd met really liked to rub things in – and tell their friends, too. Like pulling the wings off insects, making you squirm. Donna wasn't like that.

'Stay here with you in your place? Yeah, fine.' He hugged her and planted a cautious kiss on her hair. Then he remembered something urgent. 'But first *please* do something for me, would you, Donna?'

'What?' she said suspiciously.

'Put that bloody duvet-cover on to wash!'

'Oh. Yeah, I better had, hadn't I?'

Leaning together, they giggled weakly.

14

Interview day. Alex showered and washed his hair, and then shaved himself with special attention. Leave nothing to chance, he told himself, be organised, animated yet thoughtful, and give the impression of . . . of *caring* – yes, that was it: caring, the essential attribute these days for those associating with children. He chewed a lip over what to wear: not pinstripes, clearly, but should he think in terms of a suit at all? Worn grey flannels and a shabby tweed jacket were surely out of date, but a blazer? Would a bursar wear a blazer? Perhaps the plain grey suit would be best. He laid out shirts and socks and handkerchiefs and studied them for the most desirable blend. God, how ridiculous, how deplorable, and all for an interview to secure work of a sort he had never before contemplated, at a salary, no doubt, he would find paltry. But success would make him an authentic person again. He decided on the grey suit.

The headmaster's wife showed him round the school, charmingly apologetic that things were at sixes and sevens this morning, but, she sighed, two members of staff were away and with Easter shortly upon them, well, they were all under pressure. She hoped he would understand if his interview were a touch delayed. Alex, at his own most charming, sympathised and expressed his admiration of the busily occupied small boys and girls, the good science rooms, the well-equipped computer room, the music suite and an excellent indoor swimming pool. He heard that the main building was Grade II listed. The school appeared admirable; his spirits rose.

At the end of his tour he was given a cup of coffee and then ushered into the anteroom to the headmaster's study, a room full of worn red leather chairs, framed school photographs and silver challenge cups.

'Two minutes, five minutes, certainly no more,' Mrs Hammond promised him, 'and my husband will be with you.'

Two minutes later another man did appear in the room, not the headmaster from his study, but a stocky man in grey flannels and a blazer – an all too familiar regimental blazer.

'Martin!' Alex blurted in shock. 'What are you doing here?'

Martin gave him a look of equal discomfiture, then shrugged. 'Same as you, I imagine. Being interviewed. Unexpected, not to say ironic, isn't it, that we should find ourselves in competition? How did you learn of the bursar's post?'

'Hugh Thorne, via the Manningfords,' Alex jerked out grudgingly. 'And you?'

'Sir Bernard Gough, at the Manningfords, Sunday before last. They say old Bernard's a tough fellow but we got on well.' He sat down and let out a short laugh. 'Both of us keen on the Army and neither of us fascinated by the niceties of garden design, unlike our wives. But his wife, Candida, was intrigued by Betty's efforts with the manor gardens and invited her to see some famous display of spring flowers at Chilbourne House. She went with Celia Thorne for lunch there. I wasn't included, thank God, but Betty was enraptured.'

Celia, blasted Celia, Alex thought furiously. He could feel her dubious influence in this. He couldn't make out the full linkage, but he was convinced it was there. Maybe Martin was prevaricating, maybe it was through her that he had this bursar's-post interview. Fenella, he could have sworn, had turned Celia against him, and worse, Celia was clearly on terms of close friendship with Candida Gough, Chairman of the school Governors. These networks were all wrong, he told himself, conveniently ignoring his own links through Hugh Thorne. His eyes resentfully on Martin, he remembered how obsessed Donna was these days by Betty and Celia. Not surprising that she never confided in Fenella, but he could sense his own influence with his daughter waning; it was weeks since she had talked to him with her old frankness. Women like Betty and Celia were manipulative menaces with over-inflated ideas of their own importance, and he wished to heaven they would focus their heedless elderly maternal impulses somewhere other than on his jumpy daughter. Of course, it was Fenella's fault. She had no idea of her adolescent daughter's needs, stupid, neglectful, selfish woman. If only she would vanish. Margaret would cope far better with any problems Donna might run into; he was sure she dealt with adolescent angst every day in her practice and she was informed about everything.

There was no getting round the fact that her insights into the strange variables of their youngsters' behaviour were at a different level from his. But that, Margaret said, was only natural. Maternal love had evolved in mammals to ensure the survival of the species many millions of years ago. So, come to that, had monogamy, but paternal love was unlikely ever to become as evolved as maternal, whatever overstretched working mums hoped, not given the levels of bonding that bearing and feeding a child produce. Mothers possessed instinctive understanding. And for males to express their affection was difficult these days when even a hug could be misinterpreted. 'Talk to Donna if you're worried, find out what's bothering her,' Margaret advised, but Donna was evasive. 'What do you want, Dad? Can't you see I'm busy with my maths?' Or her English, or her history or her blasted art. Celia was giving her a grasp of line, she said, whatever that meant, while they painted plants together.

It was true that Alex understood work in a way he didn't understand the domestic scene. A childhood of boarding schools, cold parents and domestic disharmony had been a poor preparation for his own parenthood. He loved Donna

and Duncan, but he was losing the courage to reach out to
them in fear of being snubbed. And the rejection implicit in
his forced early retirement had left him too vulnerable to
take more. The position of bursar would restore his bruised
ego, give him back some status. Surreptitiously he crossed
his fingers. Despite a century of feminism women still went
for men of status. Oh, Margaret.

He jumped as the study door opened. A smartly suited
woman passed through the sitting-room and out, saying
goodbye, and Alex was called in.

There were three people interviewing him. The headmaster, David Hammond, tall and genial, introduced him to the
retiring bursar, James Hill, and the head of history, Polly
Ferrison. Mr Hammond was casual in dress to the point of
being scruffy. Alex, immediately conscious of his own for-
mality, resented the fraying blazer and open-necked shirt.
Illogically he felt the man wasn't taking him seriously. But
there was no lack of serious intent in the interview. First
one, then another, they took him through every detail of his
CV, discussing his academic record, his competencies, the
problems he'd faced in implementing policy shifts within
the Lord Chancellor's Department, his reaction to the vari-
ations in strategy and doctrine brought about by changes of
government. His mind distracted from Fenella and his failures, turned to impressing them, not, he thought, without
success. 'And I have had the responsibility of day-to-day
management of the fabric of court buildings,' he added,
'some of them Grade II listed, as your handsome building is.
I am totally conversant with every sort of complication
there.' This was stuff he could deal with.

The headmaster spoke of the fund-raising work done by
the bursar. 'You've seen our new buildings and special facil-
ities, and our excellent swimming pool? All thanks to James
Hill, who's been tremendous. Have you any experience of
fund-raising, Alex?'

'Not so far,' Alex replied. He thought fast, aware of the
inanity of saying nothing, even when he had nothing to say.
He had never raised so much as a fiver, or only from his own

wallet when someone shoved a good-cause box at him in the street. Damn. He managed a smile, half joked: 'Not a skill required by the Lord Chancellor's Department, you know – the Inland Revenue obliges via the Treasury. That would be a new challenge.' He warmed to this thought, reminded of something Margaret had said recently: 'And the more challenges you have to meet, the more stimulating the job becomes. And I'd hope James Hill would reveal his sources and his expertise to me . . . if you were to offer me the post.'

A trio of thoughtful nods. Then his spirits, at once jittery and desirous, took a jolt. The woman Polly asked whether his wife worked. Discussing his CV and his competencies had taken his mind off Fenella. Now he knew he was on to a loser.

'No. She is at home. The children are both in full-time education still.'

'Perhaps she does work within the community?' David Hammond suggested.

Even *in absentia* his wife could let him down. No, he wanted to snarl, she runs around with her stupid lover and goes to exhibitions of ridiculous modern art. Of course, schools like Hamlins were invariably looking for unpaid helpers to slave behind the scenes, organising those fund-raising events, making costumes for theatrical performances, running children hither and thither to games matches and God knows what else. Fenella would be no more use to them than she had been to him. Prevaricate. 'No, not at present. She spends time in London as often as not, visiting picture galleries. She's . . . she's er, interested in aspects of modern art.'

'Is she an artist herself?' Polly Ferrison asked.

'No. No, she isn't.' Simply a full-time menace, who worked at wrecking his life.

They asked him about his own outside interests and he had to do a complete brain search to find any. Work was his real interest. Feebly he said he liked walking. Then in a desperate burst of invention he told them of a great love of the theatre and how he had often thought he would like to take part in amateur dramatics – 'Behind the scenes, perhaps. That would be fun.' If push came to shove, he supposed he could prompt the kids from the wings.

The rest of the interview he was to remember only hazily. He was drained. One remark stayed starkly clear of the blur: they would be in touch within five days.

It was the week before Easter week and the case of The Queen v. Gary Jenkyns was about to begin at Winchester Crown Court. Rape and child abuse cases were invariably nasty, tricky matters to hear and having pondered the particular complexities thrown up by this one, Hugh Thorne decided he must talk briefly to fourteen year-old Toyah Storm, with his clerk and a shorthand writer present. Judges were not encouraged to see a child prior to any hearing in the courts, but if both counsel agreed the judge should do so it was permissible in exceptional and difficult cases. This, he decided, was one such case, because of the unequivocal dislike she had for giving evidence on sexual matters, a problem clearly shown on the police video of her evidence-in-chief for the prosecution. He consulted Geraint Meredith, defence counsel, along with Roger Dodson, and both were in definite agreement with this course of action. It was essential to reassure Toyah that the people who would be putting those embarrassingly probing and unpleasant questions to her over the video-link were not themselves nasty. They were doing a necessary job while protecting her youth and defencelessness as far as was judicially possible. Hugh decided he would talk to her while robed but without his wig. No sense in overaweing the girl.

When Toyah was brought in Hugh was shocked. He was finishing a cup of coffee and almost choked. Fourteen? This child looked no more than nine, ten at most, a waif whose stick-like wrists and ankles protruded from beneath a drab green frock that had lost its shape and drooped at the hem. Her face was colourless and pinched, the sunken dark eyes over-large and surrounded by dark bruise-like smudges. In Roger Dodson's case summary she was described as, 'A girl assessed at the special school she attended in Southampton as having an intelligence in the lowest three per cent of the population, and as being emotionally vulnerable and socially immature.' The sociological jargon seemed insulting in its inadequacy. The girl looked as if she had just staggered from some third-world battlefront. When had this assessment been made? Before or after the alleged rape? He wondered whether Toyah had always been thin to the point of starvation, or whether the weight loss had happened since that night in the woods where Jenkyns admitted he had driven her in his van. The medical evidence alone would indicate a high level of trauma.

'Hello, Toyah.'

She glanced at him, a fretful, frowning look. She looked in turn at the clerk and the shorthand writer, who nodded good morning to her. She turned back to Hugh, said nothing. She sat down where he indicated by his desk.

'Toyah, you know I'm the judge in your case, don't you? Good. Now, do you feel you know and understand what's going to happen today, and for the rest of this week, so far as you are concerned?'

'Yeah. They told me, on an' on. But I told them, I don't want to be keeping on answering the questions. I done all that already and I don't like it.'

'Who has told you?'

A shrug. 'Me mum, me uncles, me social worker, me solicitor, lots of 'em, I don't know who half of them is. The police. Me teacher.' She looked away, fidgeting with a fraying cuff on the sleeve of her dress, tugging at a piece of cotton until it snapped. Her mouth worked; she spat out, 'I don't like the questions. They're about dirty stuff.'

She'd had enough. Well, Hugh had no questions to put, not now. But there were things that he must say. Talking to her averted face, he told her as gently as was consistent with being firm that he understood how she felt, that everyone would, but that she must do her very best to answer the questions. If she had a story to tell, the jury would only understand it if she told them exactly what had happened when she replied to defence counsel's cross-examination – and the jury were the men and women who would have to decide the case, having heard what both she and Gary Jenkyns had to say. He studied her, asked whether she had any questions for him.

'No,' she said, then turned her head to look him firmly in the eyes. 'Yeah, I have. If you're the judge, then why ain't you wearing a wig?'

'Would you like me to put my wig on?'

She was definite. 'Yeah, I would.'

Hugh leaned forward, took his wig from his black and gold wig tin and settled it on his head. He smiled at the pale and resentful face that looked at his. 'That better?'

She nodded, nearly smiled back. 'Yeah. If you're a judge you got to wear it. Otherwise you're just like all the rest, ain't you?'

'. . . The defendant's brother, Mervyn, lived on an estate at Hedge End, near Southampton, where the defendant had arrived four weeks earlier, talking of finding a job there. Toyah's father, his partner and their son, and two older half-sisters by a previous relationship, lived two doors away from Mervyn, while Toyah and her mother and a brother of thirteen lived in Southampton. The night of the incident, 31st October, was, as you will know, members of the jury, Hallowe'en, and the girls had decided to go trick or treating in the neighbourhood early in the evening, returning to a party, a witches and ghosts party. Toyah and her brother went by bus to Hedge End to join them. Soon after the party commenced the defendant also joined them. He was known to them through their neighbour and had on at least two occasions given the girls lifts back from the shops in his van . . .'

Roger Dodson was five minutes into his opening of the prosecution case against Gary Jenkyns when the door at the back of the court opened and a slim woman in a black suit slipped in and sat down to the rear of the public seats. Hugh's eyes flickered over her. A certain familiarity . . . but who . . .?

The woman put her bag by her feet, then sat back, lifting her face to counsel for the prosecution. Fenella Lindridge. Of course. He might have expected her. Damned female.

Had Roger seen her? A movement of the big head on its heavy neck, a widening of the eyes. Yes, he was aware of her. She shouldn't be there, it was the wrong place, the wrong time: Roger Dodson needed his whole attention plus on the matter in hand. Concentrate, man, will you! Apart from the protection of vulnerable young girls, and God knew that was vital, to secure a conviction in a difficult high-profile case like this would go a long way towards restoring the unfortunate man's image. The CPS fees would not be large, but the publicity could be substantial.

The rich baritone continued, clear and measured: '. . . By half past nine Toyah was tired and wanted to return home. Her brother said he was having fun and refused to leave the party. So Toyah left alone, planning to catch the nine forty-five bus home. She was no more than fifty yards from the house when the defendant caught her up, offering her a lift home so long as she didn't mind if he went to see a friend first. It was drizzling, and as he was known to her she accepted. He did not drive to any friend's house, but instead headed for the New Forest, where he drove the van down a rough track between the trees to where it could not be seen from the road. With the van's lights turned off, darkness surrounded them. The defendant told her the van had broken down. He made her get into the back, where he pulled off her clothes and his and raped her, despite her efforts to stop him. There were tools and other objects on the floor of the van and she was badly bruised in addition to injuries affecting the genital area. During the course of the night he smoked cannabis intermittently and raped her twice more. Toyah told him he was hurting her and begged him to leave her alone, the pain was so bad. He told her to "shut up" and "shut her face". He forced her to do what he wanted, including oral sex, and she was very frightened of him . . .' Roger gave a husky cough and took time to pour himself a glass of water from the carafe in front of him.

A good place to pause, Hugh thought, appreciating the restrained histrionics. He assessed the jury of seven women and five men with thoughtful eyes. Two of the women were also sipping water; they looked shocked, but then it was a shocking case. Only one possible young unemployed among them, he in the violent orange and lime-green sweatshirt chewing his fingernails and clearly longing to be elsewhere; next to him sat glaring the notably busty and blonde pint-puller from the pub just up the road, who looked as if given half a chance she'd beat up the defendant with her vast handbag, while the rest were middle-aged and middle-class, solid citizens concentrating with impassive faces. A reasonable jury as juries went. Hugh's eyes moved on. Fenella had a notebook with her and was jotting something down. Whatever had made her come? An urge to support her lover – or judge his abilities? Unexpectedly Hugh recalled his earlier feelings of luck in love and wondered again why he should have been so privileged. It's the fate of us all to grow old eventually, but to pass through life as unlovable or lacking that indefinable lure called sex appeal was cruel, a wasteland of deprivation. Fenella's white-faced sharpness put her in a similar position to the thousands who are ugly, or disfigured by disease, or crippled in some way. For the first time something akin to compassion for the woman flickered through him. Perhaps it was compassion that Roger felt for his distant cousin; he was a decent sort.

Roger put down his glass and continued: 'In the morning the defendant drove the van back to Southampton, where he dropped Toyah off by a shopping precinct about four hundred yards from her home, telling her not to tell her mother or the police or anybody else what had happened. By chance, two policemen who had been called to the area to investigate a burglary saw him leave her and drive off, and with an instinct that something was wrong went to speak to Toyah, who burst into tears and said that she had been raped. They confirmed that her name corresponded with that of the girl reported missing late the previous night and took her to the police station, where her mother was called. At the police station Toyah was spoken to by policewomen and questioned on video tape. In addition she was examined by Dr Amanda Colby.'

Roger gulped a couple more mouthfuls of water, took a deep breath and went on to describe the extent of the injuries found by Dr Colby. 'There were grazes and bruises on her back, in addition to fingermark bruises on her upper arms. The injuries to Toyah's genitalia were such that Dr Colby was unable to touch that area for four days and therefore could not immediately perform a digital examination. She describes the vaginal injuries as considerable, causing extensive swelling and distortion to the area and including lacerations and blood blisters. She reasons that it is highly unlikely that such injuries could have been occasioned by consenting sexual intercourse, as the defendant will be claiming, since they would have been very painful at the time.'

The jury stirred, their expressions varying from disturbance to disapproval. They stared at the defendant, who turned his head to look beyond them, his eyes flat and indifferent as though he had inwardly severed himself from some unsavoury scene in which he could not conceivably have a part.

The second he heard the postman put the letters through the flap, Alex was on his feet. He'd been on edge all morning, even snapped at his lovely Margaret. The man was disgracefully late; it was almost ten o'clock and this morning the letter from the school *had* to be there. He was out in the hall, snatching up the post. Three brown manilla envelopes, one white, typewritten with his name and his degree. At last. He tore it open, read it, read it again unbelievingly, swallowed. Rejected. Why? Could they have preferred Martin? Surely not. Had that smartly suited woman they'd briefly seen been offered the post? His heart pounded from the sickening blow.

'Alex?' Fenella calling him, interrupting his thoughts.

'What?'

'Was that the post? Have you heard from the school?'

'Yes,' he ground out, 'and it's no. Again.'

'I'm sorry,' she said quietly. 'That's a disappointment. I really am very sorry.'

He could hear Donna saying something from her room about poor old dad and what a shame. He hated her pity, hated his failure. Hell, once Judge Thorne had been the sole man in the house *with* a job, now, if Martin had been appointed he, Alex, would be the only man *without* one. Small surprise if Margaret despised him, stopped wanting him. He hadn't been phenomenal in love-making, either. He blamed that on her penchant for sex in the great outdoors; how could he control events if he was in fear of leering onlookers? His natural urge was to rush it; surely that would be any man's? He leaned against the hall wall, his breath short in his chest with shock. Oh God, Margaret. He'd had such delectably carnal dreams of their celebrating upstairs in her bed, of himself lapping Bollinger from between her luscious breasts in long slithering caresses of his tongue, of them both laughing with joy and making love in comfort. But she had a thing about keeping him away from her bedroom, even from her flat; an obstinate determination that he mustn't impinge on her other life with young Sam. Alex had become convinced that if he won himself a solid job and could boot out Fenella, thereby having a life to offer Margaret free from impediments (it never occurred to him to consider Donna or Duncan as impediments), then he could have thrown himself into passionate involvement with her as a man of worth. Such beguiling hopes, all wrecked.

Wrecked by whom? He telephoned Martin rather than face him.

'Oh, Alex, yes, I have been offered the post,' Martin's self-conscious voice said, 'I'm sorry you . . . I hadn't expected it for myself . . . Perhaps they thought you were over-qualified. Anyhow . . .'

'Anyhow, congratulations and I hope you'll enjoy the work,' Alex said stiffly. His pride would not allow him to say less. 'Betty will be pleased, too, I've no doubt.' He mumbled a few further words and put the telephone down, seething with hate.

'Donna!' Fenella was calling. 'We must go now or you'll be late for your tutorial. Besides, I'm already horribly late for an appointment in Winchester.'

Time to collect Margaret again for late-morning visits. Time to confess that he couldn't get anything right, that even a passed-over major cum failed wine merchant had been preferred to him. Alex's forehead was furrowed with mortification. She would be kind to him and he did not want kindness. He wanted back his authentic identity as a professional man with a monthly salary advice chit.

Donna was talking to her friend Georgia on the students' telephone in the hall of her tutorial college, while keeping an eye open for her mother's approach along the narrow city road in her silver BMW. Georgia had been Donna's best friend at her old school and it was awful not having her around to obsess with over vital matters like having sex with Sam, or her catastrophic parents being each involved in affairs.

'Thank God,' Georgia was saying, 'term's almost over. I wish I could leave and go out to work. Then I'd have money for decent clothes instead of the muck Mum keeps buying me, ghastly Harvey Nicholls stuff which makes me look twenty-five at least. Do you know how I envy you, with no bloody school to go to?'

'So? I have to go for coaching,' Donna said, annoyed that her friend was drivelling on in this childish way about school. 'An hour's geography this morning. And I do a ton of boring work on my own. And wearing *what* clothes I like? I don't have any. My parents moan about being broke and don't give me a thing. Dad hasn't found any work – and I'm still wearing those purple jeans I bought over a year ago.'

'But you aren't at a girls' school. I bet you have some really fit bloke hanging around you, panting for it. And if you haven't you ought to have.'

'He's not bad,' Donna said, suddenly smug.

Georgia screamed. 'Aaagh! So who is he? What is he? Getting shagged at last, are you?'

'You have a low mind, you really do.'

'We all do. Well *are* you?'

'Yeah, if you must know. And he's called Sam and he's in his gap year before he goes to the University of Exeter.'

'Great. Join the gang. Mine's gone off to America on some scholarship, the creep. I might have known it was too good to last. So now I'm on the prowl again. Oh, I wish I was you. I'm desperate for a really good shag. So how'd it go for you?'

'All right,' Donna told her, cagily. There were things you couldn't confide even to your best friend, and what half-wits she and Sam had been was one of them. And her period had been due yesterday. She didn't suppose anything was actually wrong, but there was an irritating niggle at the back of her mind. What if the morning-after pill hadn't worked? What if a condom had leaked on one of those three subsequent occasions? Nothing was guaranteed, was it? And it still hurt when he entered her. Having a real boyfriend and proper sex wasn't all it was made out to be. Or was she fucking up somewhere – as you might say?

'My first time wasn't that much fun,' Georgia remarked. 'I felt like my hips were hinged all wrong and I didn't know how to join in at all. It was awful – you know, everyone goes on about how great it is, so when the earth doesn't move straight off you get all snarled up with scary feelings that you're useless. Nobody tells you it's like any new sport; you have to keep practising!'

Donna giggled in a rush of relief. 'Well, Sam's keen enough on that,' she said.

'They all are. My stepfather breathes heavily over Mum and pats her bum while she's cooking and she tells him to get off, but she goes all giggly and wriggly just the same and it's disgusting.'

Donna had her opening. 'My parents,' she said in a tired and worldly voice, 'have both of them got lovers. Can you imagine it?'

'No. How grim. But how do you know? They haven't told you, have they?'

'No, but it's obvious. Mum makes telephone calls behind closed doors and goes off for whole days without saying where, and Dad's got a crush on the woman doctor who lives in one of the flats at the manor. He spends his time driving her round her patients, like he's some saint doing good works, but it's obvious he's doing her too. And you know what's so grisly? She's Sam's mum!' Donna didn't mind that particularly, but she wanted to impress Georgia with the horrors of her home scene.

'God, that sounds like a nightmare – I mean like incestuous. They're crazy, our parents, aren't they? I suppose it's the last hope for them. You know, grabbing some fun in the autumn of their days before the blast of winter hits them. That's what Mum said about my stepdad when they first got it together. Made me nearly throw up. It would you too, if you knew Dennis.'

'Yeah, well, they're all a bit much, aren't they?' Donna agreed vaguely. Sam had used a similarly depressing analogy. It must be vile to be old. Though she couldn't imagine it happening to her. It would be different by the time she reached that far distant time, surely? Intervening generations would have worked out how to stop people from getting fat and wrinkly. 'But what did you do when you found out about your mother and him? I mean, what?'

'I asked Mum. Straight out. I got a straight answer, too, when she saw I meant it. At least I knew what was happening, and she and Dad talked to me more like an adult. And then they asked me to choose between them, you know, who I wanted to live with most.'

'And you chose your mum.'

'Yup. Remember I was just fourteen then and it seemed natural. Wouldn't you?'

Donna thought. 'Right now I wouldn't choose either of them,' she concluded flatly. 'They're so argumentative and tedious I could throttle them. I suppose I could go with the one who moans the least. That'd be Mum – but then I can't choose her, can I? I don't know what her new man's like. He could be gruesome.'

Also if she went off to some fresh place with Fenella and her unknown man she'd lose Sam and that she definitely ruled out. But living with Alex and Margaret and Sam all tumbled and muddled together was also beyond contemplation. Her father would hate the thought of her sleeping with Sam. He'd go all possessive and heavy father and forbid him to go near her, she just knew it. Better the tiresome status quo than the worse alternatives. At least she was left mainly to her own devices. Out of the corner of one eye she glimpsed her mother drawing up outside in the BMW.

'Hey, Mum's picking me up now, Georgie. I have to go. Speak to you soon. Bye!'

'Yeah, bye!'

'You're late. Where have you been?' Donna demanded of Fenella as she ran across the pavement.

Her mother leaned over to push the passenger's door open. 'I've been listening to a case in the Crown Court. Sorry you had to wait.'

'Listening to a case in the Crown Court?' Donna repeated incredulously. 'Why? What sort of a case? I didn't know you were allowed.'

'Oh yes, anyone can. It's a rape case. A young girl.'

'A rape case? Isn't it sickening?'

'Pretty horrible,' Fenella admitted, driving down the narrow old street rather too fast.

'Then why?'

Fenella negotiated a tight left-hand turn between old flint walls before replying. 'Do you remember Holly's cousin, Roger? We talked to him at Holly and Tim's twenty-fifth wedding anniversary.'

'Yes, of course. He's sort of heavy looking and quite fun. He's a barrister, isn't he?'

'That's him. He's for the prosecution in this case and I wanted to know how a court works, so I went to listen. It's a nasty case involving a fourteen-year-old girl, and she's giving her evidence over a video-link system, so she doesn't have to give evidence in person with the defendant watching her. Hugh Thorne's the judge. It's extraordinary being there with him and Roger and the other counsel all in wigs and robed up, and the jury in their box listening to all the evidence being brought out. It's very interesting.'

'Yeah,' Donna said, thinking. 'Something different. Are you going back after lunch?'

'Yes, why?'

'Because I'm coming with you. And don't try telling me it's unsuitable, or that I've homework to do because I haven't a single piece of work due in before Easter and watching what's happening in the Crown Court has to be educational, doesn't it?' She prepared herself to bridle with indignation against refusal and fight for a wide interpretation of her human rights, but Fenella wasn't arguing. Instead there was a strange little smile on her face.

'Why not? In that case let's have a quick pub lunch here, give ourselves more time. And I'll tell you what's been happening up till now, so you'll understand what's going on. The girl's evidence was heard this morning, so this afternoon it'll be the defence counsel testing it under cross-examination.'

'Still over the video-link?'

'Oh yes.'

15

Betty was spending the afternoon in the walled garden, deadheading those early varieties of narcissus that had stopped flowering and were now looking messy. Normally she preferred to tidy up at the beginning of the day when her spine was more supple; gardening, she maintained, might be beneficial for the soul but it was also bad for the back. Today her timetable had been cast away. What were minor aches in comparison with the happiness suffusing her, the relief that bubbled through her veins? Martin was to take up his post as Bursar of Hamlins Preparatory School at the start of the summer term. He would be back in the world of work, one of the cogs in life's whirring wheel of energy and achievement, soaring over the humiliations of the past year, alert, intent, *valued*. And, please God, make him a reasonable companion once more, not a sore-headed old bear.

On reading the letter this morning he had swallowed, covered her hand with his and said almost inaudibly, 'Betty, I've done it. I've been offered the appointment as school bursar.'

Betty had closed her eyes with relief, saying, 'I'm so pleased. That's tremendous.'

'They preferred me to Alex. *Me.* I never expected that.'

'You must have been more their type. The better candidate for them.'

'Yes,' he said whitely. 'Yes, I suppose so. Here, hold me,

would you, Betty? Read me the letter aloud and tell me it's true, because I can't seem to take it in.'

They were both strangely composed. No yells of triumph, no hugs or dancing about; they were beyond that, weak with relief. The crisis was passing. Betty looked up into the blue April sky and prayed that now he had a job Martin would accept hers – and that they'd return to their old habit of talking over each day's events in bed at night. Since their move to the manor house those tender meandering discussions of the petty trials and small pleasures of life had been eroded into silence by his smouldering hostility to her gardening and her new friends, by her annoyance with him. She wanted to renew that closeness. She longed to be freed from lying beside an irritable Martin as he sighed noisily and tensed his limbs in disapproval.

Two swallows wheeled over the garden, heading purposefully for the river; the first she'd seen. From the distance Todd waved triumphantly as his new mowing machine broke into a steady whirr, ready for the first cut. 'Earthly Elysium!' he shouted. Summer was on its way.

'Hello there!'

Betty turned to see Brozie Hamilton plodding in her wellies across the walled garden, and called 'Hello!' in return. Brozie was clutching two carrier bags from which prickly stems and young leaves protruded wildly.

'Here,' she said, dumping the bags in Betty's arms. 'A couple of species roses for you, dear, *Rosa californica* 'Plena'. Do you know it? You could put them in the old orchard. This variety has those gracefully arching stems that look so right in that sort of natural setting and it'll give you deep pink semi-double blooms in June and July, and, bless it, little red-brown hips in the autumn. And the flower scent is sweet, too.'

'Lovely,' Betty exclaimed. 'Goodness, how kind of you, and I know exactly where to put them. On either side of the path beyond the entrance, set well back. I've been racking my brain for what to put there.' She clutched the prickly brutes to her chest. Life was not always brimful with pleasure, but her cup today seemed overflowing.

'And then the Horticultural Society wants to book you for
a talk on restoring the manor gardens – no, no, don't start
protesting you've hardly begun. Your talk won't be sched-
uled till late autumn, but the advance warning will give you
time to take photographs for your 'before and after' slides.
You will do it . . .? Oh, thank you. And don't forget we're discussing period gardens shortly, will you? What's that you've
put along the front of this mixed border? Ah yes, sisyrinchi-
ums with *Alchemilla mollis* – that should be pretty – and
you're filling in here with asters, penstemmons, white
phloxes, and delphiniums? How enchanting.'

At the Crown Court Donna followed her mother across a
grandiose and echoing foyer and up a wide shallow staircase
to where witnesses and onlookers, counsel and solicitors
mingled together in a great curving corridor. From a trio of
black-robed counsel Roger Dodson extricated himself and
came across to them, smiling.

'Fenny, darling, hello again. And Donna, too, mmh.' He
kissed them each on both cheeks, exuberantly. 'Lovely to see
you. Are you going to be in the gallery with Fenny this afternoon, Donna? Is this your first time in a court of law?'

Donna nodded. 'Yeah. I thought it'd be something different. Educational, you know. Nobody at school ever taught us
about how the courts work. Or about politics – like what
New Labour's third way means, or what the Tories stand for,
come to that.' She paused to identify further failures of her
past school. 'Or how the government works, democracy, you
know.' Visions of Big Ben and the Houses of Parliament gave
her pleasing thoughts of bunking off from her studying: 'You
could take me to hear question time in the House of
Commons, Mum, enlarging my outlook. Still,' she concluded
gracefully, 'listening to this case Roger's doing is a start.'

'I'm not sure what in,' Roger said. 'A rape? I hope you're
fully prepared to hear some very unpleasant evidence being
disputed in all its singularly sordid details, Donna.'

'A pertinent thought,' said Fenella. 'Are you?'

'Oh, Mum,' Donna groaned, blasé with the confidence of

the teenager who knows with certainty that she is tougher than all about her. 'It's a bit late for fussing now, isn't it? You told me about the case in the car and it doesn't sound that bad. And if you think Dad's going to start on at you for taking me, then OK, we don't tell him.'

Roger raised his thick pepper-and-salt eyebrows, looking from one to the other. 'You could always walk out,' he observed, then added with a grin, 'But I hope you won't. Having an audience to impress puts me on my mettle.' He put on the wig he had been holding in one hand. 'Time to go in, Fenny. Look, the court will adjourn at about four-thirty. We'll meet for tea together, shall we? And then Donna can cross-examine me about the evidence we've heard, really put me through it.' He touched Fenella's arm, smiled at Donna and walked rapidly away, his gown billowing out behind him.

'He's nice,' Donna said absently, liking his jokey friendliness, and pondering the change in looks and personality that donning his gown and wig made to Roger. If her friends were to see him she wouldn't mind admitting to him being her cousin. He wasn't as tall as her father, but robed he looked larger than in her memories of him, and with a dignity that was impressive to Donna, who generally resisted all attempts to awe her.

Sitting in the gallery of the court, she found herself with a similarly altered perception of Hugh Thorne. Wigged and wearing that black, purple and scarlet-sashed gown thing and sitting above everyone else at the great bench beneath the Royal Coat of Arms, he was different from the man she knew at the manor house, not alien so much as formidable. It wasn't simply the wig and stuff, it was his whole appearance. He was leaning forward with his balled fists on the shiny wood to support him, his black brows lowered, his chin jutting, his manner forbidding. Something was wrong with the video-link the girl was due to give her evidence over, and with a few brusque words, 'Keep at it, please. There can't be anything vital wrong, it was working adequately this morning!' the Judge had people jumping around checking the video-link screens and plugs before himself, before the jury, before the defendant, and before prosecution and defence counsel to determine that all was well in every case.

Fenella murmured to Donna that defence counsel would be cross-examining the girl, Toyah Storm, next, and even though she'd be in a quiet room with a kindly witness-service lady for company, she must be dreading having to answer those shamingly intrusive questions over the video-link, and the last thing Hugh would want was to keep her waiting.

Somebody called that all was working OK now, a man nodded and moved away from the nearest flickering grey screen, and in an instant Toyah's upper half came into focus. Donna sucked in an abrupt gasp of air at the meagre body and sunken eyes, the chewed looking hair.

'You said she was fourteen,' she breathed to her mother. 'She can't be, she just can't.'

Fenella muttered back: 'Unbelievable, isn't it? Fourteen's right, though. I think she's traumatised, stuck in that sort of depressed and angry state where people don't eat. You can't when you're as upset as Toyah. Food's meaningless. Even repulsive. That's why she looks like a Belsen victim.'

Donna, looking sharply at her mother's white face and the bony body that had recently become almost gaunt, experienced a further shift of perspective. Fenella was speaking of something she knew; of things that had hurt her, even if they weren't on the same level of horror. Like leaving her house and her friends and her heart-charity work in Wimbledon, like having Dad being so disagreeable and unhelpful to her while maintaining irresistible appeal and usefulness with Doctor Margaret. It wouldn't be surprising if Mum were depressed, she thought, and a spurt of moral indignation against her father went through her.

She sat peering sideways at the distorted view of Toyah on the screen that was all she could see from the public gallery, and listening to Toyah's moody replies to defence counsel, but a part of her mind stayed with her mother's plight.

Yeah, Toyah had met Gary Jenkyns before the night in

question. Three times, maybe four. OK, five if he said so, she wasn't bothered.

Yeah, he'd given her and her half-brother's half-sisters lifts back from the shops a coupla times. No, she hadn't asked him, he wasn't nothing to do with her.

No, she'd never been interested in him. He was old, wasn't he?

No, she hadn't asked him to give her a lift that night, neither. He'd followed her down the road, and she'd let him give her the lift because it was raining and then the pervert had driven her miles in the dark so she didn't know where she was and she couldn't get away.

Gary Jenkyns pursed his lips and shook his head in an almost imperceptive gesture of disagreement. His eyes turned to the jury, then down to the floor, his expression sorrowfully downcast. In a moment of shock Donna was reminded of her father, so exact was Gary's duplication of Alex's own method of discrediting her mother.

Anger rose inside her at the thought of her father's persistent nastiness, at his dismissal of everything Fenella said, his habit of making anything they were involved in together both difficult and disagreeable, like mapping out a battlefield – with Fenella the enemy to be defeated. Why? If she did have a lover, at least he wasn't prominent on the scene, not like Margaret was. And didn't Dad realise that all their neighbours must know and be talking? Like Sam, like Nancy Chubb. What had her mother done, really done, to make Dad so horrid to her? Or what had she failed to do or be? Donna wished she knew the answers.

A blast of words from Toyah Storm switched her attention back to the court. The video had shown Toyah sitting to give her evidence, but now the skinny waif was half out of her chair, and her young voice was erupting from the speakers in outrage.

No, she didn't fancy Gary, she didn't fancy anyone, and she hadn't never asked him to drive somewhere quiet. Not the Forest nor nowhere.

No, it was frightening and dark among those trees, and

there wasn't nothing romantic about the way he was grabbing at her in the van.

No! It hurt, it really did, and she'd wanted bad to get away
but she couldn't.

Leave the van? How? Gary'd locked the doors and he'd
pulled her clothes off of her, hadn't he? What did he think
she should of done? Broke the windows and jumped out –
then run for miles stark bloody naked in the rain, when you
couldn't hardly see a yard? Get real.

Judge Thorne leaned swiftly to operate switches to speak
to her, his voice firm but not unkindly. 'Toyah, I'm sorry, but
I have to remind you that however hard you find these court
proceedings to cope with, you are not here to ask questions
of defence counsel, Mr Meredith, but to answer those he
puts to you on behalf of Gary Jenkyns. If you just answer
clearly then we can move on and soon it will be over. Do you
understand that?'

Yeah, Toyah understood, but like she'd said before, she
didn't like them questions. She'd been asked too many times
already about all the dirty stuff what he'd done to her. That
man Gary, he was a pervert, and that Mr Meredith who was
on his side, he was a pervert too.

All right, all right, she'd try. But she couldn't take much
more of him trying to make her say Yes to stuff that wasn't
true.

Donna was floundering. She herself went everywhere by
car, but on that dark night no one in Toyah's muddle of a
family had even thought to walk with her to the bus-stop.
Her tale was sickening. How had she borne it? Not only the
pain and the terror of those long hours, but their persistent
memory, invading and fouling all she did? And now the man
defending Gary, a dark-faced Welshman whose tattered, elderly gown kept slipping from his shoulders like the feathers
of a moulting crow, was putting it to Toyah that she had been
the instigator of the whole thing. Donna swallowed as
another horrific factor struck her. What if Toyah had become
pregnant? Had she been given the morning-after pill or had
she had to fret and worry?

On the screen the bird-boned grey figure in the chair slumped back, the face a mask, shut in, the fingers of the hands clutched together, the nervous aggression for the moment subdued. Once more the questions came, querying her statement, once more she sullenly muttered her answers.

No, she'd never said she loved him, he was a fibber. He'd done it to her, the bastard, he'd raped her and it'd hurt and she'd screamed only there weren't no one there to hear.

She'd told him, she'd said, 'No!' over and over.

She had, she'd tried to stop Gary, but he was really strong and he'd got mad at her, saying he'd scrag her if she wouldn't belt up and let him.

Look, she'd thought he might kill her.

No, she'd never done it before. Yeah, she knew what the word virgin meant, everyone knew that, and, yes, that's what she was then.

No, afterwards he'd smoked cannabis. No, he hadn't never cuddled her.

Yeah, he'd let her put her clothes back on. But soon he'd started to pull at them and touch her again.

No, he'd made her kiss him. And do other things she'd never wanted nothing of.

No! No, she wasn't going to answer no more filthy questions about him being a pervert with her.

Abruptly the grey figure slipped from the chair and disappeared from the screen.

Hugh switched off the camera and the video-link and said to the jury with a calmness he was far from feeling: 'Members of the jury, the witness has left the witness-room and a short adjournment appears necessary. Would you go to the jury room, please.'

He watched as they filed out, torn between sympathy for the pathetic victim and a grinding worry. It was hard that the child loathed talking about sexual matters and was finding every second of the cross-examination deeply upsetting, but despite her poor vocabulary and her flat answers it was clear

from what she said that this man Gary Jenkyns should not be
let out into the community again, not with three victims
behind him, as it would appear. Jenkyns faced a life sentence, while Toyah had spoken of her fear that he would kill
her. If this trial failed for lack of her evidence and he was let
out only to strike yet again, and Hugh was instinctively certain he would, the next time his victim would die: he could
not afford to leave her alive.

Hugh had seen on his screen that the witness-service lady
had gone in pursuit of Toyah. To the usher he said, 'When
the girl's recovered, let me know and I'll speak to her.'

Three minutes later he saw that she was back and flinging
herself down on the chair, her chalk-white face screwed up
in tension. Over the link he said, 'Toyah, we do understand
that you are finding this very difficult, but the trial must go
on. Are you prepared to continue being questioned?'

'No,' the bleak voice stated. 'No more.'

'I see. Perhaps you would like a cup of tea or some other
drink and a break while we discuss this matter. Just wait for
a short while, will you?'

Hugh switched off, pondered hard for some moments,
then spoke to counsel. 'This is a highly sensitive situation,
both in regard to the defendant's rights but also in view of a
young and vulnerable complainant who to my mind is
having very genuine difficulty in coping with cross-
examination. I make no point as to your handling of Toyah,
Mr Meredith, which has been sensibly and mildly done, but
I have to say I am against any further pressure on her to give
evidence. However, first I need the views of you both.'

Geraint Meredith pointed out grimly that the defendant's
rights in cross-examination of the complainant were at risk
here. 'I have not had sufficient time to complete my questioning and this will undoubtedly place my client at a grave
disadvantage.'

'Your client's defence is that of consent,' Roger Dodson
reminded him, 'and you've certainly covered that with
Toyah. It's been no, no, no, all the way and she hasn't shifted
a millimetre.'

'But there are a great many matters still to be raised and I feel that it is imperative for my client's case that I should be allowed to continue.' Geraint Meredith appealed to Hugh. 'I'm barely halfway through my cross-examination, Your Honour. I feel I have to ask you to speak to her in person and explain the need for her to continue.'

'I'd agree to that,' Roger said, sighing. 'I doubt it'll achieve anything, but I do believe it must be done.'

'I'll see her in my room, then,' Hugh said grimly. The whole situation was a quagmire of wrongs.

As he walked to his room he saw the face of the girl, white, unhappy, deeply resentful. Effectively, while Toyah might have the general vocabulary and mental ability of a seven-year-old, she equally had the obstinacy and stroppiness of her real fourteen years – and she was demonstrably disturbed and traumatised. An unfortunate combination, particularly taken in conjunction with this case. Poor wretched child. God alone knew what her future held, what sort of life she would have. But it was no good his brooding on that. For him as the Judge in the case, she posed an intolerable legal dilemma. He sat down behind his big desk and leaned his hot face in his hands. Every fibre within him rebelled against pushing Toyah to face further examination on the horrors she revolted at recalling, yet everything depended on her. Had she given sufficient evidence to satisfy the Court of Appeal? Barely. Could he coax her to another half-hour? He mourned the necessity of it within himself.

As the footsteps of the girl and those accompanying her sounded in his corridor he remembered catching a glimpse of young Donna's shocked face as she sat beside her mother in the public gallery. She was only a couple of years older than Toyah. Why had Fenella brought her into court to listen to this stuff? Hardly the most suitable example for demonstrating to her how the courts worked in the due process of law. Could it have been to show her a very different picture of life from the one she'd receive at the manor house? Or – the thought flashed through his mind – did Fenella want her

daughter to see her lover, Roger Dodson, at work? Strange
reasons, strange necessities, hidden lives. Celia had said that
she suspected Alex of an affair with Margaret Jessop. What
was wrong with people that they all had to behave so badly,
hurting and destroying one another, and upsetting their children? These were bad times.

'Sit down, will you please, Toyah.'

Hugh spent several minutes with her, trying with his reassuring manner to steady her while he explained once more
the necessity for her evidence, cursing as he did so the need
for circumspection. She was not convinced, but finally she
gave an indication that she would answer more questions –
yeah, she might. Looking at her wire-taut body Hugh was
pessimistic, but he asked for her to be sent back to the witness room, returning to court himself. The jury was recalled,
Geraint Meredith was on his feet once more, his eyes on the
screen that showed him the emotions distorting the girl's
face.

'Now Toyah, you told us in your evidence-in-chief that
Gary Jenkyns moved into the front seats of the van to smoke
cannabis and you sat there too? Is that correct?'

'Yeah.'

'You then encouraged him to cuddle you, didn't you?'

'No. I never did.'

'You said that another sexual act took place there. What
position were you in then?'

Silence.

'Did you hear me, Toyah? How did this sexual act in the
front of the van take place?'

Silence, then, 'I'm not saying no more,' in a voice of furious protest.

On the screen Donna saw her crouched in the chair like
some small animal caught at bay and snarling defiance. She
felt Fenella's arm touch hers, then they were holding hands.
'This is awful,' Fenella muttered.

Hugh was leaning forward, operating switches; he spoke
to the child. 'Toyah, is there any likelihood of you answering
these questions from Mr Meredith?'

'No. I've had enough. I'm not saying no more.'

The faintest of pauses. 'Very well. You are released from giving further evidence. You may leave.'

Toyah stared, blinked once, then disappeared from the screen; everything was switched off. The court stirred with emotion, eyes avoided eyes. A juryman blew his nose, trumpeting.

Defence Counsel was on his feet once more, clutching at his bedraggled and plummeting gown, his Welsh voice lilting wildly with agitation as he applied for the jury to leave again as he had a question of law to discuss.

Hugh nodded, sighing. 'Very well, Mr Meredith. Members of the jury, as you've heard, we have a question of law to discuss. Would you go to your room, please.'

The jury plodded out once more, the busty pint-puller rolling her eyes disgustedly at the youthful nail-biter in the orange and green sweatshirt.

The defendant straightened himself and looked at the Judge, his round red face glistening with sweat and rising hope.

Hugh turned to defence counsel: 'Yes, Mr Meredith?'

'In view of the complainant's refusal to submit to further cross-examination, I wish to apply for Your Honour to direct that the Crown should not offer any further evidence against the defendant. However, I shall need time to prepare my submission and look up the law.'

The Judge glanced at the clock and nodded. 'It's too late now to hear it, anyway. Very well. The case will be heard tomorrow morning, at ten-thirty.' He nodded to the usher and asked her to inform the jury that they would not be required again before midday tomorrow.

'Court rise!' the usher called.

Roger pushed the last of his papers into his briefcase, closed it and straightened himself, grimacing, as Fenella and Donna came towards him. 'Hello. God, what an afternoon. Strong stuff. Whatever did you make of that, Donna?'

'I don't know what to say except the obvious – it was

awful. But it had a horrid sort of fascination, too. The court – it's like you see on TV or films, but then it isn't. Here it's real and you can feel everyone's tension. It didn't seem fair to ask Toyah those questions and yet I knew it had to be done. It made me feel so sorry for her and angry for her too – but then I was still willing her to carry on and do it properly.'

'I know. One gets torn – even I do after years of it – but it's what has to be. And there are a lot of Toyahs to be seen in the courts. The trouble is, people like her are such obvious victims. They're not streetwise, whatever they think, neither physically nor mentally. They're the sort certain types of men prey on.'

'Yeah, that's right and it made me angry. The family was split up and all over the place and no one was keeping a proper eye on Toyah.' It occurred to her that Toyah would have rejected any attempt to watch over her with vigour. She could look after herself, couldn't she? It's amazing how tricky people can be when they're determined to have their own way. Donna had never seen anyone like her before: was she effectively fourteen or seven? How did anyone struggling to teach her deal with her obstinacy or those flashes of antagonism? Yet she had been powerless against Gary Jenkyns, who had put her through hell – and still might go free. She asked Roger, 'Are you cross with her? I mean she's messed things up by refusing to answer the questions, hasn't she?'

'She's certainly made it more difficult, but I don't think all is lost yet. The medical evidence of her injuries I believe does go to prove a lack of consent. Only the most crazed masochist would have consented under those conditions.'

'But the Judge won't stop it, like Mr Meredith wants, will he?' Donna asked anxiously.

'That'll depend on how convincing Geraint Meredith's arguments are tomorrow morning. The girl has given evidence to show that she resisted Jenkyns and Geraint's tested a fair percentage of it. I think we'll go on. In view of what we know of the defendant I certainly hope so.' He picked up his briefcase and turned for the door. 'Come on, let's go and gossip over tea and biscuits. I've had enough of this place for one day and I want to turn my mind to more pleasant matters, such as what you and my lovely cousin Fenny plan to do over Easter.'

16

'Here's a GCSE paper from last year,' Todd said to Donna at the end of an hour's coaching next morning, handing her the printed paper. 'You'd better work through it over Easter.'

'Over Easter?' asked Donna, outraged and holding it at arm's length. 'I'm having a break then, not doing maths!' and she turned the searing heat of her glare on Todd, to find him struggling with laughter. 'You're not serious,' she said uncertainly. 'You don't expect . . .'

'No, no. No need.' He let out a chuckle. 'We'll work through that paper after the holiday, when we've both had a break. So, what are you and your family doing over Easter?'

'Too much,' Donna said, her head bent as she collected up her books.

The bleakness in her voice reached Todd. 'How d'you mean?' he asked.

She shrugged, hesitating for a moment before answering. 'I want to do things with Sam and Duncan,' she said.

'Like what?'

'Like lying around listening to the latest CDs, or going for walks along the river. And then there's an art exhibition I fancy seeing. But Dad and Mum have a new fixation on us all doing things together. It's called "being a family", they say. Wasting time is what I call it, being where you don't want to be and having to do what you don't want to do. It'll be awful and we'll fight. Imagine my mother around horses, or my father coping with conceptual art – elephant dung with beads and glitter on it or . . . or sculptures in pink suede!'

Todd shook his head. 'Togetherness,' he agreed, 'can be overrated. But, Donna, would it be so very bad? Maybe they feel mean at having dragged you away from your friends and your school in Surrey, maybe they want to make amends.'

'But it's all from their point of view,' Donna objected. 'They don't ask me or Duncan what we want.'

Duncan had admitted to her on arriving home that he'd had a bad term and he was behind with his A level revision programme. He thought he ought to spend every morning revising, 'I mean but genuinely, not just staring at a book and fantasising about girls. And then I need to slump around doing nothing. Recovering my inner poise, blah, blah. What is all this organising us about, anyway?' He'd thought it as hopeless as she did and added that it must be because Dad's lack of work had left him with such a gaping psychological hole to fill. 'We only have to say no, Donna. We aren't so young that they can make us.'

But Donna thought they could, mentally if not physically. Going to the art gallery with her mother effectively forced her to the point-to-point with her father. But each was insisting on the other coming so there'd always be one of them about rolling jaded eyes and heaving heavy sighs. And her father was burbling on about the glories of Easter Sunday in Winchester Cathedral and how Margaret and Sam should come too. And there was worse still: Margaret had invited Donna to lunch with her and Sam that day, but while she'd liked Margaret all right as a neighbour and Sam's mum, the idea of her and Dad in bed together was horrific, and she wasn't going to be wrong-footed into disloyalty to Fenella by accepting any such sneaky invitation. Yet, then . . . what about Sam? But the thought of discussing the situation with him opened even greater chasms of doubt beneath her feet. She wanted to be adult and blasé, but everything seemed so loaded. Anyway, Sam was away until Maundy Thursday, mucking about on his scaffolding. And her period still hadn't come. Once she had thought it would be great to be a real

experienced woman. Now the responsibilities of that state
had descended on her shoulders Donna didn't think she
could cope with any of it.

It was the chaos at the Abbotsbridge surgery that jerked Alex
from his absorption over the Easter weekend arrangements.
The receptionists were fighting over the holiday rota; Kylie,
the girl who dealt with fund management matters, had rung
in sick with food-poisoning, from, she said, eating a Thai
takeaway; and Tina, the district nurse, was limping lugubri-
ously and unable to drive after a kick from an elderly
reprobate whose senile dementia had increased rather than
lessened his natural bent towards violence. Margaret's partner, Dr Jane Field, threw all this at Margaret and Alex
through the car window as he parked outside the
Abbotsbridge surgery.

'For God's sake, Alex, you'll have to help us out,' Margaret
said when the full weight of the accumulated problems hit
her. 'Drive Tina round her patients, or man the computer, or
something, *please*!' She leapt from the car and grabbed her
doctor's bag from the back seat. 'Oh hell, just when we were
praying for a peaceful period so we could concentrate on
organising our move to the new surgery.'

Jane Field gave him a rueful smile. 'You don't have to do
anything, Alex. But any offers would be received with
immense gratitude.'

It was an unaccountably mild day; the sky blue, the air
smelling sweet and full of birdsong. The thought of being
useful flared within Alex. He would be a part of their team,
smiled upon and appreciated. He liked Jane, liked her for
much the same reasons that he loved Margaret. They both
had the same talent for life that Fenella lacked. Purposeful
women, happy in the careers they'd always planned; they
shared, too, the same half-hidden glint of sensuality, the
same dangerously attractive long-legged walk. Jane was married to the local rector, a man ten years her senior, and they
had two exuberant children. Today her normal aura of well-
being coupled with womanly competence had vanished. She

looked ruffled and hot and out of humour. It disturbed Alex. These two women coped so well with their exacting lives: taking their surgeries, visiting the seriously ill; supervising clinics, giving their patients' complaints their full attention; bouncing professional ideas between themselves at regular meetings, and then on top of it all, somehow finding the time to monitor the conversion of the old Victorian house into a modern surgery. It gave him pleasure to witness daily such skilled performances. Now he resented the unfairness of life that placed these additional burdens on their shoulders. He eased himself from the car.

'I'll certainly drive Tina round her patients. Mums and babies today, isn't it?'

'Would you?' Jane said, her relief evident. 'Would you really? Oh God, you are wonderful, Alex. Heaven sent.'

'Thanks, Alex,' Margaret said.

Driving Tina, plump, big-bosomed, thick-legged Tina in her nurse's uniform and her heavy flat shoes, was no great chore. Professionally impersonal, she directed him around the sprawling local villages in monosyllables, checking her patients' records as he drove and showing no desire to discuss them with him. In consequence he had time to ponder the pressures besetting Margaret and Jane, and the other two doctors, as they worked towards their move. This wouldn't take place until late summer, Margaret had said, or possibly early autumn, since so much had to be done by way of repairs and alterations to the old house. 'Plus blasted builders being notorious for never finishing on time.' How would they cope with that particular imponderable? Alex had advised them to run, as it were, to two dates: the builders' estimated completion date, and their own more realistic but undeclared date six or eight weeks later. 'Then,' he'd told her with a grin, 'you can plan sensibly, unbothered by the hang-ups and hitches that would otherwise drive you mad.' She'd called him brilliant; so had they all.

He parked outside yet another elderly cottage and watched Tina limp up the path.

The doctors needed a coordinator, someone to guard them

from the Bodgit and Scarpers of this world. Having dealt with building firms on big projects during his time as courts administrator, he knew the snags and pitfalls only too well, even among firms of some standing: architects' specifications ignored for something cheaper, vital materials with replacement dates as long as your arm being stolen, go-slows on site – no wonder his hair had gone thin on top. Alex knew what long hours Margaret worked, and wondered whether any of these country doctors would actually, physically, have the time to deal with such disasters?

It was then that his splendid thought came: he would offer himself as manager of their move, forestaller of disasters. And since savings would accrue through his expertise, they must surely pay him. Energy flowed through his veins. He would search for the best buys in furniture and equipment; he would check the conversion work daily, keeping the men on schedule; he would be invaluable. His face exploded into rapture; he would have endless reasons for discussions with Margaret. Yes!

'Was that your last call, Tina?' he asked as she shoved her records back into the bag she held on her plump knees; he could not wait to impress Margaret with his idea. 'Great, let's speed back to the surgery then.'

Fenella and Donna were laying the table for a quick lunch when Roger telephoned to say that the trial would be recommencing with the jury back in place at two o'clock.

'You're going on? Good,' Fenella said. 'Because we're on course to come and listen.'

Outside, a car came to a stop on the gravel. Car doors were opened and shut. Alex bringing Margaret back, no doubt, silly besotted man.

'I'll look out for you both,' Roger was saying in her ear. 'We've had much heated argument over whether the jury should be discharged, as you can imagine, but Hugh Thorne came to the conclusion that it would be satisfactory for the trial to continue without further evidence from Toyah Storm, provided that he, as Judge, gave a direction to the jury that if they thought that defence counsel had not been given sufficient opportunity to test the reliability and truthfulness of the complainant, then they should acquit the defendant.'

'And you thought there had been sufficient opportunity, didn't you?'

'In essence, yes,' Roger said. 'And I agreed his approach.'

'I don't suppose defence counsel did, though!' Fenella commented.

'Absolutely not. But the ruling was given and on we go. You're sure it's all right for Donna?'

'I don't see why not. She insists it's educational, that she's up to date with her revision work and that the evidence is so intriguing we have to hear the trial through.'

Alex appeared in the doorway, with Duncan behind him. 'Which trial? What evidence? What's this you're talking about?'

Fenella cut short her telephone conversation: 'We'll see you shortly. Bye!' She put the receiver down and started to explain: 'My cousin, Roger, is prosecuting a case in front of Hugh Thorne at the Crown Court and Donna and I have been there listening to it . . .'

'It's amazing,' Donna interrupted her, continuing fluently, 'I've never been in a court before and listening to a real case is quite different from what you get on television or in films. I mean, we've been hearing this fourteen-year-old girl, Toyah, giving evidence by video-link on screens in the court and she's so thin and traumatised you can hardly believe anyone could be that bad. Nothing like the appealing baby-faced actress you might see on TV with her face dramatically painted with white make-up, but someone who's all flaky and angry and in a real state about being asked questions that she thinks are dirty. Perverted, she calls them. She doesn't understand the need for proving the case beyond reasonable doubt, she doesn't seem to understand much at all, so she can't cope with the demands on her. I've heard of natural victims but I thought people were being condescending because nobody'd explained to me properly what that meant. And then when I saw this girl, Toyah, and I heard her talking, it put the word victim into a different category for me. It's something that's kind of hidden, because her sort are never seen on telly, are they? It's terrible.'

'What's terrible?' Alex demanded. 'What is this case about?'

'Didn't I say?' said Donna. 'It's a rape case. The brother of a neighbour of her father's, someone she'd met before, offered her a lift home and she thought he'd be all right, only he wasn't and he took her in a van to the New Forest and raped her.'

'I don't believe this,' Alex said in an ominous tone, his face flushing with anger. 'You mean your mother's been taking you, at your age, to listen to some horrific paedophile rape case simply because her cousin's cousin is appearing in it as counsel?'

Donna went rigid, infuriated by his instant offensive against Fenella. She wanted to rage at him and throw cutlery about the place. 'No, I heard about it and I insisted on going. I'm nearly seventeen and I want to learn about our justice system.' Recollecting Sam's views on attack being the best form of defence, she added in sharp reproach: 'You know how the courts work, Dad; you could have taken me to hear a case being tried, only you've never bothered.'

'I should certainly not have taken you to some disgusting sex case,' Alex began, but he was interrupted by Duncan, who strolled forward into the room, hands in pockets, hitching at his jeans.

'Why not? Donna's right. Girls like her should hear cases like that – make them more careful about who they go around with. Besides, it couldn't be worse than what's on telly. Hey, I've worked hard all morning, I think I'll join Mum and you, Donna.' He nodded at his mother, standing still, her face expressionless. 'I've never listened to any cases in court either. Hearing old Roger at work should be interesting, too, and we'll be showing some of that family solidarity you're always talking about. We could do with it.'

Fenella nodded back to him. 'Lunch is all but ready,' she

said, and walked swiftly, silently, to the kitchen. On her cheeks two red spots bloomed.

At two o'clock the court heard the brother's evidence: 'Yeah, Toyah often goes home early from parties and things, she likes watching telly better.' And then her mother's, encapsulated by two sentences: 'No, she's no raving sex maniac, far as I know she's never even had a boyfriend.' 'No, you've only to look at her to see she's not mature that way, she's just a kid still.'

Donna whispered to Duncan, 'That's true, she looks like a skinny ten-year-old.'

'Yes, you told me,' Duncan muttered back. 'Ssh! It's the police on now.'

Sergeant Randle, a heavy, seen-it-all-before man in his late thirties, was concise in his replies to Roger Dodson's questions. 'As Police Constable Hansford and I were driving down the road in a patrol car on our way to investigate a burglary, we saw a man standing by a white van, talking at a young girl. I sensed something wrong. I told my colleague, "That girl's in trouble, stop a sec, will you?" He slowed and said, "Here, haven't we been warned about an abduction of an underaged girl?" and I said, "Yeah, good thinking. I forgot about that."'

The Judge leaned forward. 'Your reaction was not prompted by that, either subconsciously or consciously?'

'No, definitely not. It was . . . when I looked at them together, well, I sensed something very wrong and incompatible between them. An instinct. So we pulled over. But as we were doing that the man jumped into the van and drove off without the girl. I got out and said to her, "Are you all right? Have you had some trouble?" She started to cry. She said, "I've been raped."'

There was a pause. The jury stirred. Then Roger moved him gently onward. 'Did anything in particular strike you about her?'

'Yes. She was shaking all over. And her face was dead pale.'

'Did you deduce anything from that?'

'Well, I thought she was in severe shock. I asked her who had attacked her and she replied that it was the man in the van.'

'Did she name this man?'

'Yes, she did. She gave his name as Gary Jenkyns and she was able to give my colleague and me his current address. We drove her to the police station and telephoned her mother, who had reported her missing.'

Time passed. Roger pressed on with his witnesses, building the evidence against the defendant brick by brick. In contrast Geraint Meredith was valiant in cross-examination, even theatrical, giving the impression that he wholly believed his client's story and that the witnesses must have some dubious reasons of their own for giving such discreditable testimony: 'Did it not occur to you that Toyah could have cried rape because she was angry that Jenkyns had spurned her wish for a long-term relationship with him?'

While Dr Amanda Colby was taking the oath before giving her evidence, Duncan murmured in Donna's ear, 'That Mr Meredith is a bit over the top, don't you think? But Roger's clever – being low key, I mean. His questions are right to the point, but his voice is mild and he looks so bland that the witnesses relax and they give out more. Riveting stuff, isn't it?'

Dr Colby, short, ruddy haired and broad shouldered, gave her evidence succinctly as to the injuries that she had found on Toyah, but was cross-examined on her findings in some detail. She would not be budged from her original statement that the swellings and lacerations she had found on Toyah were most unlikely to have been caused by normal consenting intercourse, because of the high level of pain it would have inflicted. 'No, no normal woman would consent to that.' No, from her clinical experience she could only deduce that Toyah was a virgin at the time of the injuries. Donna and Duncan sat in silent concentration.

Late shafts of April sunlight fell across the lanes as Hugh drove home at the end of the day. He slowed the car, allowing his eyes to linger over the pale primroses among the tussocky grass, the hawthorn coming into tentative flower, the rooks settling in the tree tops. Sanity. Eternal renewal. Even in the last week the change had been considerable. The winter wait was over; spring was here.

He lowered his window and breathed deeply. Dear God, he was tired. It had been a long day and not easy, not with those tense and lengthy legal arguments between Counsel this morning. And he had taken great pains with his judgment, writing it out in longhand, page after page, weighing every paragraph, every word. It had to be capable of withstanding the scrutiny of the Court of Appeal, should a guilty verdict be appealed. He thought, I am doing all I can to guide the court in a challenging case. And I have good Counsel in front of me. Roger Dodson is doing an excellent job, he understands how to handle a jury, how to bring out the points at issue and explain them to the jury as if he were one of them. He's better than I expected, improved rather than the opposite; perhaps the break from that over-ambitious wife of his was not such a disaster after all. A reassuring thought. Hugh would not have liked to see the man go downhill, he was of the straightforward and kindly persuasion. Was he really having some sort of affair with Fenella Lindridge? Would she have brought her adolescent children with her to hear him in court if that were so? But then, Hugh wasn't at all sure that Donna should be listening to this sort of case at her tender age. This whole business was more than a touch worrying. He might ask Celia for her thoughts on it.

Along the lane a cock pheasant emerged from the tangled hedge, took fright at the car, and ran agitatedly for several feet along the bank before disappearing in a last flash of coppery feathers back into the hedge. A handsome bird and not one seen on the North Circular! He slowed the car still further and on the breeze caught faintly the caws of the rooks, the cries of sheep calling to their lambs in the meadow. He began to distance himself from the stresses of the day, from Roger and his dilemmas, from the judgment in the Jenkyns case, from Donna and her dysfunctional family. The evening light glowed on the haze of fresh green leaf that was spreading over the hedges and the trees, and he was filled with gratitude for the unspoiled beauty of the Hampshire countryside and for his luck in being able to live there.

On turning into the manor house drive he saw Fenella, Duncan and Donna walking into the house. Only just back? Why so slow? Ah, been talking to Roger Dodson probably. He frowned. Who knew what about whom among them, though? What a muddle people's lives got into these days. He drove his car into its garage, praying that he could avoid his neighbours in the hall. He craved a quiet session with the day's paper over a glass of claret.

When Celia returned to the flat from running Lena home ten minutes later, and glimpsed through the drawing-room door her tired-eyed husband drooping over *The Times*, she turned and made instead for the kitchen. Better leave him to unwind. From the descriptions she had heard downstairs from Fenella and her family, Hugh's day had been a hard one. Though they had all agreed that the case was being well handled.

Celia occupied herself at the sink with vegetables, washing, peeling and chopping, her hands expert. From the window she looked down at the ancient church and its surroundings. The black cat was grooming himself on the flint wall and the pigeons were settling in their trees. In the churchyard there were flowering bulbs in great drifts; earlier there had been snowdrops and winter aconites, now she saw daffodils and narcissus, and the lesser celandine. In the dusk the yellow and white blooms glimmered against the tombstones, taking on the romantic dimensions of a Pre-Raphaelite painting. A pretty thing, the celandine. Celia had painted a plant of it, quoting beneath it the seventeenth-century herbalist Nicholas Culpeper, who had used it in treating his daughter for the 'king's evil' or scrofula – successfully, he'd claimed. People enjoyed such gems of information, and so did she.

Donna had tried her hand at conveying the delicacy of the

celandine and the wood anemone recently, working in the studio with Celia between bouts of her own studies, dissecting the little plants, comparing them and probing with her into the best methods of capturing them in paint. According to the Roman writer, Pliny the Elder, Celia told her, the anemone was nicknamed the windflower because the flowers open only when the wind blows. Celia caught a look of delight on Donna's pale, tense face as she followed a line of stalk downwards with her brush. 'Pliny was examining them, doing just as we are now, two thousand years ago. That's amazing,' she said. Celia had considered that Donna's studies of the plants were pretty good, but the girl had dismissed them as rough in comparison with her own, rejecting all praise. 'I can't be that meticulous,' she'd said finally, 'I haven't your touch. They're fun to do, but they aren't what I'm aiming for.' Then she'd spent a couple of frosty lunchtimes sketching the River Test to produce a week later a picture that captured exactly the beauty of the river flowing darkly between its whitened, stiffened banks, the pollarded willows standing sentinel above, and far beyond them a glowing strip of colour that showed the sun setting behind the distant low hills. Celia had registered as she scrutinised it that Donna's perspective was exact, conveying an impression of recession into distance and serenity that was remarkable for a girl of her age. Though Celia had been warm in her admiration, Donna's sole response had been to remark that her family's move here, resented at the time, had not been altogether bad because living in the country was fine and capturing the downs or the River Test in different moods was an endless challenge.

'I'd never really thought about the countryside, because I didn't know about it. But I think landscapes are going to be my thing. Here there's so much more sky, and the fields and hills and the woods have shape, like you don't see round London. Then there are contrasts, patches of dark trees, and half-hidden lanes and gateways in a gap where you can see for miles. And there's something about the space and the quietness – watching the heron stand waiting for fish in the river – that goes deep into me.' And then she'd produced the usual Donna scowl, so that Celia had simply said, 'That's how Hugh and I feel. That's why he looks forward to fishing with James Manningford and why I paint. For that sense of peace.' A moment's thought and she'd added, 'And it's why I told you when you first showed me your work that your landscapes were good. You catch atmospheres, convey that remoteness.' And then Donna's face had softened and flushed with pleasure.

Celia put her vegetables into pans and moved them to the hob. She had an urge to show Hugh something of Donna's work, to discover his opinion of it . . . and of Donna. Celia was concerned about her. On the surface things were going well; Todd said that she was pulling up pleasingly in mathematics, would probably attain an A-grade, and, from what he'd heard from her other tutors, she was expected to do well generally. She had Sam as a boyfriend. But despite that and despite Donna's fascination with the case she'd been listening to at court, Celia sensed something was wrong. Donna was too jumpy, too tense. Celia conjured up the claustrophobic quality of the Lindridges' life in that dreary flat where disparate items of furniture sat as frigidly refusing to blend together as its inhabitants, and she recollected the sounds of the rancorous squabbles she'd heard as she passed up and down the stairs.

She began to lay the table. So strongly had she brought the Lindridges to mind that she could have sworn to hearing their angry voices even as she put down the knives and forks. It was a rotten atmosphere for Donna. Celia pondered. Did she understand about her parents' affairs and resent them? Was she afraid of a break-up? Did she know that Roger was her mother's lover? She was at an age when such matters could assume an overwhelming importance, especially with someone who had so recently undergone her own initiation into sexual concerns. Were things right between her and Sam? Was the rape case upsetting her, whatever she said? Celia was far from sure that she should be listening to something as brutal as the attack Hugh had described to her.

Talking such matters over with Celia was Hugh's outlet for the tension and horror of much of his work. To whom could Donna talk? Sam was away every week on his scaffolding, earning the money that would help him through the financial stringencies of his university years, her brother Duncan was only intermittently at home. She seemed reasonably close to her mother, but if Fenella's mind was all entangled with her failing marriage and the difficult circumstances of her affair with Roger, she could well not have picked up on her daughter's adolescent trials and tensions. Celia, uneasy, decided she must try to discover more. She sighed. Such boggy, treacherous ground would have to be trodden with the greatest of care. She poured double cream into a bowl, whipped it up briskly and began grating the rind of a large lemon. Lemon syllabub tonight, she had decided.

Hugh should have unwound sufficiently by now that she could persuade him down to the Lindridges' flat to look at Donna's pictures. He'd be appreciative of their charms. But he wouldn't stay long, he was tired, and besides, he'd never been a man for social chitchat. He'd leave, then perhaps she could manage to talk to Donna in her bedroom, out of earshot of her parents. She would see how Donna appeared then, assess the situation. Not brilliant, but the best she could devise. After dinner, or before? Before, Celia decided, squeezing the juice from a lemon. Now, white wine and caster sugar. She was ahead of herself with dinner and it was early yet. First she'd finish making the syllabub. Then she would telephone to check that what she proposed would be acceptable to the Lindridges in terms of time and place. Tact was a necessity with them.

It was Donna who answered the telephone. 'Hello?'

'Hello, Donna, it's Celia.' Even as she spoke she was aware of sharp voices. So she hadn't been imagining those acrimonious sounds. For a moment she was aware of flagging energy, and falling spirits. Why do couples fight? Had circumstances been different, had Hugh and she not met, she too could have been venting bitterness with sharp comments, dwelt like those two in alternative circumstances of little money and less love. She remembered with a shudder the Peters and Georges of her youthful days, the possible Mr Rights who would have made such treacherous Mr Wrongs. But she had avoided the mistakes somehow, thank God.

Donna was hissing, 'Ssh. Keep your voices down, can't you? I'm on the telephone.'

Momentarily knocked off balance, cringing for Donna, Celia struggled: 'Donna dear, sorry if I've telephoned at an inopportune moment, but I wanted to ask whether I could bring Hugh down, you know, some time, any time, to show him some of your pictures . . .'

'Tonight?'

'Well yes . . . I suppose. The landscapes.' A deep breath. 'But not if it's inconvenient . . .'

'Don't come down here,' Donna interrupted decisively. 'I'd rather bring some up. Give me ten minutes.'

'Fine,' Celia said, recovering. 'I'll make sure Hugh has a glass of wine ready for you.' The girl would like that. For herself, she'd prefer something on the stronger side.

17

After fifteen minutes relaxing in his favourite wingchair with a glass of excellent claret, and softened by an article in *The Times* so close to his own views against European integration that he might have penned it himself, Hugh was beginning to feel pleasantly benign. Of course he would look at Donna's paintings if the girl felt his views were worth having. After all, being married to an artist, he kept in touch with the latest trends in conceptual art, in new visual imagery designed to jolt the mind to fresh perceptions – works utilising rubber gloves or strands of barbed wire, clunking rotating beacons or strange collages, video projections that were observations on themes of healing. Challenging? Childish and gimmicky, he thought. But nobody asked him to live with the stuff and he prided himself on a large tolerance. Besides, Celia had assured him that the work he would see had no connection with such trends.

He reached out to pour himself a second revitalising glass. A lively girl, Donna, attractive too – when she wasn't looking moody. A pity she was mostly the sole youngster here; her brother, Duncan, and the doctor's lad, Sam, were away far too much. It must be dull for her, particularly since she was studying alone. Hugh would never have permitted such a situation to happen with his young Anna. Clearly Alex had failed to take his daughter's needs into account when he decided to move to a manor house deep in the country – or his tight-lipped wife's wishes, either. Celia

hinted at an increasingly barbed relationship with Fenella,
of Alex determined to purge her from the family. Hugh
recoiled from the thought. He had invariably found Alex
helpful, if a touch grey – but manipulative? Callous? Never!
It was a shame his efforts on Alex's behalf had failed to find
him suitable employment. He must ask Celia what, if anything, she had garnered on the subject of the bursar's post
that had gone to Martin Upcott. Women were wonderful at
half-hints and allusions: pointers to the causes of Alex's
rejection were bound to have filtered through on the female
network from the school through Candida Gough to Arabella
and on to his Celia.

When she joined him she turned down an offer of claret,
demanding whisky instead, 'God, I'm low tonight!' and
shook her white head seriously in answer to his query.

'My informant – entirely off the record, naturally – told me
Alex Lindridge had been generally considered too uptight,
too stiff, but that even had he been all easy charm, queries as
to the solidarity of his marriage had emerged, even rumours
of infidelity.' She sank on to the sofa, looking at Hugh over
the glass he pushed into her hand. 'Not good. Small children
need adults around them of unassailable probity.'

Hugh grimaced. 'Fenella's affair has become public
knowledge, presumably. Oh dear.'

'Oh no!' Celia retorted promptly. 'Alex's with Doctor
Margaret. Fenella is highly discreet.'

'Alex?' Hugh looked first startled, then dubious. 'Well, I
have wondered once or twice as to the exact nature of the
devotion there. But you think something is actually going on,
do you?'

Celia nodded, taking several gulps of her whisky and water
and then putting her glass down. 'Definitely so, according to
village gossip. Lena the cleaner is a Fenella fan, and she tells
me a farm lad perched up on a tractor reported seeing Alex
and Margaret *hard at it* in a small spinney on the far side of a
hedge. Lena's upset about it. "Mind you," she says, "we've all
known it 'ad to 'ave bin going on for weeks. No one can be
that kind to someone and not expect summink in return, can

they? Be against nature. But it's not fair on Mrs L. Everybody knowing and giggling. Not nice." She'd have thought better of him than that, apparently. How are the righteous fallen!' She gave Hugh a cynical glance not entirely devoid of triumph.

'How singularly stupid of Alex!' Hugh said. 'The last person I'd have expected of such a public performance.' His voice was calmly disdainful but inside he was churning. If this rumour was true, the good, the upright and invaluable civil servant, Alex Lindridge, the man whom he had strongly recommended to several influential people in good faith, had let both himself and Hugh down in the most ludicrous fashion. Perhaps he considered such bucolic sex-activities romantic: love in a pastoral paradise or something of that silly sort. Possibly he had been lured to the area by some mushy image of the country as an Arcadian idyll of endless sun-filled days, where the corn is eternally golden and the apples hang for ever ready to be picked for your delicious picnic by a haystack. Hugh, who had shot and hunted over many years, thought the romantic view of rural life naive, moronic even. Murder and havoc existed in the peaceful countryside as well as in the inner city; he'd seen it, engaged in it himself, helped pluck the limp birds, skin the bloody rabbits, gut the fish. He'd also seen the results of the fox's murderous depredations in the hen-run. Had Alex Lindridge? He doubted it. Certainly his unrelentingly urban wife would abominate such matters. Well, he would do no more on Alex's behalf. The besotted idiot must be turning half-witted – and at the age of fifty-odd, too, when even the most errant of men should have grown reliable. A further distasteful thought struck him: could Donna know? Was she miserably aware that both her parents were playing around – her father with the doctor, her mother with Roger – all of them leading the covert, opportunistic lives of those who believe in the regular gratification of self-indulgent desires? Now was a time when Donna needed both her parents' attention centred on her. He hoped she didn't know, but he was disagreeably certain that she must and that this knowledge was the reason for her strained looks.

The doorbell sounded, but it was Betty, not Donna, at the door. Betty had a problem of taste in connection with historical accuracy, she told Celia. 'A gardening matter. Brozie Hamilton and I are locked in furious argument with two ladies from the horticultural society. They really are ridiculously rigid in their ideas. I have to marshall my own arguments against theirs and I'd value your opinion. Can you spare me a moment?'

No, Celia thought, no she couldn't, it was the wrong moment. She wanted to talk to Donna, and having organised the opportunity she was damned if she'd be put off, despite feeling queasy about it. Quite why she felt so impelled was puzzling. Perhaps it was because she had grown fond of Donna, who had shown an interest in her own work that she recognised as real, something wholly different from the gushing surface enthusiasm of so many of the clients who came to buy her delicate botanical paintings. She also, flatteringly, asked for advice – and took it. Donna wanted to learn; she was aware her work had weaknesses and looked for techniques to overcome them. She aimed high and in consequence grappled with self-doubts when she failed to reach a target, arousing almost forgotten protective instincts in Celia, whose own children were young adults convinced they could learn no more from their aged parents. She was a gifted and responsive girl, Donna. Celia pushed back her hair. Being fond of people was risky, it impelled one to venture into areas that all too probably would become highly embarrassing. Nor did she need Betty, however sweet and well-intentioned, overhearing.

She was about to suggest Betty should come to coffee the following morning, when Donna ran up the stairs to appear behind her.

'Oh, hiya, Betty. Hello, Celia.'

'Hello, Donna,' Betty said promptly, smiling at her, 'I haven't seen you about for a day or two. What have you been doing? Painting? Or has it been long hours at the books?'

'Neither of those. But I have been learning. I've been

listening to a rape trial in the Crown Court. One of the Judge's cases.'

'A rape trial? Why that, of all things?' Betty demanded to be told. 'Isn't it rather sordid?'

'Some of it's vile,' Donna admitted, shifting her portfolio of paintings across her arms. 'But it's Mother's cousin, Roger, who's the counsel for the prosecution and Mum was there listening, so I insisted I had to go, and now Duncan's come along too.' She shook her head as if emphasising her earnestness. 'The girl's younger than me, just fourteen, so it's underage sex as well. It's terrifyingly real and serious, you can't imagine.'

'And you want to know the outcome,' Betty commented dryly.

'Yeah,' Donna admitted, 'well, there is that too . . .'

Their chatter had every chance of developing into a protracted discussion. Groaning inwardly with frustration, Celia gave up and stepped back, holding the door wide and interrupting their conversation with an edge to her voice. '*Do* come in, both of you, please. We'll go into the drawing-room.' She whisked herself ahead of them. 'Hugh, here are Donna and Betty.'

Hugh was urbane, hiding his puzzlement at seeing Betty. He proffered Chardonnay and poured it. Donna looked self-conscious, clutching her shabby portfolio.

'Prop your paintings up on the sofa,' Hugh suggested, removing from it the stuff of Celia's evening preoccupations, the latest PD James, a handsomely presented *History of the Rose*, and a marked-up catalogue of artists' materials together with its order form.

'Is Donna going to show you her work? You'll have a surprise,' Betty said with a proprietorial air.

Donna hesitated, then put the portfolio down, taking from it three paintings of a moderate size, the first the one that Celia had already seen of the river and the distant hills icy with frost, the second a painting of the fields and cottages to the east of the manor house under a slanting late afternoon sun. The third, since there was insufficient room on the sofa, she propped up on a nearby armchair. Then she picked up her glass of wine and went to lean against the marble mantelshelf of the fireplace, sipping slowly, her face unreadable.

Hugh's dark eyebrows twitched and rose. 'Those aren't bad at all,' he exclaimed, standing back to observe the two on the sofa. 'In fact, they're pretty good. How do you manage to produce such a feeling of tranquillity, Donna? Of evening calm? Mmm. You simplify shapes and soften angles, yes, and you erase from your subjects all non-essential detail. It's very effective.'

'Mum suggested that I should do that. Eliminate anything that detracts from the main theme, she said, like Keith New does. She's taught me a lot since we've been here. I think she'd have liked to paint herself but she says she never had the dexterity.' Donna contemplated her works, chewing her lip, then added: 'She said that Dad called a watercolour sketch she'd done on their Venetian honeymoon a daub and she was hurt, but she knew he was right so she gave it up. But she loves going to galleries and exhibitions, looking at other people's work. And then sometimes she buys.'

Celia and Hugh exchanged glances, knowing their thoughts were similar.

'She certainly has an eye,' Celia said.

Hugh drained his glass. 'But she's not fond of the country, is she?'

'She doesn't dislike it,' Donna said protectively. 'I mean, like with snow, she says it's fine to look at. For a weekend, perhaps, mostly through a car window. But she no more wants to live in it than . . . than in Siberia.'

Hugh chuckled. He was beginning to look as though he was enjoying himself. 'But she takes an interest in how you depict it?'

'Mm,' Donna was definite. 'She always has.'

Betty was still pondering the second picture. 'I haven't seen this one before. You're making strides in technique, Donna, you truly are.' She gestured with a hand. 'Those deep curving shadows at the sides establish the shapes of the trees and the cottages in their surroundings, so that they look convincingly solid and rooted in time. It's good.'

'Thanks,' Donna mumbled, her stiff young face struggling to remain cool.

Betty moved on to study the lone picture propped on the armchair and startled them all with her shriek. 'The herb garden! Look, Celia, Hugh, she's painted our west wing and the herb garden! Goodness, it looks exactly as I've been imagining it. Or better.'

Hugh swivelled and stared. 'I'm impressed,' he responded, stepping nearer to examine its detail. 'Impressed by you both. You, Betty, you've rightly allowed the old wing to determine the style of your design, while Donna's painting shows how the design will enhance that part of the house.'

'And she's put in the little bay trees in pots I fancied to flank my sitting-room window!'

'It's all in accordance with your plans, is it?' Celia asked, her eyes amused.

Betty was still giving little cries of joy. 'Yes, yes. It's great! Do look, both of you! Donna's even put in the garden bench I thought we'd have at the back – isn't that an Edwin Lutyens design, Donna dear? Wherever did you find it? And on either side the great ornamental pots I've dreamed about, planted with their rosemaries and thymes. You remembered. And the sundial, too! Goodness, I'm inspired all over again, seeing it like that. I must hurry to put the herbs in.'

'Yes indeed,' said Hugh.

Donna had portrayed the Jacobean west wing of the manor house from an almost aerial perspective, looking down on it not as it was now, with Betty's herb garden still barren, its beds barely completed, but as it would come to bloom in future summers, with its lavenders and rue, sages and artemesias blending their silvery foliage in front of the sunwarmed, time-weathered old bricks, a restful place of subtle shapes and textures.

Betty was hugging Donna, her plump weather-lined face

pink with her excitement. 'I like it, I really do! But however did you make the scale of it so accurate?'

Donna gave her a distinctly smug smile. 'It's based on your planting plan that you made to show Candida Gough. You know, all drawn to scale . . .'

'And you plotted the herbs in as I'd shown them, then painted the whole thing to look three-dimensional? Scaling it up must have taken you hours of work, though.'

Donna shook her head. 'Martin let me use your special ruler when you were out at one of your horticultural society evenings, so it wasn't too hard. You know, you showed me how to use it when you were drawing it all up, and you'd written in what plants you wanted where, so I only had to borrow a couple of illustrated gardening books from Celia and I was away.'

'So this is what you wanted my books for!' Celia stepped back to study it with a professional eye. 'Stippling in the shapes and texture of the plants as you've done is very effective, particularly in suggesting the tiny leaves of box or santolinas – and those lustrous grey-blue patches in the knot must be rue, and the gold, marjoram? Yes. I have to say I'm impressed. You've taken thought and trouble over this, Donna. Well done.'

'I'd like to buy it,' Betty announced, suddenly solemn. 'I think it's gorgeous, and what's more it would look absolutely right on my sitting-room wall. Could I, Donna? How much would you take for it?'

Donna looked almost shocked. She eyed her painting dubiously, sucking in her breath and running her fingers through her thick hair . 'I couldn't sell it to you. I mean, it's all right, but it isn't good enough to ask for money. I suppose if you really like it, well then, you take it.' She looked at Betty and then away in embarrassment.

Clearly she had not learned graceful responsiveness from her parents, Celia mused, but then it was not an art they practised themselves. She smiled encouragingly. 'Don't turn a good offer down, Donna. Think of the expensive paints and brushes you could afford to buy.'

'And books,' Betty added. 'You think about it, Donna. Ask your parents for their views. Tell them I think it's so good that I'm willing to venture to a hundred plus.'

Pangs of hunger reminded Celia she must move Betty on. 'Ah, I'm sorry, Betty, we've been so busy discussing Donna's work that I've quite forgotten to ask what it was you wanted to discuss with me. Something about historical taste in plants, was it?'

'Oh, yes. Yes, it was. Briefly, last night the Abbotsbridge horticultural society had a talk with slides on restoring period gardens, and naturally the discussion afterwards brought in queries about our views here. But I ask you, what date and style of gardening would you settle on for this place?'

'Frankly, I couldn't. Its various parts contain such a muddle of styles and dates it's impossible to fix on any particular period. Pushed, I'd say any style that was in fashion between 1660 and 1820 would be "in keeping" as they say. Even a Gertrude Jekyll style wouldn't look out of date, would it?'

Hugh interposed, 'Isn't it a matter of being faithful to a style and plantings that won't look anachronistic? No more, no less.'

'Exactly my view,' Betty said with emphasis, 'which is why the herb garden's by the old west wing. For the rest I ban those horrid bedding plants with lurid orange or shrieking puce-pink flowers that garden centres push at you, together with coy miniature conifers and those fearsome shrubs they love with violently variegated leaves . . .'

Celia laughed. 'I can think of certain euonymuses—'

'Exactly! And no modern bright-purple-leaved shrubs either, not here. But this is where I run into trouble with those two horticultural society pests.'

'They don't demand purple leaves, do they?' Donna asked.

'Oh no, these ladies demand the elimination of *everything* purple leaved as vulgar and anachronistic, even lovely *Rosa rubrifolia* and the purple-leaved sage. One of them said that green was clearly God's intention for plants and it was wrong

to interfere with His intention. I think that's sheer silliness
and Brozie Hamilton agrees. I've planned to have *Rosa rubrifolia* at the sunny end of the big bed in the walled garden and
the purple sage to contrast with the other sages in the herb
garden. Like it is there.' A stubby forefinger touched the
greyish-plum of the sage in Donna's picture. 'But I need to
know if you're in agreement, Celia.'

'Totally,' Celia said. 'Besides, I'm positive *Rosa rubrifolia*
predates 1830. It originated in central and southern Europe
and it's been about for ages.' She turned to Donna. 'Do you
know it? No? It's an arching species rose, with soft bluish-
purple leaves and little pink flowers. It *looks* old-fashioned.'

'Precisely my point,' Betty nodded, looking relieved.

'You shouldn't take any notice of people like that,' Hugh
commented.

'No, you should trust your own good taste,' Donna said.

'And frankly, when push comes to shove,' Celia added,
'what in hell's it got to with these people? If anybody is to sit
in judgment on Brambourne Manor's gardens it is its own
inhabitants and the lady from the National Gardens Scheme,
not mewing old biddies.'

She was suddenly tired of being reassuring and positive.
Donna should sell her picture and be grateful. Betty should
put down silly females with ill-conceived pretensions to
high-mindedness. But then in a switch of mood she recollected how often Betty was snubbed by that resentful
husband of hers, rebuffs sufficient to undermine the confidence even of the most determined woman. She patted
Betty's arm. 'You are in the right, you know.'

Donna was picking up her two landscape paintings and
placing them in the portfolio. Celia saw how she edgy she
looked, how tired-eyed. At the third picture she paused,
glancing round, uncertain. Celia moved purposefully to
remove it from her hands, thrusting it at Betty.

'Look, show this painting to Martin. If you're thinking of
buying it he should see it.' Martin was starting work in his
new post shortly, he'd already spent several days at the school
in discussions with the old bursar and other members of staff.

He ought to be more relaxed now and approachable, especially with money being easier for them. 'Talk it over together,' she advised. 'That's all right with you, isn't it, Donna?'

'Yeah, sure.'

Hugh had turned away and was picking up empty wine glasses; Celia suggested into his ear that he should telephone their daughter Anna to discover what present she might like for her birthday, 'In the bedroom, I think, don't you?' Then she shut the door behind him and took her chance, Betty there or not, keeping her voice muted.

'Now, how are things with you, Donna? I've not seen much of you these last few days but when I have you've been looking pale and strained.'

Donna shrugged, muttering, 'I'm OK.'

'But are you? Is it headaches? Eye strain?'

'I'm busy,' Donna said, grabbing her portfolio from the sofa. 'There's a ton of things going on in my life.'

'GCSE revision and all your painting, and now this case you've been listening to in Hugh's court – and then there's the lively Sam at the weekends. You're piling on the pressure a bit, aren't you?'

'No. I'm fine. Really.' Donna, reddening, tied the frayed tapes on her portfolio, mumbled distractedly, 'My old art teacher, Mrs Peel, gave me this to put my work in. She had it at art college.'

'Very kind,' Celia said. 'Ah, and then tell me, your predicament of earlier in the month necessitating that dramatic Sunday dash to the doctor and the chemist – can I take it that all was swiftly resolved? No further panics?'

Donna's face closed up, her lips tightened. She shook her head.

'Does that mean that all is well – or not well?' Celia asked crisply.

'My period's not come.' Her voice held mingled resonances of drama and anguish.

'Oh dear,' Betty murmured inadequately.

'How much is it overdue?' Celia wanted to know. 'And what about a test?'

'I'm nine days over.' A voice of deepest gloom. Donna straightened herself to scan their faces, the awkward portfolio clutched against herself protectively. 'I did do a test that was negative, but you can't trust them early on, can you? And I've never been so late before.'

Celia shook her head. 'Doesn't necessarily mean anything. Shock, upset, a change in your normal pattern of living; any of those can upset the hormone balance and cause periods to come early or late.' She added caustically, 'Whichever is the most inconvenient and worrying, naturally. But you took that pill, you should be all right.'

In a rush to add her reassurances to Celia's, Betty said, 'It happened to a friend of mine once just after she'd split from her boyfriend. It was a torn condom that had caused her panic, and by the time she was three weeks late I can tell you, she was in tears of despair. But then it came and we celebrated with champagne. You'll be fine, Donna, as Celia says. I'm certain of it.'

'I wish *I* were,' Donna muttered, staring past them at the windows that were darkening by the minute. She looked as though she was weeping inside, swearing and cringing, her face sheened with sweat from the ordeal of their discussion. She added: 'I keep on telling myself, it'll come this afternoon, tonight, in the morning . . . But it doesn't. I don't want a baby, I'm too young. But I don't want an abortion, either.'

As if by unspoken agreement all three sat down and leaned forward, hands resting on thighs, faces serious.

'Have you told your parents?' Celia asked. 'Either of them?'

'No way,' Donna said. She raised her eyes to Celia's and added with bitter candour: 'They'd fight even more than they do now. Each of them blaming the other. Never mind about Sam or me having been stupid.'

As if to demonstrate the truth of Donna's comment Celia heard from the floor below their voices start up again. The words were unintelligible, but the force of the anger and hate behind them came over with a shocking clarity, carrying with it an irritation factor as grating as the revving of a biker gang's rowdy machines, aggressive and malicious. Both women looked at Donna and then jerked their eyes away.

Donna shifted the portfolio in her arms. 'See what I mean. They just go on and on.' She looked down at the floor as if somehow they might be visible through the expensive pale grey carpet and the centuries-old floorboards. Quietly she added: 'I didn't know you could hear them like this. It's dreadful. I'll tell them.'

Celia said gently, 'It's only recently that I've heard them. I'm sorry.'

'Sorry?' The girl looked up. 'What for? That my parents are so grim? They should split. They really should. But they won't, because of Duncan and me. They're all wound up with self-sacrifice, reeking of it. Before anything else, they say, they have to see us through our exams.'

'But that's putting more pressure on you,' Betty pointed out. She too had heard bitter voices.

'And pressure on Mum. I feel bad about her. She ought to go. She pretends to be OK, but she's so isolated here, I know she must be feeling terrible. And Dad's around the flat too much being morbid. That's when he's not running Margaret around. And that's too much in another way.' She looked from one carefully blank face to the other and heaved an exasperated sigh. 'Don't tell me you haven't heard the rumours about Dad and Doctor Margaret, when everyone in the villages is sniggering their heads off. And then,' she added desperately, 'Sam being her son, that's unfair on Mum too. It makes things utterly impossible and horrific if I am . . . you know . . . pregnant.'

'Yes, I can see that.' Celia hesitated, then added carefully, 'I understand what you're saying, but Fenella's not a mean person. And besides, as Betty said, I doubt you could be pregnant. It's simply that you're under pressure and your hormones are rebelling. But Fenella, has she somewhere, someone, to go to, if she should leave?'

'Dad says she has a lover. That she's had others, too. I

don't know.' She looked at her clasped hands. 'She does have telephone calls but mostly she doesn't say who it is.'

From the ground floor came the sound of a crash followed by a cry: 'Oh no!' and then silence, a silence that was the more complete for the sounds that had come before. Celia and Betty's eyes communicated briefly and were lowered.

Donna's hands writhed together. She said sadly, 'I've never wanted a split. When we were little and Duncan and I were pulling a chicken wishbone between us, I was always mad to win so I could wish for them never to argue again. Sometimes we've had goodish patches, but not for long. But I think it's too late now. It wouldn't be so bad if they could live apart but near so that Duncan and I could see whichever we wanted when we wanted. And if they could be calm when they met, instead of going on like snarling pitbulls and biting chunks out of each other's psyches. Even Toyah – that's the girl in the rape case Mum and I've been listening to – even she had her father and his new family not that far from her and her mother and brother. They were pretty basic and what my father'd probably call dysfunctional and despise, but,' she said bitterly, 'are my parents any better? At least Toyah's parents seemed to be able to talk without being loathsome to each other. And they still ran visits and parties between the families. It was just they didn't realise how vulnerable Toyah was with her being so dim.' The familiar scowl appeared on her pale face. 'I don't know how my parents can carry on in this foul way. They make things worse every day they do it.'

Celia saw that she was right. Donna's own family was dysfunctional and the girl, vulnerable and anxious for the companionship and affection of someone of her own age, had inevitably fallen into the arms of the nearest attractive male, young Sam, and now might well be pregnant. Not as painful and shocking an awakening to sex as Toyah's viciously brutal initiation, but nevertheless, with the atmosphere in the Lindridge's flat building up towards explosion point Donna must be under heavy strain. Oh hell, what was there to do with people like the Lindridges who couldn't talk without fighting?

As if reading her mind, Betty said, 'Donna, you must have a word with your parents. Let them know that the bad atmosphere is upsetting you. You can't go on like this, and they shouldn't either. It's terrible.'

'I can't do it,' Donna said flatly. 'I just can't. They'd turn anything I said straight against each other and make me feel awful and I couldn't take it.' For a moment she looked as if she might burst into tears.

'Poor love,' Betty said protectively. 'You've had enough haven't you? You go on downstairs, it must be nearly supper-time . . .' she glanced at the Thorne's ebonised bracket clock above the fireplace and leapt to her feet, 'Oh goodness, look how late it is. I must run and rescue my casserole. Anyway, maybe I can say something to Alex about you and Duncan worrying over the bad atmosphere between them. He's often round at our place, after all. Don't worry, just a hint is all I intend.' She smiled reassuringly at Donna, who was also standing now. 'And I'm going to talk to Martin about buying your lovely painting of the new herb garden. I'm serious, I want it on my sitting-room wall.' She hugged Donna, enveloping her in her comfortable plumpness, then turned to Celia. 'Delicious Chardonnay, Celia. Thank you so much, and Hugh, of course. Now I really must rush. No, don't come to the door. Bye. Bye, Donna.'

As she trotted out with the painting Celia called goodbye to her, then nodded seriously at Donna. 'Congratulations. I think you've made your first sale there.'

Donna managed an embarrassed smile. 'Maybe.'

Celia took a deep breath. 'Tell me, does Sam know your period hasn't come?'

'No, I haven't said. Well, I've kept hoping it would.'

'You tell him, let him take some of the strain,' Celia said vigorously. 'I don't see why the men should get away with everything, do you?'

'It's difficult over the telephone, when you don't know who might be listening – at his end or mine.'

'Won't he be back this weekend?'

'No, he has to go to his dad. He says he'd rather be here

with me, but that's how it is with divorced parents, you're supposed to be fair to them both. Sam says it feels more like you're a bone they're both chewing on.' She thought for a moment. 'But then I feel like that chewed bone now, and it's not just for the occasional weekend, it's all the time.'

18

Over the many years of their marriage Hugh and Celia had observed small rituals. They mapped out times of the day; they made occasions for exchanging morsels of personal news, for exorcising worries, for small intimate jokes. One such time was Sunday morning tea-with-the-papers in bed, while others were pre-dinner drinks and their after-dinner coffee ritual. For this last, Celia was sent to luxuriate upon the sofa in the drawing-room while Hugh loaded the dishwasher prior to making coffee as they both liked it, with freshly ground coffee from the best coffee beans and no adulteration by way of milk or sugar. Then they would unwind together, listening to Mozart or Bach, or reading. It was all very ordered and comfortable.

Tonight, though, Hugh had heard Celia answering the telephone's summons while he made the coffee, and as he loaded the tray he had a grim feeling that it boded ill for his peace of mind, that it would be some busybody determined to involve him in some local legal problem, the sort impossible to reject without appearing churlish. Or if not a legal snarl-up, then something similarly unwelcome, neither ordered nor comfortable. He recognised a particular note in Celia's voice. He shouldered open the drawing-room door and carried the coffee tray to the sofa table to hear her concluding the conversation.

'Yes, of course you're right to be concerned. One wouldn't want this sort of bad feeling, still less scandal, hovering about the manor house like the reek of foul drains. I'll discuss your suggestion with Hugh and – though God knows I loathe the thought of it – I may do a bit of intervening myself . . .'

Hugh lifted his eyebrows and poured the coffee with disgruntlement. He had more than a grim feeling now, he had a certainty that he was going to be dragged into unpleasant matters and he was ninety-nine per cent sure he knew who and what. Why should he be the one to sort it out? The answer came prompt and pat: because he spent his days dealing with society's most dire matters; because he was the expert, the man of judgment. He put Celia's coffee down beside her. He felt weariness creep over him; a bleakness that drained his vitality, already lowered by the nastiness of the case he was trying. Why couldn't people leave him in peace? He was a judge, not a social worker. He struggled to keep professionally impartial. Yet constantly he was asked to lecture on this, to chair that, to evaluate, weigh up, recommend. The last thing he would choose to intervene in would be something not just 'on his doorstep', but actually here in his house. Damn Alex Lindridge.

What was Celia saying now?

'Yes, I know, Betty, and I agree entirely. No, no, you were right to raise it. I have to admit it's been on my mind also. No . . . no. Good night.' Her conversation ended, Celia slapped the telephone down and ran agitated fingers through her hair. She picked up her cup to gulp at the coffee as though it were whisky. Then she flung herself back against the sofa cushions, her face flushed, to look at Hugh.

'Tell me all,' he invited her, his heart contracting in sympathy, but then in abrupt contradiction shook his head and groaned, 'No, on second thoughts don't, please don't. I think I know what this is about and I refuse to be dragged in.'

She looked at him with contrition. 'I think we are both in already, out of sheer decency and because you've spoken to people on behalf of Alex.'

He sighed noisily. 'You're right. Go on, tell me the worst.'

'It's this: Brozie Hamilton rang Betty to tell her she'd heard much tut-tutting about certain newcomers to the village on her horticultural society network. The tale we've heard is going the rounds. Betty and Martin have been discussing the Lindridges' position and they've raised various points for us to consider. Like us they were already worried by the way Alex's too obvious infatuation with Margaret Jessop has led to such bad feeling between him and Fenella, and it concerns the Upcotts that the three of them may well create a scandal.' A deep breath. 'They are concerned not only on behalf of those immediately involved, like the unfortunate Donna, but also on behalf of other inhabitants of Brambourne Manor who could feel tainted by it.'

Hugh raised eloquent eyebrows. 'Taint by association? Euogh, my deah!'

Celia made a deprecating gesture with her hands. 'Yes, I know. But it mustn't be forgotten that Margaret is—'

'Oh God, yes, a doctor! So their frolics aren't simply a passing incident for the village to snort at or snigger over, they could involve the doctor-patient relationship. The million-dollar question being: *is Margaret in actual fact Alex's doctor?* Incidentally, I can't help wondering how seriously the BMA would take it. Originally the law was promulgated to protect the flustered female patient from the predatory male doctor! Can you see Alex as the complainant?'

Smiling at the farcical notion, Celia added, 'That Margaret has taken advantage of her position to force his trousers down and leap on top of him?'

'On her narrow surgical couch? Perish the thought. Besides, they clearly prefer bosky rural surroundings.' A pause. A sigh. 'But seriously, my love, it is grossly unprofessional behaviour and I hope to heaven Donna hasn't picked up on it.'

'Betty was strong on that point. But how can Donna be protected from gossips like Nancy Chubb or Lena? I hate to think how mortified she must be if she has heard. Betty says that in the Army this sort of nonsense would be jumped on at once by the man's commanding officer, while his wife might well have words with the woman concerned. And on an overseas posting the offender would be put on the next plane home. Hugh, I think she has you down as the commanding officer here and me as the CO's wife. In fact she didn't so much hint as demand that I should have a stiff talk with Margaret – and also discuss with Fenella the traumas that her daughter and possibly her son also, may well be suffering from the parental fights. So, my love, how do you fancy descending in wrath upon the sinful Alex?'

'I don't. Not at all.' Gloomily he added, 'This is a problem of living in the country, you know. One is forced to intervene, even to take sides. In London no one cares, there's too much going on, but in village communities one's under a microscope, and those like us are expected to uphold standards. I had a feeling something of this nature was going to be dumped on me when I heard you on the telephone with Betty. Oh hell, Celia, do I *have* to be involved?'

Looking at his appalled face, she almost laughed. 'Darling, it's not compulsory,' she said.

'But everyone concerned will think it is. After all, I'm the one who has known Alex Lindridge for years, who's tried to help him in his search for a decent appointment. So probably they're right. Well, you'd better fill me in on the details. And then I shall have to work out how best to tackle this to avoid repercussions.'

He recoiled from a precisely focussed distaste for this task, into real annoyance. He had treated Alex as a friend, been concerned for him, even silently sympathised over the man's difficulties with his snappy wife. Now the situation had taken on new aspects; startling secrets had emerged from the woodwork. Alex was far from the upright, immaculately behaved character Hugh had believed him, on the contrary, he was involved in an adulterous affair, not at a discreet distance like any sensible man, but beneath the same roof as his family; an affair that was becoming notorious and worse still, that could result in professional disaster for Margaret Jessop. And on top of that the man was distressing his wife and daughter, and embarrassing his neighbours. The very air of the manor house crackled with the venom that existed between Alex and Fenella. Celia was right; a stop must be put to this – but it was not so simple. In court everyone hung on his words, there he had the power to intervene and put an end to wrongful behaviour; here he had none, indeed, the whole business would be socially hazardous. His best path must be to alert Alex to the rumours, caution him as to his behaviour, mention in connection with Doctor Margaret those blood-chilling words, 'struck off the Medical Register'. And finally he could express his genuine concern about the stupid man's wife and daughter, upon whom the strain was falling.

Well, he certainly wouldn't tackle Alex here and now. He must shortly take his coffee to his desk and start work on his summing-up of the Jenkyns case. That held problems quite enough for this evening. At the forefront of his mind was the complication that Toyah had left the video-link room while being cross-examined. How could he best direct the jury? He would have to tell them that they must be sure they had been able to assess her credibility and reliability when giving evidence, as a whole. This was new law, an untried area – he must weigh each word to leave no avenues for appeal.

How was the weekend looking, then? Celia reminded him that they were spending Saturday at the Richmond house with their son and his wife and their grandchildren, but, she added, they were due to return here earlier than usual on Sunday to join a lunch party with James and Arabella at Abbotsbridge House. Right. Sunday it must be.

'Yes,' he told Celia. 'Leave Alex to me, I'll deal with him in due course.'

The defendant was giving evidence. Seated in the gallery at the back with her mother and Duncan, Donna stared down at him with frowning eyes, struggling to assess him from the jury's viewpoint. He wasn't very attractive, not with that bristly sprinkling of dark hair on his close-cropped skull and that round red face, but then he didn't look rat-faced and vicious either. He looked like the men you saw on building sites or driving the buses – Mr Anybody.

Mr Meredith, his hands clutching at his robes as usual, was taking Gary Jenkyns from the evening when he and Toyah had first met, roughly a month before the incident, until that evening among the dark trees of the New Forest. Gary said he had met Toyah and her sisters through his brother and he'd thought they were an OK family, lively and good fun. They'd been places together, like karaoke evenings or the cinema, and he'd given them a lift home in his van. On the evening concerned Toyah had been making up to him, coming on really strong and then she'd asked him to take her for a drive; yes, it was definitely at her request and no, she hadn't asked him to take her home. Without emotion he described how they had driven to the New Forest and how she'd wanted him to stop somewhere snug and out of sight, and then, as he turned the engine off, how she had moved into the centre seat of the van and put her arms around him.

No, he said, she had kissed him first, not him her, and then she went on kissing him passionately, and he described how for three or four hours they had had sexual intercourse in first one position and then another. Yes, he insisted, it had been not only with her consent but with her leading him. No, in his opinion she was not a virgin. Yes, he'd had a feeling Toyah might be under age so he had pleaded guilty to that. 'Put up my hands right away I did. But I wasn't the first, she knew what it was about all right, she was wild to act and be treated like an adult.'

Finally his counsel said: 'Are you quite certain she consented?'

'Yeah, I am,' Gary Jenkyns replied in an injured voice. 'Wanted it again and again, she did, and all the time she was saying she loved me.'

When Judge Hugh Thorne summed up to the jury he did so with slow care, putting the facts of the case, stressing that the jury must look, in particular, at whether they had been able sufficiently to assess Toyah's credibility, remembering that she had refused to conclude the cross-examination by defence counsel, Mr Meredith. They must weigh her evidence of a night of pain and fear against the defendant's tale of a night of passion. Also most importantly, they must consider the evidence which either supported or failed to support the crucial issue of consent. He concluded: 'In order to find the defendant guilty of rape you must be sure that she did not consent, and if you are sure, you also must be convinced that he did not believe that she consented, in accordance with my directions on the law. Members of the jury, please retire now and consider your verdict.'

'They convicted, the jury convicted,' Donna told her father breathlessly on their return from court late in the afternoon. 'It took them more than three hours, though. Roger must have been terribly on edge, though he didn't let it show. Mum was saying he's had a bad time recently with his divorce and everything, and he needed an opportunity to show how good he was. And he was, too. He didn't miss a point. It was shocking but it was riveting.'

'I'm glad you found it interesting,' Alex said stiffly. He wanted his darling daughter, and Duncan too, to find their lives stimulating and full of possibilities, but he would rather have been the contributor himself, not Fenella, especially not through repellent matters like child rape. 'So Roger won. Well, that's something. I'm glad to hear it.' He had no particular objection to Roger Dodson; among Fenella's awful café-society family and friends you could rank him as reasonable, a person you could mention in public with confidence.

'We had some tea while we were waiting for the verdict,' Donna told him. 'And Duncan asked Roger what sort of sentence Gary Jenkyns would get if he was found guilty and Roger said it must be life, with the judge stipulating the minimum number of years that he must serve, because he'd done it twice before, taking under-aged girls into woods like he'd done with Toyah and he would be considered dangerous. Next time he might kill the girl so she couldn't give evidence against him and put him back in prison. Roger said he had only been out for a month before he attacked Toyah. And you

wouldn't have known he was vile from his face, no way. But
he was.'

'Roger reckoned he convicted himself,' Duncan said, 'with
his weird fantasies about a night of passion with a nympho
that came out when he was giving evidence—'

'Yes, that's right,' Donna interpolated. 'What he said didn't
fit with anything about that poor traumatised little girl.'

'It sounds horrific,' Alex said, 'and I'm still not at all sure
you should have been there listening to it.'

'Oh, don't be daft, Dad,' Duncan said impatiently. 'We
both learnt a huge amount. I know you've taught us more
than most kids know about how the law and the courts work,
but seeing the law in action in a desperately tricky case like
that is something totally different. It's . . . it's so *there*, listening to both sides fighting it out and hearing arguments
over points of law, and realising what the rules are there for.
And anything we didn't understand Roger was terrific at
going through afterwards, like who can speak when and why,
or when a witness can be led. He's great. Why don't we see
more of him?'

'We could, actually,' Donna contributed. 'He said he's
spending Easter here, staying at the Wykeham Arms. He has
barrister friends in Winchester, so he's out to lunch on Good
Friday and dinner on the Saturday, and said he'd enjoy the
Easter Service at the cathedral. Why,' she enquired enthusi-
astically, 'why can't he come to the art exhibition and the
point-to-point with us?'

A dozen fors and againsts jostled for position in Alex's
mind, finally resolving into two fors: that Roger's presence
would ensure reasonable behaviour from Fenella *vis-à-vis*
his Margaret, and that, should the Manningfords invite them
to join their party at the point-to-point, Roger would be more
than acceptable in their company.

'Would you like that?' he asked his wife and Duncan, feeling saintly.

Duncan nodded his agreement. 'Yeah, he's all right, he
really is.'

'Kind of you,' Fenella said in a voice that shook oddly. 'I'd like it – and I know I'm speaking for Roger when I say he would too.'

It was mid-morning on Sunday when Alex was running upstairs in the hope of a quick word with his Margaret that he was confronted on the first floor by Hugh Thorne emerging from his flat to block his way.

'Ah, Alex, we need to talk,' he said in a brusque tone. 'Free now, are you?'

Alex hesitated, cursing beneath his breath; he ached to discover whether the doctors had come to a decision about his offer to manage their move to the new surgery, and he was certain they'd had a meeting the previous afternoon. Besides, he longed to give his Maggy, Meggy, Megs a kiss. But the Judge was crucial to him as his most valuable supporter in the job market and he spoke as if he had something of importance to communicate. The two men looked at each other; Alex groaned internally and let his eyes drop. It was vital that he should retain a good relationship with Hugh, vital too that he should not suspect the delicious relationship he had with Margaret. This was especially important since he clearly took pride in his odiously exemplary relationship with the arrogant Celia.

'Of course,' he said. 'I am at your disposal. Would you care for a coffee at my place?'

'No. I have some freshly made. Come in, will you?'

Following him, Alex wondered whether Hugh Thorne might have a lead on another appointment vacancy. That could pose problems if the doctors had decided they wanted to take his offer up, but on the other hand he had to move on, he simply must. Perhaps he could combine both, working in the evenings and at the weekends. Yes, that would be the answer; a wonderful excuse to get away from Fenella, to spend time with Margaret. And at the thought of Fenella's impotent irritation his face relaxed into a grin of pleasure.

He was steered into the dining-room, where an aroma of excellent coffee hung on the air. Unsmiling, Hugh pulled out a chair for him, seating himself at the head of the table. He poured coffees from a cafetière, pushed one at Alex, indicated milk and sugar with a twist of a black eyebrow, then leaned back in his big carver chair, his hazel eyes on Alex, cool and assessing.

Feeling unnervingly like a schoolboy summoned to the headmaster's study, Alex waited to hear what he had to say.

'Are you by any chance Margaret Jessop's patient?'

'No. I'm not. Why?'

'You haven't registered with her?'

'No.' He sipped from his cup. What was this? Without knowing why, Alex felt perspiration break out under his arms. The coffee was too hot, the room was stuffy. He stared at Hugh, registered the cold eyes, and then an idea began to take shape in his head. But surely the Judge couldn't be thinking . . .? 'I rarely succumb to illness. I've registered with neither doctor.'

Hugh took a deep breath. 'I'm relieved to hear it. You'll want to know why I'm asking you this. The reason – and I intend to be frank – is that it is being said in Brambourne and Abbotsbridge that you and Margaret Jessop are having an affair. Were you her patient and a complaint was made, this could put her in a most difficult situation as regards the BMA. In short, she could be struck off the General Medical Register. But I accept your assurance that this is not your position.'

Alex flinched with shock that was followed immediately by resentment. He tried to moisten his lips with his tongue, but his mouth was dry. He took a gulp of coffee so hot that it scalded his throat. Hell! Fenella, it must be her doing, this spreading of evil gossip; the self-righteous Celia the channel of its foulness spreading to Hugh Thorne. He struggled to reply with calm disdain, his brain searching urgently for the words to persuade Hugh of the irreproachable nature of his relationship with the doctor.

He looked him in the face. 'I can't imagine who or what you may have heard but I can assure you my relationship with Margaret has been precisely that of chauffeur.' He permitted himself a faint self-deprecating smile, 'I've been

happy during my own excess of free time to help her cope
with the pressures which arise from running a busy rural
practice.' He was suddenly burning with anger at the frustrations of his position, caught as he was between Fenella
and Margaret, and in that moment he quite believed in his
own innocence. In his view, the relationship was one of great
purity and beauty, filled with the most idealistic intentions.
He added with all the indignation of that position, 'I do find
your report of such rumours singularly unpleasant. I'm
shocked at hearing what you say and I'd be glad if you would
tell me who says it.'

Fenella, inevitably; it had to be her. She was the source of
all his unhappiness, of any and all of his failures. She weak-
ened his strength, sapped his pride. At his age he should
have been at the zenith of his success. Martin had spoken
recently of his luck in acquiring a worthwhile appointment
'in the autumn of his life'. To Alex that was rubbish; he considered himself to be at the height of his powers, in the
summer of his strength. As he took another mouthful of the
coffee he thought with sick longing of beating the tattling
Fenella up, of thumping her with his fists until she passed
out in agony. Dear God, she was causing him pain enough,
the bitch, the mean trouble-making hypocritical bitch. When
she had a lover all the time herself. He could have relished
strangling Celia, too, throttling her until she choked and her
eyes bulged.

Hugh was still looking at him, saying nothing, and Alex
felt himself begin to shake. Bile rose in his throat and he
wished he hadn't drunk that over-strong coffee. Why was
the Judge staring, no, glaring so? Was he waiting for him to
commit himself? To confess? Well, Alex had nothing to be
ashamed about.

'Is it my wife who has been saying things that could be
misinterpreted? She does have her paranoid moments. She
could be foolishly worried about the appearance of my relationship with Margaret.' He smiled faintly, shrugging his
shoulders. 'I've reassured her, indeed our two families are
doing things together over Easter, but it's her age, I suppose.'

'Your wife has said nothing whatever to me,' Hugh said, his voice glacial now. 'However, the person who has, the cleaner shared by our two households, reports that her cousin Glenn has recently seen you and Margaret from his tractor seat, ah, hard at it, I believe was his expression, on the edge of some copse on the far side of a field hedge. Since Lena, as you'll probably know, happens to be Nancy Chubb's sister, the tale of that lad's fascinating glimpse will no doubt be circulating through both Brambourne and Abbotsbridge even at this moment.'

Alex, shattered by this bad luck, sat speechless with shock. He also felt quite startlingly angry with Margaret over her zany idea that love was at its most natural and fulfilling in the wild outdoors, and revolted to think that her folly had handed to some probably illiterate oaf on a tractor such an opportunity for lurid gossip. Women had the most vexatious power to compel a man to sexual passion in hazardous situations. God, he felt sick. How in hell was he to defend himself?

Finally he half-shouted. 'This is all quite ridiculous. What can I say? Hearsay and malice and exaggeration; it's like Chinese whispers – did you ever play that game at school? I do remember we once had a quick picnic lunch among the trees on a fine day. Between visits to patients, that's all. I would never do anything that would bring Margaret into disrepute. You must believe that, Hugh.' His breath quickened with indignation. 'You've known me for many years.'

There was a pause while Hugh regarded him rather as he might some thuggish defendant who persisted in denying his offence in the face of indisputable evidence. Finally he said, 'I have known you some time. But not socially. Not . . . intimately.' There was a cool irony in his voice. 'There are other matters to be considered also. Others who are involved whether they like it or not. Or may become so. Your son and daughter. The doctor's son.'

'Donna,' Alex said. His darling clever Donna. She must never hear of this sickening development. One day Margaret would become his wife, but whatever happened he must keep Donna free from the nastiness that had enveloped his own parents while they went through their rancorous divorce. He would never allow . . . What was Hugh Thorne saying now in that curt voice?

'. . . I think we've all noticed Donna looking pale and troubled recently. Betty Upcott and Celia – and I myself – are becoming concerned that the extreme tension between you and Fenella is reacting on her, quite apart from the inevitable stress she's under from the approach of her examinations. She's still a young girl struggling to cope with her transition to adulthood, with her first real involvement with a boyfriend – and in what miserably tangled circumstances? You have to face your responsibilities, Alex, it's a difficult situation you've put her in.'

Alex stared at him in horror. Could someone have told Donna of this rumour about himself and Margaret? No, no, impossible. No one would be so cruel. And they had always been careful around the manor house. He was furious that Fenella should have run to their neighbours whining of their disagreements. She must have; how else would they know of any of this? His shock was increasing with every second, and his disgust with those interfering females, Celia and Betty, for airing their views and their half-baked theories on whatever psychosis they imagined his children might be suffering from, ruining his all-important relationship with the Judge. He had thought better of Betty at least.

He told Hugh, his resentment clear in his tone, 'Donna's care is at the forefront of my mind each and every day. I help her with her GCSE work, I am always available for her, and if she has had any worries or problems I am certain we'd have talked them over together. Her relationship with her mother is another matter. Fenella is not interested in living in the country and she is given to complaining about my current lack of a job, to making her unhappiness known, but I cannot believe that is traumatising Donna. On the contrary, Donna loves the countryside as I do, and wants Fenella to see it from our point of view.'

'Alex, you are missing the point. The sounds of raised

voices do rise up through the floorboards, you know. We hear them – and yours is the dominant voice. Had you realised that? I have seen Donna's face when she has been up here with us at such times. She hates it. And it's clear she's embarrassed in a way that's hard for a girl of her age to cope with.' His lips tightened. 'Her own parents! Don't you think that Fenella and you should try talking in reasonable terms to one another rather than indulging in raging battles? Or if you can't do that, agree to disagree and part? To stay together for the sake of your children may be burdening them both with a terrible feeling of responsibility for your unhappiness. Shouldn't you ask them how they feel?'

Alex gazed about the room with a hunted look. He did not know what to say. He had never been so disconcerted in all his life. He felt as if the aloof voice had somehow stripped him naked, leaving every flaw in his nature visible for the world to gloat over and despise. He no longer knew how to respond to Hugh Thorne's charges; he found them loathsome and the Judge was vile too. Everything in his life had become twisted as Hugh spoke; everything put in an ugly light. Worst of all, for the first time it had been borne in upon him that he might bear a part of the blame for the present horrors, that however good his intentions, he and Fenella were doing no better than his parents had in their break-up. They, too, were visiting their traumas on their young.

No, no, not true. The Judge must be exaggerating. Alex loosened the tight knot of his tie, licked his lips. He could smell his own sweat now. He had no words and the silence was becoming unendurable. He must escape, tell Margaret of these horrors he'd heard, force her to take him seriously so that she'd rely upon him to solve their crises, lean on him for once. Somehow, burbling he knew not what, he managed to get across the room to the door and escape through it.

19

He was running down the stairs to his flat when he heard Margaret calling him. 'Alex! He looked up, shaking, his feet still rushing him away from his humiliation beneath Hugh Thorne's cold words, from a situation he could only see as a total disaster, to see his foolish careless love, the source of this disaster, leaning over the top banisters, beckoning and opening her mouth to call down. No, please no!

His finger tapped his lips urgently, his face fell into lines of anguish. There couldn't have been a worse moment. She looked at him, eyebrows lifted, then beckoned again, vigorously. He mouthed, 'Two secs', ran to his own front door, opened and then loudly closed it again, swivelled on his heels and tiptoed back up to her, catching her by the waist and jerking her into her own little apartment, closing her door with a trembling and silent care.

His hands gripped her arms. 'Darling, it's awful and I hate to tell you this, but all hell's broken loose.'

Margaret blinked and frowned. 'Calm down, Alex. What hell?'

'Over us, for God's sake. Remember when we were making love in that little spinney and I heard a tractor nearby and you pooh-poohed me? Well, I can tell you now there was one, and what's more the driver saw us and now the tale is round the villages in no small way!'

'Christ, no! So who told you that?'

Alex crunched out the words: 'Judge Hugh Thorne.' He

remembered the icy voice grating like a shifting glacier, the eyes that censured him, his own almost total deficiency in countering the Judge's attack. 'He has such a tortuous clever way of going about things, that man. He started off by merely mentioning rumours, about the dangers of a doctor in your position being struck off . . . I brushed it off, said I wasn't your patient, simply your temporary chauffeur. Trouble was, I couldn't imagine where he could have heard this from except Fenella, possibly via Celia, so I murmured something about Fenella's age and paranoia, and I thought he was accepting that because he was just looking at me and listening, but then suddenly he comes out with this sickening stuff about the lad on the tractor . . .'

Margaret stopped him. 'Exactly how far has it gone then?'

It was her fault it had gone anywhere, her and her folly. He wanted to shock her, savagely. 'That lad, Glenn, is a young cousin of our cleaner – and since Lena is Nancy Chubb's sister, I leave it to your imagination where it won't have gone.'

He had jolted her. She backed away from him. Her knees seeming to buckle under her, she sat down abruptly in a chair.

'You see what you . . .' he began.

'Shut up, will you, Alex,' she snapped. 'I have to think. Rumours like this could affect my practice in particular and the new group practice in general very badly. Folk round here are self-righteous about the imperfections of people like their doctors, however dubious their own conduct.'

He could feel his whole self rejecting her, feel his face settling into censorious lines. How narrow was the range of her concern. What about his own most valuable asset, the good will of the Judge? He had little hope of winning a new position without his recommendations. Did she realise how much damage she had done to his future?

Margaret rose and the sea-green eyes focussed on him. He recognised that sharp knowing look of hers, but before he could speak she anticipated him. 'No. Don't say anything. Yes, I know you're vitally concerned too, but I'm thinking this through for both of us. We'd better have a glass of wine each for the shock, and I must concentrate. I've the germ of an idea that could work. Wait, and don't see yourself as the focus of everything, Alex, because you aren't. There's a way round every setback, if you have the nerve to find it and use it.'

Alex sat, every muscle clenched rigid. He was shocked that she did not regard this as the utter catastrophe he did. She had not turned to him for advice, she had not leaned on him; on the contrary, he was expected to wait upon her ideas, her solution. So far as he could see there was nothing to be done, except to remain disdainfully silent and let himself be seen on amicable relations with Fenella. It would be hell, but an essential hell. At least, he remembered, relieved by his own skilful anticipation of trouble, he had made plans for all his family to go to events over Easter together with Margaret and Sam. Members of the local community like the Manningfords would see them all in company at the Hackwood Park point-to-point, to all appearances in complete amity.

Margaret reappeared with two glasses of wine, her hair rumpled, but the look on her face slyly demure. She pushed a glass into his hand. 'Eureka! I think it can be overcome, Alex, if we act in unison.' As if guessing his own ideas she offered him a derisive smile and added in an almost light-hearted manner, 'Not, my dear, by facing it out and hoping that Fenella will assist us in a spirit of self-protection, but by admitting to everything *and more.*'

'What in hell do you mean?' He could feel fear running along his nerves. He was brutally over-exposed already. 'Go on, what?'

She gulped at her wine, dropped down onto the bamboo sofa, leaned forward and actually laughed. 'We make a non-sense of it, Alex, an over-the-top joke. If the locals mention certain rumours about us, we chortle and ask if that's all they've heard, because if it is, they haven't heard the half of it – how about the story that has us swinging naked through the branches of The Bull's old oak tree only the other night . . .'

'. . . yodelling like Tarzan and Jane!' Alex contributed, half aghast, half laughing, and perceiving – while fearful at her nerve – the first dawning of hope.

'Got it in one. Or that if they climb Flintpen Ring at dawn on Easter Sunday they'll see us and our friends offering druidic sacrifices – then flinging off our robes and indulging in orgies!'

'Brilliant, my Maggy Megs, wholly scintillating – if I were a different person. Can you honestly see me, the dignified ex-civil servant, carrying that sort of thing off?'

Margaret considered him. 'Why not? You'll do it ultra dryly, looking down your nose. And giving people thin smiles. And then you'll ask, with just one eyebrow raised, whether it wasn't Glenn who'd been burbling about someone seen in flagrante with Brozie Hamilton among the church-yard tombs!'

'Brozie in her wellies, naturally. Yes!' He found huge comfort in Margaret's humour. 'And then we ask who's the joker who's been spiking a certain lad's drinks.' He raised his glass. 'Here's confusion to the gruesome Glenn.' He drank with a zest that would have astounded him only seconds previously.

'That deluded lad,' she said, finishing her glass of wine. 'I'll teach him to spy and gossip. We must polish our tales a touch first, but once we get going the tittle-tattle will soon die. There'll be chortles in the pubs for a day or two, but no one will be too sure who or what at. We'll outsmart the gossips, we'll simply brazen it out.'

Alex's smile had energy in it. The allure she held for him had taken on a new dimension with this glimpse of her wild sense of mischief. 'You're so clever. God, you've taken a weight off my shoulders. I drink to you!' He held out his glass for a refill and drank deeply. 'Listen, my lovely, on a different matter – have you and the other doctors decided yet whether to accept my offer to manage the move?'

'Oh yes, that's what I wanted to discuss when I called you up.' She kicked off her shoes, tucked her feet beneath her on the sofa and leaned against the colourful cushions.

'But things have moved on since we spoke of it. Remember that girl Kylie who rang in a few days ago saying she couldn't work because she was writhing in agony with food-poisoning? It turns out the lying cow wasn't sick at all, simply that she had an interview for a similar post in a practice in Romsey where she lives, and decided not to tell us in case she didn't get it and we turned against her for looking elsewhere. But she was offered it and now she vanishes in a month – at this time of all times! She's not half bad, that lass, and the masses of rules and regulations and returns the Health Service lumber us with are fiendish for anyone fresh to cope with. So, at our meeting we were all feeling pretty frenzied about how to replace her until I thought of you.'

'Of me?' He blinked, startled.

'Well, yes.' She eyed him uncertainly. 'I mean, we were all for leaping at your offer to co-ordinate our move in any case, but then I thought, well, you're more than computer competent and you have to be used to dealing with complicated sets of regulations and rules, and – well, to cut a long story short, dearest Alex – we wondered if you'd be interested in the position of our practice manager from a month hence. Plus we would like you to deal with the move from next week on. We'd pay you for that separately. How about it?'

It was the most improbable offer in the world and it had happened to him – the chance to work alongside his Margaret! He was awed by the random nature of luck. But wait, he must be certain what was on offer. Luck wasn't normally his bosom companion. He asked what the doctors envisaged by way of salary and what exactly the post entailed. At Margaret's reply his sallow cheeks bloomed and his eyes brightened in their shadowed sockets. Such earnings would double the pension he considered so meagre (and would certainly be on equal terms with Martin's earnings), while the post itself, if hardly at the level he had risen to in the Lord Chancellor's Department, held interest and scope sufficient to be well worth exploring.

'It'll be a hefty enterprise, controlling and administering the whole affair when we have the new group practice up and going,' Margaret told him. 'The job will be considerably more serious than anything Kylie's handling now – and twice the size for a start. That'll mean twenty-five or more of us to keep tabs on. Not just us doctors, but the five receptionists we'll need and the secretarial help, as well as the pharmacists for the dispensary, and two practice nurses, two midwives, two district nurses and a couple of physiotherapists all coming and going. And cleaners, of course.'

Alex was filled with relief and euphoria. His horizons had shrunk, now they were expanding almost tangibly. He would be employed, a person of status within the local villages. Not in the eyes of the wider world, perhaps, but would that matter? Here was where it counted, here where he lived, and where he could love and work with his Margaret.

'My sweetheart, I should be very interested indeed.'

'Only one drawback.'

'What's that?'

'We'll have to behave terribly properly indeed.'

'Only in public, please.'

A soft laugh. 'Naturally.'

Happiness vibrated through him. 'I revel in being natural!'

When Alex eventually arrived back with his family he found them in a state of excitement, all talking at once. Duncan called out, 'Look! Look, Dad!' picked up a small piece of paper and waved it in the air at him.

'What is it?' Alex asked, startled.

'A cheque for—'

Donna snatched it from her brother's hand and pushed it beneath her father's nose. He stepped back to focus his eyes on a cheque made payable to Donna Lindridge for one hundred and twenty-five pounds and signed by Martin Upcott.

'Dad, I've sold my first painting! Martin's giving Betty one of my paintings as her birthday present. Isn't that amazing? Look. They left it here for me to sign for them, as if my signature were worth something!'

The painting was lying on the table and he turned to see which it was had received this startling honour. To his shock he had no memory of it. But surely Donna showed him everything she did? Had done so since she was a small child dabbing colourful splodges of fingerpaint at her paper? The sound of wood pigeons came through the window. He saw a knot garden beside an elderly house, apparently painted from an almost aerial perspective, a scene that was gently formal, patterned, full of charm. It rang a bell in the recesses of his mind. Was it in Brambourne? In Abbotsbridge? For a moment his mind flagged and he pushed at it, searching urgently. Fenella would be full of scorn if he admitted to ignorance of one of his Donna's pictures. The wood pigeons' cooing filtered into the room again; they must be up in the big horse chestnuts to the side of the house. And then he recognised those very horse chestnuts in the painting and in a flash of relief saw that he was looking at a futuristic glimpse of Betty's herb garden. Of course, and that was Martin's reason for buying it for her birthday. Well. He licked dry lips, struggling to find words to express his pleasure and pride.

'It's great,' he said. 'You've conjured up Betty's vision of her herbarium, placing it beside the reality of the old west wall of the house. It's where it should rightly be, I can see that. She's talented, Betty, like you, at transforming the ordinary but it's you who've brought its charms to life in your deft painting. No wonder Martin bought it. And at a generous price too. Well done, sweetheart. You'll be finding yourself with commissions soon!'

'She's painted it in an old-fashioned style, which suits that old wing and the herb garden well, don't you think?' Fenella said. 'And her proportions and perspective are exact, as always.'

Today had started terrifyingly, vilely, for Alex, but now everything appeared auspicious. His Donna's talents as an artist had been recognised, and recognised financially (the only way most men and women appraise such matters), while she was still only sixteen. In addition he and his

Margaret had found a way to outface the traducers and the malicious, to joke off the slanderous rumours. Together they'd achieve a new future, a special image for the practice (he'd turn it into a shining example of how such things should be run), and for themselves. In his rising relief he felt almost warm towards Fenella.

'I agree with you that the style is absolutely right for Betty and her sitting-room. It looks as though it were meant for it. Ah, and we must open a bank account for you, Donna. I'll drive you into Winchester – and we'll add something in from us. After all, you're going on for seventeen – and to mark the occasion we'll change your pocket money into an allowance payable monthly. Rites of your passage to adult status. How's that? Do you agree, Fenella?'

'Yes, I do. I was thinking along those lines too. You're quite right, Donna's old enough to deal with her own finances.'

'That'd be great,' Donna said, looking startled but pleased. 'Thanks.'

'You're sounding very cheerful, Dad,' Duncan said. 'Has something good happened?'

Alex hesitated whether to tell them of the job possibility. They'd seen him fall flat on his face before when he'd thought he was on to a virtual certainty. He hated to be pitied, knowing such pity all too often covers scorn. He had, of course, as Margaret had said, to be interviewed, checked and agreed as suitable by both doctors from the other practice, yet this was something different, he knew it internally. Margaret and Jane Field were already all for him, while he had spoken to the other two doctors on several occasions when he'd run Margaret over to look at the new surgery building, looking with them for solutions to unforeseen problems. And then he had twice sat in as their note-taker on long meetings to thrash out their guidelines for the organisation and running of the new practice. There had been no difficulties between him and Bruce Matthews or Peter Dickson; on the contrary, when he had raised points, 'as a patient might see it', they had been grateful for his contribution, nodding their approval, deferring to him where details of administrative and financial matters were concerned. Smiling to himself, he recollected how last week he had ended up acting more as chairman than mere note-taker when the women had disagreed with the men, defusing a suddenly loaded dispute over how and when doctors should cover one for another. And they had been grateful for his intervention, shaking his hand warmly as they left.

'Well, I wasn't intending to say anything, but since you've asked, the possibility of an interesting post has come my way.'

'What?' Duncan asked.

'As practice manager for the local doctors' new group practice.'

'What does that entail?' Fenella this time, her voice neutral.

'It's concerned with the day-to-day running of the doctors' and staff hours and work responsibilities. There'd be regular contact with the local health authority, with social services and community care, all that sort of thing. Then there's the pharmacy side to be kept running smoothly. And I'd be in touch with the accountants and the bank – book-keeping, financial matters . . . On the private side, there'd be reports to insurance companies, occasionally to solicitors.' He paused, not knowing quite how to put it to his waiting family. He said: 'I've all the qualities and experience necessary – and they've approached me, not the other way around.'

He was abruptly dissolved in yearning. He could not remember ever feeling such an overbearing need to become a part of a group of people as the need flooding through him now. He felt young again, uplifted, idealistic. He was too far gone in years to become a doctor, as he had told Martin he might once have liked, but he knew he could work at his best with this team – small, close-knit and intent – taking his place among them in the care of their patients. The thought of it cheered him massively, quite disproportionately, he admitted to himself, as the menace of Hugh Thorne flashed through his mind. Nevertheless he felt his cheeks flushing with anticipatory pleasure. And he must, he knew he must, be winding Fenella up wonderfully. Surely she must leave him soon, give Margaret and him the chance to be discreetly content together, and, in the fullness of time, openly so.

Aloud he added that Bruce Matthews and Peter Dickson, the doctors from the practice at Litton, would have to interview him, but Jane and Margaret seemed to think there'd be no problems. 'They said they'd be lucky if I took the post. So it's not certain, but I'm . . . I'm cheering myself with hope.'

He looked at his family, at Duncan and Donna, warily alert, their faces somehow clenched up, sliding glances between him and Fenella, now oddly silent. He saw clearly that his children were anticipating an outburst from their mother, anticipating and dreading it. But Fenella's expression was one of unnatural calm and detachment.

'It's certainly something you could do,' she said. 'And appropriate for you.'

What in hell did she mean by that?

'It would be full time, wouldn't it?' Duncan said.

'Very, especially to start with,' Alex agreed, still watching Fenella.

'Would it pay a reasonable salary?' Donna wanted to know.

'Reasonable enough. Added to my pension it would increase my income considerably.'

'Then,' said Donna on an inborne breath of triumph, 'I could have a clothing allowance as well as a pocket money deal. I need new jeans and things urgently.'

'We could certainly do that, in fact I already had it in mind,' he said, and saw Fenella nod her agreement. 'Keep your fingers crossed for me, won't you?'

He smiled benignly upon them. This was all good – except that Fenella's lack of antagonism seemed unnatural. A vague feeling of let-down crept over him and the thought flitted through his mind that subconsciously he'd been awaiting a row that would demonstrate to Donna and Duncan how unfair she was to him; always ready to put him in the wrong, objecting even to a perfectly good offer of a post. But nothing had happened. If it had, he would have been forbearing, gentle in his murmured replies, yet subtly antagonising her to the point that Hugh and Celia would have heard her voice noisily dominate the argument, not his. Only she'd been agreeable, taking him aback. He frowned. Why?

Donna telephoned Sam at his father's house, impelled by her twin news items, both of huge importance.

'Do you want the good news or the bad news first?' she asked.

'Worst first is what my father always says. Go on then, what's so awful in your life?'

His voice was flippant and it annoyed Donna. She told him, tersely, and his reaction sounded gratifyingly appalled. 'But it can't have not come! You took that pill. This is awful. Does it mean . . . you know . . .?'

'That I'm pregnant? I don't know. Could be.' Let him sweat too.

'But hold on, what about a test? You must have taken one.'

'Of course I did and it was negative, but that doesn't always mean anything.'

'What do you mean? Why not?'

She was muttering, anxious that her parents should catch nothing of this call. 'A girl I know took a test when she was five days late and it came out negative, so she thought she was all right. But when her period still hadn't come days later, she thought she'd do another – and then it was posi-tive and she was pregnant after all. She had to have an abortion.'

'You must take another test. We have to know, don't we?'

Donna was suddenly invaded by fear, heart thumping, breath shortening. Images flashed through her of angry voices, more rows, of impossible decisions to be taken – of sickness, pain and blood. 'I can't. I couldn't bear it if it were

true. What would I say to my parents? What would I do?'
She had to push the decisions away. As long as she didn't
know she was pregnant the worst wouldn't have happened.
She could hope. Sufficient unto the day is the evil thereof.
Her grandmother used to say that, Grandma Lindridge who
had good and bad ghosts lingering in her Devon cottage.
Tears pricked Donna's eyes at the memory. Dad had disliked
his mother, rarely visited her, spoke of her as a bad wife
and a bad mother, but Donna had loved her. She wished her
grandmother were here now, a tough but comforting old
lady.

'Look,' Sam said, 'I'm sorry you're going through all this,
very sorry, but you'd feel far better if you knew you weren't,
wouldn't you?' His urgent voice conveyed his amazement at
the illogical nature of her approach to so worrying a problem.

'But suppose I am? I'd be suicidal. I can't take the risk.'

'Donna, you have to be joking . . .'

'No,' she snapped. 'Leave it. You don't know what it's like
here. Look, Sam, I'll see you at Easter. That's only days away.
We just have to hope.'

She put the telephone down. The thought of his anxieties
gave her something approaching comfort. Two seconds later
she realised how their conversation had never shifted on
from the bad news to the good, that they had never discussed the wonder of the sale of her painting. She
contemplated picking up the receiver again, only to dismiss
the idea. A miserable brag. No, she would tell him about
that amazing first cheque at the art exhibition on Easter Day.
Her work, like the great works on the gallery walls, had been
held to be of value; perhaps Sam would link the two, con-
juring up images of early success, anticipating a glowing
future for her.

In her room she lay on her bed. She had a feeling of refuge
there. Tension's claws were gradually loosening their grip:
Sam knew of her anxieties, Celia and Betty, too. She was no
longer aching alone. She lay for a few minutes, eyes closed,
trying to push out unwanted thoughts. Then she turned
impatiently to reach for a French textbook. She would

sustain her mind with something positive. She'd check up on those stupid irregular verbs.

On Easter Sunday afternoon Roger arrived at Southampton Art Gallery ahead of the rest of the party. When Donna failed to see him as she peered around the ground floor, with its inevitable little marts for buying postcards, for choosing reproductions of pictures and mementos, she agonised that perhaps he wasn't coming. She needed him there for his large and easy sanity, to keep the warring parts of the group separate, to amuse and charm them into good behaviour.

'We won't wait for Roger,' her father decided. 'Let's find this exhibition. He'll discover us easily enough.'

The art gallery was a place of echoing halls. Someone, a curator she supposed, told them that the exhibition was on the first floor, and an unusual open staircase of shining wooden treads and chrome tubes took them up to the splendid gallery there, where sturdy rectangular pillars, painted in green stripes on white, rose from their large and solid bases to soar in great arches far above their heads. The few people looking at the pictures seemed lost amid their immensity. Donna stood rooted to the floor to take it in; this was really different, so massive in design, so light in colour. Except, she decided, that the pillars and the side aisles reminded her of Brambourne's mediaeval church.

'Very nineteen thirties,' Alex observed in neutral tones from behind her, staring round.

Thirteen thirties, nineteen thirties, what did it matter? 'It's great,' she said.

Roger emerged from behind a pillar across the room, waved vigorously and called, 'Hello, Alex, hello Fenella, good to see you. Hi, Donna, come and see this!'

Donna started off across the floor. 'Hi, Roger.'

Behind her, Alex muttered, 'Tsk. Bring him over to meet everyone, will you?'

Roger gave Donna a bear hug and with an arm still round her swung her towards an exhibit: 'Here, look at that picture, will you!'

Donna saw a pattern of yellow, cream and white stems and leaves reaching out gracefully across the big canvas, in a design that reminded her of the curlicues painted around mediaeval illuminated manuscripts. There were tiny faces like seed cases, and also, two by two, what she thought at first were large glittery mahogany knobs, quite out of scale and colour with the rest of this creation, but finally, in a leap of inspiration, identified as, 'Elephant dung! It's a Chris Ofili,' she said, drawing in her breath in mingled surprise and hilarity. 'I didn't know there was any of his stuff here.'

'It's called *Two Doo Voodoo*,' Roger said, 'and it consists of acrylic, oil, resin, paper collage, glitter, map pins and elephant dung on canvas. I shall await your judgment.'

Having examined from near to the straw-flecked dung bedecked with its glitter and pins, Donna stepped back. 'The dung lumps are sort of attractive,' she allowed. 'Rather like big Victorian pincushions. But I can't make out any relationship between those pretty painted curlicues that cover most of the canvas and the glittery brown lumps. They may hold deep psychological meanings for Chris Ofili, but onlookers like us aren't necessarily going to pick up on his subtleties, are we? I think they look out of place.'

Roger nodded and looked round. Since Donna had not immediately taken him to meet the rest of the party, Alex and Fenella and the others were now advancing on them, Alex frowning at this failure of his daughter's manners.

'Good afternoon, Roger,' he began, holding out his hand, but Roger side-stepped him to take Fenella in his arms, hugging and kissing her with the same enthusiasm he had shown for Donna.

'Ah, Fenny, my lovely cousin, how are you today?' he asked fondly before turning to shake hands briefly with Alex and more cordially with Duncan: 'Well, it's a long time since I last saw you, Alex. Been going through a bad time recently, I hear. Hard luck. Not the only one either. Still, I'm cheered in my loneliness in coming to this gallery with you. A good thought from Fenella. I shall be able to boast to my friends of seeing the works of famous artists.' A faint mockery entered his voice. 'One always feels one must keep up a wide range of interests, doesn't one? But in a busy life like mine I'd miss out on matters like this if I didn't have Fenny to keep me up to the mark. I hope you realise how lucky you are yourself.'

He swivelled his attention to Margaret and Sam and before Alex could open his mouth to introduce them, made him appear lacking in manners by addressing Margaret, 'Now you must be the doctor Fenella speaks of to me – Margaret, isn't it? – and . . . and Sam, I believe.' He shook hands. 'And I'm Roger, distant family one way or another to the rest of the party.' He examined them closely, not quite smiling, yet offering an appearance of geniality. He spoke directly to Margaret. 'How are you and your son liking life at Brambourne Manor?'

'It's a delightful place,' she acknowledged, returning his inspection with interest. 'And we've such pleasant and help-ful neighbours. Alex in particular has transformed our lives with his kindnesses.' The words were spoken with a drawled nonchalance that was almost a challenge.

There was a second's pause broken by a childish voice behind them. 'Mummy,' it asked, 'what's the brown stuff on this picture?'

They swung round. A slim young woman in a smart navy tracksuit, accompanied by a skinny blonde girl of seven or eight, had halted in the aisle to study the Ofili. She caught their eyes, raised her own heavenward, then bent to her child, responding in a toneless voice, 'It's elephant poo, Amy.'

'It's *what*?' The child frowned at it, then turned to look at the group behind her, startled, embarrassed lest her mother, now walking on, might have been making fun of her.

Roger reassured her. 'It is elephant poo. Funny, isn't it? But it's true.'

The child studied the brown lumps again, pulled a face and ran off after her mother.

Alex denounced the work. 'That stuff's pathetic and dis-gusting. The public health authorities ought to take action.'

In an expressionless voice Margaret remarked, 'It's amazing how close disgust and attraction can often lie. To some eyes Ofili's decorated dung would appear beautiful. It's what we perceive from objects and their juxtaposition that is said to matter, Alex.'

'Yes,' Donna said rather crossly. 'They say he's telling us about being black in a predominantly white community.'

'Yeah,' Sam said. 'Most of the picture's covered with attractive whitish elements that stretch and twine over all the available canvas, but then there are solid dark entities we might react against . . . unless we study them with an open mind for their different appeal, and don't simply see them as shit.' He hesitated before adding: 'They mark key compositional points, I read somewhere. But the two don't look right together, they contrast rather than complementing each other, there's no simple connection.'

'Perhaps that's what he's trying to say,' Duncan suggested, his head on one side. 'Anyway, Mum can explain it to us, can't you, Mum?'

'Frankly, no,' Fenella said, smiling, 'though I suspect Sam's analysis is a good attempt. Conceptual art does tend to demand explanation – by way of a text – before it's given full meaning. But the idea is that it should challenge your way of viewing the world. A commonplace object taken out of context and put in a gallery can alter our ideas and perception about it. Damien Hirst did this in a way that caught the public's attention with his pickled cow and he's holding sway – but there are many copyists who are gimmicky and trite rather than challenging. Ofili's dung has been his way of challenging the media used on paintings. He stumbled on the idea in Zimbabwe – quite literally – and hurled it at his canvas when he was stuck and frustrated. Then he saw its potential for symbolism.'

Alex said sourly, 'Great art should be self-explanatory, but Fenella learns her texts so she can supply a meaning to the meaningless.'

Donna rounded on him. 'And you condemn without knowing anything, which is far worse.' She added in a beat-that-one voice: 'And Chris Ofili won the Turner Prize, too. What prizes have you won, Dad?' She seized Sam's arm and tugged at him. 'Come on, let's go and look at the exhibition by ourselves.'

'Sure,' Sam said, following her to the far side of the gallery and then pulling her behind one of the great pillars. 'Quick, has it come yet? Say it has, please.'

'Well it hasn't,' she said. 'And don't keep pestering me. You asked last night and I told you it still hadn't.'

'That was eighteen hours ago and I worry. I've a right to be worried about you, haven't I? I feel bad about it.'

They stared unseeingly at a painting of large and luscious distorted fruits.

Donna mumbled. 'Yeah, OK. Sorry. But it bothers me to keep saying, "No, it hasn't".' Her face was red, then she burst out, 'Look, Dad's wrong about great art being self-explanatory. Lots of the eighteenth-century classical pictures illustrate old Greek stories or stuff from the Bible, and if you don't know the tales then you can only see what the characters are doing at the moment of the painting, but you've no understanding of the undercurrents or the real passions. They need a text too. I hate Dad when he snubs Mum in public. He's so awful he makes me cringe.'

'I know. My Dad was like that when he and Mum were breaking up. Vile.' Sam tugged at her hand to pull her onward from the exaggeratedly fruity still life, then halted, flinging his hand up to stop her. 'Hey, ssh, don't say anything, but just look at that!'

'What?' she hissed, annoyed, then stopped too, staring, her mouth open.

In the shadow of a pillar at the far end of the side aisle, Fenella and Roger stood facing one another, hands clasped like actors about to begin a love scene. He was urging something, his eyes and looks expressive, she was smiling, shaking her head, lifting his hands to hold them against her cheeks. A sweet fatalistic deceptiveness seemed to be all about them, and, Donna swiftly saw, a simple friendship, a warmth, of a sort that she'd never seen between her parents. Indeed, it seemed incredible that her mother, that thin tense woman in her dark clothes, could ever look like that, soft-eyed and fond.

A fat man and a skinny woman arrived to peer at the pictures nearby, a couple of teenagers trailing behind them. The lovers' hands dropped.

Donna tugged Sam back behind their own pillar. '*He*'s her lover! I never thought of him,' she whispered huskily. 'Christ, talk about being stupid. Look, Sam, I must talk to Mum, I have to – this changes everything. Roger! That's . . . it's so different – they're great together.'

'Shall I go and talk to your father? Distract him?' Sam was looking mirthful.

'Yes . . . yes, go away and keep him away.' Donna rubbed absently at her lower back which was suddenly aching. She must have been standing awkwardly. 'But don't you dare say a word to him or Margaret. Go on then.'

She watched him cross the wide room to where Alex was standing with Margaret and Duncan, Alex holding forth over – and doubtless criticising – the exhibits there. She coughed loudly and paused before walking from the cover of the pillar into the side aisle, where she found her mother standing alone in contemplation of a large painting that apparently depicted a volcano in full eruption, huge splashes and spots of red and orange and near black springing across the canvas. It struck Donna as having the same vicious energy as the fights between her parents.

Hearing her steps Fenella turned and smiled. 'Hello, darling. Enjoying these works?'

Donna stood facing her: '*He*'s your lover. *Roger*. Why didn't you tell me?'

Fenella blinked. 'What are we talking about?' she fenced, her voice low.

'Roger.' Donna lowered her own voice. 'Your lover. It's so obvious now I've seen it. Doesn't Dad know – not at all?'

'Well . . . He's certain I have someone, but I don't think it's dawned on him who.'

'Mmm. Look, why don't you leave and live with Roger? You should. He's great.'

Fenella stared at her. 'I can't possibly go until after your exams. They're important. You have to have someone looking after you, feeding you properly.'

'But why you? That's unfair,' Donna said passionately. 'Dad's so mean to you. You should dump me and Duncan on him. He can take the responsibility. And then I can give him hell while you go away and be happy. You deserve some happiness after these last few months. You really do. Go off with Roger. He's right for you. Anyway, it's better for Duncan and me when you and Dad are apart. We hate all your fights. We'd rather visit you in turns or something . . . We're virtually adults . . .' She stopped, her eyes distant. Something was happening to her . . . 'Look, go on, get Roger behind another romantic pillar and tell him you'll go and live with him *soon*. Get organised. You do want to, don't you?'

'More than anything,' said Fenella, tears suddenly standing in her eyes. 'He's the most loving man I've ever known. But you have to come too, and you can't yet – and then there's Duncan, who he should be with . . . We've been talking about it, Roger and me – but it can't be yet.'

'Why not? We have to sort it all out together, then deal with Dad. But you tell Roger, that's the first thing. And I *must* go to the loo, now.' She scuttled off down the stairs.

Five minutes later she arrived at Sam's side and tugged at his arm. 'Two pieces of news for you – great news.'

'Not your . . .?' He hardly dared say it.

'Yes, it's come! We're all right. No more worries.' A huge sigh of relief, a tremulous smile. 'And listen, see all these pictures, by all these artists? Well, I'm one now. I sold my first painting, to Martin Upcott for Betty's birthday present from him. More than a hundred pounds he's paid me.'

'That's terrific. Congratulations. You'll be able to save up for your college days like me, if you go on like that. It's . . . it shows you're worth something, doesn't it? Hey!' He spun her round exuberantly, his arms round her waist. 'Everything's going right!'

'And there's something else right – and if you breathe a word to your mother, or worse still, my father, I'll kill you,

Sam Jessop – Mother and Roger are planning to go off together. Quite soon. I told her to get it sorted.'

Sam hugged her again. 'Then that's all fine. Mum'll feel better if they do. She feels bad about you . . . Here, what are you all shaky for . . . why are you crying? Oh, girls!'

20

'We'll see you at the point-to-point tomorrow, then,' Alex instructed Roger as they left the building. 'Park your car as near to the winning-post as you can and save us a place if we're not already there, no, two. Margaret and Sam will be joining us again.'

'Don't tell Roger what to do,' Donna muttered, regarding her father with a mixture of revulsion and rage. She was well aware of his doting fondness for her, but that did not exonerate him from the offence of wearing a dreary grey suit accompanied by an even drearier navy tie, while Roger was looking right for the occasion in his open-necked green and cream checked shirt, dark-green pullover and casual grey slacks. She considered that Alex was inflicting shame on the family: in addition to making a public spectacle of himself over Margaret, and being persistently vile to her mother, he was pompous, bossy and boring. And he knew *nothing* of art.

'I'll arrive early,' Roger said. 'I'm looking forward to it.' His expressionless eyes swivelled to meet Donna's, and he gave her an almost imperceptible wink. He slid into his car, called, 'Bye, everyone!' blew kisses to Fenella and Donna and drove off.

Donna tugged Duncan in the direction of Fenella's BMW, and informed Sam he'd have to go in the car with Alex and Margaret. Realising that her young lover was about to balk, she added crisply, meaningfully, 'Look, I just must talk to Duncan. I'll see you back at the house.'

As they followed Fenella's neat dark back across the car park, Donna challenged her brother, her voice low, 'Have you worked out who Mum's lover is yet?'

Twice recently they had discussed the possibility of Fenella having someone, as their father kept insinuating, but Duncan had admitted to having no more idea who that special person might be than Donna. Now he gazed at his smug sister with a frowning, almost antagonistic stare, then his face changed. 'Christ, you don't mean – Roger?'

'Ssh. Yes. Mum admitted it when we were in the gallery.'

'Aah! Him!' The exhaled exclamations signalled deep thought. 'But that's all right,' he concluded in a voice of almost comical relief. 'He's OK, isn't he? I mean, it could have been someone awful . . .'

'Yeah. You were dreading knowing, weren't you? Like I was.'

'Dad's always been so rude about Mum's friends.'

Donna nodded. 'Yeah.' She wrapped her arms round herself and shivered. The April air was cooling rapidly. Somewhere over the docks an invisible seagull was screaming.

'But Roger's different. I've always thought he was great. Not his wife, though. Annie's a bitch. He must be glad she's left him. Tell you something, Donna. She's the sort Dad makes Mum out to be – not in her looks, I don't mean, though they are alike with all those smart black clothes – but in the way Annie's so self-centred and greedy. Predatory, that's the word, and a show-off. Mum's not like that, she's quieter and much softer than she likes to let on. Only Dad'll never see it.'

'I know! But that's because he works her up to the point where she starts playing up to his warped view of her so she can exasperate him in return. It's bizarre, but it's true.' They were close to the car now and their footsteps slowed. 'You're right about Annie being a bitch. Celia told Mum that she made Roger look a complete fool.'

'Why? How did Celia know? What did Annie do?'

Donna told him, ending tersely, 'So the gossip about her

and that QC in the lift went the rounds of everyone at the Bar and on the Bench – including people like Hugh Thorne. Annie just grinned and shrugged, but Roger must have felt awful.'

'Yeah, God, terrible. Makes me cringe to think of it.'

'And Mum must be cringing over Dad and Margaret and that tractor driver I told you about who saw them over the hedge. Come to that, I am too . . . and I'm furious inside. But that doesn't matter now. What does matter is us getting Mum out of the manor house and out of her misery.' She thought of her parents' flat, of its strange hodgepodge of furniture representing yet another clash of tastes between them, of her father dashing upstairs to Margaret every morning, of Nancy Chubb's innuendos, of her mother's bleak face and the tensions that sprouted like loathsome fungi from the dark corners of their lives. Angrily she said: 'I think she's been needing us to tell her she must leave. She won't go unless we do, because of feeling guilty. She's beginning to plan it in her mind but she thinks she'd be letting us down if she ran off to Roger now, mucking things up for us before our exams – you know.'

'You reckon?'

'I'm certain. And I've told her she doesn't have to worry about me. We managed a quick talk in the gallery.' She looked at Duncan and saw he was looking at her, not doubtful, but hesitant still. 'Look, you can't know what it's been like. You've hardly been home. No, I know you couldn't help it, but it's a fact. They've been tearing each other to pieces and it can't go on. Mum's been in a pretty bad state, but Roger'll look after her. She's hovering now, it's your approval she needs. Come on.'

'All right, I'm with you. But no, wait, Donna! Once she's told Dad she's going it'll be a worse hell. They'll squabble over every piece of furniture, every last duster. And worse – they'll fight over us.'

'No, they won't. I'm not stupid, Duncan, I've thought of that – and I'll tell you and Mum about my absolutely ace plan in the car. It'll solve everything. Go on, get in.'

*

Donna sat cross-legged on her bed, eating home made fudge from the box Sam had bought her at the point-to-point and listening to her friend Georgia on the telephone, complaining about the awfulness of the Easter weekend.

'My father said that he and Lavinia hadn't seen nearly enough of me and I must spend Easter with them. I thought, I truly did, since they were so determined to have me with them, that they must be laying something special on to amuse me. You know, their idea of something special, like theatres or the latest films with Hugh Grant and things in them, but generally all right.'

'And weren't they?' Donna popped another fudge lump between her lips.

'Bad joke! It was them for the special fun and the theatres, me for the baby-sitting! Poor darling Lavinia had had such a dreadful time having that baby, Dad knew I'd love to babysit for my new little brother and give her a real break. Well, if the silly cow must have a baby at forty-one, what's she expect?'

Donna was startled. 'I didn't know there was going to be a baby! You never said. How old is it? What's it called?'

'It's about eight weeks old and it's called Frazer and it screams most of the time.'

'Poor thing,' Donna said vaguely, chewing. 'It's probably collicky.'

'And how! I keep telling Dad and *her* that I need peace to revise for my GCSEs, but all they can talk about is diddums baby's problems. Actually, it's not too bad. The kid, I mean. It beams away at me when I talk to it – when it's not stuck in screaming mode – but it's them I can't stand, getting me over to their tedious house on false pretences. They should ask you straight out, shouldn't they? Could you stand an Easter of dirty nappies, dear kind daughter? Then you could make up your own mind whether you felt like being a saintly martyr, not have it thrust upon you under false pretences. Huh! Never mind that, how are your lot?'

'Unbelievable.' Donna swallowed the fudge to ensure total clarity for her own version of adult direness. 'Dad decided

Easter must be for maximum togetherness. But that meant
the sanctimonious bastard then had Mum *and* his girlfriend
Margaret in the same party, which you have to admit is maximum monstrousness. And then – listen to this, will you? –
I persuaded Dad that Mum's sort-of-cousin Roger, the one
who's a barrister who prosecuted the rape case I told you
about . . . yeah, him . . . that he should come to the art gallery
and the point-to-point with us and then Sam and I – yes,
Sam was in this hellish gathering too – what do we see? We
see Roger and Mum behind a pillar at the gallery gazing all
adoringly into each other's eyes – and it turns out he's her
unknown lover!'

'No! Really? You said the lover could be gruesome,'
Georgia reminded her. 'But this Roger isn't, is he?'

'No! That's what's so amazing. He's sweet, sort of jokey
and cuddly, but bright with it. I've always thought he was
about the best of all our families.'

'So then what happened?'

'So then everything turned into an absolute farce. We were
all together at the point-to-point. Once you know the inside
story to something like that and the rest don't, then things
they say or do all unknowingly somehow turn screamingly
funny. Like Dad introducing Roger to people as if he were his
best friend, instead of the man who's shagging his wife
behind his back.'

'Don't you mind about that, Donna? Really?'

'No, I don't.' The thought occurred that it was interest-
ingly cynical of her not to mind. 'Dad's been vile to Mum,
including having Margaret behind her back. Or worse, not
behind her back, because everyone here knows, including
poor Mum. Roger evened up the score and that serves Dad
right. Sam and I had to keep struggling to suppress our gig-
gles. And Dad was ultra careful with his betting, and that
was comic too. He backed favourites mostly, so even when
he did have a couple of wins he hardly made a thing. Roger
said we should watch the horses run down to the start and
then nip to the bookies to back the one that looked the most
fit, you know, ready to jump out of its skin, but I don't know

about horses so I couldn't judge and Sam's not much better. So then Roger was teaching us and we backed the winners in the last two races at nine to one and twelve to one. Then some girls from Abbotsbridge House came across – the Manningfords, they're called, Dad introduced them and they were great, not a bit snobby – well,' Donna concluded breathlessly, 'they thought Roger was terrific and they wished they'd met him sooner when they heard how much we'd won, Sam and I.' Donna's fingers searched for the last of the fudge. 'Over a hundred pounds. Oh, and I nearly forgot to tell you, I've sold a picture I painted to a lovely neighbour for – wait for it, Georgie – a hundred and twenty-five pounds.' She pushed the fudge into her mouth and chewed with immense satisfaction.

'Why,' Georgia asked crossly, 'why is it that when everything's apparently going all wrong for you, you still manage to make it sound fun? And make money, too.'

'I'm learning to make life work for me,' Donna said. 'Only stupid kids let it get them down.'

Sitting with a mug of hot coffee on her bench in the garden, with the warmth of the sun on her back and this morning's letter from Adam once more in her hands, Betty felt euphoric and a mere thirty – well, maybe forty – years young. A grandchild on the way as well as a wedding to come! '*A bit of a mistake there, Mother dear,*' Adam wrote in his funny self-deprecatory way, '*but as Laura and I had already decided we made a good item, this tiny he or she will merely arrive a touch earlier than anticipated. We're thinking of flying to England for a three-week holiday in June and we want to come and see you and Dad at Brambourne – and approve your famous manor gardens. And Laura's parents are naturally anxious to meet her seducer as well as checking up on the condition of her condition, as you might say. Laura's your sort, plant mad. She's also a clever architect. You'll like each other, I'm sure.*'

Betty sat day-dreaming. A wedding in the offing. But when and where? Laura was English, not American, a

Berkshire girl. Perhaps they would return to England, even settle near enough for her to visit them often and babysit. That would be wonderful. She recollected Adam's infant smiles and his chubby limbs and sticky kisses. Her Adam, a father!

'Glad to hear Dad's getting down to his new job and enjoying it. A prep school sounds just his sort of place. You'll be better off, now, won't you? That's great. I'll telephone soon to arrange our arrival dates and so forth.'

Her face crinkled up with pleasure. 'My Adam's coming home with his bride,' she told the robin triumphantly as he alighted on a nearby spade, sparing her a moment from his own fatherhood. 'And soon he'll have his own nestling, like you, boy. How about that?' And the robin twittered as if he understood before darting back to the old orchard.

She drank the last of her coffee. Martin would be pleased, too, and thankful that the pair of them were old-fashioned enough to think in terms of marriage. She must write to Adam tonight. No, better, she'd telephone him and then they could talk and talk. Betty wanted to know when the baby was due, and where and when the marriage would take place, and whether the unknown Laura was plagued with morning sickness, poor dear, like she herself had suffered. She had to know everything.

And then, too, she could tell him about the National Gardens Scheme, and how the lady whose section of Hampshire the manor garden was in had come to visit and been quite delightful in her praise of her plans and their implementation so far. 'Of course, it will take a while to mature to the point of approval,' Mrs Amanda Shaw had said, 'but I'm certain you're on the right lines.' She would be keeping in touch, she assured Betty, and she'd be happy to help her with the Yellow Book's description in due time. 'A matter perhaps of a more lyrical style than might come naturally to some gardeners, and of course, the atmosphere it conveys must be right.' More down to earth, she checked the outside loo, and told Betty that she would send her an invitation to the new garden owners' lunch. 'A lovely time to talk over problems and pests and how to organise your Days! Ah, and you expect the garden to peak each year in early July? Yes, that should fit.'

Amanda Shaw had asked whether Betty might be at the Chelsea Flower Show this year. Yes, indeed, Betty had assured her, and not only for her own enjoyment but to help her friend, Celia Thorne, the botanical artist, with setting up her exhibits and selling the delightful paintings and prints, at which Amanda Shaw had exclaimed that she loved Celia Thorne's work and herself owned two paintings on vellum of her favourite roses: '*Blanc double de Coubert* and *Penelope*, you know. Wonderful. I'll look out for you there. We must have tea together.'

It was on a bright morning in May that Lena the cleaner scurried in a state of shock to find Celia. Mrs Thorne was a lady who knew what was what, someone you could take your troubles to, even if she was a bit short with people sometimes. And she had to take this shattering business to someone sensible; she wasn't having the responsibility landed on her shoulders, no way! Besides, it really was the tastiest bit of gossip she'd ever come across, she had to try it out on someone worthy of the news. Wait till Nancy heard it.

A removals van! The big burly foreman said he and his team were booked to clear a load of furniture and pictures and stuff from the Lindridges' flat, 'Got the lists here, see!' but not one of the Lindridges was around to confirm this tale. That was strange – unnatural like. Mrs Lindridge had driven off in that lovely silver car of hers as soon as Lena arrived, saying she couldn't tell when she'd be back, but, with a smile, said she knew she could trust Lena to look after the place. Never said a word about removals vans, though. And Alex Lindridge had gone off with the doctor; working at the surgery with her all the time he was now, bold as you like, even after all the gossip, and young Donna was taking the first of those GCSE examinations and she'd left in Mr Todd's car . . .

Emptying the flat! Well, near as made no difference, Lena

had thought, peering at the foreman's lists, and so she told Mrs Thorne.

'I couldn't take the responsibility, now, could I?' she pleaded to Celia.

There was a funny look on Celia Thorne's face and an odd note in her voice as she asked Lena whether she'd been able to contact Mr Lindridge by telephone. 'I'd imagine it was fine if Mrs Lindridge has signed for this . . . but I suppose we could check with him.'

'Not so easy,' Lena said, shaking her head portentously. 'The girl what spoke to me when I tried, she said he was over at the new surgery all morning, checking on the builders' work, and of course, there's no phone connected there yet, nor he hasn't got a mobile.'

'Oh dear,' Celia lamented, strangling a rising chuckle in her throat, 'and here am I right in the middle of checking a late delivery of various sets of prints I've had made, and if I leave them now I'll never remember where I'm at. I tell you what,' she said, looking out of her window, 'I'll have a quick word with your foreman chap and verify Mrs Lindridge's signature. If that's there, it must be fine, mustn't it?'

'Should be,' Lena accepted doubtfully. Then she cheered up. 'If you say so, Mrs Thorne, I'm sure that's right.'

Alex was far from sure of that; in fact he rejected it with venom. He had been appalled on walking into his big high-ceilinged sitting-room to find his shoes echoing on bare boards, the walls bare, the space between them denuded of everything but the mahogany drinks cabinet and the off-white leather sofas with their smoked-glass coffee tables. No handsome Biedermeier cupboards and tub-shaped chairs . . . bare walls . . . Shock hit him; his breathing rasped in his chest and there was a roaring sound in his ears. The early summer sun coming through the uncurtained windows radiated the room's emptiness at him, its beams highlighting the drinks cabinet and the twin sofas so that they gleamed at him in all their intrinsic vulgarity, an odious shininess he'd never noticed before. What in hell . . .?

In those first terrible moments he thought of burglars, he imagined some horrific mistake, but as he stumbled on leaden feet through the flat and saw that the other rooms, only Duncan and Donna's excepted, had been similarly emptied, he remembered his scheming wife's unnatural calm of recent weeks. Fenella planned this, he thought; she set me up and savoured the thought of making me look an idiot. It goaded him into a fury. Where was she? Clearly she'd decided to move on, as he'd longed for her to do for God knows how long. But where? Was she still skulking here, upstairs with Celia, perhaps, listening and laughing with her? Or was she with that creep, her unknown lover, after robbing him of almost everything in the house? His house.

A fresh horror entered his mind and he rushed to check his clothes, his precious good suits, pulling their hangers to and fro in his wardrobe with agitated hands. No, thank God, no scissored suits. All were intact – no missing arms to the coats, no trouser legs chopped short. Back in the sitting-room he poured himself a large whisky – at least she'd left the drinks untouched in their cabinet – and went to the kitchen for water. Gulping whisky as he worked, he flung open the cupboard doors there to discover a modicum of china and cooking pans still in situ, and in the fridge, two plates of food, neatly swathed in cling film. The ironic thoughtfulness of those salmon salads struck him like a blow in the face.

He opened the tightened slit of his mouth to swear and blind at maximum volume, only to shut it again. Others in the house would overhear, learn of this débâcle – if they didn't know already – split their sides with laughter over his latest discomfiture, spread tales about him through the two villages. Worse, tales that would confirm the earlier gossip. His mouth was suddenly dry, nausea hit him and he began to shake. No, he must ensure silence over this. He had barely dragged himself free from the terrible mishap with Margaret and that leering tractor-driver, only dared this week to go into the Abbotsbridge post-office stores without first peering round for corners safe from the sniggers he knew followed him everywhere that the agricultural louts lurked.

He didn't deserve this, not just as things were beginning to go his way at last, his post as practice manager commencing next week, confirming him as a real person once more. He stood by the window and stared out in a flurry of confusion. Real? Everything was unreal now, the ground shaking beneath his feet. Donna was due back from her examination at the tutorial college any minute, but who would be driving her? Fenella . . .? Or had his wife vanished from his life entirely? She might reappear briefly to gloat, but he doubted it. But what about his darling daughter? What was happening to her? Oh God. From shivering he changed to sweating; he was suddenly frantic with worry. Fenella couldn't have taken Donna with her, not with her vital exams due over the next three weeks. Or could she?

He heard a car outside, but it was Todd's. Damn! And then he saw his pretty daughter jumping out, slamming the car door and calling her thanks for the lift. So she had been abandoned in Winchester, left to make her own way home! This was atrocious. He turned to run out to her, then forced himself to stop; there must be no dramas. He heard her opening the front door of the flat.

'Donna, are you all right? Come here, quickly.' His voice was high with temper.

She walked into the room, flung her book bag down on the carpetless floor, glanced around with a half-smile on her lips. 'Looks a bit bare, doesn't it?' she remarked calmly.

'Your mother's left us, taken most of the furniture with her too. It's the most contemptible thing I've ever heard of.' But even as he spoke his heart was thumping in anticipation of further shocks. Donna was regarding him, not with sympathy, but with the same aversion she showed for buzzing wasps; worse, since there was no surprise on her face, she must have been aware of Fenella's plans.

'Contemptible? Get real, Dad. It's what you wanted. You've told Mum enough times that if she didn't like it here she should damn well go. So she went.'

'What, in this sneaking sort of fashion?' he blustered. 'Stealing away without a word and taking the contents of the place with her? And in the middle of your exams, too, when she's always said how much she cared about you?'

'She's only taken her own stuff, things she'd been given or bought.' A grin flashed. 'She's even left the marital bed ready for your love life with Margaret. And if you want to know how my exam was this morning, Daddy dear, it was fine, no problem. And Mum did leave a word, several, in fact, and here they are.' Donna bent down to her book bag, extracted an envelope and held it out to him.

Alex tore the envelope apart, its shreds falling to the floor as he snatched at the letter, gulping at its contents, his hands trembling. He read it a second time and swallowed noisily. He shook it at her. 'You . . . you knew about this and you encouraged her. My own daughter. You've given me the worst shock, the most terrible hurt I've ever had in all my life! How could you have done this to me?' The words sounded theatrical even as he said them, but his hurt was real enough. He was conscious of a dull pain invading his entire head, while his belly griped and his eyes felt bruised and tender. Donna had backed Fenella in making a fool of him; the last person in the world he would have expected to treat him so badly, to have betrayed his trust. But with whom? Clearly Fenella was not acting on her own here; her letter spoke of 'we'. What was Donna saying so coolly?

'Mum's organised everything, thought of everything. Todd's taking me to and from Winchester on the days when he teaches at the college. Other days Margaret can use her own car for a change while you run me in. And Mum's put plenty of frozen meals in the freezer – they'll be useful on my exam days – and there's food for today in the fridge. She's been really considerate. She's taken the dining-room furniture because that was hers, but we can eat in the kitchen. She's left us the table and chairs there.'

His voice shifted to a snarl: 'Decent of her! But who's she gone off with?' His fingers slapped the letter. 'All she says is,

"We . . .", that "we've" taken a short lease on a flat, and "we" hope to buy a little place in Richmond or Twickenham . . .'

'You are dim, Dad. You don't see what's in front of your nose. We thought you must surely have realised.'

He stared at her. His pained mind clicked sluggishly over. 'Not . . . not Roger?'

A shrug. 'Who else?'

More nausea, more pain. He'd been so stupid. 'But I've always thought of Roger as a decent chap . . . I trusted him. It's unbelievable.'

Donna said steadily, 'Mother trusted you. But then there was Margaret. In the same house and *everyone* knowing. At least Mum didn't rub your nose in it like you did hers, with both villages full of sniggering people making snide remarks and you telling filthy lies and shouting at her. She was discreet.'

Alex struggled to fight back. 'She can't have been so very discreet. You evidently became aware of what she was up to. Or did she tell you about her affair – and Duncan, too, no doubt? A big joke against me!'

'No,' Donna said, her equanimity varying not a jot. 'She said nothing. It was Sam who spotted it, if you must know, at the gallery. He took one look at Mum and Roger smiling and talking together and he saw love. And then I followed his eyes and I saw it too.' Unexpectedly sentimental, she added, 'It came from them like the scent of flowers – the warm scent of real old-fashioned affection.'

Alex's face wore a look of revulsion. 'Do you mind?' he said acidly.

'Affection and trust,' Donna said pointedly.

'And what about her leaving before your examinations? How do we manage? Fenella fussed enough over those – and now she isn't even here. It's so selfish.'

'She had to go, exams or not,' Donna told him. 'You were giving her a rotten time here and if you'd had any sensitivity at all – never mind about sympathy – you'd have understood how down she was. Don't you realise how much Duncan and I disliked the foul way you were treating her, setting up all those endless arguments. She was looking ill and losing weight, and Betty and Celia were saying they were worried about her. We all were.'

That damned woman, Celia. 'So you and those bloody interfering women set all this up . . .?'

'No,' Donna said. 'You did that, making Mum's life such hell that you forced her out. Not so different from how your father behaved, was it? Mum's often done things that've annoyed me, but everyone's mothers do, and I love her as well as you – if I do still love you or even *like* you, that is – and I wanted the torture to stop. So Duncan and I told her she didn't have to be a martyr, because I could cope here for a few weeks. No bother. And we'd be happier if she was happy.'

'What right had you . . .?' Alex began, but Donna overrode him ruthlessly.

'Put your thoughts on this, Dad. I'm almost seventeen now and soon my GCSE examinations will be over, and then it won't be long before I can get my driving licence – and I'll be the one who'll choose where I go and whom I live with.' She met her father's angry eyes coolly. 'I could do my A levels in either Winchester or London. I could take the degree I want at either Winchester Art College or the Slade. Both have equally good courses to lead to the sort of life I want.'

'It's like that, is it,' Alex ground out, 'blackmail? Do as Donna says or she goes off to her mother and the new lover?'

'Don't be stupid,' Donna said. 'I want to stay friends with you both. And Roger and Margaret too, if that's what you each want. But I want nothing to do with bullying, nor does Duncan. You've always said you cared about us, well, now start caring about how we feel, and that means behaving decently to Mum, talking family things over with her and bothering about her views, not putting on the snarling pit-bull terrier act.' She turned and walked away, adding over her shoulder. 'I'm going to have my lunch and then I have to revise for my next subject, English literature. And you can go off and tell it all to Margaret and milk her for sympathy. But no way do you bring her into this flat, not till Mum's ghost has had time to get away. That means not till after the holidays, at the very earliest. For someone who's supposed to be caring, someone who you say suffered over her own husband's infidelities, Margaret's shown very little caring or sympathy over Mum's feelings, has she? She should have been aware of her embarrassments . . . and her unhappiness.'

He stared at her in stunned silence as he adjusted his view of his daughter's levels of perception. He had never been so taken aback in all his life.

'You know what I mean,' Donna told him. 'Put *all* our feelings into your love equation. And if you don't like what I'm saying, well, we can talk about that too, Father dear.'

With a flourish of her pen, Celia finished signing and numbering her prints of this year's best paintings, recently arrived from the printer in Verona. She packed them with careful hands in readiness for the Chelsea Flower Show, tidied her studio, and then went to make herself a cream cheese and watercress sandwich and a cup of coffee and wondered where to consume them. Indoors or out in the garden? One fifteen. That awful man, Alex Lindridge, would by now be well aware of how his wife had turned the tables on him. She had almost choked from the effort of suppressing her laughter when she'd heard from Lena what Fenella had done, and she'd been chuckling to herself all morning in the studio. Good for Fenella.

Eat outside, she decided, picking a good firm apple from the fruit bowl and humming to herself. The sunlight was inviting and Betty might be there, sitting placidly on her garden seat. Some company would be pleasant. Should she do anything about Donna? The girl could be shocked and upset. No, Celia decided. She disapproved of interference, she would await developments. In the meantime she would be around, were her presence needed.

In the event, she discovered Donna sitting cross-legged on the lawn in front of Betty on her garden seat, tucking hungrily into a salmon salad while divulging to her the morning's fascinating developments, adding that her mother had left the manor house to live with her lover in Richmond.

'So I've come out here to escape Dad, who's in a foul mood, not because he wants Mum around, but because she's made him look a fool.' She took a mouthful of salmon and chewed with great good cheer.

Betty looked at once shattered and disbelieving. 'She's gone? Truly gone? Now, when you've your examinations immediately ahead of you? Oh, Donna dear, I am sorry . . .'

'It's all right,' Donna reassured her, swallowing. 'I told her it was OK to go. She'd had enough of Dad and the country-side to last the rest of her life. And the shouting and the rows between them about Dad being so *obvious* over Margaret was upsetting us all. Anyway, her lover needs her more.' She turned her head up to smile at Celia. 'Hi, did you know? Mum's finally left Dad.'

'I saw the removals lorry,' Celia told her. 'There was a sur-prising amount of furniture going into it.'

'It was all hers,' Donna assured her.

'I don't doubt it,' Celia said, seating herself next to Betty, and putting the tray beside herself on the lawn. 'She's going to live with Roger Dodson, is she?'

'How do you know about him?' Donna asked, slightly deflated.

'I met him with her once. It was at an exhibition in London.' She added kindly, 'He seemed very pleasant and clearly fond of your mother.' She took a preliminary bite of her sandwich.

'They're lovely together. He told me once he'd fancied Mum for years. It's like he still sees her as twenty- five, the way he raves on about her.'

Betty stared at Donna with incredulity. 'You mean, you knew about this? That they were planning to go off together?'

'Yeah. I organised parts of it, well, the ideas bits, you know, like Mum simply vanishing.'

'Let me get this straight,' Betty demanded. 'Roger's the barrister who was prosecuting the rape case you listened to, if I remember rightly? The one who spent quite some time with you at Easter?'

Donna nodded. 'That's him. But we didn't know he was Mum's lover until nearly the end of Easter. It was Sam who saw that.'

Betty closed her eyes despairingly. 'I don't believe what I'm hearing. It's all such a mix-up. And then there's Margaret. And you and Sam. How are you going to cope with all this, you poor girl?'

'Better than before, I should think,' Celia said, sipping her coffee. 'Less pressure and trauma all round. And Donna won't be over-fussed about having two sets of parents, she's a modern girl, aren't you, Donna?'

'Yeah,' Donna assured them. 'Most of my friends have two sets, some even more. I quite like Margaret, even if she has been a bit callous and detached about the whole thing. But then Mum and she never had anything to do with one another. The main thing is that Margaret would be better for Dad to live with, like Roger for Mum. Dad alongside Mum wrecked them, made them both stunningly nasty, which they aren't when the other's not there. It's like a chemical reaction, I suppose,' she added grandly, 'with the mixture fizzing off poison gases. But I'm not having Dad and Margaret living together in our flat for a while yet. It'd be too embarrassing and distracting all round.'

When Hugh arrived home after court that evening he was amused to learn of the day's events from Celia. 'Well, that's moved things along with a jolt. A salutary shock for Alex, I imagine. Though it's what he was asking for. And Roger does need someone to look after him. They'll be fine, he and Fenella.'

'You amaze me,' Celia said truthfully. 'Firstly, I thought you didn't like Fenella, and secondly, I can't help wondering why you would think her the right person for Roger.'

'I've learned a great deal more about them both,' Hugh admitted, 'and I've come to the conclusion that despite Alex's frequent allusions to Fenella's lack of education and

her shallow mind, she has a great deal more to her than he
has ever brought himself to acknowledge. Friends and neighbours here who have met her say that her knowledge of art is
extensive, but more than that, she is intuitive about people,
even if she can be awkward with them. I can't think that
Alex's attitude has ever helped her self-confidence. Roger
told me that when he discussed his cases with her, she was
remarkably perceptive and constructive, often suggesting
subtle lines of questioning he might not have arrived at
himself.' A faint chuckle. 'I thought both his examination-in-
chief and his cross-examination of the defence witnesses in
the Jenkyns case were admirable, definitely above his previous standard.'

'You think his ex-wife Annie was pulling him down? She
was too tough and ambitious for someone as basically kindly
as Roger. Is that what you think?'

'I think . . . yes, in essence. While Fenella, surprisingly,
considering our original view of her, seems to bring out the
best in him. But more than that, he confided to me that she
had been a generous angel to him financially, relieving him
of horrendous pressure.'

'How do you mean? How did that come out?'

'I invited Roger to see me in my chambers after the
Jenkyns trial to tell him how impressed I'd been by his
performance and to enquire how he saw his future. He said
he'd like to go on the Circuit Bench as I'd done, but the
competition's fierce and there was a problem in balancing
the finance in the meantime. He needed to become an
assistant Recorder straight away. I said I would recommend
him strongly. He thanked me and it was then he told me
how, like many at the criminal bar, he was having cash-flow
difficulties – in other words, he'd reached the stage in his
career when most of his work was long fraud and drugs
cases on Legal Aid. Unfortunately they're paid by a central
taxing authority which normally pays out eighteen months
to two years after the case – and not always then – even after
considerable argument. This allied to the new personal tax
requirements for a barrister to pay tax on his income in

the financial year he's *earned* it – whether he's been paid or not – has resulted in many in his position being made bankrupt.'

'Yes, you've mentioned that particular horror before. And then Roger's been in an impossible position over the division of the equity in the flat he and Annie owned, something Fenella is enraged with Annie over.'

'Yes, I heard how Annie's lover had abandoned his wife and children to live with her in the flat, but that Roger could neither persuade Annie to put it on the market at a reasonable price, nor to pay him his share in the equity. She said they should wait for prices to rise, since between all their needs they had to make decent money on it. In the meantime Roger was caught every which way – a recipe for horrific stress, and one that would have been disastrous for him but for Fenella's help. She probably saved his position with regard to a possible judicial appointment.'

'Go on, this is fascinating.'

'Roger made no bones about it, he told me that he hadn't been able to pay his VAT because he was more than a hundred thousand pounds overdrawn and his bank manager had refused to up his borrowing level, because of the impasse with Annie over the equity in the flat. In other words he was facing bankruptcy, despite the fact that the Legal Aid fund owed him more than one hundred and twenty thousand pounds.'

Celia grimaced in sympathy. 'What a hellish situation! Go on.'

'Fenella lent him the money to pay the VAT – and this, so he assured me, happened before their affair started – together with what he needed to buy Annie out and then sell the flat himself and sort out the worst of his financial problems. He even had some difficulty in persuading Fenella to charge him a reasonable interest. He thinks she's an angel of goodness, can't say enough in her praise.'

Alex hadn't been able to contact Margaret until the end of the day. When she didn't return for her usual late lunch at her flat he'd attempted to telephone her, only to have the receptionist on duty at the practice report with ghoulish relish that she hadn't the time to eat, that she'd had an unbelievable morning coping with the results of a nasty head-on car crash in one of the narrow country lanes. 'She had to perform a tracheotomy on the spot – you know, to keep a man's airways open – and she saved his life. Lucky she happened to be near the scene, wasn't it? And then she had to wait with him for the ambulance and there were two lads in a right state whom she was able to help, and then when she got back from that there was first a nasty miscarriage she had to go an' deal with and then an old lady with a stroke . . . Oh dear, yes, and I'm so sorry, Alex, in all the flurry I forgot, but she did ask me to tell you she wouldn't be back for lunch. But then you must understand that with all that going on I never had a second free even to think of it. Its been a dreadful time, you can't imagine . . .'

'That's all right,' Alex said, cutting short the effusions and feeling thankful that he and Margaret had each taken their own cars today. 'When you do see her, tell her I won't be in again until tomorrow, would you? Some problems have occurred here that I must deal with.' He replaced the telephone before the garrulous girl could ask what problems. In an odd way he was thankful Margaret wasn't here. He wanted to pour his exasperation out to her, but on the other hand he had to think how he was to sort out the hundred and one complications Fenella's vanishing act had produced.

How were Margaret and he to work out their new life together? Move into her flat or his? Nothing could happen until Donna had finished her examinations, she had made that painfully clear. What then? Where would Donna eventually decide to live? He refused to give her up to Fenella and that treacherous Roger Dodson. What about an early divorce? Would Fenella make his life hell by fighting over every clause, by petty squabbling over the value of her share in the flat? Would she lure Donna away from her rightful home with expensive presents, even – frightening thought –

her own car? Right now he felt angry enough to do battle over anything and everything but then he remembered with discomfort that it was Donna who appeared to hold the strongest position and she'd already set out her own terms, implying that she could choose to stay here.

Was that because of Sam? Were they having sex? No, surely not; not after the firm but tactful warning he'd given the boy. But this idiotic situation Fenella had thrust upon him had opened the way for Sam to spend a great deal of time with Donna this summer – and without any supervision now that he himself would be working full time at the surgery, and he hated the implications. With Margaret and him as they were it would be indecent for Donna and Sam to be similarly involved. He shuddered at the thought. More gossip, more salacious leers – Lena the cleaner would never miss out on such juicy revelations.

'No,' Margaret said. 'I don't think we should move in together.'

It was late in the evening and she had just finished her usual scrappy meal and come to sit beside him on the worn bamboo sofa.

Alex looked annoyed. 'I haven't asked you yet.'

'No, but you were going to, weren't you? After Donna's finished her exams, you were going to say.'

'Possibly. Why shouldn't we?'

'It's too soon,' Margaret said, kicking off her shoes with a sigh of relief, and tucking her feet beneath her. 'We have to see how we get on once we're working together full time. I need to check you over objectively. We haven't exactly had what you might call a normal relationship so far, have we?'

'We've had no chance—' he began defensively.

'No, we haven't. But what I have had recently is the chance to see you in your relationship with Fenella. You've been super to me, nobody could have been kinder or more affectionate. But where Fenella's concerned I have to say that her walking out and taking all that furniture with her without warning served you right. You were a bastard to her like Boyd was to me. And if I'd thought of it with Boyd I'd have done it myself.'

Alex stared at her in silence.

Margaret smiled somewhat grimly. 'And I'll tell you something else in regard to your sharpness to Fenella. All right, you detest her. But whatever the cause, if you ever even once speak so venomously to me I'll poison you in return, give your system the clean-out of a lifetime.'

'You wouldn't!'

She laughed at his stunned expression. 'Wouldn't I? Don't try me.'

'If you think that badly of me I'm surprised you're considering continuing our relationship at all,' he said angrily.

'Oh, the choice is small at my age,' she said flippantly. 'And then you're not so very bad. I had my moments of being foul to Boyd, too. Look, I'll tell you straight. I'm fond of you, Alex, very fond mostly, and I do want to be with you. I think we go well together. But I'm never going to marry again. When Donna's away, when she goes off to college, whatever, we'll be together – I hope. For the moment I think we should continue as we were, don't you? Including sex, naturally.'

'That was,' Alex said, taking a deep breath and trying to speak lightly himself, 'roughly what I had in mind myself. Donna has been straight-talking me. And then there's Sam. I agree tact is necessary in these circumstances.'

'What does Fenella have to say? I take it she left you a letter – it's generally considered to be the thing in such circumstances!'

'She did, damn her. She admitted the lover she'd denied having had did exist all along and that it was Roger. Then there were various boring remarks about his wonderful qualities – as opposed to my lack of them, I suppose. Finally she divulged that Roger and she had taken a short lease on a flat in Richmond while they look for something more permanent in the same area: it has all the right road and rail links for a barrister regularly dealing with cases in different courts. Fenella will work at the Heart Foundation as before, her bit of charity work with a friend. Wimbledon's within reasonable distance, so she'll take up with her old acquaintances once more, I suppose – and have her righteous friend Celia around at the weekends as well. More to the point, she says that Duncan and Donna must choose which of us to spend their time with, but that must be dependent also on how their educational needs develop. Termtime with one, holidays with the other, I suppose.' His voice was flat.

'It sounds all right. Better you both have a partner you care about and share the children.'

Alex was aware of the dull pain in his head once more, of a dry mouth. 'I'll see so little of Donna.'

'Nonsense. You'll share her and it won't be so bad if you can agree the arrangements sensibly with Fenella. Besides, Donna's growing up, she'll be gone soon of her own accord, don't try to kid yourself any differently. And you'll have me.'

'Shall I?' he asked, made uneasy by her brisk common sense, her refusal to wrap him in her sympathy.

She pushed back her untidy pewter-coloured hair with an impatient gesture, then she laughed. 'That's up to you, Alex darling, that's up to you. We all of us make our own futures. Come on, let's celebrate Fenella's vanishing act, open a bottle and make love. We've just time before you need to go back down to Donna.'

TRIALS OF FRIENDSHIP

Hazel Hucker

Five friends from college, now in their early 40s, hold an annual Sunday lunch party. This year it's Polly Ferrison's turn and she is dreading it. As year succeeds year, she has become all too aware of just how far her friends' achievements outstrip hers: Candida has married extremely well and now runs a minor stately home as well as a successful business; civil servant Jane has a high-flying career in government circles, while much-divorced Vanessa is a solicitor with a smart flat in town. Even Mary, a farmer's wife, has exploited her assets and created a profitable home business for herself. Polly's only achievements are her two daughters – one now at university and the other about to follow her. When they've both left home, what will remain for Polly but a dull teaching job and her failing marriage? The reunion party, however, foreshadows changes in all their lives.

THE REAL CLAUDIA CHARLES

Hazel Hucker

Flora Monk, a promising but struggling novelist in her thirties, plans to make her name known with a biography of Claudia Charles, a distant cousin of her mother's, described in her recent *Times* obituary as 'an early feminist, and one of the world's finest writers of twentieth-century prose'. But this project is not one to please Flora's aunts, nor her elderly widowed mother Primrose, who vehemently opposes it, for reasons Flora cannot fathom.

Finding herself pregnant by her lover, and harassed by her mother to give up her project and marry, Flora struggles to achieve the task she has set herself. It seems that the more she unravels the secrets of her famous relative's life, the more her own sense of identity is called into question.

When Primrose dies, Flora uncovers shattering truths about her family history, and finally begins to understand, too late, what her mother has had to suffer throughout her life, and why their own relationship was such a difficult one. But from these revelations emerge, at last, the real Claudia, and ultimately the real Flora.

Other bestselling Warner titles available by mail:

☐	The Real Claudia Charles	Hazel Hucker	£6.99
☐	Trials of Friendship	Hazel Hucker	£5.99

The prices shown above are correct at time of going to press. However, the publishers reserve the right to increase prices on covers from those previously advertised, without further notice.

W

WARNER BOOKS

WARNER BOOKS
PO Box 121, Kettering, Northants NN14 4ZQ
Tel: 01832 737525
Fax: 01832 733076
Email: aspenhouse@FSBDial.co.uk

POST AND PACKING:
Payments can be made as follows: cheque, postal order (payable to Warner Books) or by credit cards. Do not send cash or currency.

All UK Orders   **FREE OF CHARGE**
EC & Overseas   25% of order value

Name (BLOCK LETTERS) . . . .

Address . . . .

. . . .

Post/zip code: . . . .

☐ Please keep me in touch with future Warner publications

☐ I enclose my remittance £ . . . .

☐ I wish to pay by Visa/Access/Mastercard/Eurocard

Number ☐☐☐☐☐☐☐☐☐☐☐☐☐☐☐☐

Card Expiry Date ☐☐☐☐